THE RISE O

Sharath Komarraju is a Bangalore-based author. He began life as a software engineer but has since jumped the fence to write full time. His first novel, *Murder in Amaravati*, was longlisted for the Commonwealth Book Prize in 2013. Perhaps his best known work is the *Hastinapur* series, which attempts to tell the story of the Mahabharata through the thoughts and lives of the epic's lesser known female characters. When he's not writing, he's either watching cricket or talking to his wife, or trying to watch cricket *while* talking to his wife.

The Rise of Hastinapur

SHARATH KOMARRAJU

HarperCollins *Publishers* India

First published in India in 2015 by
HarperCollins *Publishers* India

Copyright © Sharath Komarraju 2015

P-ISBN: 978-93-5177-376-4
E-ISBN: 978-93-5177-377-1

2 4 6 8 10 9 7 5 3 1

Sharath Komarraju asserts the moral right
to be identified as the author of this work.

HarperCollins *Publishers*
A-75, Sector 57, Noida, Uttar Pradesh 201301, India
1 London Bridge Street, London, SE1 9GF, United Kingdom
Hazelton Lanes, 55 Avenue Road, Suite 2900, Toronto, Ontario M5R 3L2
and 1995 Markham Road, Scarborough, Ontario M1B 5M8, Canada
25 Ryde Road, Pymble, Sydney, NSW 2073, Australia
195 Broadway, New York NY 10007, USA

Typeset in 10.5/14 Bembo Regular at
Manipal Digital Systems, Manipal

Printed and bound at
Thomson Press (India) Ltd.

BOOK ONE

PRIESTESS

PROLOGUE

Ganga Speaks

The wise men who reside at the foot of these mountains say that desire is the root of all evil. For hours every day they stand on one leg in their soiled white loincloths, and they join their hands above their heads. They wish to conquer desire, they say; desire for food, for water, for the flesh of another. Only a man who has conquered his desires has conquered all, they say, with their kind smiles in their dulcet tones.

And yet, these men who serve the gods tour North Country and become guests of honour at various kingdoms for three months every year, when the wind from the Ice Mountain becomes so chilly it turns the skin blue at a mere touch. It is during these tours that they perform acts for the betterment of the world: acts which have, over the years, prevented the disappearance of the race of kings from Earth. In return for these acts of kindness, the kings offer their silk beds and their nubile waiting-women so that the sages do not experience the discomforts of winter.

Up on Meru's slopes we defer to the will of the Goddess Bhagavati, She who is present in a drop of water, in a grain of sand, in a mite of dust. If She has decreed that living beings shall

3

be ruled by desire, that desire must be the one thing that drives their lives relentlessly forward, we do not question it. All that the Goddess has given us, we accept, we covet, we revere.

But now I am no longer on the Meru. I am no longer Ganga, Lady of the River. I am but a woman whose skin has pale yellow patches and parched green spots. I do not speak often now, but when I do, my voice is like the cackle of a crow. Every morning, I walk up to the great white boulder that now covers the Cave of Ice, and I whisper the incantation that would have once opened it. My son, Devavrata, would have laughed at this foolishness, and he would have said that the world of Earth was nobler than the world on Meru; but perhaps this is the difference I speak of. I do not fight my desires. I give in to them.

They say that the Great War has brought about such destruction in North Country that it has hastened the end of the epoch of Dwapara, and that the Crystal Lake has all but dried up. Indra's explorers, however, must have found lands and lakes further up north, for they seem to have forsaken all interest in the sixteen Great Kingdoms – or what remains of them. The salt route continues to exist, shrouded in magic. The dead lake is covered in mist that only a Celestial can clear. Devavrata's old Mystery has doubtless been enhanced, and I doubt that now even he could find his way to the lake.

What shall happen from now is not in my hands. I know that the door to the world of Meru shall remain closed, at least until my death. What will happen thereafter is not to my concern. They teach us on Meru – though not many of us listen – that the future is but an illusion which no man can know. The past is unalterable, but at least it is real. The two worlds are different in this, too; here on Earth, men and women fixate upon their futures, and in doing so they forget to spend a little time, every now and then, reminiscing about the real, rigid – and often pleasant – memories of the past.

They say in the new epoch (the wise men call it the age of Kali) earthmen will kill each other, that the gods will shun them, that they will descend from Meru at the end of it all to populate North Country with life of their own kind. But how quaint is the idea. North Country lays barren of life *now*. Brother has killed brother in the Great War. The cleansing has already happened. The Meru people have already forsaken the earthmen. And yet the wise men look ahead – as I have said, on Earth, the eye is forever on the future, the one thing it cannot see.

But I, from sheer force of habit, must look unto the past.

I must go back to the time before Vichitraveerya's passing, back to the time when Devavrata, perhaps vain of his strength, won all three princesses of Kasi for his brother. Ambika and Ambalika fulfilled their destinies in their own strange ways, and bore sons that carried forward the line of the Bharatas. But what of Amba, the first princess of Kasi who should have become queen? Her tale is a long and tortuous one, but in the end it is she who had a bigger say in the fortune – and fall – of Hastinapur.

Fortune, because she brought about the great marriage alliance of the age which merged Kuru and Panchala into one. Fall, because her child would grow up to be the warrior who killed Devavrata, the undefeatable champion of the throne of Hastinapur.

I used to hear it being said that no warrior in North Country could drive a chariot as swiftly as Devavrata. No one could fight with a sword as skilfully as he. No one could shoot arrows as rapidly as he. He read the scriptures and understood them; he debated with Brahmins and was hailed as their equal. In politics and battle strategy he was peerless. It warmed my heart to hear such things, but I was also wary. I was wary that Devavrata's destruction would come about from that one place men scarcely care to look: from within. He would be destroyed – as all powerful men eventually are – by the consequences of their actions, by the ache they cause through their choices.

Amba's tale, then, is also the first chapter in the tale of Devavrata's ruin.

ONE

When she was ushered into the waiting room, Amba saw that the floor carpets were of the wrong colour. Seating herself on the edge of the blue-cushioned teak chair under the central lamp, she nodded at the attendant waving the fan to go a little faster. The autumn had been pleasant this year; pleasant enough to allow her to sleep on the palanquin the previous night – but somehow, in this forbidding country she found a layer of fine dust on every surface. That morning, when they had first arrived at the border of Saubala after skirting along the edge of Khandava, her head palanquin bearer had asked her to cover her nose and mouth with a cotton cloth dipped in cold water.

Her breath had caught in her throat in spite of the precaution, and even now, surrounded by washed silks and sparkling brass vessels, her eyes pinched. 'Once I begin living here,' she thought, 'I will make sure this place is cleaned with soap water at least three times a day.' She undid the clasp of her gold arm-bands and laid them aside, signalling to the servant in the corner of the room to come take them away. She removed her coronet and laid it on her thigh – one that Mother Satyavati had given her on the eve of her departure. 'Until you are wedded to someone else,' she had said, 'you are the queen of Hastinapur. And it is important that you look like one.'

6

Amba slid off her ivory hairclips one by one, placing them in a row beside her on the seat. She shook her head to loosen her hair and let it fall in a heap over her shoulder and upper back. As she first became aware of the faint whiff of jasmine and sandal coming from the incense sticks the attendant had lighted on her arrival, and as the catch in her throat eased somewhat, she felt grains of sand in her hair brush against the back of her neck, and grimaced. 'Make arrangements for my bath,' she said.

'Yes, my lady.'

Sand and dust, everywhere. When Salva was courting her in Kasi she had once asked her courtiers to tell her about his kingdom. They had said it was situated on the banks of River Saraswati, which flowed for half the year and remained dry for the other half. It had once been a large kingdom, Saubala, back when the Saraswati was one of the Great Rivers, when its current was strong even through the summer. But now that fertile land had become a desert. Wedged in between a mountain and an endless sea of sand, Saubala was no more than a vassal state.

She had heard about all that, but now that she realized just how it was, she wondered if she would ever get used to it. One must make small sacrificesfor one's love, she told herself. Surely Salva would find her different to the maidens of his own land. Would he not learn to like her ways too? Was that not what love was about?

She leaned back on her hands and looked up at the ceiling, yellow and bare. The walls were adorned with paintings of camels and horses. The men of Saubala, she had heard, were great riders. Indeed, on the day she turned fifteen, Salva had taken her riding on the vast northern plains of Kasi on a white stallion. He had ridden, alone, all the way from Saubala to Kasi through four nights to be by her side on her birthday. That was the day she had let him hold her hand, and that night he had kissed her on the cheek in the blue light of the new moon.

Ladies at the court of Kasi would not dare say anything to Amba's face, but she knew there had been rumours about Salva's intentions. How dare the king of a vassal state be so presumptuous as to show affection so openly to the first princess of a Great Kingdom, they asked. In the eyes of people who could not see beyond the material, all motives were black, all gestures were fake. Salva, they said, wanted her only because she was the princess of Kasi, the kingdom that, after Hastinapur, boasted the most fertile lands in all of North Country. Even her father, who had permitted all of Salva's advances toward her, had asked her once: 'If you were not the princess of Kasi, my dear, would he still wish to be wedded to you?'

And she had said, 'He would, father.'

She had, however, never asked Salva that question. How could she? It would amount to her doubting his love. When he had been nothing but kind, generous, thoughtful and compassionate throughout the time she had known her, how could she slap him in the face like that? There were things in love that ought not to be spoken about.

Even now she wished that Salva had defeated Devavrata in battle and won her. But Devavrata hailed from Hastinapur, where princes were taught first to handle a sword and a spear before they were given toy wooden horses to play with. And they called him the finest warrior of the land. Salva had his gifts, but valour and skill in battle were not among them. Amba had known that during their courtship too, and it had not mattered to her.

It did not matter to her now, either, except – it would have been *nicer*, that was all.

It would have meant that she would not have had to beg Devavrata and Mother Satyavati to let her go. It would have meant not having to listen to Mother Satyavati expressing doubts about Salva's love. She pictured herself on the bank of the Ganga at Kasi, where Devavrata and her suitors fought one another. If only Salva had won, she and he would have stood on his chariot, side by side, and pointing at the vanquished Devavrata with the tip of his bow Salva would have said: 'I only desire Amba. You can take Ambika and Ambalika with you, Son of Ganga.'

Yes, indeed, that would have been nice.

She clapped her hands once, and a vessel of water was brought for her. She drank a thimbleful, then another. Water in this country had a queer, salty taste to it. She sighed to herself. Her skin was used to the fresh-water springs of Kasi; did she have to bathe in saltwater too? She hoped that her skin would not blotch.

An attendant came to her, bowing low. 'Your bath is ready, my lady,' he said.

'So why has the queen of Hastinapur journeyed through the night to visit a vassal state?' asked Salva, after they had both sat down. He had taken the chair opposite her, ignoring her gesture that motioned him to her side. When he sat he looked no more than a raw young man of seventeen. Like all riders, he was strong in the thighs and calves. His hips were supple and sturdy, so that when he stood he had the appearance of a resolute mountain, but now that she was sitting face to face with him, he looked like any of the stable boys she had seen in the castle. She knew he wore shoulder pads under his robe to broaden his stature.

Amba gave him her hands, but he stayed unmoved. His long fingers were wrapped around the balls of his knees, and in his gaze she found no love, no concern; only mild curiosity, and, perhaps, a respectful distance. 'I am not the queen of Hastinapur, Lord,' she said, drawing her hands back a little. 'I am your Amba. Do you not recognize me?'

'The day Devavrata won you and your sisters in the battle on the riverbank, all of you became Hastinapur's queens, my lady – Your Majesty.'

'But Devavrata did not want to keep me there against my will. He gave me leave to come here, my love. To your arms.' She peered into his stone-black eyes to guess what he was thinking. 'You *do* love me, do you not?'

His eyes softened, and Amba's heart leapt. In that one moment she saw the old Salva, the king who had wooed her at her father's house with lotuses and love songs. He was concealing his true feelings for her, she thought. But why? What was the need when she was here, ready to fly into his arms at a mere nod?

'Love is not the question here, my princess,' he said, and after waving the attendants out of the room, took her hand in his to pat it. 'You do know how much I love you. Today, ever since I saw you in court, I could not think of anything else. My courtiers would have me speak of how to store Saraswati's water, but all I thought of was how to send them away so that I could run up here and sit with you.' He ran his fingertips on her knuckles. 'You do know I love you, do you not?'

'I do,' said Amba, 'but why do you say that love is not the question? If we love each other and want to be with each other, what else matters?'

'Everything, my dear! Oh, if only Devavrata had not come to the groom-choosing and that you had garlanded me. Would it not have been a happier state of affairs then? But now...'

'Nothing has changed now,' said Amba. 'Believe me, nothing has changed.'

'Has it not? Did Devavrata not win you in a fair fight against all the kings of the land? Did he not take you as prize for Hastinapur's throne, to be wedded to High King Vichitraveerya?'

'He has, yes, but it was he who has sent me here, my lord! Even Mother Satyavati – she blessed me that I should make you a good wife and your kingdom a good queen.'

Salva did not stop caressing her hand, and she noticed that her own fingers were small and thin next to his. His voice dropped to a low whisper, and he said, 'Amba.' She should have liked it because it was the first time that evening he had said her name, but the tone in which he said it – she felt her eyes smart, and she blinked rapidly, hoping no tears would drop.

'Amba,' he said again. 'You're such a dear little girl. You are too innocent to understand the ways of the world, my dear. Do you really think that Devavrata sent you here just so that he can see you happy?'

'Yes,' she said, raising her head to him. 'He said he would not keep a maiden in Hastinapur against her will.'

'And he would not, I give him that. But you do belong to Hastinapur. Why would Devavrata give you away to me, without wishing something in return?'

She tensed. 'What did he ask you for?'

Salva broke into a sad smile. 'Your riding companions brought with them a parchment. After you were shown to your quarters this afternoon, they read to me Devavrata's message.'

'Bride price?'

Salva nodded. 'As you perhaps know, ours is a small city. The Saraswati feeds us but for six months of the year. Plants do not grow on our sandy lands. But we do have the mountains behind us, and on top of them we have set up quarries. Devavrata wants our mines for six months, until midsummer next year.'

Amba recalled bits of conversation between Devavrata and Satyavati, something about weapons and how the kingdom of Panchala was forging them by the thousands out of their rocky lands. If marble, granite and sandstone could be taken from Saubala, could Hastinapur not match Panchala in weapon-making, at least for the next six months?

'That is too dear a price, my lady,' Salva was saying, as though from somewhere far away. She could only feel his fingers wrapped tight around her hand. 'This is the wrong half of the year for us to be giving up our mines. If we do not trade our stone with Kunti and Shurasena, they will not give us food and water. My people will starve.'

'Then do not give him the stone he wants,' said Amba.

'And suffer the consequences?'

'What are the consequences?'

'Well,' said Salva, 'nothing immediate. But it is not well for a kingdom of my size to cheat Hastinapur of what is rightfully hers.'

'Rightfully hers?' Amba said, her voice rising. 'Are you saying that I rightfully belong to Hastinapur?' Her eyes filled with tears, and her voice quavered. 'I am a person, not a thing.'

'A person ... who was won fairly by the champion of Hastinapur in an open fight to be wedded to his brother.'

'A person!' she said resolutely. 'I do not belong to any one kingdom. I belong to the king of Kasi, who bore and bred me, and I belong to you, the one whom I chose to love, to marry.'

His fingers resumed caressing her hand. 'Dear girl,' he said. 'You do not understand the ways of the world.'

'Fight him,' she said suddenly, and felt his hands retreat in shock. 'Fight him for me, my lord.'

'My lady,' said Salva, with a nervous laugh. 'You must be jesting. Did you not see how convincingly he fought us all? He is the foremost warrior in all of North Country, and you want me to fight him?'

'For me,' said Amba.

'It shall not be a fight, my dear. I shall be walking to certain death.'

'Then let us die,' Amba said, her breath heavy and fast, eyes glistening. 'Let us die so that in our next life we are united.'

'My lady! Think of my people, of my wives–'

'But it is me that you love! You told me you would happily die for my love. Or were they just lies, then?'

He hesitated; only for a moment, but he did. He let out a smile that was meant to disarm her, but it only made her skin crawl. 'What you ask is impossible,' he said. 'I cannot forsake my kingdom for you.'

'Why? Do you not love me?'

'Not as much as that, no.'

She was reminded of Mother Satyavati's quiet voice and dark lips mouthing the words: *Will he take you back?* Then she had jumped to Salva's defence, but now, she found herself wavering. If he was neither ready to pay the bride price nor to fight for her against Hastinapur, he could be saying only one thing.

'Are you going to send me back?' she asked.

'My lady, I am afraid I am left with no other choice.'

She pulled her hand back and looked at it as if termites had been chewing on it. A wave of disgust washed over her. The king withdrew out of her reach, watching, and his left hand rose to signal the attendants to become alert.

'Stop,' she said, raising her own hand. 'You have nothing to fear from me. I carry no weapons. Even if I did, I would not have sullied my knife by stabbing you, O King.'

'I understand your anger—'

'You understand *nothing*! All you understand is to treat a maiden like she were property, to be fought over, to be won, to be given away in return for a price. I now know that when you pursued me in Kasi, you did so because in your eyes, I was a prize to be won. But now that someone else has won me and is offering me to you, you want nothing of me.'

'Amba, you do not understand. All of North Country will laugh at me—'

'If you accept my love?'

'To accept you as a gift, as alms, without giving them anything in return!' Salva sprang to his feet and clasped his arms behind him. He puffed out his chest and looked down at her. 'You do not understand a man's world, Princess. There are bigger things than love that the world cares for.'

Amba looked up to face him, her lips pursed tight. 'Like duty, you would say, would you not?' She got up slowly. 'Like honour.' She stood to her full height. 'Accepting me would drag you down, would it not? You would not be able to stare Devavrata in the eye if you take me into your court and accept me as your queen. People will say that the king of Saubala had to be bestowed a wife by Devavrata, who defeated him and stole her from him first! That is your concern, is it not, Salva?' She had never taken his name before. But now this man appeared to her stripped of title. He was no king.

Salva squared his shoulders. False bravado, she thought. She could spit in his face now and he would take it. He knew that she was right; she could see the admission in his furtive, ferrety eyes. A long-gone whisper sounded in her ear, that of an old maid who had reared her since she was a babe. She had said that the king from Saubala was fine and mighty, but he had eyes that could not be trusted. Amba had then laughed her away as a whiny old woman, as she had done with Mother Satyavati. How right they both had been! How stupid was she to have thwarted the opportunity to become High Queen of Hastinapur for this lout.

'Hastinapur will look after you well, Princess of Kasi,' said Salva. 'You can stay here for the night as our honoured guest. We may be a small kingdom, but we treat our guests as gods. Early tomorrow, you can ride.'

Amba broke into a laugh. She turned away from the king and signalled for her coronet and clips to be brought. 'We will ride tonight, Your Majesty,' she said. 'Please make arrangements for us to leave in an hour from now.'

'Tonight? It may be dangerous crossing the Khandava at night.'

'My riding companions will protect me. If you have any gifts for the court of Hastinapur, I shall be glad to carry them.'

She was aware of the stillness behind her for a moment, but she did not look back. Then she heard his step recede from her toward the door that opened into the corridor. When the attendant came bearing the silver bowl with the coronet on it, she lifted it carefully with her fingertips and looked at the big green emerald that stood atop the snaky arrangement of diamonds and rubies. It looked very much, she thought, like a peacock's feather.

She set it on top of her head. Then she walked to the mirror.

TWO

Amba kept her lips woven together with an iron will for as long as she could, but eventually emotion won over pride, and soon after the palanquin had reached the edge of Khandava, she buried her face in her hands and sobbed like a child.

The song of the palanquin bearers carried an easy, joyful rhythm. As Amba wiped her tears she tried to follow the words but realized that she could not. The fishermen of Hastinapur spoke Sanskrit mixed with strange guttural sounds and wheezes. Even today, Mother Satyavati's speech carried those marks.

Thoughts of Satyavati brought back thoughts of the royal court. Before stepping out, she had checked herself in Salva's mirror. She had never, until this evening, thought of herself as a possible queen of a kingdom. She was taller than most women her age, and she still had at least a year or two of growing up. Her cheekbones were the right height, and though her forehead was a bit too broad for her liking – which meant that she liked to place the spot of vermillion further up above her eyebrows instead of between them – her hair was richer and darker than that of either of her sisters.

She was big-breasted, bigger than most women she knew. That was the one thing that Salva had liked about her body. That night on the terrace of the north fort, after they had got past the guards and were lying on their backs together, looking at the crescent moon, he had slid his hands over her breasts and caressed them.

She had big hips too; someone had told her that big hips were good for child-bearing. Her legs had once been strong and shapely, when she had been thirteen and had been used to riding her ponies on Kasi's fields, but in the last one year she had neither ridden nor run very much. Once she got to Hastinapur she decided she would get back to exercising her body – an hour of weaving for the arms, perhaps an hour of spinning to keep her back from tightening up, and an hour of riding, even if it was within the palace walls. During her short stay there she had once inspected the stables, and had been impressed by the dark horses that had come from Kamboja, the rocky kingdom up north.

She had never been called beautiful by many. It was her mouth – too wide to ever curl into a pout no matter how much she tried – that gave her whole face a grotesque, mannish appearance. As a child she had hated standing in front of the mirror, especially when accompanied by Ambalika, easily the prettiest of the three. But as Amba had grown into a young woman, she had taught herself the art of making her eyes and nose assert themselves more – by wearing kohl and nose rings – and of downplaying the mouth – by not applying any beautifier to it at all.

The palanquin stopped, and Amba heard the gruff voice of the head rider. 'Enough with your singing!' he barked at the bearers. 'We shall pass in silence. And pray to your gods that we do not run into a pack of wolves.' The palanquin bearers whispered to one another in hushed tones for a few moments, then fell quiet. Amba noticed that the sounds of the forest had died too.

She hoped that the bearers would begin their merry singing again, because the quietness made the voice inside her head that much louder. One thought had been nagging her at the corner of her mind, a thought that she had deliberately pushed aside every time it piped up. But now she had to let it come out, for her very future may depend upon it.

It was to do with what people had been telling her for quite some time now. Mother Satyavati said it, Bhishma said it, her old maid in Kasi said it, so did her father – and even Salva today said it: *she did not understand the ways of men.* Now she was going back to Hastinapur with an emerald coronet perched on her head, assuming that she would become queen, but would she? Vichitraveerya was a man, and so was Bhishma. After she had kicked at the honour that had been placed at her feet, would either of them allow her to just walk in and take her place by Vichitraveerya's side?

If Salva was right, if Bhishma thought that Amba belonged to Hastinapur, then he would have no qualms in taking her back. But if Salva was wrong, and if Vichitraveerya thought the same way as Salva and rejected her because she was 'another man's property', then she would have to face the same predicament again. Only then she would not have a palanquin to sit in and cry. Perhaps the regent of Hastinapur would be kind enough to send her off to her father's palace, but alas, her father too, was a man.

Where would she then go?

Her hand went up to the coronet on her head and fingered the fine diamonds. A nameless fear took root in her heart. It slowly swelled in size and grew so heavy that she had to lie down on her bed, bobbing up and down to the beat at which the bearers walked. Suddenly she was thankful for the silence. It may not come to it, but she had to be prepared for the worst. Now she had a night ahead of her to plot her way to Hastinapur's throne.

Ambika and Ambalika would be her rivals, but she had no fears about them. She would trounce them because she knew how they thought. No, more than her sisters, she would need to know how Mother Satyavati would think and move, what

Bhishma and Vichitraveerya would say. She would need to enter, and fully understand, the minds and worlds of men.

It could not be impossible. Mother Satyavati seemed to have done it. Her old maid in Kasi had once told her that men were simple beings with straight, narrow desires. It would be nice if she could be taken back lovingly at Hastinapur, but if she was not, she would have to be prudent and bargain for a place to stay instead. If she were to get for herself a section of the palace – no, even just a room in the palace – if she could just place herself so that she would be part of Hastinapur's first family without being *in* it, perhaps with time, she could manoeuvre some pieces here and there and see what would happen.

For instance, one immediate advantage that she enjoyed over her sisters was that she was more sexually mature. Ambika's breasts were only just forming. Ambalika still had puberty marks on her cheeks and forehead. They could flame passion in the loins of no red-blooded king. But she, Amba, was another matter. Being a waiting-woman in the court of a kingdom she was supposed to rule would be a hitch, but it would be a temporary one if she did the right things. It was not unforeseen for a king to have children by waiting-women; such born babies were sent away to fostering in distant kingdoms. But what if the king had a son by a waiting-woman who was not just of high birth, but was the eldest princess of a Great Kingdom? What would happen then?

Her spine tingled in spite of the warm night breeze that flapped the yellow side curtains of the palanquin. Her eyes grew heavy– a sign, she thought, that her mind had ceased to worry. She had drawn her battle lines. She drifted away on the sounds of wheezes and grunts from the palanquin bearers, and as she teetered between sleep and waking, she saw herself walking through a dark and tortuous tunnel, at the end of which, in the distance, she saw the stone-studded, glittering throne of Hastinapur. Vichitraveerya sat on it to the left, resting his arm, and when he saw her he smiled and beckoned to her to sit by his side.

Amba rubbed her stomach with her palms three times – the way her old maid had once said women should while praying for sons – and went to sleep.

'You have come back, my lady,' said Vichitraveerya. He had the slender build of the Kuru kings. His wrists bore the marks of a bow-string, and his fingertips were rough and brown. The vast plains of Hastinapur encouraged open warfare, and her kings learnt to ride a chariot and to string a bow before they knew their way around their mothers' breasts.

'My lord,' said Amba, bowing low. 'I have realized the folly of my ways.'

'Did you? Or was the king of Saubala not able to afford the bride price that we demanded for you?'

His small eyes were peering at her. He wore his hair long so that it grew all over his ears and covered them. He had a firm nose, an inquisitive and charming mouth, and eyebrows that looked like they were carefully drawn with a kohl pencil. None of his features by themselves appeared like Mother Satyavati's, but the manner in which he carried himself reminded Amba of her. He would have made a fine maiden, she thought, if he had been born one.

'I cannot lie to you, my lord king,' she said. 'I had given my heart to Salva, and he said he had given his to me. But today I have known what a poor illusion love is.'

'Oh, you have, have you?' said Vichitraveerya, motioning her to sit down. He adjusted his white morning robes so that they would not get entangled between his legs. 'I do not bear you any ill will, my lady.'

Amba tensed. She placed both her hands on top of each other on her laps, and waited.

'I did not bear you any ill will when brother Bhishma told me of your wish to leave. I had not even met you. Perhaps I should have; I would perhaps then not have let you go.' As he entwined his hands, Amba saw that his fingers were bereft of rings; strange for a High King. 'But what is the need to mull over the past? The truth is that I did let you go, and you did go.'

'But I have come back, my lord.'

'You have, but only because the man you wanted rejected you, my lady. Is that not so? If the king of Saubala had pride enough to reject you because you were won by another, how much pride must I, the High King of Hastinapur, possess?'

'Since you are the High King, Your Majesty, and since you are a much bigger man than Salva, I thought you would see it prudent to rise above your pride.'

'Ah!' said Vichitraveerya, laughing shortly. 'You speak well, better than your sisters. How much older are you than they?'

'Ambika is two years younger, my lord, and Ambalika one year younger still.'

'It shows. I would have liked nothing better than to take you as my queen, but for your journey across the Yamuna to Salva's court.'

'He has not touched me, my lord king, of that I swear,' said Amba.

'That is not my concern!' said Vichitraveerya, anger rising in his voice. 'The men you lay with are entirely your choices, Princess. In the Kuru line we believe a maiden is free to choose her men.'

'Then can I not choose you as my husband, my lord?'

'We *also* believe in a man's free choice,' said Vichitraveerya. 'If I take you as my queen now, my name across North Country will be sullied.'

What name was he referring to, Amba wondered. North Country did not so much as mention Vichitraveerya's name. Whenever Hastinapur's throne and her great plains were spoken about, people sang praises of Devavrata the valiant, of Bhishma the heroic. Men from smaller kingdoms, especially further down toward the Eastern Sea, even thought that Devavrata was the

High King of Hastinapur. When the champion had ridden at the head of his army a few years back along the length of the country, demanding salt and fish from the kingdoms of the shore, he had been received in a manner befitting a High King.

Vichitraveerya, however, did not have a name outside of Hastinapur. Did he not know that? Or perhaps this was just another of those games that men played. She restrained herself from speaking of this matter; she would do well now not to anger Vichitraveerya.

She said, 'I shall give you a son, my lord; a son that would match Devavrata in battle.'

His eyes lit up at her words, and she knew at once that she had hit a spot. How humiliating it must be for a king to be overshadowed by his brother in all aspects? Chitrangada and Vichitraveerya were, after all, sons of a fisherwoman; how could they ever become kings, even though circumstances may have placed them on the throne? She saw from his eyes and his suddenly rigid posture: she now had his attention.

'I do not ask for favours, my king,' said Amba, looking up at him beseechingly, her hands still placed on her lap. 'If you take me for your wife, I will give you a son for whom even Devavrata shall have to step aside. In my veins runs the blood of the great Rama, the mythical king of Kasi who once united and ruled over all of North Country. I shall bear you a son who will be the Rama of this age.'

'But you cannot know that. You don't know that you will bear a son.'

'Ambika and Ambalika are but children, Your Majesty. You must have already lain with both of them. Did they please you as a king ought to be pleased? Or did you have to guide them by their hands and tell them what to do?'

Alarmed, Vichitraveerya looked away at the door and motioned to the attendants to leave. After they did, he turned to Amba and said, 'Ambika and Ambalika have the same blood in them as you do, my lady. If you can give me a son, so can they.'

'Only women in the peak of their womanhood can give birth to valiant sons, my lord. Do you see signs of womanhood in either of my two sisters? Look at me.' She opened her arms on her sides, palms facing out. 'Look at me, and think of them. Ask yourself with a calm mind, then, about who can give you a better son.'

'Will Ambika not be your age in two years?'

'Yes,' said Amba, and though it pained her to speak so of her sister, she said, 'but can you be certain that she will come to be as I am today? Even if she does, my lord, I can give you a son right now, not in two years. Why do you still hesitate so?'

'I cannot take you as my wife,' he said looking so utterly helpless that she pitied him. 'Hastinapur's honour will be lost. Brother Bhishma will surely say no.'

'Is Brother Bhishma the king of Hastinapur, my lord, or are you?' she asked.

'He is, no doubt. I am but a figurehead, the puppet of a man who happens to sit on the throne while he rules. I do not like it, but what shall I do? Brother Bhishma is a great warrior, and he does know a lot more than me about matters of state.'

'He is older than you are, my lord. With the passing of time, I am certain that you will rule as well as he does. But you shall need a son of Kshatriya blood, of a woman who is in the fullness of her youth. Ambika and Ambalika are Kshatriya princesses of the best kind, but they are yet to reach that age where the womb is at its supplest.'

'Yes,' said Vichitraveerya, 'perhaps you are correct. But I cannot marry you after having given you away.'

Not relenting, Amba said, 'You do not have to, my lord. Not now.'

'Eh? What do you say, Princess?'

'I do not wish you to marry me and soil your name. All I wish to do is give you a son. Once I do that, you can either choose to take me as your wife and seat me by your side on your throne –

or you may not. But please let me give you a son who shall be king after you.'

'Why, why, that is unheard of – a princess staying at the court of the king who is the husband of her sisters.' His eyes, which had been shifting all this while, came to settle upon hers, and then they travelled down to her neck. Amba saw desire in his eyes; not desire for a son, but desire for her body. For a moment she wondered if she had played the wrong way, whether she should have seduced him instead of promising him a son, but she steadied herself. It did not have to be one or the other.

She lowered her voice, her gaze, and said, 'Do not look at me that way, my lord.'

He looked at the open door to make sure that no one was approaching. Then he turned to her and said, 'Do you know what a man needs from a woman, my lady?'

Amba did not know what to say, and she did not want to be wrong. She lowered her gaze further and said, 'Mmm?'

'A man needs a woman to parry with him. Not with swords and spears, no, but with words, like you do with me. And he needs her to parry with him in bed. Do you know why it is so common for the kings of North Country to sleep with their waiting-women?'

Amba shook her head, her gaze still lowered.

'Because waiting-women are whores in bed, oh yes, they are. They give the king what he wants, and they take from him what they want. But women bred in royal households are not like that, my lady. They are too demure, too soft, too giving. They relent when they have to rebel.' He pushed aside his robe and pointed her to the red marks on his shoulders and neck. 'You see these marks? Let me tell you, these were *not* caused by Ambika and Ambalika.'

'I understand, my lord.'

'That is what a man needs, more than sons or victory in battle or any of that nonsense. Brother Bhishma is an impotent fool; he neither has desire nor the ability to sire sons. No wonder, then, that he values valour and violence. But I – I possess the hunger, and I possess the means to satiate myself. And I will.'

A slow realization came to Amba, by the way Vichitraveerya's voice dropped a notch when he mouthed the words 'impotent fool', even though he knew they were alone. This was how Vichitraveerya got back at the world, then, for putting him second to Devavrata in everything: by indulging in the one thing that Devavrata could not – or would not. No matter how many more men Devavrata defeated in battle, Vichitraveerya would always have more women. The more ruthless Devavrata became in strengthening Hastinapur's hold on North Country, so did Vichitraveerya become in his pursuit of women. One would never acknowledge the other as right, and each would assume that he had won over the other.

Amba wondered if there was any truth to what Vichitraveerya said about Devavrata – was he, indeed, impotent?

She decided that it was not her concern. Vichitraveerya had told her what she must do. She got up to her feet, went to the door, and locked it. She came back to the chair on which Vichitraveerya sat, and with her hands on his chest, mounted him.

THREE

AMBA SPEAKS

Vichitraveerya's wedding to my sisters was the first wedding in the Kuru household for nigh on twenty years. It was as if the festival of lights and the festival of colours had come together to the city of Hastinapur. I did not venture into the city, but my companions told me that every house had been painted in elaborate patterns of red and green, that every temple had rows of lamps lining the walls of its courtyard, that bulls were decked with silk and vermillion and turmeric, that legs of calves were tied with anklets so that the air would fill with jingles. Doors had divine chants written on them with sandal paste, and men and women broke into songs and dances as though it were the harvest season and they had been blessed with a bountiful crop.

The gates of the royal palace were thrown open to let in the throngs of people. Kings and regents from all sixteen Great Kingdoms attended as guests, even those that Bhishma vanquished in Kasi. (King Salva sent his minister, who read out a lengthy message in court on his king's behalf, wishing the threesome a hundred valiant sons.) My own father was there too, and though I tried to catch his eye during the ceremony, not once did he turn from my sisters to look in my direction. Some of the other kings did, but whenever I met their gaze they would look away, and they would lean to the person next to them and whisper something.

This was no more than two weeks after Vichitraveerya and I began to see each other in our bedchambers. Watching him perform the holy rites with my sisters while I attended to their hair and jewellery ought not to have made my heart heave – Vichitraveerya and I had, after all, become one in the one way that matters – but it did. I resolved to myself then that my own marriage to him would exceed this one in pomp, and the dances on the street would be more passionate because I would be mother, by then, to the future High King.

Wise men who had visited the court of Kasi long ago often told my father that if you truly desire something, that if you work for it, the gods will make sure that you get it. In those days, when I was still a maiden, I believed it. But now, on the cusp of death with my newborn child next to me, I do not. Enough has happened in my life to make me certain that the gods do not care for you at all. Even if they do, they take pleasure in making you run after this or that all your life, and when they tire of it they let the thread snap and allow you to wither away.

On the night of their wedding, Vichitraveerya came to my chamber. Ambika and Ambalika had gone to bed, he said, because they were tired after the day's duties. This was the fifteenth night in a row that he had slept by my side, and I remember laying awake at night long after his breath had slowed, staring at the dark ceiling and counting the days of my month. It was the fertile period of my cycle, so if all had gone well, this month – and for the nine months following it – there would be no blood between my thighs.

But come the night of the full moon, I woke up from a deep afternoon slumber (you sleep well during the day when the nights allow you none) with a headache, a cramp in my back, and an unmistakable moistening between my legs. That saddened me, but I let it pass since this was yet only the first month of our union. That night and for the four nights that followed, the king came to my chambers, and I did not desist lest he became angry with me.

It was only after two or three more moons had come and gone that I began to wonder if something was wrong. The king, by all accounts, was virile and strong, and when I surreptitiously asked Ambika and Ambalika about it they told me that he would make love to them every morning. The number of lovers that Vichitraveerya had taken in his early days of adulthood was by now already legend. If that were the case, should my stomach not have slipped by now? I now know how foolish I was, and with my child by my side I can say that I had always been worthy of being a mother, but back then I was but a young maiden, and Salva, when he made love to me, had not entered me with his organ. So as women are taught to do, I blamed myself, and resolved to strengthen my efforts to bear a child.

I began actively pursuing the king now, sending word for him when he was at court, when he was out riding, when he was engaged in mock battles with Bhishma – and he always came. Two or three times a day he came to my chambers now, and every time he left me I would lie on my bed, awash with sweat, certain that *this* time he must have sown his seed in me.

But every time, as the month rolled over, I would wake up with blood on my undergarment. In my frustration, once or twice I contemplated seducing a stable boy just to see if it was me or if it was the king, but prudence stopped me. I think, even back then, in the heart of my hearts I knew that there was nothing wrong with me. The king had lain with so many women and he had yet to bring a son into the world. Ambika and Ambalika too were barren. It was impossible that Vichitraveerya himself did not doubt his ability: the venom with which he spat out the words 'impotent fool' when he referred to Bhishma was perhaps nothing more than despair at his own condition.

All of these are still mere speculations, of course, because six months into his marriage, Vichitraveerya fell sick, and by the end of the year he had breathed his last.

I nursed him through his illness, even as Ambika and Ambalika shied away from the white bubbles on his skin, the pale lines on his cheeks, and his withering limbs. Once you have lain with a man, something akin to tenderness takes birth in your heart, and you cannot will it away. I saw that with Salva too; on the day he betrayed me, I had been angry, yes, but now, as I look back, I only remember the sprightly rider who took me on moonlit walks. My relationship with Vichitraveerya, meanwhile, was never a loving one – he did not stay back after our passion had abated to hold me close or to whisper in my ear – and yet, when he fell sick and his own wives deserted him, I could not find it in my heart to do the same.

Perhaps a doubter may say that it was hope that drove me. One could say that I saw my hopes of becoming the queen of Hastinapur ebb away with the life in his body, and that I nursed him only to resurrect my falling plans. But I – only I – know what I felt. Once you have lain with a man, you become one with him. Mother Nature makes it so. And when he slips away in front of your eyes, it is as if a part of you is slipping away.

After Vichitraveerya died, after I had mourned his passing for nine days – really mourned, unlike my sisters – Bhishma summoned me to his chamber. His face showed no signs of sadness. His eyes, like two perfect spheres carved out of blue sapphires, looked at the portrait of Vichitraveerya that hung on the wall opposite. Years ago, when he was yet a youth, Bhishma must have been like all of us, with ambition and desire. But something must have happened for him to shun it all, to step away from it and choose to just stand by, watching. 'Impotent fool,' Vichitraveerya had called him, this man who chased desperately after every woman in sight.

'Brother Bhishma,' I said, bowing low.

'My lady.'

He pushed back his red cape and held his arms behind his back. His eyes did not leave the portrait of the dead king. Outside, even though it was past sundown, the lamps had not yet been lit.

'My servants have told me that you nursed the king in his poor health,' he said.

'I did what any subject would do, my lord.'

'You did much more than even his wives. For that I am thankful.' He paused for a moment. Then, summoning some purpose, he said, 'Vichitraveerya was a fool to have not taken you as wife, Princess.'

'We all have our foolish moments,' I said.

'The day you came back, I told him that if you ask to be his wife, he must say yes. But he … he has always been a child—always seeing, but never knowing.'

As the shadows lengthened, attendants stole about the room, lighting lamps in every corner. On each side of Vichitraveerya's portrait were kept two small earthen pots with oil-dipped wicks leaning to the side. Once they were lit, Vichitraveerya's eyes seemed to look down upon us eerily, and I felt, just for a moment, that he passed by the room like a shade.

'The court doctors told me that the disease that afflicted the king was brought about by excess time spent in the company of women,' said Bhishma. 'And I think in the month or two before his death, he had been spotted visiting your chambers almost three times a day.'

'The king wished it, my lord, and I could not say no,' I said. It was not a lie, not strictly, because he had wished it as much as I.

'That may be so,' said Bhishma, 'but the whole kingdom now knows that you were his lover. The rumours may not have escaped you.'

'They have not.'

'After these ten days have passed, after the people of Hastinapur wake up to their king's death, they will all look for something – or someone – to blame.' Bhishma turned to face her. 'They will ask for the price of their king's life.'

I met his gaze, only fully understanding now. 'Brother Bhishma, are you saying that I am responsible for the king's death?'

'The people will say that, not I,' said Bhishma. 'The astrologers at the court will curse you and brand you as a witch who cast a spell on the king. The doctors will nod along. So will the courtiers, and so will the people.'

'And you? What of you, sire? Can you not tell them what truly happened?'

'What truly happened,' Bhishma said, his eyes narrowing at her, 'was that you lured Vichitraveerya into your bed in the hope of becoming queen before your sisters, my lady. I shall not judge your actions; I am merely telling you how *the city* will judge you.'

'But surely I, the princess of Kasi, cannot be called a murderess!'

'You are no longer the princess of Kasi, my lady. You are but a waiting-woman at our court. Your father disowned you long ago.'

I looked into his eyes, wishing there was something behind that cold facade he always hid behind. He could make all this go away, I knew. If he were to stand in front of the court and declare me innocent, all of Hastinapur would go by his words. Better still, if he would take me to be his wife…

'I will not take you for a wife, my lady,' he said, as if reading my thoughts. 'Please do not ask me that.'

'But why?' I said. 'You won me by fighting my suitors. You brought me here against my will when my heart was with another. You caused me this heartache, and now you brand me a witch on behalf of the people. You accuse me of murdering the king. Do you not feel responsible for my plight, my lord? I, who was meant to be a queen of a kingdom, am now a witch because of you. Does that not weigh on your heart?'

Bhishma's lips fused together, and in a low, controlled voice, he said, 'I did not call you here to debate with you, Princess. I have called you here to warn you of your future. I shall not marry you – indeed, I shall not marry anyone – nor shall I question the will of the people of Hastinapur.'

'Then allow me to die!' I said. 'What have I got to live for, now?'

'That is up to you,' he said, turning away from her. 'But Hastinapur shall not have your blood on her hands. Years from now, all of this will be forgotten, but the fact that we have killed a scheming princess, a witch of the land, shall not be.'

Of all the things that he had done to me, this was perhaps the worst, I thought. He did not care about my present or my future. He would shed no tear on my death, just as he shed none at his brother's. All he thought of was what would happen to Hastinapur, to her legacy, to her name. Who was Amba when placed against Hastinapur? Nobody!

'I have a horse and a riding companion waiting. You shall ride straight away, after retiring to your room to gather your belongings. I have given your companion instructions to take you wherever you wish to go.'

'But where shall I go, Brother? Where have I left to go?'

'I shall give you a sack full of gold coins carrying Hastinapur's seal. That should provide for your food and shelter anywhere you go in North Country.'

With those words he sent me away. To this day, I do not know if he truly believed that I was under danger to my life in Hastinapur. But many years later, when I passed through the city on my way to Panchala, I spoke to a few cloth traders in the kingdom, and they still told tales of the witch from Kasi who stole the life of their beloved king. So perhaps he was right; perhaps he acted to protect me. Or perhaps it was he who sowed the doubt in people's minds to get rid of me, for had I milled about the palace with my sisters, my jealousy would only have driven me against them. Perhaps he foresaw that. People even say that the blue moonstone he wears around his neck shows him the future and guards him against it. Perhaps they are right.

Now, in the throes of my death, I can forgive Bhishma his sins – and who on earth is truly sinless? – but on that night when he banished me from the kingdom, I was but a maiden of seventeen, sharp of tongue and heart and not as quick of mind. If I had then possessed the prudence that I do now, I would have taken his gold and gone to one of the neighbouring kingdoms as an heiress to a dead nobleman, and perhaps, someday, I would have married someone and have had a respectable life of my own.

But I spurned his gold and his companion. I gathered my clothes into a bag, put my riding clothes on, and set off on the back of a dark colt with nothing more than a few days' food in my knapsack. I also took a sword with me. I did not know where I wanted to go, but I set off eastward, in the direction of Panchala.

FOUR

Amba tethered her horse to one of the wooden poles outside the cowshed. She filled the feeding box with two bales of hay from the corner. Then she ran her hand over the white streak on the animal's forehead and whispered something into its ear. The horse snorted, shook his head free of her, and buried his face in the box.

She drew her hood over herself and stepped into the shed. To her right, seated on an inverted water vessel, a thin young man with a straight nose had his lips to the mouth of a flute. To her left, a portly middle-aged woman washed a dirty brass utensil in a tumbler of dirty water. In the middle of the room were three tables set in a triangle, and men sat hunched over their glasses of barley juice. As she entered, all of them stopped what they were doing and looked up at her.

Amba crinkled her nose and kept to the edge of the wall, where the light of the torches was the brightest. She made her way to an old wooden casket by the corner, closest to the woman washing dishes, and sat down, taking care to cover her legs. She told herself that she would get used to the smell of cow dung and foul breath; she just had to sit there for a few minutes. She kept her eyes low, and wrapped her cloak tighter around herself. Into the heavy air, someone said from the centre table: 'Who is the piece of lightning, Asvini? Never seen her around these parts.'

'Shut up and drink your juice, Sirisha,' said the woman from behind the table. Bending towards Amba, she asked, 'What will you have, dear?'

Amba found her voice. 'I will have some goat's milk, please.'

A cackle of laughter shot through the men's huddle. 'Drink some barley juice with me, lady,' said someone in a thick voice, 'and I shall follow you like a dog.'

The man with the flute, sitting along the opposite edge of the room from her, lifted his instrument back to his lips. The shed fell silent for a few seconds, then the men began to wave together, singing along to the notes and holding up their glasses.

Amba drank her milk, tapping her feet to the rhythm, and kept the empty glass beside her. She narrowed her eyes at the group of men, but she could not make out their features. All the fire torches in the room were perched on the walls, leaving the middle of the room in shadow.

'Asvini!' one of the men called. 'Fill me up again with some of your nectar!' A giggle went around the group, and the speaker looked up and threw up his eyebrows at the landlady.

'Only if you show me how many coins you have on you, Kavasha. Your woman told me today that I should not give you more than a glass no matter how much you plead with me. And you have already had four by my count.'

'Eh! This is my second one, I swear to the gods.'

'Show me your money bag,' said Asvini.

The man called Kavasha slumped in his chair and played with the rim of his glass. 'Asvini, you know how bad the rains have been this year.'

'Aye, I do. That is why you must not drink so much, Kavasha. Why do you not go back to your wife and sleep with her? Go. Make love to her tonight.'

'Eh, I make love to her every night. But I do not get any love from you, Asvini, and I have been coming to this shed all my life!'

'When my man comes back from his travels I will send him to you, and he will give you all the love you need.' Asvini's reply sent a hoot through the group, and the men banged on their tables with their glasses, drowning out the mellow tone of the flute. She filled up the men's glasses one by one, collecting a coin from each and depositing them into the little yellow cloth bag that hung off her waist. When she came to Kavasha, he rummaged his pockets but came up empty-handed.

'I have nothing, Asvini,' he said, blinking up at her.

'Then I have nothing for you, you good-for-nothing oaf.'

'At the next harvest, I will give you all the rice you need for the whole winter if you fill up my glass just this once. I pray to you, Asvini. Your hands are those of Annapurna herself, and your barley juice – ah, the gods can keep their nectar, I tell you.'

'Shut up,' she said, but Amba saw that he had broken her. She had begun to smile, and she filled his glass even as she said, 'That field of yours will not yield anything this season or the next, Kavasha. We have not had rains the whole year. Where are you going to get the sack of grains from?' She got back to her place behind the table and began to wash a fresh batch of vessels. As she wiped the first one, she looked at Amba and asked her if she wanted another pail.

Amba nodded. 'Yes, please.'

She heard whispers from the men, and then one of them nudged Kavasha and giggled. The latter got up, cleared his throat, steadied himself, and bowed in her direction. 'My lady,' he said.

Amba bowed too, without removing her hood or cloak. Somebody thumped him on the back and he sat back down. 'What if my field does not give me anything?' he said, after taking a big gulp of his new drink. 'I have my cattle which will give me milk, and I will open a shed just like this one, and I will only allow maidens to come there – maidens that would drink nothing but goat's milk.'

Asvini motioned to one of her servant boys to attend to the unwashed utensils. She came to the edge of the table and said, 'What self-respecting maiden would come to your shed, you idiot?

And you speak of cattle – let us see if that cattle lasts this year, shall we? If you have not heard, Hastinapur is readying for battle, they say. Once they come and go, neither will you have cattle nor a wife.'

'Eh! Hastinapur will never take Panchala!' Kavasha replied. 'And they will take my cattle only over my dead body!'

'So they will,' said Asvini, filling up Amba's vessel up with milk. 'They shall have no trouble killing you, and all you men who sit here – go and protect your women, because if Hastinapur comes, even the royal house will have nowhere to run.'

'Yes,' said a big man with a long beard and smooth head, brooding over his glass. 'The king of Hastinapur is getting married to the princesses of Kasi, they say. If that is true then Panchala is caught in the middle, is it not? If only our king had a daughter to give in marriage to the king of Hastinapur. Being relatives is much better than being enemies, if you ask me.' He downed his glass and brought it down with a thump on his table. Asvini hurried over to fill it up. He tossed her a coin, which she caught and slid down her bag.

'If you ask *me*,' said Kavasha, 'the king should give us a son who will lead us in war against Hastinapur. All that land between Ganga and Yamuna – just imagine how many sacks of grain will grow on that land every year.' His eyes watered at the thought, and he gave Asvini a sly look. 'Then you shall have no say in when I come and when I leave, Asvini, huh? I shall be rich, and I shall shower you with gold coins.'

'Hah, you make me laugh, Kavasha. Do you think I will be here by then? Long before Hastinapur fights with us I will shut down this cowshed and go eastward. They say Kosala is a kingdom that seldom fights, and that the merchants there are rich. If I open a barley-juice shed there, I suspect I shall not need to deal with people like you lot!'

Amba raised her head, just enough for her mouth and nose to be visible. 'You are right, madam,' she said. 'Kosala is indeed full of rich merchants.'

'Aye,' said the man Asvini had addressed as Sirisha. 'How would you know that, lady?'

Amba stopped. 'I … I was the waiting-woman at Kasi for the three princesses until Bhishma won them over in battle. I have visited them in Hastinapur, and now I am on my way back home.'

'Wait a minute,' said the big brooding man. 'That sounds like a lot of rot! Waiting-women are taken on palanquins, and they never travel except with riding companions.' When the rest of the men turned to look at him, he said, 'My sister is an errand-girl at the court to the waiting-women. She tells me what it is like.'

Amba's heart leapt when she heard that, and she asked the man, 'Will your sister be able to guide me to the king?'

'Eh? But you are going back to Kasi, are you not?' he asked.

'I tell you,' said Kavasha, 'something about this woman smells bad. I saw her horse outside. It is not of our kind. It is of the kind they have up North, where the rocky kingdoms lay.'

Asvini said to the men: 'Hush, boys. Sit down and drink up in silence.' But Amba saw that her face had turned suspicious too. The sooner she got out of there, the better, she thought. As she rose to pay, her scabbard undid the knot of her knapsack, and her crown tumbled onto the wooden ground.

Everyone watched in stunned silence as the coronet came to rest a few feet away from her. Then someone from the huddle whistled. The men got up one by one, and leaving their glasses behind, circled her and looked down at the ornament. One scratched his head, another opened his mouth in a circle, yet another touched the jewel with the tip of his foot, as though he expected it to blow into pieces any minute. 'Whoa,' said Kavasha. 'Look at that!'

'You are from Hastinapur,' said one of the men.

'You want to see our king,' said another.

'Are you here to kill him?'

'No!' she said. 'No, you do not understand. I ... I am the princess of Kasi.'

Kavasha laughed. 'A few minutes ago she was a waiting-woman to the princess. Now she *is* the princess.'

'I am the princess of Kasi!' she said. 'I am banished from Hastinapur for having killed the king.'

'Hastinapur's king is dead?' said the big man, looking around him. 'Why has this news not come to us yet?'

'Because it happened but a few days ago. If Panchala invades Hastinapur now…'

'Nonsense. Hastinapur's king is hale and hearty. He is cavorting with his three wives as we speak!'

'He is not,' Amba replied. 'And he never got married to three princesses. He only married two. I am the third one.'

Kavasha leaned closer to her. 'You are the third princess of Kasi? You look too old for that.'

'I am the *first* princess of Kasi. I am the eldest of them all.'

'Gah! Another story,' said Kavasha. 'I think you are a spy.'

She saw them all nod, one after the other, and at the end she saw Asvini's face, set in disapproval. 'I ... I ... well, why don't you take me to your king? I shall explain all.'

'No,' said the big man, grabbing her by her arms, 'you tell us first who you are and why you are here, spreading lies about Hastinapur.'

When she felt the man's iron grip close around her arms, when she saw him lift her up in the air as though he was handling a dried twig, Amba, for the first time in her life, felt that she could die. The man's chest heaved every time he took breath, and when he breathed out it sounded like a snort so heavy with the smell of barley that it made her head pound. The other men had closed in around her now, and one of them was looking into her sack. Another one pulled back her hood and removed her cloak. A collective gasp went up.

'Say what you will, she looks as pretty as a princess,' said one.

'Oh, sweet as honey, ripe as corn,' said another.

'Hush!' said the man holding her. He leaned in so that his nose almost touched hers. She closed her eyes and drew back as much as she could. He shook her, once, forward and back. 'I am asking you for the last time, "Princess". Who are you? And what are you doing here? If you do not answer me, I will leave you to this pack of wolves here. By the time they are finished with you, you will have wished you were dead.'

Her breath quickened as though she had run here all the way from Hastinapur. How foolish she had been not to take Hastinapur's gold. If she got out of this, she thought, she would go back to Bhishma and take the gold he had promised her. She would just set up a new life for herself in one of the kingdoms and live comfortably, under a new name. Revenge was not for her; she who could be broken in two by this man's bare hands. She prayed to the Destroyer with all her devotion, even as the brute's fingers burned into the skin of her arms. She prayed for something to come and rescue her; anything . . .

'There,' said a voice, and to her ears it sounded like Shiva himself. 'That is enough. Put her down and leave, all of you.'

'Aye, and who might you be, sir? Bhishma himself, I suppose, come to rescue her?'

'No,' said the man, stepping out of the shadows into the light. 'I am enough for scum like you.' He held up a ring with a large red stone, and immediately the fingers around her released their grip. She was placed on the ground, and all the men fell to the ground, bowing. He held out his arm in her direction. 'Come over to my side, my lady. I shall protect you.'

It was only then that she looked at his face – a web of marks and scars through which two keen eyes looked out. His lips were so thin that when he spoke, it appeared as if someone had cut into his mouth with the thinnest of blades. 'I shall not catch sight of any of you again. If I do, I shall make sure I put my sword to work. Do you understand?'

'My lord,' said the big brute that had lifted her. 'We were concerned that this woman is a spy from Hastinapur.'

'You are but a peasant,' said her saviour. 'What do you know about spies and such? And did your mothers not teach you to treat a woman with respect? What shall come of Panchala if her men see a whore in every woman? The king shall be displeased with you, gentlemen, if I were to tell him of this.'

Amba heard them howl and hug the ground more closely, and the big fellow said, 'Pardon us, my lord. Perhaps we have misbehaved with the lady.'

'Perhaps?'

'Pardon us again, we *have* misbehaved with the lady.' He turned to her and went down on one knee. In a low voice, he murmured, 'We beg your pardon, my lady. I do wish you forgive us.'

'Enough!' said the nobleman. 'I suggest all of you oafs run home and get some sleep. Perhaps in the morning, after the fog has cleared a little, you will know what you would have done had I not been passing through.' He took her hand in his and led her out into the chilly night, closing the door behind them. 'Come, my lady,' he said to her. 'Get the horse out on the road!' he instructed the shadow of a man to her left, who went scurrying away.

The nobleman walked in front of her, the reins of her horse in one hand and his in the other. To their left, corn fields stretched out as far as she could see. The moon had already set for the night, and she could not tell what time it was. She had left Hastinapur on horseback no later than an hour after sundown and had maintained a good pace; it could not be much later than midnight now, she thought. Of course, if she had not been consumed by anger at Bhishma, she would have stayed the night and started in the morning. Now once again she bristled at the thought of that man. If she had to be here, riding on a horse with a stranger for company at midnight in a strange land, was he not to blame? If she had her way, she would see to it that the head of Hastinapur's regent would roll in the dust.

'I must thank you, my lord,' she said out loud, holding her cloak from flying away in the west wind. 'You saved my life in the cowshed.'

'My name is Jarutha,' said the man, without turning back. 'Your ladyship must not be accustomed to travelling by herself, for otherwise you would have known that it is a bad time to be about in town.'

'Allow me to introduce myself, my lord—'

'I heard what you said before I came to your rescue. Are you indeed the princess of Kasi?'

'I am, my lord, yes. You can send word to King Kasya, who rules over Kasi, and he shall only be glad, I think, to confirm it.'

'I think we shall do that, yes,' said Jarutha. 'But you said something else, madam, which was interesting. You said that the king of Hastinapur is dead.'

'That is the truth, Lord Jarutha,' said Amba. 'The king of Hastinapur died nine days ago to this day, and if you do not know that perhaps your spies are not as good as you think they are.'

Jarutha laughed. 'We do not have spies in Hastinapur, my lady. They do not take lightly to strange people over there. Here in Panchala, you at least got two glasses of goat's milk. In Hastinapur, they do not allow you to enter unless you bear a message or a seal.'

'Is that so?'

'Yes, they look after themselves well. They defend themselves well too, so I am not certain that you are right when you say this is a good time to invade Hastinapur.'

Amba said, 'The king is dead, Lord Jarutha. If this is not a good time, then what is?'

'As long as Bhishma is alive, Princess, Hastinapur will not fall.'

'Bhishma is only one person, my lord. You have a whole army. Surely you do not think that Bhishma can rout your whole army single-handedly?'

Jarutha did not reply. He led their horses out of the cornfields up a hill. Her horse began to pant and protest, but Jarutha's appeared fresher and ready for the climb. Jarutha asked her to mount his horse so that hers could rest for a while. After they had made the switch and resumed their trek, Amba looked up to see the outer wall of the fort a few hundred leagues ahead of her. The breeze had picked up as they gained in elevation, and now she had to hold her cloak with all her might to prevent it from flying away. When she turned around she saw that the fields lay below her, dotted by scarecrows here and there. The starlight and the wind made the fields look like one great purple ocean.

She turned around, and as they approached the wall in silence, as the first warmth of the firelight touched her skin, Jarutha said, 'Our king, I think, will have a word with you, my lady.'

FIVE

The High King of Panchala, Drupad, appeared cross with the world. Amba could guess why. A king's day ended much later than that of most of his subjects, but once it did, they liked to be undisturbed till the next morning. She had heard it said that kings lived short lives because they could be killed in battle at any time, but to her mind it was the daily grind of duties that wore them off, bit by bit. The methods of relaxation they employed did not help, either. Was there a king in the land who was not addicted to alcohol or women or dice? A man may think, foolishly, that he could sleep with as many women as he wanted, but he would only end up learning what Vichitraveerya did – that there was also such a thing as too much pleasure.

The soft fragrance in the room suggested that a waiting-woman or two had been driven out just before her entrance. On the table she saw three gold-plated glasses and a jug with a long, narrow mouth. Red rose petals covered the large circular bed, and a glass of milk sat on the stool to its right, half-empty. Milk – from buffaloes, especially – was believed to strengthen a man's virility. Tell a man that it would make him a God in bed and he would even drink poison willingly.

'Jarutha tells me you may have something to tell me, my lady,' he said, waving her to a chair. He was big and broad-chested, and wore a moustache that drooped down over his cheeks on both sides. Like most kings from the plains, he wore his hair long, over his shoulders, and seemed to like tucking it behind his ears every now and then, much in the manner of a lady preening herself. He had two or three zits on his forehead, one of them fresh and the other two fading away. Amba guessed he could be no older than twenty.

'That is so, my lord,' she said, bending low and taking a seat. 'I bring news that Hastinapur's High King, Vichitraveerya, breathed his last nine days ago to this day.'

'Indeed? We do not have spies in Hastinapur, alas.'

'Jarutha has told me so. If you wish to take Hastinapur, Your Highness, I do not think a more opportune moment than this would present itself.'

'Taking Hastinapur will be good, yes,' said Drupad. 'But it has not weakened as much as you say it has. Bhishma still commands her armies and guards her gates. It shall not be easy getting past him.'

Bhishma, Bhishma, Bhishma! Wherever she went she heard his name, no matter how much she wanted to run away. 'Talk of this kind does not befit a warrior like you, my lord,' she said coldly. 'The challenge of battle should spur you on, not scare you away.'

Drupad smiled at her. Despite his moustache, he had a nice, impish smile, she thought. 'What you say may be true if it is indeed a challenge we speak about, Princess. But fighting with Bhishma is not a challenge. It is sacrifice. You forget, perhaps, that he is old enough to be my father. He has been fighting wars for as long as I have been alive!'

'He is old. His limbs are weary. Yours are fresh and young. I am certain that if you take him on—'

'I shall do no such thing,' he said. 'But tell me this — why are you so eager to send me to my death? What harm have I ever done you, Princess of Kasi?'

'I wish to see Bhishma humbled and killed,' said Amba. 'And I thought North Country was a land of great kings, not cowards garbed in royal silk.'

He refused to rise to the bait. Still smiling, he said, 'I am sure many in the land wish the same thing as you, Princess. If Bhishma were subdued, the fertile lands of Hastinapur will be up for grabs, with no king on her throne. Which king of North Country would not wish to have granaries overflowing with wheat and corn throughout the year?' He paused and looked away for a second. Then he shook his head. 'But Bhishma still stands. And that is the truth.'

'But Your Majesty,' she said, 'you are admitting defeat even before taking up arms against him. He is but a man. Surely he is not invincible.'

'I am certain you know the tales they tell about him. He is the son of King Shantanu and a river nymph that came down the mountains of ice up north. If what they say is true, then he has divine blood flowing in his veins. Perhaps it would take a god to defeat him.'

'Do you hear yourself, King?' she asked, her eyes suddenly ablaze. 'Panchala's High King fears attacking a king-less city because of one man. Your whole army against one man, my lord – surely he cannot subdue your whole army on his own?'

'He who subdued an army of kings at your groom-choosing, my lady, can subdue any army of men.' He got up and walked to the window, where dark satin screens hung from the sill. He pushed one to the side, and a blast of wind sent his hair flying. He seemed to be looking far up north, toward the mountains. 'But I do think we can make use of your information, my lady. We cannot take Hastinapur, but we can take back our quarries that Bhishma has captured.' He closed the curtain and turned back to face her. 'At the northern tip of Panchala, where our boundary merges with that of the Kurus, we have quarries that fell rock to forge weapons. Over the last two years, the Kurus have inched their way into our territory, and now they hold two of our eighteen quarries – not many, I admit, but it would be nice to take back what is ours.'

Amba twisted her hands together. 'Won't Bhishma come to defend them?' she asked hopefully. 'And if he does, will you fight him yourself?'

'No, my lady,' Drupad replied, adjusting his hair. 'I shall only send Jarutha with a band of men to drive the usurpers away. From what I know of Bhishma, and if what you say is true – that Hastinapur is kingless – then they will not respond to our attack, at least for now. We can take back what is ours, and we can continue to make weapons that will one day,' he looked away into the distance, 'make us the supreme kingdom in North Country.'

'Not as long as Bhishma is alive,' she said, trying to goad him.

Drupad merely shrugged. 'Perhaps you are right. But he cannot live forever, can he, Princess?'

'He will, perhaps. Have you not seen how well he wears his age?'

She saw his eyes twitch and his moustache bristle, and knew that her words had hit their mark. No one who saw Bhishma even once would fail to notice how the man seemed to grow young with every passing year. It fed the myth – and Amba did not think it anything more than a myth – that he was, indeed, the son of a god. Perhaps when white hair begins to show in his beard, she thought, people will realize that he is but a man.

'You wish to kill him,' he said, 'even more than I do. What has he done to anger you so?'

'That, Your Majesty, is none of your concern.'

'Perhaps you are right. But you are still young, Princess, no more than twenty, I would assume. You have your whole life ahead of you. Would it not be prudent to go back to Hastinapur and stay there? God willing, you may still bear the future High King, and become queen mother.'

'I was not wedded to Vichitraveerya.'

'Even so,' said Drupad, 'you carry the blood of Kasi in you. Bhishma and Satyavati will be fools not to allow you to bear sons for Hastinapur's throne.'

'I wish to see the death of Bhishma,' said Amba simply.

'That, my lady, shall only come in the wake of Hastinapur's destruction.'

'Then I wish to see Hastinapur destroyed.'

Drupad came to stand by her. 'I would not like anything better than to see Hastinapur destroyed and under my rule, Princess.' He placed a hand on her shoulder. His palm was bruised and callous; the hand of a swordsman. 'But there is a time and place for everything, is there not? Hastinapur shall fall, it is written in the stars; but not now.'

Amba looked up, and she heard herself say, 'Take me as your wife, Your Majesty.'

Drupad withdrew his hand. 'My lady!' he said with a short laugh.

She got up to her feet. 'Why? Both of us want the same thing, do we not? Take me as your wife, and together we shall plot the death of the fiend that champions Hastinapur's throne.'

Drupad took another step back. 'My lady, I am betrothed to the princess of Chedi. We are to be wedded this midwinter.'

'So what? It shall not be the first time a king takes more than one wife.'

'But you are not just another princess—'

'Yes, I have the royal blood of Kasi flowing in me. I shall continue the line of the great king Rama himself, who is said to have united all of North Country in his time.'

'Yes,' said Drupad, 'yes. But taking you as my wife will only anger Bhishma. He may come to attack us.'

'He would not!' she cried, reaching for his garment and tugging him toward her. 'He banished me from the kingdom.'

'That does not mean he will sit idle while Panchala and Kasi become allies, Princess. It may be true that we do not have spies in Hastinapur, but Hastinapur has many in Panchala. They will carry news of our wedding to Bhishma, and I promise you that he will wage war on Panchala and take you away.'

'Only to banish me again!' she said.

'That may be so, yes. You can stay here in Panchala, of course. I shall not deny you that. But as long as you stay unmarried, or stay married to an obscure nobleman – I shall see to that, if you allow me – Hastinapur will be quiet. But if you ever were to wed a High King, I am afraid they will not allow you.'

'Who are they to allow or disallow me, Your Highness? They do not own me.' She wound her fingers tight around his garment. His own hands were wrapped around her wrist, gently but warily. She could see in his eyes that he was alert to any quick movements on her part. 'They do not own me.' Her grip loosened, and she moved away to cover her face with her hands. In her mind she saw herself as a cowering speck over which the large, dark, lanky shape of Bhishma's shadow loomed. She shivered.

'The day Bhishma won you in the fight, my lady,' said Drupad, 'you became Hastinapur's property.'

She heard the words that Drupad did not say but meant to, that lay hidden beneath his kind, avuncular tone: She did not understand the world of men. She had thought she had grown more aware, but the fact that she had persuaded herself to come to Panchala and meet the king, the fact that she had thought she could goad and threaten the High King of Panchala to wage war on Hastinapur for *her* sake, the fact that she had asked the king to marry her – this did not show *understanding*. This showed foolishness; and a childish delusion that she could turn men around her little finger, that she only needed to ask them to marry her and they would jump at it.

No, she thought, none of the Great Kingdoms would see her as anything more than a petulant child. No High King worth the title would even consider marriage with her as long as she was

Hastinapur's castaway. She had to leave. She had to find means within herself to gain her vengeance.

Drupad, as though reading her thoughts, said, 'In the Madhuvan forest west of here, Sage Parashurama has made his hermitage.'

She lowered her arms and looked up at him, eyes bloodshot and filled with tears.

He turned away from her. 'He will look after you well, my lady. He is a knowledgeable man too, so you may find his advice useful. I will ask Jarutha to take you there at daybreak. You can spend the night here, if you wish.' He turned to face her. 'You should not cry, my lady. You are still young, as I said, and your life lies ahead of you.'

Amba wiped her tears and bowed to the king.

'Jarutha!' Drupad called out.

Jarutha appeared at the door with his head bent.

'Yes, my lord.'

'Show the lady to her room. And before day breaks on the morrow, you shall take her to Parashurama's hermitage.'

'Yes, my lord.'

SIX

But for the faint streak of grey over the western horizon, the sky was black. Amba looked up and saw no stars because of the heavy, low-hanging clouds. Whenever a breeze blew from over the corn fields to the north, she smelled rain in the air. It reminded her of the monsoons of Kasi and tugged at her heart; growing up in Kasya's castle, had she ever imagined that today she would be seated on a lone horse, about to embark upon a journey into the woods? Even now she could tell Jarutha that she had no will to seek out Parashurama, to exact her vengeance on Bhishma, that she wanted to return to Kasi, to her father's arms; but she stopped herself. Her father would not take her back. She remembered the cold mask he had worn at Ambika and Ambalika's wedding, how he had made sure that he would never be caught with her alone, how he had not once looked into her eyes.

'We will journey on horseback, my lady,' said Jarutha, gathering the reins of her horse in one hand and his in the other. 'We would have arranged for a palanquin for you, but we need to cross the Yamuna on our way, and the ferries do not allow palanquins on board.'

'That is fine, Jarutha,' she said. 'We shall go.'

'At any time you feel the need to stop and relax, please tell me, my lady.'

At her nod they began to descend the slope down from the castle, across the corn fields. The stirrups of her horse had been padded with cotton so that her feet could rest against them. Her saddle, too, had been propped up with silk and satin so that she would not feel any discomfort during the journey. She passed a sidelong glance at Jarutha's horse, trotting along bare-backed on her right. The stirrups were no thicker than mere metal wires, and the saddle was a thin slice of browbeaten leather.

On the streets of Panchala she saw maize heaps in front of each house, sorted by size and shape, ready for peeling and plucking of the kernels. In a week or so, leaves would begin to fall. The second crop of the year was the more expensive one. It would require employing water-carriers to transport water from the river to the fields. It would require oxen and carts to distribute water evenly. It would mean digging and preserving water pits, ensuring that stored water did not get lost to the sun, and many more such headaches. Even for a city on a riverbank, rain afforded the least difficult way to water crops.

They reached the gates of the city, where Jarutha spoke a few words in a barely understandable dialect to the turbaned man on guard. The door swung open, slowly, silently, to let them pass.

By this time the grey had spread to the rest of the sky.

The rain she had smelled at the top of the hill that morning must have passed in another direction, because by the time they reached the bank of the Yamuna, the sun was out. As the two fishermen led their horses away toward the ferries, Amba asked Jarutha, 'Are all the stories about Parashurama true, Jarutha?'

Jarutha bowed. 'If you are referring to the tale in which he is said to have killed his mother on the order of his father, people say that it *is* true, my lady, yes.'

'Then why did your king send me to see him? Why would a man who did not care for his own mother care for me?'

The fisherman laid a plank of wood to bridge the gap between the boat and the bank. Jarutha stepped on it, tested its strength with two light skips, and then turned to give Amba his hand. Once they had both seated themselves, Jarutha said, 'There are two reasons why His Majesty has asked you to see Sage Parashurama, my lady. The first of them is that the sage is said to have trained Bhishma in the craft of weaponry when he was being fostered atop the Meru.'

'Jarutha!' Amba said. 'Surely you do not believe in such tall legends.'

Jarutha's voice was grave. 'If you had seen Bhishma fight, my lady, you would find it difficult *not* to believe in tall legends such as this.'

'So you really think, then, that he was fostered on the Meru, along with the gods?'

Jarutha signalled to the ferryman to be careful as they lurched into the water. Turning back to her, he said, 'They say that Sage Vasishta himself tutored him about the Vedas.'

'Yes, and Brihaspati taught him about the tenets of justice,' she said. 'I know the tale.'

'Then you know the reason why we are on our way to see Parashurama. If, indeed, the sage tutored Bhishma when he was young, he may have a certain way with him to make him obey his command.'

'Ah,' said Amba, 'are we not being foolish to assume that Bhishma would put aside his vow just to honour his old teacher?'

Jarutha shrugged and rubbed his beard. 'What can anyone say? If he does not succeed in making him marry you, he may at least ask him to let you back into the city. Would that not be agreeable to you?'

'No,' said Amba, 'it would not.' She turned her gaze northward, where the river turned a sharp bend and disappeared. Mother

Satyavati's village would be on the same bank a few hundred leagues upstream, she thought, and when they passed an island she wondered if it were the same one on which she had given birth to the man who had taken to dividing the Vedas. They said the boy sprung from her womb fully grown, and that Mother Satyavati had only to spend a few minutes in labour.

How nice it would be, Amba thought, if it were truly that easy to bear a child.

'Are these islands ever covered by mist?' she asked the ferryman.

'Only in the winters, madam,' said the ferryman without looking in her direction, using his hefty arms to twist and turn the paddle. 'At midwinter we do not ferry people across until it is a good time past noon, for the morning fog has often caused many a boat to crash against the bank and break in two.'

They finished the remainder of the journey in silence. When they got off, Jarutha paid both the ferrymen with a silver coin each and helped her back on top of her saddle. Jarutha tied together the reins of both horses and took them into one hand. He then drew his sword and said in a whisper to Amba: 'We shall not confront any wild animals as long as we keep to the eastern edge of the forest, my lady. But if fate would place one before us, and if I were to be conquered by it, I bid you to ride northwest of here in a straight line for four miles. That will take you to the hermitage of Parashurama.'

Amba said, 'I shall not leave you to the beast, Jarutha. I know my way around a dagger and a sword; in fact, in Kasi the princesses are trained in hand weapons. So if you have one on you, give it to me and I shall stay on the alert too.'

Jarutha looked back at her for a moment, then turned around and resumed walking. 'My lady, if a beast gets past my sword and reaches you, I doubt if your hand knife will prevail.'

As the two made their way through the forest, Amba heard lizards and squirrels among the leaves strewn around her. Her horse was undecided too, only stepping forward after he had tested the ground first with his hoof. Jarutha grunted commands at both animals, but they pulled away resolutely and snorted every time he tugged at their bridles. Amba had never been in the woods on horseback, and though she had once dreamed of being carried away by a prince on a white horse to the waterfalls that lay in the middle of a forest far away, in her dream there were no wild beasts and lizards and spiders; only koels and peacocks and prancing fawns.

After they had gone some distance, Amba said to Jarutha, 'You spoke of two reasons why we are seeking out Sage Parashurama. What is the second?'

'The second reason why we seek the sage,' said Jarutha at length, 'is because he has a natural enmity toward the Kshatriyas. They say he has obliterated their clan twenty-one times.'

'Twenty-one times?'

'That is so. The Haihayas killed his father, and his mother struck herself twenty-one times in grief. So Parashurama took an oath to kill all Kshatriyas in the world twenty-one times.'

Amba asked, 'But each time he killed the clan, how did they replenish themselves again?'

'The blood of the Kshatriyas runs down the line of the women, my lady. If the sage wanted to wipe out all Kshatriyas from the planet, he should have killed the women.'

Amba's dislike for this sage grew sharper. 'But I suppose some vow or the other stopped him from doing so?'

'Yes, my lady. Raising a hand on a woman is a grave sin.'

She wanted to ask if sending her away on horseback to fend for herself was not, and even as she considered the question, anger welled up inside her. But what was the use? Jarutha was just a nobleman, no more than a slave that could fight.

The hermitage was a clutch of five huts surrounding a well and two banyan trees. As they made their way to the clearing in the middle, Amba noticed there were no mythical animals about. She saw a group of squirrels gorging themselves on a heap of nuts by the well, and two or three crows hopping over discarded plantain leaves dotted with grains of cooked rice. She heard the occasional screeching of monkeys and the call of a nightingale, but that was it. No golden deer or a talking tortoise was to be seen.

The central hut was built of mud and it had a large, sturdy teak front door with a latch fashioned out of metal wire. Jasmine and chrysanthemum garlands hung from one corner of the doorway to the other in an inverted arch. At each end of the doorstep sat half a coconut, spotted with vermillion and turmeric. Somewhere near its middle, the word 'Aum' had been written in white chalk.

Amba opened her mouth to say something, but Jarutha turned back and gestured at her to remain silent. Once she got off her horse, he pointed towards the door and nodded. Leaning on its side was an axe, with a dark wooden handle so large that it appeared as thick as the frame of the door. Both its heads were of the same size, and the silver blades gleamed in the morning light. For a moment Amba thought she saw them dripping with blood, but when she shook her head and looked again, they were stainless.

The presence of the axe meant, of course, that Sage Parashurama was in the hut.

Parashurama took a pinch of brown powder from his palm, placed it on the tip of each of his nostrils, and took a deep breath. Then he squeezed the tip of his nose, shook his head, and closed his eyes. He was seated cross-legged on the porch of his hut, with his staff underneath his right elbow. He addressed Jarutha first.

'Your king is doing well, Jarutha. The rain gods have not been unkind to Panchala this year.'

'By your grace,' said Jarutha, bowing.

'Ah!' Parashurama waved him away. 'I never prayed for your kind, and I never will. If I ever think of Kshatriyas in my prayers, Lord knows I only ask for their destruction. What did you bring for us from Panchala?'

'I beg your pardon, Sage. We have not yet harvested our crops. My master pledged you a tenth share of the kingdom's corn.'

'Tenth share!' said Parashurama. 'What shall I do with so much corn, Jarutha? If you could get us some sesame seeds to plant in our garden, and some peanuts for our squirrels and monkeys, we shall be more than grateful. Did you know that Shurasena only grows paddy?'

'That is true, my lord. They have the biggest stretch of land along the Great River among all the Kingdoms. They have to make use of it to grow paddy.'

'I sent Bhargava last week to Shurasena to get some nuts and pulses, and they said they did not have enough to give away. They offered us elephants loaded with sacks of rice, but what shall I do with them?'

'Your grace,' said Jarutha.

Parashurama took another sniff of the substance in his hand. As he inhaled it fully, his nose and head shivered with what Amba could only call ecstasy, and his eyes, when they reopened, looked at peace with the world.

He looked at her, and the brow again creased with a frown. 'I do not care for your like either, princess. Oh, how much simpler life would be if the world was populated just by Brahmins?' He looked up at the sky and said, as though he were speaking to someone, 'Lord, give me strength.' He picked up the tiny painted container by his side and fingered the contents. He applied it to the edges of his nose, inhaled again, and reopened his eyes, peaceful and happy.

'I know who you are,' he told her. 'You are the princess of Kasi who got married into the royal family of Hastinapur.'

'I did not, your grace,' said Amba, inclining her head. 'I got sent away to Saubala where King Salva rules.'

'Is that by the foothills of the Western Mountains, where River Saraswati is said to flow?'

'Indeed, my lord.'

'I have not been there in a long time. The last time I passed by, the mountains were not as high as they are now, and the land beyond them was greener than it now is.' His mouth twisted, and his face turned grim. 'I see hard times ahead for the kingdoms in the far west. River Saraswati will dry up completely in the years to come, and the land will crack and be covered with sand.'

Amba said, 'What do you see in my future, your grace?'

Irritation spread on Parashurama's face. 'Do you mistake me for an astrologer on the streets of Hastinapur, Princess? I do not tell people's futures, because I do not see them. No one can see the future, not even the people on the Meru that we call gods.'

'But you just saw the future of the Western Kingdoms.'

'One can predict the futures of kingdoms with certainty, girl, because one knows the factors that will come to pass. But the fortune of a single person has too many things entwined with it. It cannot be foretold.'

'But your grace,' said Amba, joining her hands and falling to her knees, 'King Drupad said you will be able to help me.'

'Help, I can offer, yes,' said Parashurama, raising his hand to bless her. At once his voice became kind. 'I sense in you a great anger, my girl, and I see in you my own self when I was your age. Even now, my anger triumphs over me too often for my liking.'

Amba bent her head. 'That is so, my lord. I feel my anger is so strong that it can burn me alive.'

'Then you know what you must do, child. You must conquer your anger first. For that you must first conquer your vanity.'

'My vanity?'

Parashurama turned to Jarutha and said, 'Tell me, Jarutha. Tell me this maiden's tale, and we shall see what we can do to assuage her fury.'

Jarutha sat down at the sage's feet, by Amba's side, and began to narrate. Amba corrected him whenever he went wrong, and all the while Parashurama listened, now stroking his beard, now frowning.

After Jarutha had stopped, Parashurama said to Amba, 'You have suffered in the hands of men, have you not, my child?'

Amba bent her head and said nothing. She thought of Salva, who had seduced her, taken her, and left her to the whims of Hastinapur. She thought of her father, who first raised no murmur of protest when Bhishma abducted her and her sisters, then spinelessly attended the wedding to bless his daughters, and then made his displeasure felt at *her* for choosing her own path. She thought of Vichitraveerya, who failed in sowing in her his seed in spite of one whole year of amour. And last of all she thought of Bhishma himself, the lynchpin, the one man who was the sole reason for everything that her life had become today. And over all these thoughts Mother Satyavati's voice spoke again and again: 'You do not understand the ways of men, my dear.'

Tears flowed down her cheeks.

'Yes,' said Parashurama with a sigh, 'that is the lot of women in our world.'

Jarutha said, 'It seems to me, your grace, that lady Amba here was particularly wronged by Bhishma, who abducted her and then failed to provide her the home she deserves.'

Parashurama nodded. 'Not just Devavrata. All the men in your life, my child,' he said, turning to her. 'All of them seemed to have wronged you in one way or another. Do you not fear, then, that I may fail you? For after all, I am a man too.'

Amba said, 'No, your grace. You are said to be a learned man. You have studied the scriptures, you have taught the Vedas to the gods that live on the Ice Mountains. You are said to have trained

Bhishma in the art of war when he was a young lad. You are the only man in North Country that I know of, my lord, who can stand up to Bhishma with a hope of winning.'

'I am certain,' said Parashurama. 'I am certain of that. But I wonder if that is the right path for you to choose.'

'I shall walk any path you direct me to, your grace.'

Parashurama smiled. 'We shall see.' He turned to Jarutha. 'You can leave the maiden here with me. I have come to stay on Earth for at least six moons from now, so she will serve me here. Let her live the life of a priestess for some time.'

'Yes, my lord,' said Jarutha, getting up to his feet.

'And tell Drupad that I understand his intentions very well,' said Parashurama, his face clouding over suddenly. 'Tell him that I do not like being manoeuvred this way, but I shall do it, this one time, for this maiden.' The muscles of his wiry body tensed, all at once, and his lips fused together. 'But tell him this is to be the last one – the *very* last.'

'Yes, my lord,' said Jarutha, retreating two steps.

'You may go.'

After Jarutha had left, Parashurama said to Amba, 'The life of a priestess is a tough one, my girl, but it gives you victory over the one thing men have always failed against – the self. Will you stay with me and serve me? I promise you a way out of your pain.'

Amba bent down so that her nose touched the ground, and she laid the very tips of her fingers on Parashurama's feet. She heard the murmur of the sage's blessing, and she felt a certain warmth enter her through her back and fill her, loosening her muscles and clearing her mind. She felt like she had come home.

SEVEN

AMBA SPEAKS

In Kasi, when I was four or five years old, we used to play a game with a wooden bow and a ball of flowers. The attendants would place the bow on top of a wheeled table, covered in drapes, and they would hide the ball underneath. Ambika, Ambalika, and I would then fight each other to push aside the table and retrieve the ball. Because I was the eldest, and because I always liked to win games of this sort, I generally emerged with the ball in hand, and my father, King Kasya, would arrive and gather me up in his arms to hug me and shower me with kisses while Ambika and Ambalika enviously looked on.

That, my father's hug, is my oldest memory of warmth – not the kind that touches your outer self, but the kind that lights you from within. I felt the same warmth on that morning I knelt in front of High Sage Parashurama; my own father had discarded me, but it looked like I had found another.

I did not fully understand what the High Sage meant when he said the life of a priestess was tough. I did not quite comprehend what it meant to conquer the self, either. Some of the people in Panchala who now call me a witch would perhaps say that I have not yet conquered my self. They may be right. My father – that's what I call him now – Sage Parashurama, never conquered his self, either; even today, he is given to losing his temper and admonishing his disciples for the smallest transgressions, and if a High Sage himself has not attained that state, I shall make no claims to it.

I have heard it said that happiness lies in the things that you already have, not in the things that you want. But I think not that people who say this have ever had their lives snatched away from them – not by nature or some such unseen foe – but by a living, laughing human being. If happiness indeed lies in the things that you have, what happens when so much is taken away from you that you have nothing?

My tale is a tale of despair and loss. Years from now, people writing down the tale of the Great War will make my life a mere appendage to the main event. They will look for purpose in my life, they will look for something within my character that is redeemable, they will look for those thin rays of hope every tale is said to possess, but they will not find any. And they will turn back and say this is a tale not worth telling, and they will confine it to perhaps two or three torn leaves.

But tales of despair have their place too, I think. When one is a child one may hanker after stories of heroes triumphing over villains, of good triumphing over evil, of all things coming together to end well. But as one grows, one finds in tales of despair a certain pull and solace, for these tales resemble life the most. It is only in these tales that you understand that happiness and hope are no virtues; and sorrow and despair are no vices. The universe knows of no vice and virtue. It is as it is. Only in our minds have we set up these opposite forces and declared they should forever be at war with each other.

This is perhaps the knowledge of self that High Sage Parashurama meant to teach me that morning when I knelt by his feet. He wanted me to look at my life from the outside. He wanted me to shrug at it. He wanted me to embrace it, to accept it, to admit that it was not ideal, but also to realize that nothing in the world was.

So I am no longer scarred by sorrow, or fearful of despair. They have been my companions for life, and I know they shall be with me in my final moments too. But on that bright morning when I touched the sage's feet, I remember how my heart leapt when he said he promised me a way out of my pain.

That day, after lunch, the sage summoned me to his hut. He motioned me to the ground, and after I had taken my seat, said, 'I will tell you the ways of a priestess now, my princess.'

'Yes, my lord.'

'A priestess is a woman that has given her life to the Goddess, the mother of all things that you see around you. We call her by the name of Bhagavati. She has no image, She has no form, She has no shape. But you see her everywhere you look – within you, without you. You know she is there, do you not?'

'Yes, my lord.'

'A priestess of the Goddess fasts during the first half of the day on the rising cycle of the moon, and during the second half of the day on the falling cycle. On full-moon days, she will have all three meals, and on no-moon days she will have none. This is to learn the first lesson in life: your bowl will be full on some days and empty on others. That is just how the universe is; the moon herself is not the same from one day to the next. Why should your life be so?'

'Yes, my lord.'

'A priestess of the Goddess sleeps on the floor with no pillow under her head. Three times in a day she will wash herself, but will change her clothing no more than once. She will look at all of life as her brethren, and that means she will not eat meat, nor will she kill any animal unless in self-defence.'

'Yes, my lord.'

'A priestess will look after herself at all times. She will make her own food, make arrangements for her own drinking and bathing water, and she will keep her house clean. She shall not depend on anyone else for her needs, be they related to food or water, no matter what period of her cycle she is in.'

'Yes, my lord.'

'A priestess of the Goddess shall at all times accept the gifts of nature with open arms. She will never be ashamed of her desires, because they are given to her by the Goddess; nor will she question the outcomes of her actions, because they too are given to her by the Goddess. She will train herself to always accept and never question. She will train herself to possess the wisdom to choose well, the strength to persevere in pursuit of her ambitions, and the detachment to accept the result.'

'Yes, my lord.'

'We shall begin with this,' he then said, 'and extend your training after a month. A priestess also studies the Mysteries, but for that you will need a good teacher.'

'Are you not a good teacher, my lord?'

'No, my dear, not for the Mysteries.' He lifted both his legs onto the ledge so that he could sit cross-legged. He waved me away and instructed me to get my mind ready for the ordeal ahead. As I was about to leave to collect my things that Jarutha had left by the well, the High Sage called out to me and said the words that I would remember all my life.

'Remember, Amba,' he said, 'a priestess is slave to no man. She only answers to the Goddess.'

EIGHT

Amba woke up and tied her hair in a knot over her head, keeping it in place by means of a timber twig. She folded the mat and rested it against the corner. She picked up the broom and cleaned her room, humming to herself a chant she had heard on the lips of one of the sages the night before. Mentally she counted the days of the month so that she would not miss the fast of the *Amavaasya*. Four more days to go.

Picking up the leaves and fallen grains in a straw bowl she went out to the well to dump it by the fence. Squirrels and badgers would come by after sunrise and eat some of it. The rest of it would get blown away by the wind. She craned her neck to see if the baby doe had come today. She reminded herself to pluck an extra apple or two from the orchard for her, just in case she would return. Sage Parashurama had advised her against pets, but she told herself that this was not a pet, just a recurring visitor.

The last month – her first at the ashram – had not been as much a struggle for her that Parashurama (and she) had feared it would be. The first few days she had woken up with a rash on her waist and a catch in her back. Bending to sweep the floor of her little hut had hurt her thighs so much that she could not sleep at night. Without a mirror she had at first not been able to tie her hair, so she had wandered about the hermitage – to everyone's amusement – in loose, undone locks. So what, she had thought. Did the sage not say that a priestess ought not to be concerned with vanity?

Gradually, the aches ebbed, and she taught herself to tie up her hair one morning when she went to the lake to get water. One of the sages in the hut adjoining hers had taught her how to cook, and she had begun to boil rice and vegetables to arrange for herself a decent meal. There were days when she had not adhered as religiously as she should have to the fasting rules, but ever since that day when Sage Parashurama had caught her munching away on a guava behind the hut, she had been steadfast.

The one thing she could not get her mind away from, even amid all this, was Bhishma.

Every now and then, she would either be on her way to the orchard or in the middle of a meal or at the well drawing water, and something would come over her suddenly and she would sit down and weep. At nights she would go down to the bank of the Yamuna, some three or four miles away, and sit there watching the ferry come and go, people stepping out, stopping for a moment to look at her, then passing on their way. She would sometimes lie down on the sand and look up at the moon floating by, and she would hug herself and think of her father in Kasi. Sage Parashurama had said that if you thought of someone with all your heart, you would make them think of you. She would hear her father's voice in the river's waves, and she would wonder if he ever thought of her.

Today Sage Parashurama had summoned her to his hut immediately after the morning prayer, which was one of the reasons for her good mood. She had not spoken to him in the last one week or so, and if he wanted to speak, it must be because he would tell her how he was going to show her a way out of her pain.

She walked back from the hut and stood by the door. She removed the stick holding her hair together and shook her head, letting her tresses fall over her shoulders. As she fingered the stick in her hand, her mind went back to Bhishma in the palace of Hastinapur, and Ambika and Ambalika seated on the throne. Her lips tightened. She snapped the twig in two.

When she entered, she had to twist her nose against the pungent smell of burning incense. From somewhere deep within the cloud of smoke, she heard Parashurama's voice.

'Come, my child,' he said.

From memory she went in the direction of the platform on which he generally sat, and lowered herself onto her knees first, then folded her legs under her and came to rest on the back of her heels.

'You look well, my child,' said he. 'Better than I thought you would after a month of being a priestess.'

'I am getting used to it, my lord,' she replied.

'It does not bode well for a priestess to leave her hair open, my dear.'

'I beg your pardon, your grace. I lost my pinning stick this morning. I will make one for myself after the midday meal.'

Even from such a short distance he was visible only as a grey shadow, and his voice seemed to come at her from a deep, cool well. She saw the dim outline of his jaw, his long beard, his hair gathered together into a ball over his head. He looked a lot like the keeper of time himself.

'I did not summon you here to speak of your hair, though,' he said. 'I think it is time we spoke about Devavrata.'

A lump appeared instantly within her throat. 'Do you bear bad news of him?'

'No, dear,' said Parashurama, in a smiling voice. 'I wanted to know if you still wished to take revenge on him.'

'That is the very reason I still draw breath, my lord,' said Amba.

For a few moments the High Sage did not speak. All Amba saw were floating wisps of white smoke and a blurred image of a man's face drawn in hazy black lines. She could well have been speaking to a statue.

'Amba,' he said finally, 'you think of me as your father, do you not?'

'My lord.'

'Then shall I advise you on something, with your good at heart?'

'Yes, my lord.'

'Let it go, my child.'

Amba raised her head. 'My lord?'

'Let it go,' he said. 'Your thoughts of vengeance and anger are your own. You have a choice to kill them, and to live a happy life.'

'I do not want to kill these thoughts, your grace,' she said, not raising her voice, matching the hollow tone of her master's. 'I have lived with them for so long now that they have become part of me. Killing them would mean killing a part of myself.'

'A bad part of yourself. You are merely severing a deceased limb, and by doing so you save the rest of your body.'

'My lord—'

'You must trust me, my child. Your anger will one day burn you to ashes. Your vengeance will one day turn to you and ask for your life.'

'If it takes Bhishma's life, I will gladly give up mine, your grace.'

Parashurama smiled. 'This is not about Devavrata, child. No matter what happens to Devavrata, even if you were to hack him into pieces and throw him into the Great River, the fires that burn within you shall not die. Anger has taken much from me, my child, and it has given me nothing in return. I do not wish the same for you.'

'Bhishma has robbed me of my life, my lord,' said Amba, blinking away tears. 'How can I not punish someone who has taken everything from me?'

'No one can take everything that you have,' said Parashurama. 'Today you have much to be thankful for, do you not?'

'I? What do I have for which to be thankful, my lord?' Amba's voice finally snapped, rising a pitch higher. 'I have lost everything that was mine – my father, my sisters, my lovers, a right to be queen of Hastinapur – and you say I have to be thankful for it? Pray tell me a few things that I must be thankful for, your grace.'

'Your mistake is to think that all those things were part of you, Amba. Your father, your sisters, your lovers, your servants – these were all things that you had, things that existed outside of you. You thought – and still think – that all those things made you what you were, but it is not so. It is when we lose everything we have that we truly find ourselves, my child.' He paused for a moment. 'In your last one month, did you not get a glimpse of who you really were?'

Amba thought of the girl who drew water from the well and chanted verses to herself. She thought of the doe that frequented the hermitage and ate the apples that she left at the fence. She thought of the squirrels that picked out nuts and grains from her house, and stood up on their hind legs while scurrying here and there to look up at her, as if to say thank you. She thought of the girl who tied her own hair, who boiled her own rice, who grew her own vegetables, who slept on the hard floor, who sat by the sages at night and listened to their discourses.

But then she thought of the girl who went to the Yamuna alone and wept, who broke her pinning twig into two out of rage for a man in a far-off land.

'No,' she said resolutely. 'What I need to quench my thirst, your grace, is not empty words that serve no purpose. I will only see happiness the day Bhishma's head rolls in the dust.'

Almost to himself, Parashurama said, 'Perhaps one month is not enough.'

'You promised me a way out of my pain, your grace,' said Amba, her tone now accusing him. 'But it has been a month and you have done nothing.'

'I have been trying to show you a way out, my child, but you refuse to see it.'

'Your way out is for me to forget my vengeance? Did I need to come all the way inside the woods to this hermitage to be told that, your grace?'

Parashurama sighed. 'Perhaps you are right,' he said. 'When I was as young as you, I scoffed at my father for having asked me to forget my rage. And today I look back and see how right he was. But perhaps that is the folly of age, of youth. We run after all the wrong things, and we refuse to see what is important even when someone points them out to us.'

Amba lowered her head and said nothing.

Parashurama got to his feet. At two waves of his hand, as though by magic, the air in the room cleared and sharpened. Amba, on her knees, looked up at him and saw his face set in cold, hard stone. Not even the loose strands of hair on his scalp and chin appeared to move. A raised staff in his left hand, he opened the palm of his right to bless her. She bent to the ground, her hands laid out in front of her, each one touching one of his feet.

'I gave you my word that I will guide you out of your pain,' he said gravely. 'Over the last month I tried to show you *my* path, but your path may be different, and it ought to be so. Each of us has to walk our paths alone.' He controlled his faltering voice. 'If you insist on walking your path, I shall help you do so.'

'I thank you, my lord,' said Amba.

'I shall go to speak with Devavrata,' said Parashurama, taking her by her shoulders and rousing her up to her feet. 'I shall ask him to right all the wrongs he has done to you.'

Amba said, 'I will come with you!'

'No, I know what Devavrata's reply will be. I may have to fight him to extract your vengeance for you, my lady. It will not be safe for you to be present.'

'But my lord,' said Amba, 'I wish to see your victory. I wish to see his fall. I wish to laugh in his face.'

Parashurama smiled kindly at her. 'You do not know yet what a great warrior he is, my girl. He may be more skilled at arms than I am. After all, I have not touched a weapon besides my axe in a long while. Do not take my victory for granted, though I assure you that it will take all his might to defeat me.'

The air in the room was clear now even as fog had begun to collect outside. The sage went to the corner by the fireplace and fiddled with a cloth bundle. When he came back, in his palm he held a brown stick with gum oozing out of its sides. He handed it to her and said, 'You shall sit here in this room while I am gone, and you shall light a fire by the window. You shall feed this stick to the fire, inch by inch, until it is all consumed, and while you do it, you shall chant a verse that I have written down in the parchment here. If you have lived your last month as a true priestess, you shall be able to see me fight your enemy.'

Amba bowed and took the stick in both her hands. She touched it to her eyes and said, 'Thank you, your grace.'

He raised his hand again to bless her. 'I must make haste now. Today is four days away from the day of the no-moon. I shall take my axe, and I shall stop by on the bank of the Yamuna. All my weapons are atop a fig tree there. I shall collect them, and I shall make for Hastinapur to plead your cause to Devavrata.'

'I wish I could come with you, my lord,' said Amba.

'You shall, if you make the fire on the morning of *Amavaasya*, and if you keep a clear mind as you feed it.' He took a step back from her. 'Now I must go.'

Amba bowed and closed her eyes. She waited for his touch on her forehead, but when it did not come after a full minute she opened her eyes to see that she was alone in the room. She had heard no footsteps. The outside fog was now beginning to creep into the hut through the window. The cloth bundle from which the sage had produced the gum stick was no longer in its corner. Amba walked out to the front door and looked in the direction of the fence. Everything looked as it always had – the chatter of squirrels, the screeching of monkeys, the rustling movement of lizards under fallen leaves, and the gentle sounds of sages as they went about their daily chores.

There was just one thing missing: Parashurama's axe that used to lean against the door.

NINE

Amba sat in front of the heap of firewood and joined her hands in reverence. She had heard many a tale about how sages and gods saw events that happen in different places and different times. They always began, she guessed, by praying to the dead firewood, for without its will no fire would burn, and without a fire no magic could happen. She chanted no verses because she had not yet learnt the methods of fire worship, but she willed the Goddess with all her heart to keep the fire from dying.

'Mother,' she thought, 'keep the fire alive for as long as I need to see, and see to it that the sage vanquishes my foe.'

She rubbed the flint stones over a fist of dry hay, and when she saw smoke rise, she blew over it gently through a sooty pipe. She had never made fire before this; she had never been the first to wake at the hermitage, and whenever she had needed fire, all she had had to do was step out and hold a piece of parchment to the altar in the courtyard. But the sages had been adamant about this: she had to create fire on her own when she performed the Mystery of the Sight.

The first few times, the smoke in the hay fizzled out as though someone had sprinkled water upon it. The last few days had been cloudy, so she had been unable to dry the hay adequately. She thought how ironic it would be if she were unable to watch the battle between the sage and the king because she could not start a fire. Elsewhere, the two warriors must be getting into their armours just about now, and she imagined them in their respective chariots: Bhishma's drawn by black horses that looked grotesque and diseased; Parashurama's by white ones with silvery wings and angelic faces.

She drew a particularly large spark from the flint, and as it struck the hay it gave birth to a tiny, steady flame. Amba put her pipe aside and fed it with handfuls of straw dipped in oil, and within a minute the flame grew sharp, hungry tongues that licked and spread.

Amba picked up the mass of burning hay with her hands with care and dropped it on the firewood. The flame seemed to die upon touching the wood, but a black smoke rose into the air in a thin line. Amba blew upon it till the whole room filled with it and made her cough, but she kept at it until she spotted a weak, orange glow emerge from underneath the wood. Now she poured oil and ghee upon it, strengthening it till it began to devour the wood and shrivel it into a black, lifeless mass.

She did not realize she had begun to mouth the incantation without her knowledge, and as soon as she sat down she began to see shapes in the swirling grey smoke. She thought she saw a bearded man on horseback with a spear in hand, and though she first thought it was Bhishma, the smoke thinned to reveal Jarutha. All about him were armed warriors chasing peasants and workmen. 'Do not kill anyone,' said Jarutha, and his voice echoed in her ear, as though he were speaking from inside a cave. 'Drive them out, and we shall set up our outpost here to guard against setbacks.'

Amba felt her hold on her mind ebb with each passing moment. Vacantly, she remembered Drupad's words which referred to a stone quarry up in north Panchala, which the Kurus had captured and were using to make weapons. Around Jarutha she now saw the dead bodies of four or five men who had deep stab wounds on their backs. Jarutha's horse kicked one of them in passing and turned him over, and Amba saw that the hard, handsome face was littered with red sword cuts.

Her nostrils twitched and her eyes watered due to the smoke, but she stared up at the apparition, fumbling with her hand to find the block of rubber wood that the sage had given her. She broke off a piece of it and tossed it into the fire, giving rise to a fresh ball of smoke that dissolved into the shape above her and sharpened it. Now Amba could see the crags in the rock surrounding Jarutha, and she could see the grimness in which his features were set – far removed from the easy, smiling countenance that he had sported with her.

Touching his beard, he surveyed the terrain around him.

Amba remembered the words of admonishment that Parashurama had used with Jarutha, that he did not like being used, and at the time she had wondered what he had meant, but now she saw: Hastinapur's rock quarries could be safely ransacked if Bhishma could be distracted, and Drupad had used Parashurama – through her – for the purpose. Despite what he had said, he must have spies in Hastinapur that told him that Bhishma had left for a battle, so he had sent Jarutha up north to take back their rocks and cripple Hastinapur's weapon factories.

She saw twenty or thirty villagers now surround Jarutha, and at his command they began to dig the ground and lay the foundations for a defensive structure. From within the shadows many more men emerged and set to work, while Jarutha and his men stood guard. A dozen or so archers positioned themselves behind the working men, their quivers brimming with arrows.

Amba wondered vaguely where Bhishma must be, and at once the shapes in the smoke dissolved and arose again to reveal a large circular clearing in a dense forest, at the either end of which stood a chariot, one drawn by white horses as in her vision, and one drawn by black. In the former she saw the sturdy figure of the sage, clad in saffron and with lines of sandal paste on his forehead. In his left hand he held a bow fashioned out of crude wood.

He looked out at the other end of the clearing, where at the wheel of his chariot stood Bhishma. His face had not changed from the last time she had seen him – she had ceased being surprised about that – but in stature he seemed to have grown. His frame was still wiry, much like that of the sage he was facing, but he seemed to have acquired this air of resplendence about him. Amba had heard that gods, when they descended upon Earth, appeared to mortal eyes as though a light shone forth from behind them. Bhishma looked the same. His eyes too seemed to have turned into a darker shade of blue.

'I do not wish to fight you, High Sage,' he said, and Amba felt the voice had become softer since she had heard him last. 'I pray to you; let us not allow the matter of a woman come between us. Let us put our differences aside and part as friends.'

'The time for words is behind us now, Devavrata. I have told you what I wanted. You have said you cannot do my bidding. Is that still your answer?'

'Yes, my lord,' said Bhishma. 'I have taken a vow that I shall never touch a woman, and I must abide by it.'

Parashurama grunted in disapproval. 'Then you can certainly take the maiden and give her shelter in your city. She lives as a priestess at my hermitage; no place for a maiden used to the comforts of palace life.'

'I shall be only too happy to give her shelter in Hastinapur, my lord.' Bhishma picked up his bow, wore his quiver around his shoulder, and ascended his chariot. 'But doing so shall put her life in danger. The people of Hastinapur believe that their king would not have died but for her, and if they see her living amongst them, I am afraid they will name her a witch and stone her to death.'

'Ah,' said Parashurama, 'if you desire to have her in your city, you can. You are the champion of your city's throne, and if you said one word in support of Amba, your people would accept her. But you do not.'

'I cannot but bow down to the will of the people, my lord,' said Bhishma.

Even with her mind at the mercy of the images in the cloud of smoke, Amba felt anger stir within her. Bhishma was not afraid of her being stoned to death; he was scared of what might happen if she, Amba, were to stake a claim to the throne ahead of her two sisters. With Vichitraveerya now gone, they were bound to look for a Brahmin to father the future king. It would be messy, indeed, for Bhishma and the royal house if she were to bear a child through the Brahmin before Ambika and Ambalika. If that were to happen, Bhishma and Mother Satyavati would have no choice but to accept her son as the future king, except for the fact that she had never wed Vichitraveerya. It would raise some questions that would surely be interesting; questions that Bhishma would rather prefer not to ever have to answer. It would be so much more convenient if Amba did not live in Hastinapur at all, if she were to be banished with one flimsy excuse or another.

Right now he could end this all, crown her the first queen to Hastinapur, and allow her to bear the future High King. But he would not. He would rather fight his teacher and kill his men in meaningless skirmishes with Panchala than see her ascend the throne. Why, she could not fathom. Had she hurt his pride so much when Mother Satyavati, on her behest, ordered him to release her? She had heard it being said that men least liked to give away their prizes of war. She remembered that her father had a whole palace built of marble to display the various shields and swords he had won during his conquests.

Men lived by these strange symbols of honour. Bhishma was the foremost man in the land, so his sense of honour must be tougher than most, his pride more vulnerable than most. Had she hit it on that day when she first told him about Salva? With all his talk of being the champion of Hastinapur, was he anything more than a petty man who could not rise above this disgraceful notion of nobility?

The neigh of horses and the blowing of a conch shook her and brought her eyes back to the image in front of her. Bhishma raised his bow and sent an arrow flying into the ground. 'I still do not wish to fight you, my lord,' he said, 'but I do not think we have a choice, either of us.'

'No,' said Parashurama, tying around his forehead a thread of twine. 'We do not.' He picked up his bow and set an arrow to it. 'May you fare well, Son of Ganga. We shall see how well you have learnt my lessons.'

TEN

The horses dug into the dry earth with their hooves, and at the cry of the charioteers and the crack of their whips, they charged at each other, raising a cloud of dust that shielded Amba's view. For a while all she heard were sounds – of Bhishma and Parashurama calling out to one another: 'Rain your arrows on me, Son of Ganga. Let me see if any of them can pierce my skin.' 'I am ready for you, Venerable One, my armour wishes to taste the tip of your spear.'

Then all of a sudden the mist cleared, and Amba found herself between the two chariots. She turned to face Bhishma only to see a lance being hurled directly at her. Before she could do anything other than throw her hands up in the air and shriek, the lance passed through her without hurting her and flew in the direction of Parashurama, who nonchalantly brushed it away with his mace.

The High Sage stood in his chariot with his legs apart, his chest puffed out, with all his weapons on his person. Amba saw a bow slung over his shoulder, a mace in one hand, a jagged sword in the other, a spear in a sheath of deer hide at his waist, his axe fastened to his back, and two combat knives at either wrist, ready to be drawn out of their pockets any second. But of all this, the biggest transformation was in the face. The eyes smouldered with the red fire of bloodlust, and the naked joy of a king drunk on wine, of a child at play. His arms and legs pulsated with energy, as though he could not wait to throw himself into the midst of this and draw the blood of his favourite pupil.

At this moment Amba realized what he had meant when he said he had his own demons to fight. This Brahmin, whose favourite activity ought to be the study of the Vedas and the unlocking of the Mysteries of the Goddess, loved to fight and to kill. He was a Kshatriya born in saffron clothes, a king with sacred ash smeared over his forehead and arms. His hands, which held the staff and brass vessel, wanted nothing more than to wield an axe or a bow. He always seemed to her to be out of place at the hermitage, as though his mind were perpetually on something else.

It was only now that he seemed to be at home.

As the lance fell to the dust by him, Parashurama smiled, not one of kindness that she had become used to seeing at the hermitage, but one of delight. He said something that Amba could not quite make out, and when she floated closer to him so that she could hear him better, he shot an arrow in her direction that followed her as she swerved out of the way and sliced through her with a whoosh.

Bhishma warded it off with a shield and instructed his charioteer to drive along the periphery of the clearing, raining arrows on Parashurama, shooting them such that they appeared to be flying away from him for half their flight but changed course and curved toward him. Parashurama's chariot began to move too, in the opposite direction to Bhishma's, and the arrows began to miss their mark now but only for a moment that it took Bhishma to adjust to the sage's motion. Once again the arrows began to swoop in with precision, and each one fell to the ground, blunted by Parashurama's mace or sword. Amba looked at one of the fallen arrows and found that it was curved to one side, and there was a smattering of lead on the left edge of the tip.

She had heard that archers from the Kuru kingdoms had pioneered the art of applying weight to selected portions of their arrows so that they would swerve in mid-flight if shot in a precise manner. Other kingdoms of North Country had picked up this technique by now, but no one was yet able to shoot such arrows with the skill of someone from the plains. She noticed that Bhishma was not fully drawing back the string of his bow, and that he was releasing his arrows up into the air instead of aiming them directly at the sage, and yet each one dived in with unerring accuracy and hit Parashurama's moving chariot. And each time Bhishma drew back the string of his bow and released it, he cocked his wrist a certain way, sometimes to the left, sometimes to the right.

The first rule of archery, from her own lessons as a child all those years ago, was to pull the string back to one's ear and release the arrow at the highest speed possible. But she had heard that archers from the plains deliberately slowed down their arrows so that they would have enough time to bend in the air. Not only did this make it difficult for the target to defend himself, it enabled the archer to keep shooting for longer.

Now arrows seemed to rain down on Parashurama as he scrambled with both his weapons to mow them down. Amba could not believe that Bhishma was shooting only one arrow at a time; such was his speed. Since each arrow required only half a draw and since each one travelled only at a fraction of its highest speed, at any one time Amba saw five or six arrows in flight, each one dipping toward the sage one after the other like a group of hawks descending upon a lone, scurrying rabbit.

The sage kept up his defence admirably enough, though a few of the arrows scraped his shoulders and hips. Bhishma looked like he had just stepped off an oil bath, drenched in sweat but his armour unscathed and spotless. Even his horses and his charioteer appeared fresh and purposeful; no wonder, for none of Parashurama's weapons had yet reached within ten feet of the regent. Parashurama hailed from the woods and the mountains; his weapons were the mace, the sword, the axe; with a bow and arrow he was no more than a journeyman, she guessed, which was why he had chosen to defend himself against Bhishma's cunning arrows with hand weapons.

Then Amba saw that Bhishma's arrows let up in numbers – whether fatigue had started to tell on him or whether he wanted to give his teacher a chance, she did not know. She could distinctly make out moments of silence between successive twangs of his bow now, whereas earlier it had been one continuous buzz, like a bee hovering over its comb. His chariot stopped too, and Amba saw the front two horses buckle to their knees with a short neigh and a snort. The charioteer yelled at them to get up, but they bucked and pulled with their heads and refused to relent to whiplashes on their thick, black manes.

Parashurama recovered enough to untie his bow and quiver and shoot arrows of his own, but most of them buzzed harmlessly past the flag of Bhishma's chariot. Amba noticed that his arrows swerved too in mid-flight, but they did not have the same merciless aim, and all Bhishma had to do to defend himself and his chariot was to stay still, watch for the rare arrow that found its target, and decimate it with short, straight shots. When defending he used another bow and arrows from another quiver. Amba guessed these were straight-flight arrows, and sure enough, this time when he drew back the string of his bow, he did so right to his ear, and took that extra half a second to aim properly. His wrist pointed dead straight, like the tip of a sharpened spear.

Not once did he miss.

With Parashurama's growing anger she felt restlessness well up within her too, and she wished she could take arms and support the sage. She flew close to Bhishma and stood in front of his arrows, hoping to disturb him in some way, but neither he nor his arrows saw her or stopped for her. Parashurama's chariot stopped now too, and his charioteer panted, nursing the bruises on his

arms and chest caused by Bhishma's arrows. His horses did not
buckle, but their breath came in hard, heavy bursts. One of them
had a long, curved arrow sticking out of its side. These horses and
the charioteer must have been loaned to Parashurama by Bhishma
for this fight, so he would not kill them, Amba thought; but he
would certainly cripple them as much as needed to win the duel.

'Let us fight on land, Devavrata!' cried Parashurama, setting his
bow aside and raising his hand.

Shooting down the last of his teacher's arrows, Bhishma said,
'Yes, my lord, our horses and our men need rest and nursing.'
He was just being polite, thought Amba. His man and horses
did not need nursing; they would be ready to fight after a few
minutes of rest. But Parashurama's horses needed to be tended to,
and Bhishma knew that the sage wanted to draw him out of the
chariot onto the ground. And yet he agreed. How confident must
he be that he would win? All this was just a game to him. After
all this, not one mark on his body, not one scratch on his armour,
whereas Parashurama appeared as if someone had sucked out all
the air from within him.

They descended from their chariots and stood by them for a
few moments. Parashurama gathered his weapons and made his
way to the center. Bhishma carried a mace and sword in either
hand. His sword was not jagged like Parashurama's was; men from
the plains fought with light, smooth-edged swords, and their
maces were light too. In hand-to-hand combat they relied on
defence and endurance. Her archery trainer had once told her that
the Kuru princes trained with maces for days on end at a time,
without stopping for food or for water. Amba wondered what that
meant during this battle, both for her and for Parashurama.

As they approached each other, Amba thought she saw a hint
of a smile on Bhishma's face as he looked at the sage, haggard and
sweating. 'Let us not fight over a woman, my lord,' said Bhishma,
extending his arm towards the sage. 'What you ask of me, I cannot
do, and you are no longer the warrior you once were.'

Parashurama spat at the ground. 'I am still the same, Devavrata, but you seem to have grown into a man since the last time I saw you. Do you remember the bouts we used to have on the slopes of the Meru, by Vasishtha's hermitage?'

Amba hovered from one to the other, listening but still thinking of how the regent had twice appealed to Parashurama to not fight over a woman. Yes, she thought, a woman was not worthy enough to be fought over, and yet this man had once done the same thing when he wanted a queen for his city. One rule for Kshatriyas then, and another for the rest of the world. Amba wished she could pick up the sword in Parashurama's hands and slit Bhishma's throat then and there. Hastinapur would be truly without a protector, she would get revenge, North Country would have its emperor in Drupad, and all would be well with the world.

'I do, my lord,' said Bhishma, 'but then I was but a boy and you were in the prime of your age. Now – now I do not think it fair that I should take up weapons against you. The gods know that I have sinned enough today by taking up arms against a Brahmin. Do not make me strike my teacher too, I pray of you.'

Parashurama stood up to his full height – and when he did, he stood almost eye to eye with Bhishma – and said, 'You are not the only one that has words to keep, Son of Ganga. I give promises too, and I must do my best to keep them, whether you allow me or not.'

Bhishma turned to look in Amba's direction, and for a moment she wondered if he could actually see her. Then he turned away from her and reached for his mace. 'If that is so, High Sage,' he said, 'let us both keep our words and do what is right.'

ELEVEN

All sages trained themselves in the craft of weapons, though it was not their primary goal. Their daily lives – in the midst of forests and mountains teeming with wild animals and game – were much more eventful and prone to accidents than those of kings, and it was only prudent that they equip themselves with skills to defend against chance encounters with hungry predators. It was part of folklore that they cursed animals and intruders with death and disease, but a curse would only come true in due course of time, at Mother Nature's own slow pace. For immediate dangers a curse was useless.

This fact did not surprise Amba. Upon some thought, it only seemed natural. If kings broadened their minds by the study of religious scriptures, why should Brahmins not educate themselves in the art of warfare and weaponry? She had heard that Vasishtha, the first High Sage of them all who tutored Rama and his brothers all those years ago, was a fine hand with the staff and spear.

Because they lived in places dense with rocks and trees, and because they wanted to defend themselves against animals, they wielded hand weapons like knives and axes. Parashurama's axe had been the biggest she had ever seen in her life, and if legend were to be believed, it was with that weapon alone that he went on his killing spree, wiping out the bloodline of the Kshatriyas twenty-one times.

Now it was the blade of the same axe that Amba saw glisten in the afternoon sun as the two men, Bhishma and Parashurama, circled each other, one holding the axe, the other a mace with the tip pointed at his adversary. She felt as though she were standing close enough to reach out and touch either of them, and yet she saw only in grey smudges and dusty shapes which threatened every minute to crumble to powder if she so much as made a quick movement.

The first salvo came from the sage. He held his axe in both hands above his head and jumped high into the air in Bhishma's direction. The latter took a step back and warded him off with a deft block. Parashurama turned a full circle to aim at Bhishma's unprotected ribs, but he only met his pupil's forearm that absorbed the full force of the blow, then pushed it down to the ground, throwing him off balance and sprawling in the dust. Amba thought this would be the best opportunity for Bhishma to keep the sage down on the ground, but instead he pulled back a couple of paces and waited, breathing evenly.

He is only playing with him, she thought bitterly, and willed the sage to his feet.

Parashurama sprang up with his axe in one hand, and with the other he drew a hand knife. Watching him, Bhishma transferred his mace to one hand and kept the other free to defend himself. A mace was traditionally a weapon used to overwhelm enemies with weight and momentum, and it was generally accepted as a weapon of choice for men with thick heads and broad shoulders. Perhaps the Kuru line of kings was the first to wield the mace in one hand and use it as a defensive weapon. In hand to hand combat the men from the plains all behaved the same way – they never struck first, preferring instead to wear out their opponents and wait for the right moment to strike.

Parashurama lunged at Bhishma, showing his axe but attacking with the knife, but Bhishma was equal to both, knocking off the axe with one hand and letting the knife fall on his metal wristband with a clang. When it slid off the polished metal and scraped his forearm, Bhishma cried out, and punched the sage with his fist full on his left cheek, sending him reeling onto the ground.

Amba began to realize that this was no match. Even though Bhishma looked slender and graceful, his closed fist resembled the paw of a grown panther, and the way in which he waved the mace with one hand bespoke the strength he held within his shoulders and arms. Where Parashurama was dragging his axe with both hands, Bhishma just lay in wait, watched, and swatted him away. This had never been a match, she thought sullenly; apart from feeding the sage's ego, this fight was not going to accomplish anything — besides, of course, distracting Bhishma from the northern stone quarry where Jarutha was right now driving Hastinapur's miners away.

Parashurama got up to his feet again and shook his head this way and that, and Amba saw that his right cheek had swollen to twice its size. Standing a good ten feet away from Bhishma, he reached for his spear and threw it at him. Bhishma caught it, broke it in two over his thigh, and cast it away.

'You have become too strong for me, Devavrata,' said Parashurama, panting. 'But I shall fight you to death.'

'No, my lord,' said Devavrata. 'I shall not let you.'

Amba stopped feeding the block of wood to the fire and got to her feet, turning her head away in disgust, allowing the image to fade away into the shadows of the gathering dusk. She had not eaten the whole day, but she was not hungry. A dull thud knocked at her head from inside, and she felt like screaming out at the top of her voice. With a grunt, she hurled the piece of wood against the mud wall.

She went to the window and looked up at the black, moonless sky. Today was meant to be the day Bhishma would be vanquished.

Today was meant to be the day on which all her wrongs would be righted, said the sage. But how pitiful was his duel! Was this the same man who had once single-handedly vanquished the whole race of kings? How could he be defeated by his own pupil with such ease? Perhaps it was true what they said: Bhishma was invincible.

Now what else was she to do? She had no one to support her. Once again, the man whom she trusted broke her faith, though she did not feel anger toward the sage; just pity. He had done his best, and he was still doing his best, willing himself on against her enemy in spite of knowing that it was fruitless to do so. He would learn soon enough, she knew, and he would come back, his body bruised and his soul shattered, and he would ask her to go elsewhere if she still wanted to have her revenge.

Or, she thought with a sneer, he would tell her to forget it all and live in peace.

She called out: 'Mother!'

An answering breeze touched her face and cooled it. Outside, each of the huts had lamps burning at their front doors. Only hers was dark. She felt a shadow move across the doorway, but when she walked out and stood under the stars she found no one. 'Mother!' she called out again, 'why do you place me among impotent men who can neither wield weapons nor study the scriptures? Where must I turn now? Is there not a man in all of North Country who could stand up to Bhishma and subdue him?'

Another breeze blew from the direction of the well, and she ran to the fence, looking out to see if she could hear anything. All she heard was the faint hiss of the Yamuna flowing in her own unfettered way. The smell of night queens made her nose hair tingle, and when she picked one up, she saw that it had been trampled upon. She smoothed the petals tenderly and set it in her hair just above her right ear, and looking up she said again: 'Mother, give me a sign that you hear me speak!'

A third gust of breeze blew, this one so strong that it sent her hair flying and knocked off the flower in her ear to the ground. From far away in the woods, she heard the distinct call of a nightingale. She looked all around her to see if anyone else was present, and when she looked back at the tree, she heard the call once again. She took two steps toward it, but she hesitated and stopped, for it was dark and cold out there. 'Mother,' she whispered, 'whom shall I turn to now?'

A fawn sprang out of the woods, startling her, and blinked at her with big blue eyes. When she extended her arm to him he merely held her gaze for a long minute, then turned and skipped away into the bushes. Amba followed him.

The fawn led her to the riverbank where she had often sat with her head buried between her legs, weeping at her fate. The stars seemed to have drawn closer this night, she thought, looking about herself, marvelling at the blue light that bathed the trees, the silver sparkle in the calm waters of the Yamuna, and the white heads of wildflowers that waved this way and that in the breeze. When she neared the shore and extended her arm for the fawn he once again bounded away out of reach, and looking at his thick purple coat she thought of the corn fields of Panchala.

As she sat on the edge of the bank, with her feet immersed in the water, she repeated the question, this time to herself: 'Whom do I turn to now?' At the same time the fawn came and sat by her, stretching himself out on the sand such that his chin came to rest upon her thigh. She leaned forward to run her hand over his head, and in so doing she caught her reflection in the water.

She had perhaps changed more in the last one month than she had throughout her life, she thought, looking at her naked toned arms, her loose hair, her unruly skin. Once a princess, now she had become half a priestess. And what had the High Sage said? *A priestess is slave to no man. She only answers to the Goddess.* Why should a priestess, then, depend upon men to do her bidding?

The fawn closed his eyes and nuzzled against her hand. His fur was cold and soft to the touch. She had raged against Sage Parashurama and blamed him for not giving her what she had wanted, but she had not realized that he had given her all that she needed. She had held him responsible – like she had held Drupad responsible – for not being brave enough for taking on her problems on his shoulders and delivering her to her goal, but she had not stopped to think for even a moment why he must fight her wars. By starting her on the path of a priestess, he had given her all the tools she needed; now it was up to her to find her path and walk along it, wherever it may lead.

She could not – she would not – stay on at the hermitage and rely on the sage. The longer she stayed on, the more she would resent her life and his inability to fulfil her dreams. She had to move on. She had to learn to look inward in times of strife and find the solution within, and she had to remember that a true priestess bowed to no man.

She got to her feet, and looking up at the sky she murmured: 'I am coming to you, Mother.'

TWELVE

AMBA SPEAKS

I remember that night as if it were yesterday. People who claim to hear the gods are either mad or are lying, but on that night when I sat by the Yamuna and looked up into the dark blue sky, I felt the Goddess's smile warm on my arms, and she seemed to whisper to me that I must go to her. Perhaps I was at the edge of my own reason. Still, as I sat caressing the forehead of the fawn, I was aware of no other sound but the Yamuna's soft gurgling, of no other smell but that of the wet grass beneath my feet, of no other touch but that of the Mother's caress.

I waited till the Sage's return to tell him of my decision, and though he warned me again that the path of a priestess was a long and arduous one, he blessed me and said that I should set up my hut a mile or so northward, closer to the riverbank where the green-apple trees stood. Although he said that I was not yet ready to live on my own, I left him the very day he returned, accompanied by two of his younger sages who would help me raise my hut. I did not tend to the sage's bruises and wounds; I was too eager to go where the Goddess promised to lead me. I would look back at the oversight later as evidence that I had not yet learnt to step out of myself, and I would offer my nursing care to the sage, but by then all his wounds would have turned to scars.

In the beginning of that first year, when I went to the lake to fill up my earthen pot, every now and then, my glance would steal to my reflection, and I would set my hair in order, or lift the edge of my garment to better cover my bare shoulder. When I came upon blooming jasmines, my hand would pluck them seemingly on its own and place them in my hair, and on some evenings I would sit by the doorstep tying them together with a thread into a garland. I would apply sandal paste mixed with turmeric to my arms and hands, and I would rub them together, marvelling at how soft they became.

On the first full moon day after I moved to my own hut, I invited the sages at the hermitage for a meal – though I still took the raw grains from them – and all evening I spent restless in my mind, eager to hear from the sages how tasty everything was. I dressed up well for this occasion, I remember, and it was only at the end of the meal, when I caught my reflection on an upturned brass plate, that I wondered why the Goddess had not spoken to me after that night by the Yamuna. After everyone had left and I lay alone on my mat with my arm resting over my forehead to shade my eyes from the moon's rays, just as sleep was about to take me, it hit me like a bolt. I suddenly knew the reason for the Goddess's silence.

Beginning the day after, I cast away my hair pin and the container of sandal paste and turmeric. Whenever I went to the river or drew water from Parashurama's well, I made certain that I did not look at myself. I kept away all brass plates and began to use only earthen vessels. The less I saw of myself, I found, the less I thought of myself. The only things that remind us of ourselves are these objects, things that reflect our physical appearance, I thought, and only after about three moons of such abstinence, I saw Parashurama's scars for the first time.

'I beg your pardon, High Sage, for not nursing you when you returned from the battle you fought for my sake,' I told him, but he just smiled and brushed his beard with his fingers. That night, after I had said my prayers and rolled open my mat, I saw in my courtyard the fawn of that fateful blue night, prancing in joy.

At the beginning of the second year, Sage Parashurama brought for me a grey cloak made of a hard, coarse fabric that burnt the back of my hand when I felt it. I was to wear the hood over me for twelve hours of every day, and for those twelve hours I was to tie around my eyes a black cloth so that I do not see. Only when you stop seeing do you truly open your eyes to life around you, said the High Sage that night, and over the course of the year I would see what he meant. In the autumn of that year I reared a calf after her mother had died in childbirth, and during that winter my fawn broke his hind leg while trying to jump over a stream in pursuit of a butterfly. I brought water from the brook and froze it with the white salt-like powder that the High Sage gave me, and I tied the ice wrapped in a piece of cotton around the fawn's leg. In that spring I also sprained my hip when the calf butted me one morning when I was about to leave to the hermitage to fill my vessel with water. But she hurt her nose too in the process, and I applied some turmeric on her bruise and allowed her to sleep next to me until the wound healed.

Sometime during this year, news came to me that Ambika and Ambalika had both given birth to sons. It did not raise so much as a flutter in my heart.

The first day of the third year began with heavy storms. The river overflowed and immersed the roots of the green-apple trees, and the well from which we drew water swelled so much that we could just lean over and reach the water. At nights I heard the boom of thunder and old, heavy trees crashing to the ground. On one such night Sage Parashurama came to my hut, his hair dripping with water, and I asked him the question that had been plaguing me for a long time.

'Am I a priestess yet, my lord?' I asked. 'Am I ready now to vanquish Bhishma?'

The High Sage said, 'If you have to still ask that question, my dear, then you are not ready.'

He gifted me a cow to rear that autumn, and his sages built for her a shed in my yard, under the big guava tree. My calf took to the cow's teat enthusiastically, and the cow did not resist. She gave me milk every day too, and now on my return from the well after filling my vessels, I would bring for her a bale of dry hay from Sage Parashurama's yard.

I would hear news of Bhishma and of Hastinapur, and as the year progressed I found that my fist had ceased closing at the mention of his name. By the time the first rain clouds of the new year had begun to gather, I found that I could think about him without my heartbeat quickening, and I even thought that if he were to come to my hermitage in need of a vessel of milk, I may – just may – find it within my heart to invite him in and sit by his side while he drank, to fan away the mosquitoes and bugs.

My fourth year began on a sunny note, for Bhishma had begun to recede from my thoughts, even as Hastinapur's news became less and less frequent now that everything was well. I went to the hermitage on the first day of the year and brought back with me seeds for tomatoes, potatoes, spinach and corn. I had no knowledge of farming and rearing crops, but I thought it should not be that difficult compared to caring for animals, and with my calf now on the way to becoming a full-sized cow, and my fawn outgrowing his need for my attention, I had begun to notice that time hung heavy on my hands. I thought that if Parashurama could have a vegetable garden, so could I.

Although it was not as simple as that, by the end of that winter, I had a patch of land behind my hut on which I grew most of the things that I needed to eat. But for rice, which I still got from the hermitage – and which the hermitage still got from the kingdom of Kunti – everything else the Goddess gave me through her land.

It is one of the great wonders how time seems to shrink when one is busy. Plants, I found, were harder to look after than animals. For one, plants could not swat away flies and mosquitoes on their own, so one had to guard them, protect them, nurture them. I built a fence around my farm, much like the one Parashurama had, and every morning, a zebra and a clutch of monkeys would come and sit atop it, calling out to me to come feed them.

All year, I woke up each day before dawn broke, and I went to sleep only long after the sun had set, with aching muscles and heavy eyes. It was probably the least mindful I had been of time in my life before or since, and it was also the soundest that I had slept.

In my fifth year, I cast off my rings, my jewelled coronet, my sleeping mat, my silk clothes that I had taken when I left Hastinapur, my arm bands, and the few gold discs that I had bundled up in my sack. I do not know why I did this; but I can say that I knew I needed to do it, and once I had done it, I felt happier, and I could feel the Goddess draw me closer to her in embrace. During that year I gave away most of the milk my cows produced to the hermitage, and my vegetable farm had grown to a size where it could quite easily feed three grown men. Sage Parashurama often sent young men from the hermitage to my hut for foodgrains and for manure, and though they smelled like heaven and carried the knowledge of the world in their eyes, I found to my surprise that I was not once tempted to draw one of them to my side. I was not beyond bodily desires yet, I knew, for I still bled between my thighs every month, but there was not the ache I once had for the touch of a man.

Once a wandering sage came to me for water, and while I asked him to wait he stared at me through the doorway and asked if I was a priestess. Quite taken aback, I said, 'No, my lord, not to my knowledge.' He said he was from the Northern Mountains and that he needed a place to stay for the night. Though I understood his meaning, I pretended that I had not, and guided him to Sage Parashurama's hermitage.

I still had desires, and I did not hide them from myself, for had the High Sage once not said that a priestess ought not to be ashamed of that which comes from the Goddess? But I no longer had the ravenous fire within me that demanded a man by my side, the fire that I had grown up with, the fire which – during my time with Salva and with Vichitraveerya – had at times threatened to devour me.

Now it just seemed to glow somewhere deep in me, blue and cold.

THIRTEEN

The queen who knelt in front of her was no more than a girl, thought Amba. She was dressed in all her royal finery – a green and yellow fabric stitched together to wrap her up like she were a silkworm. The heavy gold pendant hung off her neck and dragged it down like it was a millstone. Her mind went back, for one fleeting second, to that day eight years ago when she had come to Parashurama's hermitage, dressed just like this.

'Which kingdom do you come from, child?' she asked softly.

'My lady, I come from the city of Anga, which resides on the shore of the Eastern Sea.'

'That is quite some distance.'

'My need is pressing, my lady,' she said, bowing low.

'We shall come to it, my dear. But first, tell me your name.'

'They call me Anjasi, after the river.'

Amba nodded at the attendant waiting outside. When he entered, she said to both of them, 'You will need to cast away your clothes and dress in garments that we shall give you.'

'Yes, my lady.'

'Every spring, we keep the rite of fertility. All four of my priestesses take part in it. This year's rite is perhaps too soon for you, but if you do well, you can keep it next year.'

'Yes, my lady.'

'I must tell you that this one year will be the hardest of your life, child.' She tried to keep her voice free of derision, but she was not certain that she succeeded. A hint of scorn crept into her tone. 'This is not a palace, and you will have no attendants serving you.'

Anjasi bowed. 'I shall serve you with all my love and care, my lady.'

Amba saw the glittering rings on the girl's fingers. She had half a mind to instruct her to give away her jewellery too, but she caught herself. Amba herself had not given up her coronet until the third year, she remembered. It was one of the hardest things for a girl to do, giving up her jewellery. It was akin to asking a king to set aside his sword, even if he had never fought a war.

'We do not have mirrors in our hermitage,' said Amba, 'nor do we speak to each other unless we must. We all know our duties, and lord knows there is enough to keep you on your toes from sunrise to sundown.' She paused to look at the queen. 'Have you seen to any household chores in your father's house, girl?'

Anjasi shook her head, shamefaced.

Amba sighed. This was going to be harder than she had thought. They all came with twinkling eyes and pretty smiles, but after two days of the life of a priestess, they fled, covering their ears with their dainty little hands. She wondered if she should tell Anjasi of all the other hardships she would see in the next one year, but she cut herself short. Anjasi would learn all in due course, like she – and all other priestesses – had. It was like crossing a bridge of stones; only after stepping on one did you think of the next.

'Do you have any questions?' she asked.

The queen began to shake her head, but mustered courage and looked up at Amba. She said, 'My lady, they say you walked through fire after you had become a priestess. Is that true?'

Amba thought of the night three years ago, after her five-year period of training had ended. Parashurama had pointed her towards a bed of burning coals and asked her to walk through it. Without hesitating for even a second, she had closed her eyes, joined her hands, and stepped on the red embers with the mother's name to her lips.

Amba wondered if she would do the same today. Three years of being a priestess had dulled the keenness of her senses, somewhat. Now she had four young women doing her bidding – and a fifth was about to join them. Though she kept up her basic training, she doubted if she had been firm enough with herself to withstand the test of fire. She had thought becoming a priestess was hard enough; in the last three years she had come to realize how wrong she was: staying a priestess was the real challenge. She smiled to herself, hoping the Goddess could not hear her think.

'It was a long time ago, my child, but yes. I did walk through fire.'

'Will I … be required to do the same, when I am done?'

'Nothing will be required of you that you cannot do, my child,' said Amba, holding the girl's chin with her forefinger. 'But you shall not become a whole priestess, therefore you shall not be asked to walk through fire. You will merely be taught the ways of a priestess so that you may bring forth a son that your kingdom is proud of.'

The girl nodded, but Amba saw fear in her eyes. Smiling at her, Amba pointed Anjasi to a bundle of clothes in the corner. 'Wear them, child, and send back your clothes and chariot with your attendants.' She waved to the attendant, bidding him to leave the room.

Anjasi asked, 'My jewellery, lady?'

'You shall not wear them, but you may keep them for a moon or two. Come midwinter you must cast them off as well, all your rings and necklaces.'

'As you wish, my lady.'

Amba called out without raising her voice: 'Parushni.' When she arrived on tiptoe and bowed to her, she said, 'Anjasi will sleep with you in your hut, and she will stay with us until next year's rite. Will you show her our ways and take care of her so that she would not miss her kingdom?'

'Yes, Mother.'

'Now it is time to water my plants,' said Amba, rising up. Just then she saw the doorway to the hut darken with a shadow. She knew who it was without having to look at it a second time. 'Sage Parashurama,' she said, 'I shall be with you in a second.'

Amba met him on the edge of the courtyard by the well. She picked up the vessel full of water and gestured to him to walk with her around the hut to the farm at the back. Through one of the windows, the sage asked Amba, 'Another priestess to train, my lady?'

'Not quite,' she said. 'She wants to have a child by one of the gods.'

Parashurama fell in step with her and held his hands behind him. 'Do you really believe that, my lady, that it is gods who father children born at the fertility rites?'

'That is what the mothers believe, Sage, and that is all that matters.' They came to the fence. She opened the log gate and bent the can over her hand so that water trickled off the tips of her fingers onto the soil. 'You have something on your mind, do you not?'

'Yes,' said Parashurama from behind her. 'It is regarding King Drupad.'

Amba stopped, just only for a second. Her hands continued their motions as if she had heard nothing. She had thought – no, convinced herself – that all matters related to Panchala and Bhishma had been buried deep enough in her past, but one mention was enough to bring back those memories. She had to shut her eyes to drive them out of her mind.

'How is Panchala any of my concern?' she managed to say.

'It is not,' said Parashurama. 'But King Drupad is still childless, after all these years, and now that Hastinapur has two heirs–'

'He wishes for one too.'

'Yes, he does. He came to my hermitage yesterday, and he had a proposition.'

Amba saw in her mind's eye a blood-tipped arrow lifted by an invisible hand and, set to a bow with a string of gold. Without being told she could guess what the proposition was, and a part of her leapt at it, but she held herself back. She was now a priestess. 'But Sage,' she said, stepping to the next row of basil plants, 'I am past childbearing now. I am already six-and-twenty.'

'But my lady, that is what Drupad wants. He wishes to lay with a sterile priestess.'

Amba stood up and turned to Parashurama. 'I do not understand.'

'The priest at Drupad's court told him that laying with a priestess who was past child-bearing would bring back his virility, and he would be able to have children.'

'That is impossible,' said Amba, 'and you know that too. An impotent man is an impotent man for life, Sage, no matter how many priestesses he beds.'

'I do not know that for certain,' said Parashurama. 'The Goddess of Fertility works in her own mysterious ways.'

Amba turned back to her plants. 'Be it so, but I would not lay with that man even if I had to die.' In her mind the image of the arrow sharpened, and the string got stretched back so far that Amba wondered if the bow would snap in two. Then the arrow flew into the air and pierced a man's chest through his armour, drawing a single stream of blood that flowed downward, to his waist. Amba recognized the man with the sharp face and the beard, and his cry of pain which was but a whisper.

There will be a child, she heard someone say from deep within her. *There will be a child, and it will be the death of Bhishma.*

Amba looked up at the clear blue morning sky. She broke into a loud chuckle. Mother, she thought, why do you play this game with me? I do not care about Bhishma any more, nor do I care about the fate of Panchala or of North Country. I am yours; I have given myself to you and you have accepted me. All I want to do for the rest of my life is to serve you, and now you bid me to have a child. But how will I have a child, Mother? How will I survive having a child at my age?

'You know of enough herbs, do you not, that would prevent a maiden from giving birth to a child after laying with a man?'

She nodded, her mind still lingering over the voice that she had heard. It had come from within her, so it had to be hers, but a little part of her wanted to believe the Goddess had spoken to her.

'Then what do you fear, my lady?' said Parashurama. 'You shall not bear a child, and the High King will get his manhood back. You have helped many maidens become mothers; perhaps you can think of this as step toward helping a man become a father.'

Parashurama was right; she would lose nothing by doing this. On the contrary, doing a good turn to a High King of a kingdom such as Panchala would only serve her well in the future. All she had to do was to bear with the discomfort for one night – and if Drupad were truly impotent, it would not be a long night – and she could go back to her own world.

But there was that voice.

Deep within her, something stirred and awoke. Her mind began to race. If the voice had, indeed, been the Goddess's, it meant that She had put into Amba's hand another tool by which she could take her revenge on Bhishma. For the first time in perhaps eight years, she thought of Ambika and Ambalika atop Hastinapur's throne, playing with their children, and her eyes suddenly awoke with stinging, scalding tears.

If the Goddess willed it so that her wrongs were to be avenged, who was she to deny her? She was not right in questioning whether she would survive, either; if the Goddess gave her instructions to birth a child, she would have her own plans of looking after her. Amba was no more than a servant to her, and her duty was no more than to follow her bidding.

So she said to Parashurama, 'Tell the High King that I shall receive him at the fertility rite this year.'

FOURTEEN

The rite of fertility usually took place on the day after the first rain of the year, after the earth was made fertile by the sky. But this time Amba decreed that it be moved back by a week. No one had asked her why, but she had told them nevertheless that it had to be on the night of the full moon. What she had really wanted to do was to time the night with the most fertile period of her month.

Seated on her bed, she turned her wrists and looked at the flower bangles she had been asked to wear by Parushni. At one time she would have perhaps smiled at them, touched her nose to them and breathed in with a deep sigh, but now she just looked at them. Her hair had been set in a plait that morning, and tender jasmines had been tied to her scalp with twine. She had asked Parushni severely if she had intended to dress her up like a maiden about to be married, but Parushni had just smiled and gone on with it.

Oil and sandal paste glistened on her arms and thighs. On her forehead was a single vertical line of vermillion, and underneath it was a yellow turmeric curve. She had been given a new white sari to wear, and her undergarments had a dry, warm feel to them. Incense sticks burnt from the corner of the room where a stone idol of the Mother sat, looking at her. Amba observed all these things with detachment, as a priestess should. There was but one thing that she could not be detached about – at least she had not been able to in the last one month – and that was Bhishma.

Eight years, she told herself. Eight years of training and she had conquered all parts of herself, and yet at one word from the Goddess she was ready to take up arms against Bhishma again. She thought she had conquered envy, but her heart burned when she thought of Ambika and Ambalika. She did not know what she envied about them; she wanted neither to be a queen nor to be queen mother. Did she just envy the fact that they had borne children while she had remained barren?

Even with Bhishma she did not know what caused her anger. Her life in the last eight years had been happy and rich with contentment, and if Bhishma had been responsible for it, she ought to be thankful to him. But then another voice sprang up inside her, one that she had long ago learnt to suppress but had lately become louder. It said: whatever you have gained is by your goodness of character. Whatever you have lost is due to Bhishma. So go, get your revenge against your destroyer. Do not rest until you have seen his dead body.

This was not the Goddess; she was priestess enough to know that. The voice of the Goddess never preached death. This was her own self, that old self that had goaded Sage Parashurama to fight Bhishma, that old self that had torn apart her hair on those long summer nights thinking of ways in which she could reach Bhishma and plunge a dagger into his heart. Back then, this voice had screamed in her ears. Now, it only whispered. And yet these eight years she had learnt to silence it. Now she let it go on.

Outside she heard drums, and through the shadows on the white curtain and the chants, she could make out that Drupad was ready. As the drums reached a crescendo and she readied herself for his entry, a small thought came to her: *you can still stop this*. But she pushed it aside with a savage shake of the head and filled her head with images of the mysterious bowman who would one day shoot the poisoned arrow at Bhishma's heart. That bowman would be her son, she thought. The Goddess had told her so.

She smiled, and got to her feet to welcome her paramour.

She could not at first recognize Drupad. He had the skin of a leopard wrapped around his waist, and his body was smeared with ash. A round, red spot gaped at her from between his eyes, and a black vertical eyelid had been drawn on it, with long lashes ready to blink open. A live snake hissed from over his left shoulder, and when it looked at her it raised its hood and opened its mouth, revealing two sharp, hungry fangs. In his hands Drupad held a trident fashioned out of wood and iron, and in his wet, matted hair there stood a white crescent moon with a star at its bottom tip. His feet were grey and dusted with ash, Amba noticed, and his toes had been fitted with brass rings that clacked against the earth with each step.

Her mind went back to their last meeting almost nine years ago, when she had asked him if he would marry her. He had expressed horror at her question then, and now he had come back to her. But for the Goddess's promise of a son who would kill Bhishma, she would have spat in his face and sent him back to his kingdom. In what way was he worthy of laying with a priestess of the Mother? But that did not matter. Now, for her own sake she had to endure him and stoke in herself some of the lust that she had long ago vanquished. For her own sake, for this one night, they had to be the incarnations of Shiva and his consort.

He opened his mouth when his eyes fell on her, whether in recognition or in wonder she did not know. The lines on his face had lengthened a bit since she saw him last, and there was a childlike innocence to his face, the kind into which men often lapsed in middle age. *Especially impotent men*, she thought. Men grew up with such certainty over their ability to sire children that when the tragic realization of their inability dawned upon them, it drove the light out of their eyes.

'So we meet again, High King,' said Amba, holding her hands out to him in a gesture of welcome.

He got down on one knee and took both her hands in his. He clutched them to his lips and sighed into them. 'My lady, Amba! It is you, it is, indeed, you.'

'So it is. I have heard that Bhishma has taken back the quarries you stole using me as pawn.'

'My lady! The gods have made me suffer long and hard for that slight! I asked Sage Parashurama to tell me your whereabouts so that I could come to you and offer my apologies, but he would not.'

Amba shook her head. 'No apology is required, Drupad. We all serve a bigger force, and She is always watching. If you say you have suffered, then I grant that you have.'

'No, no, my lady, there has not been one night that I have slept soundly after I sent you to Sage Parashurama. Many a time in the last eight years did I wonder how it would all have transpired if I had taken you as my wife that night.'

'But you did not, Drupad, and there is no gain in wishing the past had been different.'

He kissed her knuckles, smelled the flowers on her wrists. 'Bhishma has been encroaching on our mountains all these years, my lady. Now he holds almost the same amount of rocky land as does Panchala. And no king in North Country dares raise his voice against the champion of Hastinapur.'

'You have not wed, have you, Drupad?' she asked, ignoring his comment. She held his chin and lifted it up so that she could look into his eyes. 'How will you have sons if you do not marry?'

'Do you think I have not tried, my lady? Ever since I was fourteen I only rarely slept alone on my bed, but never did a maiden get a belly from sleeping with me. I am known all across North Country as an impotent wretch. Pray tell me, who will give their daughter in wedding to someone like me?'

'Not even the vassal states?' Her mind went, fleetingly, to Subala.

'No, my lady,' said Drupad, 'not even the vassal states. And now that the queens of Hastinapur have given birth–'

'Let us not speak of them, High King.'

He looked up, puzzled; then remembered the 'queens' he had referred to were her sisters. 'Yes,' he said, 'yes, of course. With Hastinapur now possessing heirs, a new strength seems to have taken over Bhishma. He was once cautious and diplomatic, but now he attacks my mines without so much as a warning.'

Amba felt anger rise within her, and though a part of her admonished it and fought to allay it, another part of her relished it, especially now that she held the reins of Bhishma's future in her hands. She said, 'I will give you a son, High King.'

'My lady?' he dithered. 'I do not understand. You do not understand–'

'I understand perfectly well!' she said, silencing him. 'You have slept with waiting-women, with women of your court, perhaps sisters and wives of your noblemen, but you have never slept with a priestess.' Her voice sank low to a whisper. 'A priestess is a daughter of the Goddess, Drupad, and the Goddess never allows the rite of fertility go to waste.'

Drupad stumbled to his feet, and though he was taller than her, at that moment, he looked like a mere child, fumbling and looking down at his hands. The snake on his shoulder wrapped around his neck tighter and stared at Amba, its forked tongue sliding out and slipping back in.

'But Sage Parashurama told me that you are past child-bearing, that you would return strength to my loins.'

'I shall give you a son, King of Panchala, who will one day slay the regent of Hastinapur.'

That lit up his eyes, she saw, though his manner was still that of a knave, arms waving about as he hunted for words. She reached out, fingers outstretched, to take the snake by its neck and lowered it onto the floor. 'Come, Drupad,' she said, 'I shall show you how the Mother makes love to the Destroyer.' She took his hand in hers, and as she guided him to the bed, his eyes glassed over with desire. Under the leopard skin wrapped around his hips, she saw a round bulge take shape.

With her other hand she dimmed the lamp. Outside, the chants and drums continued.

FIFTEEN

Amba caressed her stomach. It had grown quite a bit in the last two months, and now she could not stand on her feet for very long without catching her breath. She looked at the chalk-drawn calendar on the mud wall of her hut; if her calculations had been right, her son would be born before the midsummer feast, fourteen days from now. Her body was bathed in sweat, and grains of sand and mud stuck to her palms as she pushed herself back against the wall. The sun was so harsh this year that even in the middle of the night, the breeze that flowed over the Yamuna was warm. It dried the skin and left it broken in white patches.

The house had become dirty, and she had left the plants untended for nigh on a week now. Anjasi had been around to help her, yes, but she was still new at the hermitage. Only after the priestesses kept their first rite of fertility did they become truly serene and accepting. Even Parushni had been fidgety during her first year.

She wondered if she should get up and sweep the room once, but it was late at night now. It could wait for tomorrow. A knot appeared in the pit of her stomach, and it churned and tightened, making her head swim and eyes ache. She clutched her hips with both hands and breathed in and out deliberately, as Sage

Parashurama had taught her to. In a few moments, the cramps subsided, leaving her covered in a fresh layer of sweat.

When she had first asked the High Sage why her stomach turned so much, he had said male children did that because they were in a hurry to leave the woman's womb and run and conquer countries. He might have said that just to please her, but there was some truth to his words. Her son would be the future High King of Panchala. He would need to run around a lot, and would need to fight a lot of wars – especially with the rulers of Hastinapur.

On that thought she sat up straight against the wall and bent down, so that her lips hovered around her chest, as close to her son as she could get. Then, in a low, steady croon, she began to speak. Six months of daily habit had ironed out all stutters from her speech, and the words came out on their own, one after the other, without her having to push them out with any conscious thought. Sage Parashurama had said that a child in the womb began to hear and understand its mother's words from the twelfth week onward. He had instructed her to speak to her son, to tell him tales of gods and goddesses, of kings and queens, and of right and wrong.

'He will one day rule the land, my lady,' he had said. 'His education must begin, therefore, at the earliest possible time – right from the womb.'

She had begun to tell him all that she knew of the world, but on the second or third day a thought had struck her. Why not also tell her son, she thought, of the reason for which he was being brought into the world? So she had begun to recount the tale of Amba, the princess of Kasi, the lover of Salva, the paramour of Vichitraveerya, the queen of Hastinapur, the mother to the son of Drupad, the High King of Panchala, the priestess of the Mother – and the enemy of Bhishma.

Every day for the last six months she had repeated the story to him, and now it all came out in a great torrent, like the Yamuna in flood. As she whispered, she held her palms on her stomach, rubbing them in circles on both sides. It was as though she were reading off an invisible parchment placed under her closed eyelids. Her first telling of the story had been neutral, sometimes even from Bhishma's point of view (as she understood it), but lately she had begun to stress her own feelings, her own thoughts, her own emotions. More often than anything she repeated how important it was for him – her son – to avenge all the wrongs that had been heaped on her by one man.

She stopped when the back of her neck began to ache and let her body slide down against the wall so that she could lay on her back and sleep. But her stomach stirred again, and her eyes shot open. She felt as though her son had slipped off her and was falling to the ground.

She sat up in a flash, legs spread out, and waited, reminding herself to breathe. For a few seconds nothing happened, and she thought she could go back to sleep again. But then it came again, a swift sliding motion deep inside her, as though something had snapped. She tried turning over on her side, but abandoned the idea at the sharp pain that shot up her back when she moved. She leaned back, supporting herself on her elbows, and gulped.

This was it. The moment had arrived.

'Anjasi!' she called out.

The boy was coming. Her pupils dilated, and wrench after wrench took hold of her to shake her by her innards. 'Anjasi!' She fell to the ground and began to whine as waves of pain washed over her. She dug her fingers into the dry earth, and as her stomach cramped up further, her eye lids grew heavy, and though she fought with herself to stay awake for the sake of the boy, her mind had given way, and she felt her body shutting down. With one last gasp of effort, she called out, in a voice that was no more than a hoarse whisper: 'Anjasi!'

Then she passed out.

When she next woke up, it was dark outside. She reached out with her hand and met Parushni's. She asked, 'How is my son?'

'You had a daughter, my lady. She is as beautiful as you are.'

Amba frowned, and struggled to prop herself up against the wall. 'A daughter – how is that possible?' she said, shaking her head. 'No, no. There must have been some mistake.' She turned to Parushni, squeezed her hand. 'Are you certain you are not mistaken, Parushni? Are you certain he is not a boy?'

Parushni shook her head gently. 'I think you ought to sleep for a while longer, my lady.'

'I do not!' Amba jerked her hand away. In her mind she ran over the words that had come to her that faraway morning by the plants. Had the Goddess not told her that she would bear a son who would kill Bhishma? She closed her eyes and racked her brain in frantic desperation. Was there something that she was missing? She had done the Goddess's bidding word for word, the Goddess had promised her revenge through her son, and now … and now…

She closed her ears and let out a long, shrill cry.

Parushni drew back, horrified. 'My lady,' she said, 'you are still weak, and you know not what you are doing. Please rest your eyes for a bit. Sage Parashurama will bring your child to you in due course.'

'I do not *want* to see my daughter!' cried Amba. 'I did not *want* a daughter, do you not understand? How brazenly has the Goddess betrayed me! How I trusted the Goddess, became one with her for eight years – eight years! And this is how she repays my trust. She promises me a son and gives me a daughter.' Her fingers knotted together and twisted. The toes of her feet curled and uncurled.

'My lady,' said Parushni, taking into her hands an earthen vessel, 'you must drink this. You must sleep.'

With a cry of anger Amba knocked it off, sending it crashing against the wall. The green slime that had filled it now lay on the floor, and it seemed to Amba that it made the shape of a slender man with a beard. She sprang to her feet and threw herself at the liquid, clawing at it with her fingers and digging her nails into the earth.

'Amba,' said a voice.

She stopped, hunched on her knees, her garment now soiled with smudges of green. She looked up at the door, and saw the dark figure of the High Sage. Breathing heavily, Amba rolled into a sitting position with one knee raised. She rested her chin on it, slid her hands into her hair, and began to sob.

'Amba.'

'Do not come near me,' she said, her voice steady. 'You – you are all the same! You come in different garbs, all of you; my father, Salva, Bhishma, Drupad, Jarutha, Parashurama – all of you are the same *fiend* that go by different names. You take me out by the hand, promise me something, and then you drop me in the middle of the river and ask me to swim.' She pulled at her hair with both hands and gave out a cry of anguish. 'Why, High Sage! I was happy being in my own world as a priestess. Why did you have to come and ask me to lay with Drupad?'

'I did not ask you to have a child with him, my lady,' said Parashurama, standing at a distance. He signalled to Parushni to leave. After she bowed to both of them and retreated, Parashurama's voice softened. 'But what has happened has happened, Amba. Do not question the will of the Goddess.'

'I did not, High Sage, not until today. Because that is all I have done in the last nine years of my life: always sought the Goddess's command. But even the Goddess is like unto you, my lord; or perhaps you all are like her, I do not know. She promised me a son, and she gave me a daughter. What am I to do with a daughter, High Sage, pray tell.'

'Do you forget, Amba, that you yourself are a daughter to your father? Do you not know that for a priestess, a daughter is more desirable since she can train her to be priestess after her?' He took a step closer to her. 'Perhaps that is the Goddess's will.'

'The Goddess's will is to rile me,' said Amba savagely. 'The Goddess's will is to show me how powerful she is. She is nothing more than a petty crone who wishes women to serve her blindly, taking her every action in their stride.' She looked away in the direction of the door, and she thought she saw a spot of purple flash by. Looking back at Parashurama she said, 'I no longer serve the Goddess, High Sage. She has forsaken me, and so I shall forsake her.'

'She has not forsaken you,' said Parashurama. 'And you cannot forsake her. None of us can.'

'I can!' said Amba, her eyes burning bright with fury. 'And I will. From today the Goddess is as good as dead to me.'

Parashurama raised a warning hand, and took a faltering step toward her. 'It does not become a priestess—'

'I am *not* a priestess!' said Amba, sitting up. 'Do not come near me, High Sage, and do not woo me with your false words and smiles. I have taken enough betrayal for one life, and I cannot bear to take any more. I beg of you.'

For a moment the sage said nothing. He then took a couple of steps back into the shadow, and Amba saw his figure set against the silvery starlight. 'So be it,' he said. 'I shall not be with you if you do not want me. But you must sleep, my child.'

Amba did not answer.

'You must sleep,' said Parashurama again, 'for it is late at night, and you have been through much in the last two days. Perhaps early tomorrow morning you can see your daughter—'

'I do not wish to see my daughter,' said Amba.

The sage sighed. 'So be it.' He turned and left the hut.

After he left, once again Amba thought she saw a flash of purple at the door, and with half a mind she wondered if she should go up to the courtyard and look for the fawn that had once taken her to the riverbank. But to what end? The Goddess would lead her again, somewhere, and then she would promise her one thing and give her quite another. She crawled on all fours to the corner of the hut furthest from the lamp, and curled up into a ball, wrapping her arms around her knees. In the darkness she saw a distinct shadow of a warrior raising his bow, ready to shoot an arrow at his enemy. She could not see his face, but if she could, she knew he would be bearded, and if she could hear him speak, she knew his voice would be a soft, clear, dulcet whisper.

She wept.

The next time Amba opened her eyes, for the first few seconds she did not see anything. In the daze she wondered wildly if she had gone blind with anger at the Goddess, but soon, dark shapes began to form in her line of vision. She turned her head to look at the front door of her hut; the leaves of the guava tree beside her well rustled in the night breeze, and the starlight had become sharper. Amba sat up against the wall and shut her eyes, recalling what she had seen in her sleep. It came back to her in short, white flashes.

It was the same vision she had seen earlier, that morning when Parashurama had come to her asking if she would sleep with Drupad. She had seen the same black-tipped arrow with the golden feathers set to the ivory bow by dark brown, slender hands. A wisp of raven-black hair would appear every now and then at the corner of her sight, and it would wave for a moment before disappearing. The naked arms, shorn of all jewellery, lifted the bow into the air and released the arrow with a twang.

The shaft zipped past the heavy grey air, and Amba saw a long streak of lightening in the background among the rainclouds as the arrow zoomed in on its target. It shattered the bearded warrior's armour and pierced his chest, and as a horrible cry of death escaped him, Amba felt joy surge within her. The man looked nothing like Bhishma – his hair was greyer and thinner, his skin was loose and had folds – but she thought it had to be him. No other man's death would cause her this much joy.

But it was the sight of the archer that caused her to draw back in surprise. On that morning when she had first seen this, the arrow had risen on its own, and the bow's string had been pulled back by invisible arms. Today she had seen who shot the arrow that killed the champion of Hastinapur; it was not a man, no, it was a maiden who was much older than her but looked very much like her.

She opened her eyes, and the purple-coated fawn stood at the door, blinking at her with one foot inside her hut. When she stared at him, he blinked two more times and jumped out into the courtyard. He strutted ahead a couple of paces, then looked back at her over his shoulder, as though beckoning her.

Amba got up to her feet and followed the fawn, and as he had done all those years ago, he led her to the riverbank, and as Amba sat down at the same spot by the growing grass shoots, he cavorted to her side and rested his chin over her thigh. She placed her palm over his forehead and combed him, watching his eyes grow dreamy and dull. All around her the water seemed to sparkle in brilliant white beads and waves; in the flowing river, on the tips of blades of grass, on the fawn's fur. *How beautiful everything is*, she thought, and looking up, she said in a whisper: You have not forsaken me, have you, Mother?

For now she knew that the arrow that would kill Bhishma would be shot by a woman, and who said women could not be warriors? Perhaps they could not prevail against men with weapons of the hand, but archery required no great strength; and now she remembered the lessons of an obscure sage who had come by Kasi when she was eight and had told her tales of an island far away peopled by women who fought with the best warriors of their age. She had first assumed that the woman whom she had seen in her dream was herself after she had aged a few years, but now she was sure; it was not her. She had Drupad's wide forehead, and she had his thin brow, his black lips.

Whether she had a son or a daughter did not matter, Amba thought; not all men were heroic, nor were all women docile and meek. Everyone came into the world the same way, she had learned during her training as a priestess; the Goddess did not discriminate while giving life. Anybody could become anything, so long as they had teachers to teach them and mentors to guide them. Her daughter would have the best of teachers in herself and in High Sage Parashurama. She would learn the art of war from the same man who once taught Bhishma, and she would learn the ways of a priestess from her. She would grow up drinking from her breast, so she could not fail to imbibe the wrongs that had been done to her. She would grow up wishing to avenge the world for what it had done to her mother.

Amba would make sure of it.

She got up to her feet, only noticing in passing that the shimmer on the rivers had disappeared and the fawn had woken up and gambolled away. The night had become darker and more ominous, but she felt as though the Goddess had lit her from within. She ran all the way back to the hermitage and to Parushni's hut. She entered it with a smile on her face, and rushed to Parushni's side, where a little bundle of cotton garments lay. She knelt by its side and pushed the clothes aside so that she could see her daughter.

Her hand trembled.

The babe did not open her eyes, but when Amba placed her finger on the little one's palm, the fingers curled around it. She picked her up gingerly in both her arms and carried her out. The breeze had died down now, and the trees appeared still, as though they had stepped into a painting. She touched her lips to the babe's pale cheek and smoothened her brow. She recognized the lips; they belonged to the woman in her dream. Amba looked up at the stars and said, 'No, Mother, you have not forsaken me.'

With half a mind she expected the fawn to come at her from behind the well and jump around them, but nothing happened. Amba clutched the infant to her bosom and whispered: 'I shall call you Shikhandini.'

BOOK TWO

THE BLACK STONE

PROLOGUE

GANGA SPEAKS

The hardest lesson a priestess learns is that of ignoring the voice inside her. My mother, Ganga, the Lady of the River that flowed along the slopes of the holy mountain Meru before the gates came quietly sliding down, told me this on the day I was about to leave for Earth for the first time. You shall hear voices inside you, Jahnavi, she said, but do not deceive yourself into thinking that they belong to the Goddess. Priestess or not, the Goddess does not speak in mortal tongues.

This lesson has fallen on deaf ears up on the Meru too, for I see Brihaspati and Vasishta and all the other wise men claim that they know the will of the Goddess, that she has spoken to them. Common men do not share this folly; they well know that the Goddess is beyond reach, and they see the voices inside their minds for what they are: their own selfish desires. But the wise men and the priestesses believe – just because they have undergone such hardships in their training – that they have somehow come closer to the Goddess, and they insist on others the belief that the Goddess whispers to them alone, and they alone can hear her.

119

Amba did not have a true priestess guiding her through her trials, and though Sage Parashurama guided her as well as he could, it was perhaps no wonder that she erred. She heard what she wished to hear, she saw in her surroundings what she wished to see, and instead of extinguishing the fire of hatred that burnt her heart, she chose to kindle it, telling herself all the while that the Goddess willed it so. During the five years of her time at Parashurama's hermitage, though, she was truly on the road to being a priestess, and if Parashurama had not come to her with the request to cleanse the High King of Panchala, perhaps she would have found that little clear spot within her – that spot within all men where the Goddess resides.

But perhaps I am being too harsh on her; after all, Shikhandini would go on to become the woman to cause me the greatest loss that I have ever known, and perhaps that goads me to have feelings of resentment toward her mother. This is the nature of all tales, then; it is impossible to remove the teller from the story, though I strive to be neutral and force myself to see in all colours, through all eyes.

To this day the vision of Devavrata haunts me in my sleep, and I do not think I shall be free of it even in death. I do not see him as the old patriarch who fell to his death on the battlefield, pierced by a hundred arrows. I do not see him as the spineless man – some said selfless – who stepped aside again and again for the throne of Hastinapur to be occupied by men who had no fire in their loins. I do not see him as the gangly youth who stormed out of my hut on the Meru, vowing never to return.

No, I see him as he was when he was four, when he cried after me and held the tip of my garment in his closed fist to prevent me from going up the well to offer my prayers. I see him asleep on my lap after I had recited to him – for the hundredth time – the story of the Wise Ones and the pitcher-girl. I see light in his eyes, I see contentment in his heart. In all the years he lived on Earth, he had neither. That is as it should be; for there is no light or contentment in life on Earth. If he is to live among the mortal people, he must live as they do.

Sage Brihaspati's words come to me, now and then, not in the same tone in which he uttered them, but softer, almost musical. 'Earth will shred you to pieces, Son of Ganga,' he had said. On that day I had thought that the sage was cursing my son, but later, I understood that it was no more than a proclamation of truth. When the sage's words came true, when the final arrows pierced into the chest of my son, I found myself strangely calm, neither surprised nor sorrowful. What had to come to pass had come to pass. But there was no denying the searing pain that shot through my breasts, as if that last arrow that felled him pierced my heart too.

On the day that Devavrata turned his back on the Meru, he turned into an enemy of the mountain, and when I became Lady of the River after the death of my mother, he became my enemy too. When he had to choose between me and Earth, he chose Earth; perhaps it is fair then, that when I had to choose between him and Meru, I chose the mountain, for it birthed and reared me. Devavrata fought with many a weapon during his time on Earth, but when he came to battle with me and the people of Meru, he found himself powerless, for our weapons were not swords and bows.

But I must not make it seem that the tale of the Great War is all about the death of my son. If there is one thing that I know from being a priestess to the Great Goddess Bhagavati, it is that men and their lives are fleeting. The Goddess and her creations have always existed, and shall continue to exist even after the last man on Earth draws his final breath. What the purpose of this universe is, where it began and where it will end, only the Goddess knows. Hers will be the real great tale of the ages, if she ever chooses to tell it. All other tales, like this one, are but tiny particles of sand that make up the shore on which the Goddess treads, at her own speed, quietly, speaking to no one.

That is why, perhaps, all wise men who have looked for meaning in life have found none, and that is why this tale of the Great War must be read as if there is no purpose to it. There is no good, no bad, no justice; there is just life, and there is desire. From the time they are born, men are plagued by desire, and some men – like Devavrata, like Satyavati, like Amba – are prepared to lay down their lives to fulfil their desires. I am telling this tale to bring these people out, to show the world that they lived.

Now in my ears I hear laughter, that of a sixteen-year-old girl with a large and crooked nose.

ONE

Devaki raised the golden silk hood from her face and peered out at Pritha, who was combing herself in front of the mirror. She saw the girl's lips crumple up in distaste, and smiled to herself. Pritha was at that age. Devaki remembered her own days as a maiden of fourteen in this very room, in front of that very mirror. Her brother Kamsa had grown up faster than she had; men had to put on their royal faces from the time they were ten, it seemed. He would return from a day of riding or hunting and stroll into her room, and when he spotted her turning around in front of the mirror he would chide her.

'Do not worry, sister,' he would say, 'there is no one in North Country that has hips like yours.'

'Do you not feel shame, brother,' she would reply, 'for saying such words about your kinswoman?'

He would throw his head back and laugh. In all these years, many things had come to pass, and people around the country today called him tyrant and usurper, but in her company he would still laugh like he used to when they were growing up. Once or twice she had asked him if it was necessary to keep their father in his prison, and his face had turned grave. 'Devaki, my dear,' he had said, 'our father enjoys all kingly comforts in his room.' He always insisted on calling it a 'room'; not prison, not cell.

'But–' she would say, and he would wave her arm gently at her. 'No, sister, you and I have been good friends, have we not, all our lives? Is it not enough if I tell you that I had no other choice, that my hand was forced?'

This would make her grow quiet, for what he had said was true. They had been the best of friends all their lives, and there was some truth to what he said. Devaki had visited her father now and then in his 'room', and she had seen him being attended to by three menservants and two waiting-women. She had not asked him explicitly, but his manner conveyed deep contentment, the kind which she had never seen on his face during his time as reigning king.

Devaki turned her hands over and adjusted her rings so that the diamonds faced the ceiling, caught the light, and glimmered. Still at the mirror, Pritha said, 'Hmph,' and threw her hair over her shoulder to look sideways at her neck. It was scrawny, noticed Devaki; like most girls her age, Pritha's growth had all been in her chest and hips, with her thighs yet to acquire the contours that would lend shape to her legs. She had the right-sized head, and the eyes were the shape of lotus petals with long lashes fluttering over the lids every time she blinked, but she had a nose that looked bitten by an angry bee. Her lips were thin, and when she pursed them, they set together into a pout not altogether ugly, but well short of beautiful. If only Mother Nature had given her nose's voluptuousness to the mouth and the mouth's curves to the nose, thought Devaki, Pritha would have been a beauty.

'Come here, Pritha, my dear,' she said, 'sit by my side. Will you do my hair while I set right my nose ring?'

Pritha came to the bed and sat by Devaki. She was trying to be lady-like, thought Devaki with a pang, but she was not old enough to be one yet. She wanted to tell her that her time would come, but she stopped herself. Instead, she removed her hood and untied her hair, placing the clips by her side and gesturing with one arm to the attendant at the door for a tray. Pritha took a sandal comb in her hands and began to run its teeth down her hair, and in front of her, Devaki held the mirror such that she could see the younger girl's reflection.

'You are worried about something, my girl?' Devaki said. She would be no more than four years older than Pritha, but she felt as though she were her aunt. She had been told that maidens grew up fast in their second decades, especially after they got married. Perhaps when both of them would be past their childbearing time, years from now, they would address themselves as equals. But now, it had to be this way.

Pritha did not reply at once. She held Devaki's hair in one hand and ran the comb with the other. Her fingers did not fumble once. The attendant came with the tray, took away the hair clips, and on Devaki's mute gesture he cleaned the ash from the incense sticks next to the mirror and replaced them with new ones. Devaki's eyes smarted at the fresh burst of grey smoke, and the reddish gray tips made her look away.

'Not I,' said Pritha, sullenly. 'Perhaps you have something on your mind? You will swat away all my concerns about my looks, surely, and you will say that I will be a beautiful maiden once I grow up. But I know I shall not be, sister; I know how you used to look when you were my age.'

'I? What can I have on my mind, my dear? I got married today; this is the day every maiden dreams about her whole life. And what have I got to fret over when I am marrying such a kind king as your brother?'

'Aye, how am I to know? Perhaps you are sad that you will have to leave Mathura.'

Devaki asked herself the question, and the reply did not shock her. Leaving Mathura would create a void, sure, and she would miss the boat rides on the Yamuna on which her brother took her on the night of every full moon. He would himself row them in a canoe downstream all the way until they reached the city's walls, lined on each shore with seventeen of their best war barges.

Though she would say she was not interested, Kamsa would relate to her what he had done since their last visit to improve the strength of the fishing nets and the speed of the battle boats.

Yes, she would miss that, but only a little. She would miss her brother chiding her and laughing with her, but then that time had long passed. When was the last time Kamsa had come into her rooms and spoken to her? When was the last time he had given her a gift for no reason other than to see her smile? When they were children he would pick wild flowers from the forest and arrange them in a little round bouquet in a straw basket for her. Every time she asked why, he would just shrug, fold his arms over his chest, tilt her head at her and smile.

She would miss all that, yes, but she had already lost it all. She would not miss having to go down to her father's chamber to visit him, more out of duty than love. She would still send a letter or two every moon, enquiring about his well-being, but that would be it.

So she said, 'No, Pritha, that does not make me sad, though I rather think it should.'

'But something is on your mind, is it not, sister?' Pritha asked. She set aside the comb and crawled over to Devaki's side. She turned her face to her by the chin and looked into her eyes. 'There is a certain emptiness in your eyes, my lady, which I did not see this morning when Lord Kamsa took you and my brother out on the streets on his own chariot. What magnificent horses he has!'

Devaki nodded and looked away. 'Indeed, yes.' The incense sticks made her eyes water, and she allowed the tears to drip down her cheeks. One part of her laughed at her trepidation, said she was foolish to think of her brother that way, but another part of her cowered at the memory of Kamsa's gaze directed at her earlier that afternoon.

Pritha saw the tears and hugged her with her long arms. 'My lady, sister!' she said. 'This is not how a wedded bride ought to look. Your cheeks are smudged by tears instead of turmeric. The vermillion on your forehead is falling away. Here, let me help.' With the tip of her garment she dabbed at Devaki's forehead, then blew on it softly. 'There. Now, my lady, you shall tell me what is bothering you, for if it is my brother that has caused you grief, I intend to–'

'No, no,' said Devaki. 'It is not your brother. It is mine.'

'Yours?' said Pritha, surprised. 'Lord Kamsa seems nothing but overjoyed at your marriage to my brother, my lady. He shed tears when you touched his feet this morning. I saw him when he took you around Mathura in his chariot. He drove it himself, and he yelled at the top of his voice every few yards. He was the very picture of delight.'

'Yes,' said Devaki wistfully, 'he was.'

'But then where does this worry come from, my lady?' Pritha planted a kiss on Devaki's cheek. Her lips felt cold, and Devaki shivered. 'Did something happen during the chariot ride?'

Devaki got up and walked to the window that looked out at the Yamuna. The bank had been raised some twenty-odd feet so that more fishing docks could be constructed. On one of the half-built docks, two labourers worked in the evening sun with pulleys, lifting and suspending a large block of teakwood and shouting instructions to each other. Even though Mathura was situated in the narrowing stretch of land between the two Great Rivers, agriculture was not possible because of vast stretches of wetland that housed only moss and algae. Fishing was the kingdom's lifeline, and the docks that stretched along Mathura's shoreline made not only the fishing boats that fed the people, but also the war barges that kept watch on the waters day and night.

On the flat platform that led to the dock a holy man stood on one leg like a stork, facing the sinking sun. He had his arms stretched out, and water dripped to the earth from between his hands. The white thread around his shoulder dangled in the breeze, and his orange lower garment fluttered. It was such a holy man's voice that they had heard, all three of them, that afternoon in the chariot amid the din of men and women clamouring over one another for a glimpse.

Or was it one of the labourers? Or a fisherman, perhaps? She could not be sure. It came from the crowd, and when Kamsa looked again with his ears pricked, he had heard it no more. But that one time had been enough.

A sound at the door stirred her, and Devaki turned from the window to face the approaching footsteps. Unannounced, her brother walked in. When she searched his face for a smile, she found none. Pritha, hunched on her knees on the bed, looked at him, then at her, and then back at him again. Kamsa set his black slit-like eyes straight on Devaki, twirled his moustache once, and said, 'Devaki, we need to speak.'

Kamsa had always been a boy too big for his age, and in his youth, Ugrasena, Devaki's father, used to go to some length choosing waiting-women for him that were heavy-boned. When she was a child, Devaki had not understood the meaning behind her father's words that 'they must not be crushed by him'. But as she grew into a woman, she appreciated her father's concern. In their games Devaki had always taken care not to anger her brother. Once, when she had pushed him past the edge of his fury, he had dragged her by one arm and tossed her over the bed against the wall. She had spent the next ten days nursing a near-broken elbow.

Over the years, Kamsa had learnt to conquer his anger, thanks to some training in diplomacy and trade that their father put him through.

'Pritha,' he said, 'go to your chamber, please.'

Pritha got up to go, but Devaki motioned her to remain where she was.

'Let her stay,' she said, with a firmness she did not feel. 'Whatever you have to say to me, I am certain it concerns her equally.'

'It concerns Vasudev,' said Kamsa, clearing his throat. 'Not her.'

'Vasudev is her brother,' said Devaki, glancing at Pritha for a moment. 'She will certainly care for his well-being, will she not?'

'For his well-being?' said Pritha, stepping forward, frowning. 'What is this about, my lady?'

Devaki looked at Kamsa, who returned her stare.

'Who was the soothsayer, dear brother?'

'A Brahmin of very high birth, I assure you.'

'So you believe him, then.'

'Do I have a choice?'

Devaki thought she recognized the expression on Kamsa's face. It was the same drooping, despondent look that he wore when he had told her, all those years ago, that he had had no choice but to imprison their father. Now too, she thought, like a parrot he would repeat the same things: His hand was being forced; he had no choice.

'What is this?' asked Pritha. She turned to Kamsa and said, 'My lord, what is the lady Devaki saying? Is my brother all right?'

'Oh, he shall be all right!' said Kamsa. 'But I shall not have my own usurper growing underneath my wing! If I had known this before your wedding, Devaki, I would have made you stay a maiden forever.'

'Brother,' said Devaki calmly, 'I can still be a maiden if you decree it.'

Greed filled Kamsa's eyes. 'Will you?' he said. 'Will you, my sister, do that for me?'

'No. But if you will force me to do it, will I have a choice?'

'Ah, I cannot treat a woman that way. If you swear by your word that you shall be celibate, I shall let you go free, dear sister. Go to Shurasena, rule your kingdom well, but have no children, for if you do, I shall knock on your door and take them away.'

Devaki felt her knees shiver. Out on the fishing boats they sang the tale of a man who once made a fishing net with the spine of his father. No fish could bite through the net, it was said, and the man became a wealthy fisherman. In due course he married, and the very first thing he did on the night of his son's birth was to use his slicing knife on the babe's neck. When the wailing mother asked him what he had done, he said he had a dream in which his son flayed open his back and used the marrow to strengthen the strings of his net. And then he killed his wife too, and they say he sailed off in his boat with his net into the Yamuna, never to return again. Today, as the boats floated by on silent dark nights, over the sound of crickets from the bushes, the fisherpeople swore they heard the wailing of a man, and the splash and gurgle of a net hitting the water.

Devaki saw Pritha's eyes lightening up in gradual realization, and she joined her hands in Kamsa's direction. 'My lord,' she said, 'let your sister and my brother go. I shall tell them to keep their children away from you. I shall see to it that they grow up loving their uncle so much that they would never think of lifting their sword against you.'

Kamsa shook his head indulgently. 'Pritha, my girl, you do not understand. I have only two options ahead of me. Either Devaki takes an oath that she shall forever be celibate, or I imprison them.'

Perhaps nowhere else but in the court of Kamsa, thought Devaki, would the princess be asked for a vow of celibacy on the day of her wedding. Her tone dead, she said, 'Why do you not separate us, brother, and you shall have your wish.'

'No, no,' said Kamsa. 'The gods do not forgive a man who would keep his sister away from her husband against her wishes. I do wish you see my way in this, sister, and take your oath and leave the shores of Mathura with my blessings.'

Devaki considered spitting on Kamsa's face, but stopped herself. It would only make things worse. The wedding party from Shurasena had set sail back home that afternoon. Vasudev only had Pritha and two of his personal guards from his land in Mathura. If Kamsa did decide to take her prisoner, he would not have a smidgen of regret in doing so. That would anger the people of Shurasena and Kunti, yes, but what would anger achieve? No other kingdom in North Country boasted of Mathura's prowess in naval warfare and defence. Shurasena could not even hope to lay siege to Mathura and rescue them.

'I have one thing to ask of you, brother,' she said, 'and then you can do whatever you wish with me and my lord.' At Kamsa's head inclining, she said, 'Let Pritha go to her town in Kunti. She is but a girl. She is not related to you in any way. Though she is the sister of Vasudev by blood, she is the adopted daughter of Kuntibhoja. So let her go.'

Kamsa looked in Pritha's direction. 'I shall do that, but what of you? Will you take the vow of celibacy?'

Devaki shook her head. 'No, I shall not, though I wish our mother had taken it.'

Kamsa's breathing grew heavy and laboured, and his nostrils swelled. In two slow steps he came to her and looked into her eyes. He raised his arm and struck her across the face.

'You ungrateful wretch!' he said. 'What have I not done for you all your life? How much love have I given you? And this is how you repay it? You shame me, Princess of Mathura, for I no longer think that it is royal blood that flows in your veins.'

Devaki wanted to get back up to her feet so that she could spit in his eyes, but she found that she could not. The shooting pain in her cheek dulled her left eye and closed it. When she opened her mouth, all she could utter were incoherent sounds.

'There, my lady,' said Pritha, rushing up to comfort her. 'I am here with you. Do not move.'

Kamsa sent a flower vase flying to the ground with a clatter. Next, he picked up one of the pots lining the fireplace, lifted it up above his head and crashed it into the ground. Panting, he strode up to Devaki and jabbed his finger at her. 'You! Do you think I do not have plans of my own if you do not listen to me? Do you think I am fool enough to give *my kingdom* to *your son*?'

He threw his head back and laughed, the first time Devaki saw him do so in years. He turned his back to them and walked out of the room, muttering to himself. As he passed the door, he clicked his fingers twice, and Devaki saw armed guards march into the room and stand in a single file along the wall, waiting for her with their heads bowed.

TWO

Sweat trickled down Pritha's brow, though the breeze flowing along the Yamuna was cold enough to make her teeth chatter. For the first time in her life, that evening when she had seen eye to eye with Kamsa, she had come face to face with real, mortal fear. That smile underneath his moustache had never left his face, and yet his eyes had bored into her and left her a hollow wreck. If Devaki had not come to her rescue and asked for her freedom, only the gods knew what he would have done with her. If he had planned to just kill her, it would not have been so bad, but one always heard stories of kings doing 'things' to princesses and queens from other kingdoms.

The boat heaved up and down once, and Pritha lost balance and fell back on the ledge. Mathura's two guards stood on either side of her. Though they spoke to her only in deferential tones and bowed whenever she looked in their direction, she was not under any illusion as to what their instructions must have been. 'If she misbehaves,' she could hear Kamsa telling them, 'cut her up and feed her to the river.'

She thought of what would happen now to Devaki and Vasudev. By now Kamsa would have had his men throw them into a dungeon with their hands and legs in chains. Perhaps he would treat them well, with waiting-women and such. He seemed to look after his father with a lot of love, though Pritha thought he would not think a second time before cutting off his father's head if he ever tried to escape. The same terms would probably be laid out for Devaki and Vasudeva too.

They came to the edge of the woods that marked the entrance to Shurasena, and the boatman turned the boat around so that it would align itself with the contour of the bank, grating against it and coming to a stop.

With the arrival of familiar shores, Pritha relaxed a little bit, although she began to feel a bit cold. The events of that afternoon would certainly lead to war, she thought. Shurasena would not just sit back and watch her king being held prisoner in such a manner. If Shurasena and Kunti were to join forces, they would surely crush a tiny kingdom like Mathura. She felt calmer now. *I shall come back for you, brother,* she thought. *I shall come back for you with an army by my side, and then we shall see how Kamsa will touch so much as a hair on your head.*

The first guard returned and gestured to them that all was clear. Pritha got up, and taking the guard's hand, sat down on the boat's hull and descended into the water. After she stepped on the wet sand, the guard, who had been holding her shoes, dropped them in front of her. She did not ask him to lean down and hold them up to her feet. The guards walked ahead of her and waited, whispering to each other a word every now and then. It seemed like it was now their turn to be scared and nervous, as though they were accompanied not by a maiden but by a snarling hungry wolf.

As they reached the gates of the city, the blue-armoured soldiers of Shurasena peered at them. One of them called out: 'Who goes there, by the name of the king?'

One of the guards with Pritha said, 'We come from the land of Mathura. We escort the princess of Kunti back from her brother's marriage.'

'Aye, let me see your seal,' said the guard, and when Kunti stepped out into the light and removed her hood, he knelt down and took her hand in both of his. 'I beg your forgiveness, Your Majesty,' he said, 'but how is it that you come here on foot?' He turned a hard glance at the guards. 'Did the king of Mathura not think it proper to send the maiden on a palanquin?'

The guards looked at one another. Then one of them said, 'We have a message for the king of Shurasena from Kamsa, the king of Mathura.'

The palace guard got to his feet and escorted her toward the gate. Then, facing the guards from Mathura with a raised spear, he said, 'You shall not pass without stating the reason for which you need His Majesty's audience.'

The guards thought again, but only for a moment. 'Very well, then,' said the speaker, 'your king is held prisoner in the royal prison of Mathura.'

The spear slipped to the ground, and four other blue-clad soldiers came running to the gate to flank the first man. The guards that escorted her did not flinch, nor did they raise their weapons. Their faces were deadpan. One of them extracted a roll of parchment from his inner robe and extended it toward the group of soldiers. 'If you open the gates, we shall come and speak to your king.'

The guard looked at Kunti, and she nodded at him. The gates slowly swung open.

THREE

Pritha stood in front of her foster father with her head lowered and hands clasped in front of her. Kuntibhoja had acquired name all over Kunti as a kind and loving king, but inside the palace walls, more so in matters concerning his daughter, he was a tyrant.

'This does not become of you, Pritha,' he said gruffly, marching up and down the room. 'I warned you, did I not, that you may not go to Mathura on your own? If only you had taken some of our men with you–'

'Permit me to interrupt, father, but our men would have changed nothing. The lord of Mathura would have imprisoned them too, along with brother Vasudev.'

Kuntibhoja twirled his green cape in an expression of contempt. 'The men of Kunti are not weasels like those from Shurasena.'

'Father!'

'Enough, I have heard enough. From now on you shall be within the palace walls until I find you a husband …'

'But father,' said Pritha, raising her head, 'what about brother Vasudev and his lady Devaki? Are we not going to their aid?'

'Hmph,' he said, and upon approaching her he removed his crown and placed it on the table nearby. 'Do you know, Pritha, how able Mathura is at defending herself?'

'But father, we can take the help of Shurasena. I have spoken to the king there this very morning, and they wish to lay siege to Mathura and rescue their prince.'

'Ha, Shurasena, you say! The kingdom to which we, the people of Kunti, provide men to fight. Do you mean the same kingdom, dear girl?'

'That same kingdom gave you a daughter when you most wanted one, my king,' said Pritha. 'And they give us enough bulls to till our fields every year so that our people live in prosperity.'

'Our prosperity,' said Kuntibhoja, 'comes from not fighting unless we have to, my girl. Do you know when we last fought a war? It was before my grandfather's time.'

'But sire, must we not rescue the king of Shurasena?'

'Must we? Perhaps you can tell me then, how I shall convince my men to lay down their lives for a prince that they have never seen.'

Pritha thought of Vasudev. Gentle, meek Vasudev, who had only married Devaki on the behest of his father and the request of the king of Mathura. Now he was in prison in an unknown country, and here his very kin were debating with one another whether he should be rescued. Her lips quivered with fury, and when she spoke her voice trembled. 'Your very own cousin's son has been captured unlawfully, cruelly, and you sit here in your palace telling me why you cannot fight to bring him home. Is that not a blight upon your race, my king? Is this how you wish to be remembered, as a king who would do nothing to save his very own nephew? Tomorrow if one such event were to befall you, would you like me to sit here, in your place, and wonder if there was any good in rescuing you?'

Kuntibhoja looked up at his daughter for a moment, listening. Then he said, 'Do not speak out of your turn, girl. These are not matters a maiden need concern herself with. Go to your chambers and begin your music lessons. Your teacher Susharma has been asking after you.'

'I do not wish to learn music!' said Pritha. 'I want you to fight Mathura and save our kinsman!'

'You do not decide such matters,' said Kuntibhoja in irritation. 'I have given you too much love, it appears, my lady, and now you have dared to look me in the eye and told me how I am to govern my state?'

'Father,' pleaded Pritha, touching him on the arm. 'Please do not sit idle. When good people like you do nothing in the face of evil, it only grows bigger, and one day it will take us all.'

'Do not quote the scriptures to me, Pritha. Enough trouble has come thanks to your being in Mathura all this while. Now you shall learn to be a real maiden. You are sixteen, and I regret to say that you have no makings whatsoever of a lady.'

Pritha let go of him and took two steps backward. 'Sometimes, I wish you had never adopted me,' she said. 'If it were my own father, I dare say he would have loved me more. Would you have said such harsh things about me if I were your own? I think not!'

Kuntibhoja's face softened. 'Pritha—'

'Enough, father,' said Pritha. 'I have heard enough for one day. I shall be in my chambers. You can tell Susharma that I have returned. He can give me all the training in music that he wants while my brother and kinswoman rot in the prison of Mathura.' With that she turned, and shaking off her father's fumbling arm that tried to stop her, she stormed off the room. At the doorway the attendants bowed, and one small man in a white turban and red upper garment jogged up to the king and bowed. As Pritha left the room behind, she heard, only in passing, a few words behind her.

'What is it, Kanishka,' her father was saying.

'Sage Durvasa has come to court, my lord king,' said the little man. 'And he has asked for an audience with you.'

'Saaa,' said Susharma. Pritha tilted her head and looked at the way his mouth dripped with betel juice. 'Now repeat after me, Princess,' he said, pulling the brass bowl toward him so that he can discharge another long string of orange liquid into it. Then he cleared his throat. 'It must come from the base of the neck here, Princess, here.' He pointed to his neck, and it made a little clucking sound, like a bird had been swallowed. 'Now you do it.'

'Saaa,' said Pritha.

'No, no, no, no,' said Susharma, waving his hands over his head. 'You are singing it from the top of your neck, Princess, from the top, here. But what you must do is to sing from the bottom, here. Now try again.'

Pritha tried again. Susharma again said, 'No, no, no, no.'

'I am tired, master,' said Pritha. 'Can we not resume our lesson tomorrow?'

'Oh, no, we have already fallen behind by so much, Princess, ever since you left for Magadha.'

'Mathura. I went because my kinsman was getting married.'

'Quite,' said Susharma, folding another betel leaf into his mouth. 'If you do not learn to sing by the time you get married, the noble king of Kunti will behead me, my lady. So please, for my sake, sing from the bottom of your neck, here.'

'What do you know of Sage Durvasa, master?' asked Kunti, turning a lock of her hair in her finger.

'Sage Durvasa? Hmm, I have heard of him, I have, in the ballads that they sing about him on the street. But the tales are tall, I think, woven so that the balladeers will have something to eat.'

'Oh?'

'They say he was born of the rage of the Destroyer himself, and he is said to always have a curse upon his lips, ready to fling at people who happen to be in his way.' Susharma paused to explore the inside of his mouth with his tongue. 'You must sing, my lady. Repeat after me. Saaa.'

'Sage Durvasa has come to Kunti this morning. Did you know?'

'Saaa?'

Pritha nodded. 'I was with my father and I overheard the attendant announce his visit. What do you think he is after?'

Susharma closed his eyes and frowned in effort, counting something with his fingers. 'Well,' he said, 'it is not midsummer or midwinter, so this is not the usual time when we get visited by sages. If he had to forego his prayers and come here, I wonder if he does not have something set on his mind.'

Pritha sat back in her seat, cross-legged. The arrival of Durvasa had set about a little thought in her mind, one which had begun to buzz all morning after she had returned to her chambers. She had herself heard tales of Durvasa's mad rage, of how he had once cursed Indra, the king of the gods himself, so that the ocean of milk had to be churned and the nectar of immortality extracted from it. Then there was that tale that began the Bharata race itself, whose descendants now ruled over Hastinapur with such an iron fist, of how he placed a curse on Shakuntala that she would be forgotten by her husband. And then there was that little fable about the man they called Rama, and how sage Durvasa caused the death of the great king's brother.

All these tales Pritha had heard before, in the numerous plays that artisans and singers staged on Kunti's streets every night. Kunti was the city of the arts – there were more singers and poets in Kunti alone than in all the other Great Kingdoms combined. It was sad that it was so, because Kunti had been blessed by untold quantities of land, and if only her people stopped lazing and began to till their lands, it could feed all of North Country two times over. But they would not, Pritha knew, as long as they could rely on Shurasena for their foodgrains, which the shore kingdom paid in return for Kunti's spearmen.

'Princess,' said Susharma, leaning forward, his mouth once again orange. 'Will you please sing, or else the king will behead me!'

'Susharma,' said Pritha, dispensing with respect. 'I shall give you two diamonds from this necklace.' She pointed to her neck. 'I brought it here from Mathura. You know, I am certain, how good diamonds are in Mathura.'

Susharma's languid eyes travelled down to her neck, to where she was pointing. He nodded.

'All I shall ask of you is that you leave me in peace, and if my father were to ask you how my lessons have been going, you shall say words to keep him happy. All I ask of you is that my father will not come to me again and tell me that you have gone to him with a complaint. Will two diamonds suffice for that?'

Susharma nodded again.

'You can trade them for a farm that will keep your family free of hunger for all their lives, Susharma,' said Pritha, and at the lack of interest that she saw in Susharma's eyes at that idea, she shrugged morosely. Young men in Kunti either became singers, poets or soldiers. Each house had acres and acres of land attached to it, and yet it did not occur to anyone in the kingdom that they could produce food from it. She sighed and said, 'You could do what you wish with them, of course. They are your diamonds.'

She waved him out of the room with a promise that she would have the diamonds ready for him the next day, and after he had left, she got back to thinking about Sage Durvasa. If the tales about him were even remotely true, it meant two things: that he was a man slaved by anger, yes, but also that he was a man of great power. They said that the sages who disappeared into the mountains to the north for six moons of the year went past a rock gate to the abode of the gods, and that they sat upon the ocean of milk looking at the Protector laying on his side upon the snake that went around the universe. If Durvasa drew power from there, it meant that she could use that power to launch an attack on Mathura.

Or perhaps an open attack was not necessary. If Durvasa agreed to help her, they would need to wage no war, kill no people. They could devise a way by which her brother and sister could be rescued, and Kamsa would not even know. He would not chase after them if they managed to escape Mathura; from her father's words it appeared that Mathura's safety lay in the fact that it was surrounded by well protected waters. Draw him out of his walled city and Kamsa was no more than a fangless serpent.

But now only one question remained. Would Durvasa help her? At once she cursed her plain appearance; how she wished that she could sway her hips this way and that and whisper into the sage's ear so that he would do her bidding. She had heard that sages came down to earth to fulfil their baser urges for half a year, after having denied themselves for seasons at a time. She got up and walked to the mirror. She grimaced at what she saw. She would someday take a knife and carve that nose into shape, she thought, and turned around to inspect her profile.

A knock was heard on the door, and Agnayi bounded in.

FOUR

'How does the wife of the fire god,' said Pritha, without looking at the direction of the visitor, but smiling all the same into the mirror. 'I am surprised he has not burnt you yet with his passion.'

'Oh, do stop, Princess,' said Agnayi as she marched up to the mirror and held Pritha in both her hands. 'I have not seen you for moons and moons, and yet I see you in all my dreams.'

Pritha coloured. She pushed away the other girl's hands and said, 'I have only been away a month, Agnayi, not long enough for you to narrate forlorn love poems.'

'Ah, Princess, would that I be a man so I could carry you to this bed right now and make love to you. You look lovelier than the first dewdrops of winter.' Agnayi held Pritha's cheeks in her hands, and leaned forward to kiss her nose.

'If someone were to hear you,' said Pritha, 'they would think you were getting paid in gold to praise me to the skies!' Her gaze floundered to the mirror for a moment.

'But it is true, Princess,' said Agnayi. 'Any man in North Country would be lucky to have you by his side.' She took Pritha's hands in hers, and their fingers entwined. Pritha returned the pressure of Agnayi's palm. 'Such soft hands,' the girl murmured with her eyes closed, and Pritha gave a short, disbelieving laugh.

'We continue on this path for a little longer, and there shall be scandal at court,' said Pritha, allowing her hands to relax. 'You will be the ruin of me, girl!'

'The court today is too busy to hear the words of young maidens in love, Your Highness. So if you let me, I will wave the attendants away, and we can draw the curtains over the windows and dull the lamps just a little bit…'

'What a filthy mouth you have, Agnayi. I am going to put in a word about you with my father. It is time we found a nice boy for you.'

Agnayi disengaged her hands from Pritha's and led her to the mirror. She placed her hands on her shoulders, and Pritha covered them with her own. A little pang came to Pritha's heart as they both stared at their reflection. Agnayi's nose was straight and thin, as though some lovelorn sculptor on Kunti's streets had painstakingly created it. And her lips had such divine form. Pritha wondered if she could just reach out and touch them with the tip of her thumb.

'When such beauty is in front of me every day,' whispered Agnayi in her ear, 'how shall I ever give my heart to a boy?'

'You and I cannot make children, Agnayi,' said Pritha. 'I do hope you remember that.'

'Ah, children, for whose sake do we have children, Princess? Only for ten years or so they are ours, then we become theirs.'

'Says the girl who finds a different man to share her bed every night.'

'Princess!' Agnayi leaned around and looked straight into Pritha's eyes, her face contorted into an expression of shock. Then she said, 'Well, you cannot blame me. Some of the new stable-boys know their way around a bed.' She touched their foreheads together. 'I could ask them over one of these nights, if you would like to see for yourself.'

'Again, again, that filthy mouth of yours,' said Pritha.

'Not the filthiest part of me, Princess,' said Agnayi, leaning in, and then threw her head back in laughter. 'I have missed you so, Princess. I am just glad that you are back.'

They walked to the bed, hand in hand, and sat on it. For a few minutes neither of them spoke. But their eyes kept meeting and looking away, as though something sprang up in their minds but left before they could reach out and grasp it. Their hands too fidgeted about each other, uncertain. At last Pritha said, 'What do you know about Durvasa?'

'The sage?' On Pritha's nod, she said, 'Old, for one.' She looked at her. 'Too old for you, certainly.'

'Oh, is that all you ever think of?' said Pritha in irritation. 'I need to make him agree to something.'

'With due respect, my lady, it is the man that ought to persuade the woman.'

'Not if it is the woman's work and the man has nothing to gain from it.'

Agnayi frowned. 'Do you have something in mind, Your Majesty?'

'I – well – I need to take the sage into confidence about something, and we need to go to Mathura together.'

'Mathura? But you have only just returned.'

'I shall tell you the complete story later, but now I must ask you – will the sage like me the way I look or do you think I need to – make changes?'

Agnayi's frown deepened. 'I do not like this, Princess. If you want to have the sage, that can be arranged. Leave it to me. But this journey to Mathura that you speak of – that sounds dangerous.'

'It is, my dear,' said Pritha, 'and that is why I must trust you to keep my secret.' She took both Agnayi's hands and kissed them. 'I can trust you, can I not?'

'Just promise me that you shall be careful, Princess.'

'Of course, I will. I am so glad to have you in my life, Agnayi. I promise you I will bring you such great diamonds on my return.'

'I shall be glad, Princess, if you return safely.' Agnayi got up from the bed and went to the mirror again. She looked at Pritha and said, 'Come here, and I will dress you up so that the sage cannot take his eyes off you. He will be potter's clay in your hands.'

Dressed in a blue gown with little gold spots (which Agnayi had burrowed out of her closet) and a white linen hood, Pritha stood in front of her father's throne. She kept her head bent, but every second or so she lifted her gaze to see if she could spot the sage. Only two men accompanied her father; one was the court astrologer who kept throwing serious glances at her as he spoke – she knew him well.

The other – well, he looked no more than a boy, this stranger, with a head shaved smooth but for a tail of black oiled hair that dangled over the back of his neck. Every time he turned to speak to the king it fell over his shoulder. In his hand was a golden coloured staff with a sapphire perched on the tip. His arms were lean but wiry, and his calves and thighs suggested he had walked long distances in his young life. The third time she stole a glance up at the visitor, she saw his face and thought of just one thing: light.

For a deep yellow light seemed to glow upon the boy's face at all times. Pritha knew not how the trick was achieved; she was reminded of mud dolls she had seen on the streets at the spring fair in which holes were carved on all four sides so that lamps could be lit in them and covered with little pieces of brown linen. The dolls glowed as though they were small rubies themselves, and when hung on doorways on moonless nights, looked very pretty indeed.

The boy looked like one such doll, except in yellow.

Pritha looked around the room to see if there was anyone else, and at the same time her nose perked up, alert. It was said the sages from the North had queer powers; was it possible, then, that Sage Durvasa was present in the room but was invisible? His vessel of sacred water stood at the foot of the young man, so he could not be far away. In the middle of his speech the man's eyes rested on her, and he smiled and inclined his head in a bow. Pritha averted her eyes and looked down at the ground.

'Come, Pritha,' said her father, 'pay your respects to Sage Durvasa.'

Pritha stepped forward, looking up only enough to make certain that she would not trip on the stairs. When she looked up, she saw that the young boy had stood up now, staff in hand, and was holding his right hand up, palm facing toward her in a sign of blessing. So Agnayi had been wrong, thought Pritha, as she went down on both her knees at his feet. She placed her hands on his toes and touched her forehead to them.

'You shall have sons full of valour,' said he, in a voice that had just begun to go hoarse. He would be no more than seventeen, she thought, and wondered what happened to the old hobbling sage that she had been told to expect. 'Your daughter is as beautiful as a nymph on the Meru, Your Highness,' said the sage. 'You must scour North Country for a man eligible enough to have her.'

'By your grace, my lord,' said Kuntibhoja, bowing.

'They tell me that the Kuru princes of Hastinapur are coming of age, too. I did not stop there on my way, but there was a wedding on the night of the equinox last year in the royal house there, was there not?'

'Yes, my lord,' said her father. 'The elder son of Vichitraveerya got wedded to a princess from the rocky mountains to the west.'

'Ah, yes,' said the sage, and with his hands guided Pritha back to her feet. 'Bhishma has his eyes set on the west. But an alliance with Kunti will do them good, I think. An alliance with Kuru is good for Kunti too.'

'Yes, my lord.'

Sage Durvasa caressed the jagged surface of the sapphire. He had strong hands, Pritha noticed; long wiry fingers, square stubs for fingernails. With a smile, he said, 'And it will not have escaped your notice, Your Majesty, that the king of Hastinapur, Pandu, is yet to be married. Only the blind elder brother got married, so if the eligible king finds young Pritha suitable, she may well become the High Queen of the land, and in time, queen mother.' His smile hid a hint of a child's mischief, and Pritha suddenly noticed how smooth his chin and scalp were, as though he had scraped them both with a knife just that morning.

'But as you know, my lord,' said her father, 'Bhishma only looks northward. It almost seems to me that he wishes to swell his kingdom right up to the foothills of the Ice Mountains.'

Durvasa nodded. 'Indeed. But there is enough on this side of North Country to keep his hands full, if only he knows which fights to pick and which to leave alone. It has come to my ears that King Vasudev is being held prisoner at Mathura. Is that so?'

Pritha's eyes narrowed at the young visitor. People said that sages had a divine eye that could see all of North Country. Some said they reared carrier pigeons. Whatever their sources of information were, she thought, they were reliable – and fast. Why, beyond Shurasena and Kunti, no other kingdom could possibly have known of this. And yet, a solitary sage on a long journey down from the northern mountains had got wind of it.

'If Hastinapur's help could be enlisted to fight Mathura,' the sage was saying, 'then it would afford you a chance to introduce beautiful Pritha here to young Pandu. Word is that he wishes to set out on a campaign throughout North Country. I dare say they plan to leave Mathura alone for now, unless you intervene.'

Pritha wished he would not discuss her marriage with such equanimity. The two times their eyes had met and they had traded smiles, she had seen something impish in him, as if challenging her, and she found herself wishing to respond. But then she chided herself; this was but the first time they had met, and he was a sage with wisdom culled from all the ages, though he looked no older than a boy of seventeen. If he smiled at her, it could not have been out of lust or attraction; he must have seen thousands of maidens like her during his life.

'We shall speak of that in due course, my lord,' said Kuntibhoja. 'You have come from a long way off. Pray retire to our visiting chambers and allow our women to wait upon you.'

Durvasa turned to Pritha and said, 'May I have the honour of being waited upon by this young lady?'

Pritha felt heat rising to her cheeks, and she looked away. For a long time her father did not reply, and she was too scared to look at him to guess what he was thinking. But finally he said, 'Yes, my lord, whatever you wish.'

FIVE

PRITHA SPEAKS

I do not remember much about the day on which I first met Sage Durvasa, much like I do not remember the first time I must have gazed upon the face of my mother. But I remember certain flashes – of sight, smell and sound. As I think back now, I see a flash of brown, almost orange fabric that the sage wore. My nose seems to know the faint, sweet taint of wet sandal paste, and my ears still prick up at the gruff voice of a grown drunkard on the face of an innocent babe.

It is difficult for an old woman such as I to narrate what a young sixteen-year-old girl would feel when a man of beauty smiles upon her, and sees her not as a child but as a woman. That girl was once me, but my body has now outgrown my mind. I have a faint memory of wishing to curl up into a ball that day, when Durvasa and I first smiled at each other, but I cannot now recall the shivers that must have travelled down my back, the chills that must have come over my fingers, the cold sweat that must have gathered under my arms.

I do recall though the friendship that developed between him and me, and in time I began to see him not as a boy but a full, grown man. Now, in my failing age, I do not quite see his face as it once was. I only see the shape of a yellow mud doll with little windows carved on all sides holding a lamp within it and swinging from the roof, suspended by a thread of gold. It fills me with pleasure, that thread of gold, because it is the image of the only man that convinced me of love. Many after him have come, and they claim it was all his magic and that his love was all but fantasy, but there is still a girl inside me that believes that love cannot be made to spring into being through a puff and an incantation.

That first week when Sage Durvasa came to Kunti I spent some time with him, usually after dusk when I went to serve him dinner. The waiting-women looked after him and his needs, and I heard ravenous whispers and giggles about the sage among the maids that attended to his chambers. During that week I went to the riverbed every day in my chariot – and my father would insist I have two riding attendants with me at all times – so that I could be carefree and gaze upon the open stillness of the Yamuna. After the sun was up you could see nothing but calm water, and in the distance one could see the cloudy mass of grassy knolls that led into the kingdom of Mathura. Yet I knew that if I were to tether a boat and ferry toward that shore, battle barges would converge upon me like bees on a spring rose.

So I instructed my charioteer to drive along the bank until I reached the outer walls of Mathura, where the river was again unguarded. Here the river narrowed to almost half her width, and the water gushed along at twice the speed. On the other side I saw a line of donkeys tottering toward the city gates, and when their keepers cracked their whips upon their backs, they brayed meekly.

'To whom do those donkeys belong?' I asked my charioteer, and he said that they came hither from Magadha, the Great Kingdom to the east that was said to have ambitions of conquering the whole of North Country.

That night, when I entered Sage Durvasa's chambers with curried corn and rice on my plate, he said to the girl at the entrance, 'Shut the door, will you, my girl?' Then he watched me place his meal on the table by his side, and I – well, that last week we had played enough games with our stealing glances – looked him straight in the eye and said, 'Would you like me to fan you while you eat, sire?'

'You shall not call me "sire",' he said, motioning me to his bed. 'We have not had the opportunity to talk, have we, my lady Pritha?'

'No, my lord,' I said, and sat at the edge farthest from him. 'But I trust the waiting-women have given you no reason to crave my company.'

'They teach you to speak well in Kunti, I see,' he said. 'Come closer to me, my dear, and let me gaze into your lovely eyes. Let me hold your hand, for it is cold this night in your kingdom, and I would very much like to warm myself by your touch.'

'I think it is hunger that is keeping you cold, sire,' said I. 'Perhaps I should leave and let you eat.'

'I am hungry, yes, but not for the food that you brought.'

In spite of myself I went pink at that, and I dared not look up to see the desire in his eyes, for then I would have melted and given him what he wanted. The only weapon a woman held over a man was the use of her body; put a small price over it and he will chew you up like a betel leaf and spit you out, crushed and crumpled.

So I said, 'My lord, I am but a girl who does not know the ways of men. Must you send flutters down my heart this way? Can you not sate your urges with our attendants?'

He smiled, his thin lips spreading and his eyes twinkling. 'I think you know enough about the ways of men, my lady. And as for your attendants, I sate their urges more than they sate mine, I dare say.'

When he said that, I remembered the cupped hands and whispers among the chamber girls. Envy surged through me. I moved a little closer to him, but he extended his arm, gripped my wrist, and pulled me toward him. I started to give out a little cry of surprise, but his lips locked with mine and drove it back down my throat. My eyes widened first, then a dull fog filled my head and I fell into a trance, allowing him to suckle gently on my bottom lip. When he moved away I noticed that my fists were closed tight around his upper garment, and with a chuckle, he moved in again, this time for longer; a lot longer.

When we broke apart this time, he rubbed his mouth with the side of his forefinger. 'You learn quickly, Princess,' he said. 'Not like the waiting-women.'

I flushed, and moved away again to gather myself. It was not easy to carry out your plans, no matter how elaborate and well-thought-out, when a man made you tingle in your knees like he did. I was scared that he would follow me to my edge of the bed, but thankfully he did not, for if he had, I would have either given in to his embraces or run out of the room, both of which would have been regrettable.

After my breathing returned to normal, I told him, 'I wish to go to Mathura to rescue my brother and his wife.'

His smile did not change, but his gaze became more interested, I thought. He took a piece of corn and put it into his mouth.

'My father and foster-father are both cowardly,' I said, feeling the heat rise within me. 'They do not do justice to the blood of their forefathers that flows in them. When a dacoit kidnaps their future king, they sit by and watch. They say Mathura is too strong for them to take.'

'It is true, my lady,' said the sage. 'Mathura is too strong for Shurasena and Kunti to fight on their own. Perhaps if the Kuru kings could be persuaded—'

'I do not believe in looking outward for help. Why would Hastinapur come and help us lay siege to Mathura?'

'For a prize such as you, my fair maiden,' he said, 'I would think any king in the land would lead his forces against any power.'

'Sire, will you please listen to me?' I said, trying to snap him out of his illusion. 'I was at the riverbank today, and I saw the

Magadhan trade caravan entering Mathura through its eastern gates, and while the gate itself was guarded, the caravan was not.'

Durvasa sat up on his bed. His hand reached for his staff, and he began to stroke the sapphire with his thumb. 'Go on, Princess.'

'Can we not enter Mathura that way, if we perhaps disguise ourselves as Magadhan tradesmen, and then can we not make our way to the king and rescue my kinsman and his wife?'

'If it were as easy as that–'

'I shall not venture to say it is simple, sire, which is why I am asking for your help,' I said, 'and I ask not for favours.' I looked down at my feet. 'You know more about the Great Kingdoms than I do, and I am certain that once we are inside the city, we shall find some way to get to the prison where they hold my brother.' I held my hands together and squeezed my palms. 'If you shall be so kind as to help me, I – I–'

'It is dangerous, this mission you ask of me,' said Durvasa. 'I could lose my life.'

I looked up at him, and with rare courage I met his eyes and said, 'Did you not just say, sire, that a man would face any danger to have me?'

I do not know where I got the courage to say such things to a man I had only met once, and perhaps I was no more than a lovelorn girl in pigtails. But there was something about the glow on Sage Durvasa's face – its mystery would be revealed to me later, when it was too late – which seemed to feed my soul and spirit, and I could think of nothing else but to breach Mathura's walls, break open the prison that held Devaki and Vasudev if need be, and bring them back to Shurasena.

For one whole month after my conversation with Durvasa, we set about plotting our way in. Every day we would ride down the Yamuna and look at the donkeys and their keepers. Sage Durvasa had a staff that looked like a bamboo shoot which, if you looked through it, made the riverbank appear as though it were at arm's reach. (When I asked him about it, he said it was just a trick of the light; he would say no more.) Using his looking-tube we would try and locate any guards that may be concealed by the bushes.

After two weeks of watching, we sailed across the river and landed on the other shore so that we could watch the tradesmen from closer. The donkeys appeared weary, and Sage Durvasa said that from the way the sacks hung off the animals' backs, it appeared to be foodgrain of some sort. A few tradesmen mounted their wares on little carts pulled by oxen. Once in a while, Durvasa asked me to stay back in the bushes so that he could go and strike up a conversation with one of the men, and at times he would be gone such a long time that I would make myself a pillow out of his linen sack and go to sleep, especially if it was a night on which the breeze was soothing.

So it was a month to the day, on the third night of the moon's waning cycle, about four weeks to go for midwinter, when Sage Durvasa said to me what I'd been waiting to hear: the day had arrived for us to go to Mathura in search of Devaki and Vasudev.

SIX

Devaki looked at the forlorn figure of Vasudev slouched over his gold-cushioned chair. She set aside the linen and sewing needle on the bed and motioned to the guard for a tumbler of water. Her brother had been right; but for the restrains on their freedom, he had looked after them well. She did not find this altogether different to the way she had always lived her life; once the prison was the size of her chambers, now it was the size of one room. In a way she even liked it here because her husband was by her side always, and she could speak to him whenever she wanted. During their courtship, there had been an occasional letter or an elaborate visit during which Vasudev would come to her castle for an hour or two during the day. Even now, after they were wedded, if they had gone back to Shurasena, he would have no more time for her than perhaps a few days a month.

But now was different. Yes, Vasudev brooded a lot, mostly about why the armies of Shurasena and Kunti were taking so long to mount a rescue. The first few days he had raged against the guards, as though they had anything to do with their plight. 'Mathura will be razed to the ground,' he had declared on the first day. 'My father and uncle will descend with their armies when they find out how you have treated me, and you and your families will be destroyed.'

The guards had responded to that with stoic silence, and like self-inverting hourglasses, they would come at the same time everyday to enquire about their needs, about whether they could do anything to make their lives more comfortable. In the early days Vasudev would say sarcastically that they could give them the key to the door, but they would shake their heads and say, 'We cannot do that, Your Majesty.'

As more and more days went by without word from across the river, Vasudev's excitement rose to fever pitch. 'They are assembling their troops, Devaki,' he would tell her. 'They shall be here for us any day now. I can feel it!' And she would say mildly, 'I am certain they are, my lord,' and get back to sewing another green flower onto the satin hood. But in her mind she had always known that Shurasena and Kunti would not come; Mathura had her temples to protect her, and she also had the might of Magadha to fall upon, just in case. In her castle she would often hear the young maidens speak with wide-eyed enthusiasm about the priests in the temples, and how they empowered Mathura's boats to glide over the river on their own, without needing oarsmen.

Now she folded her arms and sighed. In the last forty days she had seen her husband's spirit slip away, inch by inch, and today he seemed to have reached a new low. Perhaps he had begun to see now what she had known all along; that they would do better to plead Kamsa's forgiveness and beg for his mercy than to hope for a rescue mission from across the Yamuna.

But why would Kamsa relent, she thought, gazing at the blue figures of children that she had sewn on the white tunic a few days ago. The faces of the children were her biggest hope. She was certain that Kamsa's heart would not melt at the sight of Devaki and Vasudev. If they had any hope of softening her brother, they would have to have children; and they would have to hope that the sight of a fresh-faced babe would make Kamsa see the folly of his ways.

Otherwise how long could they go on like this, she sewing and he moping about in his chair? And what was the worst that

Kamsa would do if they had children in this prison? He would not kill them, would he? Her brother would not stoop so low as to lay a hand on a newborn infant. He would probably send him away to a far-off land for fostering, perhaps to a kingdom beyond the Southern Mountains, from where he could be certain the child would not return.

She had spoken to Vasudev about this before, and he had flatly refused. But then that had been during their first week here, when hope still flickered in his heart. Now it appeared to have extinguished itself. 'Two Great Kingdoms, my lady,' he said, 'and in unison they cannot rescue their own prince.'

'Perhaps it is as you say,' Devaki said. 'Perhaps they have sent envoys all across North Country, enlisting help.'

Vasudev snorted and ran a hand on his chin. 'It is time we faced it, Devaki,' he said. 'They are not coming for us. Cowards, all of them!'

Devaki did not say anything. She had learnt from experience with her brother that there were certain things that men said to which a woman must only respond with silence. She motioned to the guard to take away the linen and light the lamps. She looked out of the window (fastened with inch-thick metal rods) and saw that the sun had just set, and a faint shade of grey had begun to take over the sky.

'If they wanted to come, they would have by now,' he said, and she ached for him once more. It must not be easy for a king of his stature to know that his subjects would not risk their lives to save his. Loss of pride for a man and loss of shame for a woman were worse than death, she had once heard.

'Perhaps,' she said, 'there is only thing that we can do which could give us our freedom.'

'Promise your brother that we shall not have kids?'

'No, my lord, if we are to remain childless, what good would all the freedom in the world do us?'

'Hmm.'

'The only way out is for us to have a child here, my lord. In this prison. Perhaps, when he holds his nephew in his hands and sees how small he is, my brother's heart will melt.'

The last time she had said this, he had flared up as though she had uttered something blasphemous, so now she was glad that he was at least considering it. The patch of sky visible through the window had turned black now, and she saw three or four stars just beginning to twinkle. Without so much as a glance at her, Vasudev strode to the front door and drew the shutter on the glass window through which the guards could see them.

He smiled at her as she settled down on the bed. This was the first smile she had seen on his face for a month. She smiled back.

Pritha fingered her forearm and winced, less from actual pain than from the memory of it. The night was cold and quiet, and because they were outside Mathura's walls they had not yet come upon any hostile boats. Every now and then a fishing boat from a stray settlement would pass them by, and they would stare at them with fear, but then Durvasa would wave cheerfully and they would smile back. The lamps they carried had a yellow sparkly glow to them, and when they held it in front of their faces they looked like beings from another world. When they smiled, their broken teeth glowed with a brown light, and Pritha thought that if Durvasa had not been with her, they would have bundled her up into their ferry and taken her away.

She felt her forearm again. It had been two weeks ago now that Durvasa had branded her, and for four nights after she had not slept a wink. The medicine that he had given her seemed to work better on his skin than hers, and only after the seventh night did the pus stop oozing out of the seared flesh. Durvasa's wound had healed in a day; the night after he had branded himself, she had seen that the circle and star had already become black and dry.

His foot nudged hers, and though she pulled it away, she could not help but smile at the river, and from the corner of her eye she saw his mouth curve upward in a half-grin. It had not been easy these last thirty days to resist his charms, and once or twice she had succumbed and allowed him to touch her underneath her upper garment, and she had run her fingers over his bare chest and played with his nipples, but each time her sense had prevailed, and she had warded him off before they could go far enough. (Not far enough, *too far*, she reminded herself.)

But on numerous occasions his hands would find hers when no one was looking, and she would allow him to hold them. His palms felt oily and smooth, and the way he squeezed his fingers and pressed them over hers awakened every cell within her body, and she would pine for more. During dinner with her father he would seek out her foot with his under the table, and he would slide his toe up her calf. Once or twice she resisted, but on the third time she responded, and on the fourth and fifth she reached for him first.

And he would whisper such delightful things in her ear in that hoarse voice. 'Your hands take me to the very abode of the gods, my lady,' he would say. 'I know not what shall happen when our bodies come together.' The first few times she had only gulped and blushed, but soon she would find things to say, even if they were mere moans of approval.

The sound of the river brought her back, and with it she remembered Agnayi's warning. She had not been happy at all with Pritha's trysts with the sage, but what could she do? She was trying her best to resist. At least Pritha had had the good sense to stay true to her word and not sleep with him. No other man she had ever seen had controlled her this way, and even now, when she looked at him in the darkness, it appeared as though a golden light shone through from within his head.

'I had always been told that Sage Durvasa would be an old man,' she said. 'I had thought that I would have to seduce him against his will.'

He bent his head and chuckled. 'The land in the North is full of Mysteries, my dear. The Durvasa before me was indeed old, but the old must always make way for the young and the new. That is the way of the world.'

'But what of all that he knows, my sage? He must have seen a lot, and he must have been wise.'

'He was,' said Durvasa, nodding. 'Each sage, at the end of his life, gives his knowledge and memories to his successor. So I have in my brain all the knowledge that he has gathered, and I have all his memories.'

'Is that a Mystery, then? Will you teach me how one can give his life to someone else?'

Durvasa laughed. 'It does not come as easy as that, my lady. One must be worthy of it. One needs to train to become a sage.' He looked behind over his shoulder to mark the path. Turning back to her, he said, 'And it is not as charming as you think, Pritha. It is quite burdensome to remember incidents from ten lifetimes. Sometimes, I wish I could live as you do, unfettered and free.'

They rowed in silence for a time, the only sounds coming from the whoosh of their oars and the slosh of the water. There was no moon in the sky, Pritha noticed, and on a quick reckoning on her fingers she frowned, for it should have been the thirteenth night on the waxing cycle, two nights before the full moon. And yet—

'The moon is present,' said Durvasa. 'I just covered her up with a patch of sky so that people will not see us.'

'Can you do that?'

'They teach us little tricks, and this trick is truly little when you set it aside the Mysteries. But do not concern yourself with all this, my lady. Your life shall be a lot more pleasant without them, I promise you.'

They neared the bank, and they worked the opposite oars so that the boat aligned itself against the grassy shore. Durvasa drove his oar into the earth with a mighty heave and held it. Pritha also did the same, and the boat steadied. Getting to her feet, she jumped onto dry land. Durvasa threw her the rope and pointed at a nearby tree. Pritha went around it twice with her arms and secured it with a double knot.

'Good,' said Durvasa, climbing out. Panting a little, he went up to the knot and confirmed its tightness. Letting his sack drop to the ground, he kneeled down and opened it. He gave Pritha a necklace made of seashells and a silver coronet. 'Wear this,' he said, and proceeded to smear himself with grey ash. 'If you put some of this on your body, you shall look just like the wife of a trader from Magadha.'

'Wife?'

'Fine. Sister, if you like that better.'

Pritha took the garments in the sack and went behind a tree to change into a gown and a knapsack. She tied her hair in two small buns, the way Durvasa had asked her to, and put the coronet on her head. Wearing the necklace she came out, to see the sage look grey-haired and wrinkled, with ash dropping off his arms and legs. He raised his eyebrows at her and said, 'Your beauty is such that you cannot hide it with such adornments, my lady. Even in the clothes of a pauper you look like a queen.'

'I wish I could say the same about you, my lord,' she said, stepping out and tossing her clothes into the boat. 'But you do look like a beggar!'

He laughed at that, but in a moment his eyes moved away, and he frowned. 'I hear the song of the traders, and animals approaching.' He came to her and took her hand. 'We do not have much distance to cover, my dear, but I think we shall do well to run so that we may not miss the caravan.'

With that, they set off into the darkness.

SEVEN

They came upon a thirty-foot marble arch, on the centre of which was mounted a serrated disc of gold. On the face of it was written a single line of Sanskrit: 'Fire moves water'. Pritha looked down from the disc at Durvasa's face, who inclined his head to the side. The trader ahead of them got asked a few questions, and now the guards were rummaging through the sacks on his donkey. Every now and then the animal would bray questioningly when prodded in the side with the tip of a spear. Pritha noticed that the guards here wore the same red armour that she had seen on the people of the war barges on the Yamuna. One trader passed through the gate, and the queue inched ahead.

Fires burnt on either side of the entrance, and whenever a breeze blew the flame flickered, sending shadows over the taut, wooden faces of the guards. When they spoke, it seemed to Pritha that only their mouths moved, and their voices were all gruff and rude. Her hand was nestled in Durvasa's, and when she turned to him to say something she saw him staring up at the golden plate and the strange words. She looked at his eyes – two blue marbles – and wondered at where the man had taken his birth. Blue-eyed men, she had been told, came from the kingdoms further north from even the mountains of ice. She would have to ask Durvasa once about his homeland.

When they arrived at the gate Pritha became aware of a pungent smell of burning oil. She assumed it came from the fires surrounding them. The guard put his arm out and raised his eyebrows at them.

'We come from Magadha,' said Durvasa. 'I am a trader, and this is my sister.'

'Show me your arms,' the guard said.

Both Durvasa and Pritha showed their arms. The guard peered at Pritha's mark, rubbing it hard with his thumb and then examining it in the light of the fire. He then looked at her from head to toe, frowning. 'You do not look like a Magadhan trader girl,' he said. 'Even your clothes do not look Magadhan.' He turned to Durvasa. 'Have you something else from Magadha?'

Durvasa said, 'Sir, we have come from far away, please let us pass. This girl goes by the name Uddalaka in Magadha.' He lowered his voice. 'She is quite an important person in the court of High King Jarasandha.' Then he cleared his throat. 'His Majesty would not be pleased if he knew that Uddalaka was not allowed to enter Mathura.'

The guard's stony face did not yield. He repeated: 'Do you carry the seal of High King Jarasandha?'

'Ah, no, I fear Uddalaka may have forgotten to bring her seal. But I do have something for you from Magadha.' Durvasa searched in his bag. 'Let me see. Ah, there we have it.' He brought out a fistful of pomegranate-coloured flat stones and laid them out for the guard to see. 'We have come to present Kamsa, the king of Mathura, with these. We think he may like to see them. Do you not?'

The guard's eyes widened when they fell on the stones, and he beckoned his partner over to see. 'My, oh my,' he said, smacking his lips. He raised his hand and attempted to touch the stones, but Durvasa closed his fist and withdrew it just in time.

'Well,' he said, 'we came all the way here in the hope that Lord Kamsa would buy these stones from us. We know he is a lover of all things beautiful, is he not?'

'Yes, yes,' said the guard uneasily, shifting on his feet.

'Besides, these stones are said to be touched by the magic hands of Indra himself, the lord of rain and water, and they are said to have been forged in the quarry of Agni, the lord of fire. A sage from Meru once gave these to my grandfather, and it was passed down to me through my father.'

Behind them Pritha became aware of a clamour, and people crowded around them, jostling and peeping over one another at Durvasa's clenched fist. 'Show them to us!' someone said. But Durvasa waited for the sounds to die down and then said, 'High King Jarasandha said that these stones will bless Mathura so that her defences will never break, and she will rule the Yamuna for as long as the river flows in the lands of men.'

His voice had taken on a strange, echoing quality now, noticed Pritha, as though he were speaking from deep within a heavy fog. A hush fell around them, and when he opened his palm to expose the red stones to the fire again, holding them just at the right angle so that they would catch and reflect the light, everyone sighed at once. The guards, once again, leaned forward and pursed their lips in indecision.

Durvasa's fist snapped shut once again. 'But if you insist on seeing the royal seal which Uddalaka so regrettably forgot to carry with her, I think not that we shall come here again. There are enough Great Kingdoms on the other side of the Ganga who would give half their lands for a treasure such as this!'

'But sir,' said the guard, 'we have orders not to let anyone in without either a brand or the king's seal.'

'We have the mark of Magadha on our arms, my man,' said Durvasa, showing him his arm again. 'I was born there, and I dare say I pledged my loyalty to King Jarasandha when I gave up my dear sister – my only sister – up for his court. Why, Uddalaka, have I not?' Pritha nodded, and before she could speak, Durvasa said, 'And what of Uddalaka herself, her prime of youth dedicated to the service of the king and his many needs. We worship the land of Magadha as much as you worship Mathura, and do we not all want the friendship of the two lands to last till the end of time?'

'Yes,' the guard agreed, 'we do, yes.'

Durvasa drew back, returned the gems into his bag, and sighed deeply. 'Ah, but if you men do not let us pass without the seal, you shall only be doing your duties.' Upon getting an eager nod from the guard, he patted him on the shoulder. 'We shall turn back if that is what you wish, but keep in mind, my man, that this may enrage King Jarasandha, and you may get a messenger from him soon, and he *shall* bear the seal; oh, he shall.' Durvasa took Pritha's hand in his and turned his back on the bemused guard. 'Come, Uddalaka,' he said, 'let us go back and tell High King Jarasandha that his loyal servants are no longer welcome in Mathura. It will sadden him, yes, but that is the truth.' They took a few steps away from the gate, and the group of traders in front of them stepped aside to allow them to pass.

'Wait,' said the guard, after they had descended the stairs. 'Do not leave, trader.'

Durvasa stopped, but did not turn back.

'Perhaps you are who you say you are,' said the guard.

Durvasa threw him a scornful look over his shoulder. 'Perhaps? If you so doubt me, guard, let me go and you shall have your answer – *perhaps* – in a few days from the High King himself. Can the town of Mathura afford to foster enmity with a kingdom as mighty as Magadha? Ask yourself that, guard, and you shall have your answer. Perhaps!'

The guard's partner, a frail man with greying hair, who had hitherto stood watching, now sprang into action. Angrily waving the younger man into silence, he pottered down the steps and stood by Durvasa, bowing with his hands joined. 'Fie! Fie on him for having spoken to our esteemed guests that way. I beg your forgiveness for both of us, sire. Please pass, and please take with us good tidings for Kamsa, the lord of Mathura.'

Durvasa looked at him with fury in his face for a long moment. Then he relented and said, 'I do not wish to raise hell when you men are just doing your jobs. But I do wish you learn to tell real noblemen from tricksters.'

'He ... he is new, my lord, and he is quite young. Please forgive him, and please come, my lord. Please, my lady, please come.' The man clambered back up the stairs, bowing to them after each step, and he nearly stumbled and fell once or twice. Back at the entrance, under the arch, Durvasa laid a hand on the young guard's shoulder and nodded.

'I am pleased by your spirit,' he said. 'If all kingdoms had guards like you, no spies will escape alive. But not all of us are spies, my man.'

The young guard murmured: 'I beg your forgiveness, my lord.' His face was wrought tight, Pritha noticed. If it were not for the glowering older man by his side who elbowed him in the hip, she doubted if the fellow would have bowed to them.

Durvasa dove into his bag and brought out two stones, and holding them out to the old man, dropped them into his palm. 'One for each of you,' he said. 'Let it not be said that the subjects of Jarasandha have not inherited his generosity.' At this, both the guards smiled, and after slipping the gems into their pockets, they signalled to the gatekeeper to let them pass.

EIGHT

Pritha wore her veil as they entered the streets of Mathura. It was long after sunset, so the lamps in front of the huts on either side of the road had retreated within themselves. Here and there, people sat on rocking wicker chairs on their front porch, sipping buttermilk from their brass vessels, stopping their conversation to stare at them as they passed. Pritha held her veil in one hand and kept her head bowed. Through the light yellow fabric the lamps appeared to be nothing more than smudges, but she could clearly see curiosity on people's faces. Here was a city that did not like visitors, she thought, twisting her nose against the smell of cattle dung that hung in the air.

They passed the streets and made their way toward the river, where the farmhouses lay. Durvasa walked with a sure step, as though he had come here before. He did not stop to talk to anyone, but she noticed he wore on his face the smile of a priest, and the ash on his body gave him an exotic, sacred appearance. Whenever a bunch of rustic men would pass them, he would take her hand in his and pull her a little closer.

Soon the path narrowed, and on both sides of her Pritha saw open fields. Only a few of them were flourishing, though, she noticed, and she remembered someone say to her long back that though Mathura was in between the two great rivers, the soil was muddy and wet, which meant large expanses of land were infertile. Even here she could see great patches of brown splotched across the green fields.

Each field, though, had a shed for cows and a barn full of caged containers which housed hens. All along her walk Pritha had to keep her nose bent at an angle so that she could at least close one nostril against the foul smell. Cows called out to their young ones, bulls snorted, buffaloes brayed, and tiny white chickens hopped and skipped along the ground, pecking at the soil.

Most of the houses she saw were made of brick and stone, and even here, out of the way of the main streets, every house appeared as though it had been just washed. In front of most houses she saw the picture of the golden discus that she had seen on top of the arch. Here the lamps appeared brighter; whether they really were or if they appeared so because there were no fires about (as they were on the streets), she did not know. The moon was perched at the sky's zenith, and once in a while Durvasa raised his head to look at it, as though drawing strength from it.

They stopped near a house erected on a mound on two levels. An iron fence stood around it in a circle, and Pritha saw that nails had been inserted into it so that the sharp points extended outward. Even here they had the fear of theft, then, she thought, and followed Durvasa up the path leading to the wooden gate. When they reached it, they heard a low, growling sound of a man from inside. 'Turn back!' he said. 'I have a Magadhan spear in my hand, and by the gods I shall not hesitate to send it through your chest if you take one more step forward.'

Durvasa raised his hands above his head and called out, 'We are not intruders, sir. I'm just a weary trader from Magadha with my sister. We need a place to stay for the night.'

There was silence, and Pritha could imagine the man with the spear on the other side of the grilled window, chewing ominously on betel leaves or some such, mulling it over. 'Come closer to the

light so that I can see you,' he said. First Durvasa, then Pritha
went to the right edge of the gate, under the fire. 'Why is the
lady under a veil?'

'My sister has a beautiful face, kind sir, and young men now are
not as chivalrous and kind as they were in your day.'

'Do not get me started on the upstarts,' said the man from
inside. Pritha heard a lock click, and the door open. A man of
about fifty with an unkempt beard and a falling stained turban
came out, limping on one leg, carrying his spear over his shoulder
like a mace. He came to the gate and stood a good three feet away
from them, watching. His body bent one way to account for the
bad leg, and he had a curious way of looking through one eye
and cocking his eyebrow. 'Just one day, you say? You shall find
your own way tomorrow, or I shall set my bulls on you, I will.'

Durvasa bowed. 'Just for one day, sir.'

With a groan of approval he set about undoing the latches on his
gate, one after the other. While he did so he mumbled something
about the spate of thefts that had been plaguing Mathura for the
last few months, and how he had lost four cows. 'It has become a
nightmare, living in this town,' he said, swinging open the gate and
waving them in. Pritha waited at the front door, pulled back her
veil over the back of her head, and waited. 'Please go on, my lady,'
said the man from behind her, 'you may find it a little too rustic
for your taste, but I do have a lot of room, I do.'

Pritha went in, and in the light of the two oil lamps that stood
on the spinning wheel lodged in the middle of the room, stood to
one corner and watched the men walk in. The farmer hobbled in
behind Durvasa, locked the door, and said, 'They call me Nabha. I
used to have the most number of cows around these parts, but in
the great disease of *Ananda*, I lost a few hundred heads. The priests
came and gave us more of their black stones that year, so that we
could till our lands better, but no, the soil here does not hold.'

Durvasa motioned Pritha to a seat, and Nabha hurried
across the room to hold the chair for her. She did not know

why the garrulous man became so gentle in such a short time; but she bowed in his direction and took her seat. 'Pray forgive me, my lady,' said Nabha, taking off his turban and rolling the loose end around his wrist tightly. 'I have not had a maiden in this house for a whole age. I know not how to behave with them, so you shall forgive me if I do not treat you as I ought to.'

'You have given us your house, sir,' said Pritha. 'What more can we ask you to do?'

'Ah,' said Nabha. 'Ah, oh, I ... I have a tumbler of buffalo milk on the hearth. Will you two have some? That and jaggery; it will put you to sleep like babes, it will, and send you dreams that are white and sweet.'

Durvasa smiled at him and nodded. Nabha went into the kitchen and brought out two brass glasses and a plate with two yellow pieces on it. Pritha looked out of the window, and in the silvery moonlight she saw an expanse of land sloping toward the Yamuna, with clutches of paddy fields growing in pockets all over it, punctuated with huge smudges of brown. 'Is that all yours, sir?' she asked, taking the glass of milk.

'By the grace of the gods, yes,' said Nabha. 'And it is to the grace of the priests and our temples that we are able to coax crops out of such stubborn land. You are from Magadha, you said; you should know, then, what my words mean.'

Pritha began to shake her head, but Durvasa said, 'Yes, of course we do, kind sir.'

'I ... I must ask you to forgive me again, sir, for what I said when you were at the gate. It is a dark night, and my eyes do not see as well as they once did.' When he bent over the table, and his face neared the lamp, Pritha saw that his left eye was covered with a grey, smoky substance. He saw her noticing, and blinked ashamedly before turning away. 'I said you can only stay for a night, but I have a big house, my lady, my lord, and you can stay here as long as you wish.'

'We shall not, Nabha,' said Durvasa, finishing his glass of milk. 'But we have come here late, and I trust we have shaken you out of your slumber. So now I think we best retire to our beds, and perhaps tomorrow you can guide us on how to reach King Kamsa's palace.'

The man's one eye widened a touch, and he said in a whisper: 'You know the High King, do you?'

'Yes, we carry a few things that are of importance to the High King.'

Pritha saw a faint wave of suspicion enter Nabha's face, and his manner became more reserved. After they had emptied their glasses he carried the vessels to the kitchen, and on returning, he pointed to the staircase. 'If you please, go up these steps and take one bed each. I shall sleep here on my rope cot.' Turning to Pritha he said, 'My lady, I shall not brag that these are beds a lady like you is used to sleeping on. I am but a cow-keeper, and this is all that I can give you.'

Pritha got up and inclined her head at him. Durvasa's words – that nobody could look at her and not guess that she was a princess – came back to her. Until she had the veil on her face, the man wanted to chase them off with a spear. The moment she had given him a look of her face, his manner of speaking had changed. If she had but raised her veil at the gate, Durvasa may not have had to resort to all that trickery.

They went up the stairs, and when they reached the top, Durvasa looked down, waved and said, 'Sleep well, Nabha.'

'Thank you, my lord, I will.'

Pritha woke up to the sound of a rooster. Gently she disengaged herself from Durvasa and sat up to tie her hair. The previous night, after they had taken their respective beds in the loft, the sage had come to her and lain his hand on her arm. She should have brushed it away and asked him to return to his bed, but she had looked at him and smiled. 'It is a cold night, Pritha,' he had said, 'perhaps we can stay warm better if we shared a cot.'

She picked up her anklets from the ground and tied them around her feet. She got up, walked to the window. Every time she allowed him to touch her, they went a bit further than they had the previous time. Last night he had lifted her lower garment up to her thighs, and his hands had stolen underneath her robe. It would not be long before he would take her, she thought, as she stood in the red light of dawn and looked at the rising sun. As the first rays hit her cheeks, she closed her eyes and felt that the warmth of the sage's touch was somehow akin to the warmth of the sun.

When she opened them again, she saw movement at the bottom of her vision. It was Nabha wheeling a contraption into his field. It looked like a small chariot, but no horse or bull was tied to it. The wheels dragged behind them a pole whose teeth – like the canines of a tiger – faced downward, toward the earth. On top of the wheels was a wooden chair with high armrests and a thick brown rope wound against its legs. On the other end the rope held together a long thin handle that pointed straight ahead, and it was this handle that Nabha was currently pulling at.

The toothed pole dropped a touch and scraped against the ground. Nabha swore. He limped across to the water wheel and dragged across a black, rectangular stone. Halfway back to his plough, he stopped and mopped his brow, and after sitting down on his stone for a few minutes he resumed his journey. Pritha watched him with a mixture of amusement and wonder; when she had seen the field last night, she had thought it would take at least twenty strong men to till it, but here was Nabha, frail and sick and half blind, going at it gamely.

Behind her Durvasa moaned. She looked over her shoulder to see if he was waking up. But he only rolled over and went back to silent breathing. When she turned around she saw that Nabha

had succeeded in bringing the black stone to the plough, and
he began to tether it to the back. She felt sorry for the old man;
he had told her last night that it had been long since he had a
maiden in the house, which meant that there was a time when he
had family too, perhaps a wife, a son, a daughter...

What misfortune would have occurred to leave him alone at
this age, to grapple with tools that he could no longer use? From
Durvasa's sack she removed a neem twig, broke it in two, and
carried the piece with her down the stairs, to the back of the hut
where she presumed the water tumbler was kept. After cleaning
her teeth, she splashed water over her face and arms. The skin
under her upper arm smarted as water hit it, and she turned it
over to examine it. She saw Durvasa's teeth marks. She felt the
base of her neck with her forefinger, and pulled it back when it
felt rough and tender to the touch. She thought of her brother
and his wife in Kamsa's prison; while they languished in captivity,
here she was, cavorting with a sage. Angry at herself, she hurled
the water vessel back into the tumbler and walked out of the
front door and onto the field.

When she came to the doorway, the sight that met her eyes
made her stop. 'By the gods!' she said, as her eyes widened and her
step faltered. She shut her eyes once, shook her head, and then
opened them again, certain that what she saw would disappear
as an apparition would, but there it was, still. She fumbled over
to the edge of the field, not noticing the smell of dung in the
morning air.

Set against the sun, Nabha sat on the chair mounted on his
plough, slumped, as though he had had his fill of arrack. With
his hands he gripped the handle in front, and he seemed to push
and pull at it. Behind the wheels the toothed pole dug into the
earth. The wheels kept turning at a steady pace, and white smoke
rose into the air from the black box. Pritha first thought that the
plough had been set on fire, but the smoke rose only to disappear
in a second.

Then she asked herself: *Where are the bullocks?*

She ran into the sun for a closer look. The farmer worked through his field in straight lines, starting from the leftmost end and ending at the right, and then turning around. As he approached she found that the contraption moved at no great speed, and that a faint whirr emanated from it, as though a top were spinning inside. When Nabha saw her, he straightened on his perch and gave her a bow.

The sun had become stronger now, and she felt sweaty and dizzy, though at the back of her mind she knew that it was not the sun that was wringing her head. She had heard tales when she was a child that there were charioteers that cracked the whip with such speed and precision that it appeared to the naked eye as though they merely pointed with their arms and their horses followed. It was said that their horses galloped, but so smooth was their movement on the earth that they appeared to have wheels on them. Her father had laughed at these tales, and he had said that such horses and such charioteers perhaps existed only on Meru, where the gods rode winged beasts. But now here she was, not on Meru but in Mathura, the kingdom right across the river from her own home, where a sick, gnarly farmer was tilling his plough with invisible oxen.

Suddenly it came to her why Mathura was known as the kingdom that could never be defeated, how a tiny city such as this with no fertile land could stand up to the might of the Great Kingdoms. It had been blessed by the gods. She had heard the farmer speak of temples and priests; perhaps they had sought the gods' blessings with untold austerities, or perhaps they had ploughed the Goddess herself for secrets that she is said to have held within her, away from human beings.

How often had she heard in Shurasena that Mathura's boats sailed on water as if they were in flight, that their war barges cut though Yamuna's harshest currents without drifting off course even a furlong, that the boats carried twice the number of archers as other boats the same size. If boats could be persuaded to sail on their own, thought Pritha, what need was there of oarsmen? On all boats there were more oarsmen than archers, and if Mathura could make boats that did not need oarsmen, she could stack them to the brim with archers, and she could scuttle enemy ferries in a trice.

How often had she not heard in Kunti that Mathura was impregnable, and how often had she thought that it was just a tale of fancy, told and re-told by travellers on cold nights around a bonfire. But now here she was: on a bright morning on an open field, watching magic unfold. There was no fire around her, no sacrifice, no Brahmins chanting verses from the scriptures, no rituals – nothing – and yet this was magic beyond all the sages of the world.

She looked back over her shoulder and saw Durvasa, folding his wet shawl in his arms and peering out from the doorway to the hut. Even from this distance, she saw that his face was set in a deep frown. She ran across the field back to the house, her feet digging into the fresh, moist earth with each stride. By the time she reached Durvasa her toes had black mud between them, and she panted like a dog. She bent forward, hands on thighs, and looked up at the sage.

'By the holy isle and all that it stands for,' whispered Durvasa, his blue eyes shining. Beads of sweat dotted his brow. 'What *is* that thing?'

'I know not, Sage,' said Pritha, 'but I think that is what gives Mathura her strength.'

She turned around so that they could look at Nabha together. The farmer finished ploughing his field and was making his way back to them now, his turban set upon his head in a lopsided way, the loose end fluttering in the breeze. Set against the sun, Pritha felt he looked like the god of death, but the god of death rode a bull. Where was Nabha's bull? She felt fear creep into her heart as the whirring thing approached them in its steady speed. When her hand sought Durvasa's and held it, she noticed that even the sage's palms had become sweaty.

As it came nearer and the buzz got louder, Pritha saw that the smoke had a foul grey colour to it. Just as she was about to ask Durvasa what it meant, the plough lurched forward once and stopped. For a moment it stayed silent, and then it gave another sputtering cough, releasing another belch of black smoke into the air. The yoke fell to the ground, and the handle in Nabha's hand creaked and bent away to one side, refusing to yield to his frantic yanks.

'There you go, you piece of junk,' said Nabha. He aimed a kick at the side of the plough with his good leg, and spat at it. Then he turned around, adjusted his turban, and walked up to them.

'Get your things,' he said to Durvasa, while taking off his turban and bowing in Pritha's direction. 'We will go to the temple to get my stone mended. The priest will show you the way to the High King's palace too.'

NINE

Pritha and Durvasa sat facing each other in the cart amidst bales of hay and stray tomatoes. Nabha sat at the front and cracked the whip on the backs of the oxen. Between lashes he made strange sounds with his lips and tongue, which Pritha guessed meant something in the language of cattle. They went along the same path they had come the previous night, and in the morning light Pritha could see better the patches of barren land that stretched on either side. She looked at Durvasa to catch his eye, but the sage appeared engrossed in thought. Not even in the mountains up north would he have seen a sight such as the one they had seen in the field that morning.

He would stitch his lips together tight and stare into the distance for a time, then he would steal a glance or two at the smooth black stone that sat by Nabha's side. After a few moments he would shake his head and sigh, sometimes looking at her and smiling faintly, and sometimes looking through her as though she did not exist.

Finally he asked Nabha, 'Why do you not use the stone for this cart then, Nabha? Why do you torture the poor animals so?'

Nabha replied without looking back, 'Oh, we are not to use the stone for going from place to place, sir. The priests forbid it; they say the gods do not approve of such doings.'

'You only use it to till your lands, then.'

'Aye, and to milk my cows, sir. I have sixty eight heads of cattle, sir, I do, and I do not have any helping hands. I have to use the stone for that too.' He paused to snort and wedge his tongue between his lips. 'But it does not always do what it is meant to do, sir, as you saw this morning. I would love to have a farm boy, I would. Better than all the stones in the world.'

'Indeed,' said Durvasa. 'But the stone belongs to you, and you do not know how to mend it?'

'Aye, sir, pray tell me how should I know the job of a priest? These stones are gifts from the gods, they tell us, and only the priests speak to the gods, sir, not common folk like me. The priests kneel down in their temples and pray, and the gods mend the stones and they're given back to us.'

'But you have certainly tried to open the stone, perhaps, or to break it with a hammer at least?'

Nabha looked around and stared at Durvasa. 'No, sir, a single scratch on the stone and they will take all our cattle, they will. There was a man whose farms were right next to mine, his name was Mitra, and he tried to break it open, they said. The next day the priests came to his house and snatched all his cattle away, sir! And they put him in prison too!'

'But why do they do such things, Nabha? If the stone belongs to you, there is no wrong in trying to break it open, is there?'

Nabha turned back to his oxen. 'They say that if an unworthy man unlocks the secret of the stone, my lord, the gods will punish us all and take away their gift. No one in the kingdom will have the stone any more, they say, and therefore they must punish those who threaten to cause harm to all his brothers.'

'So every time it stops working, you have to lug it all the way to a temple and get it mended by a priest?'

'Aye, that is so.' Nabha's left hand went to the stone, and he caressed its surface. 'But it does not need mending too often, my lord. The last time it stopped in the middle of a till was some six moons ago. And it only takes half a day to mend, you know.' He cracked his whip with passion on the ox to the right, and it bleated in response. The cart quickened.

They entered the city now, and on signal from Durvasa, Pritha wore her veil. From underneath the fabric she saw men crane their neck and look at her from within their stores. A row of water-carrying women in red gowns turned around as they passed, and smiled. Nabha raised his whip at them in greeting.

He turned into a narrow lane and stopped in front of a mud hut at the very end of it. Pritha saw that a high wall had been erected to block the other entrance of the lane, which also prevented sunlight from entering. On both sides of the doorway, from the ground to the arch at the top, oil lamps peeked out from within small dark holes. When Nabha had said that they were about to go to a temple, Pritha had expected something grander, much like the marble temples back in Shurasena and Kunti, but this was no more than a hovel. Even Nabha's house looked better than this, she thought, getting down from the cart and reaching for her sack.

Inside the hut it was hot despite all doors and windows being open. Every ledge, every platform, every surface carried lighted oil lamps, and in the middle of the room, at the brightest point, under a hole in the roof through which a beam of sunlight entered, a basil plant stood in a brown pot of mud. A youth wrapped in a wet, white cloth was ringing a bell with one hand and muttering prayers. With the other he clutched the cloth close to his chest. On his shoulders and forearms Pritha saw lines of sandal paste and moist ash.

Pritha removed her veil and felt a layer of sweat gather under her garment. Nabha walked in front of them and bowed low in front of the plant. The priest acknowledged them with a nod and pointed them to the floor. Nabha crawled over and sat down, and motioned to them to do the same.

After a while the priest finished his worship and came over to them. He pulled for himself a chair and sat on it, one leg crossed over the other. He had a boy's certainty of step and gesture, and also his arrogance, thought Pritha. He waved his hand at Nabha and asked, 'You have brought the stone with you.'

'Yes, my lord.'

'Have you seen that the fire chamber was not empty?'

'Yes, my lord, I did.'

'Did you perform all sacrifices just as I told you?'

'Yes, my lord. I gave my best goat to the stone on the previous full moon, and for this one I was going to give it my best bull.'

The priest nodded solemnly. 'And the worship?'

'I did it just as you told me, my lord.'

'How long has it been since you first took the stone from me, Nabha?'

'About a year, my lord.'

He nodded again, and pulled the white cloth around himself. Pritha saw black smudges littered over it, some fresh, most of them faint.

'Perhaps the time has come, then, to mend it. Leave it with me and I shall pass it on to the high priests. You can return in seven days and take it back.'

'Certainly, my lord.'

For a few moments the priest tapped his fingers on the arm rest of his chair. His foot shook restlessly. He looked at Nabha. 'Well?'

Nabha began to scratch the back of his head. 'Sire, these are friends of mine ... traders from the city of Magadha.'

The priest trained his eyes on Pritha, and she lowered her gaze. 'Indeed? She does not look like a maiden from the far-east. Who is your father, girl?' He called her 'girl' even though he could not have been much older than she – he was perhaps in his twenty-first year, no more.

She raised her head to speak, wondering what to say, but thankfully Durvasa spoke up. 'We belong to a family of stone traders at the eastern end of Magadha, my lord,' he said. 'For nigh on twenty years now the royal house gets their jewels made only from us.'

'Indeed. I know of no such family in Magadha, and dare I say I know the city quite well.'

'Sire,' said Nabha, 'they wish to see the High King about some matter, they do.'

The boy looked at Durvasa first, then at Pritha, his mouth curving upward in a derisive smile. 'Indeed, who does not wish to meet the High King.' He sat up in his chair, leaning forward, trying to take a better look at them. 'Tell me what you *really* wish, Brahmin, and tell me who this maiden *really* is.'

Nabha dithered, 'Sire, it is like this …'

'Nabha, have you left your stone in my front room?'

'Yes, my lord, I have.'

'Then you may leave.' He glanced at Pritha as he said, 'I shall help your friends reach wherever they wish to go.'

Nabha scratched the back of his neck again and looked at the ground. 'Ah,' he said. 'Umm, okay.' He looked at Durvasa, and upon getting a nod, got up to his feet and bowed.

After Nabha had left, the priest went to the front door and closed it.

'Now, sir,' he said, pulling his chair closer to them. 'I am no foolish farmer to believe whatever you say. I am a priest. Now you shall tell me the truth, for if I see one more lie escape your lips, I warn you, sir, that the High King's guards are only a mellow call away, and they like to speak more with their spears than with their mouths.'

'And I suspect they do not speak as kindly as you do either, sir,' said Durvasa.

'They do not, and I tell *you*, sir; the only reason I am still speaking with you in words is because of this maiden here. I take no pleasure in your appearance or in your manner, but this maiden – I doubt not that you have cast a spell on her, for how else–'

'She is my sister, sir,' said Durvasa quietly.

'I told you, Brahmin,' said the priest, 'I am no fool. In which world do Brahmin brothers have Kshatriya sisters? Look at the form of that woman, look at her face; she should not be out of her place in the High King's palace, I dare say!'

Durvasa sighed in an elaborate manner. 'You seem to have caught us out, sir,' said he, leaning back against the wall, raising one knee, and letting his arm rest on it. 'So I shall tell you the truth. Our true aim is not to meet the High King.'

'Of course it is not,' said the priest.

'It is to meet the maker of these black stones that Nabha uses to till his fields.'

A strange change came over the priest's plump features. His brow came together in a deep frown, and his mouth flattened. His breath grew heavier, like a little dog's after a futile rabbit chase. 'If you are from Magadha,' he said, his eyes turning orange, 'you should know that the maker of these stones is more valuable to Mathura than the High King himself.'

Durvasa stayed calm. 'I am aware of it.'

'And yet you come walking into my hut and ask me about him, thinking, perhaps, that I shall take you by the hand into his chambers? One more moment here, Brahmin, and I shall call the guards, and I say you and your "sister" here shall see the blue of sky not once more in all your lives.'

Durvasa sighed again, and got to his feet in one quick motion, which made the priest draw back a little in suspicion. Pritha looked up at him, eyes agape. 'One moment, then, is all that I ask for, sir,' he said, and reached for his sack.

'Keep your hands off it!' said the priest, springing to his feet, but Durvasa had already retrieved something from his sack, something that looked like a little brown ball of string.

'Do not fear, sir, for I do not have the means to hurt you. You have called me a Brahmin, so take my word that I shall not harm a fellow Brahmin.' As he spoke he undid the ball of string and wrapped it around all his fingers. As more and more twine came out, he rolled his fingers around it, and in no time at all both his hands were tied, and as he held them up, little more than a foot apart, a black star stood between them, its spikes trembling with each movement of his fingers like the limbs of a spider.

Then he brought it close to his mouth, and with his eyes set on the young priest, he blew fire onto the star. The priest cried out, first in fear, and then as the flames travelled around the twine and left Durvasa's fingers somehow unharmed, as the flames licked his skin without charring it and danced to his whims, bending this way and that, the young man's mouth fell open, and he took two faltering steps away from the sage. Pritha walked back until her spine touched one of the teak beams that held up the roof, and she leaned back against it, thinking of all those things about Durvasa that Agnayi had said, that he was the son of the sage who descended from the lord of the Sun himself. Some others said that he came into being out of a vessel in which the Destroyer had trapped all his anger. Could any of that be true, she thought, staring at the live yellow lines trapped between his long fingers.

The charred twine dropped to the ground in dust, and the air filled with the smell of burning flesh, but the sage's hands were their usual smooth brown. Soon there was no string wrapped around the fingers, only lines of fire, and Durvasa's eyes looked on at the priest in front of him, who had knelt down and joined his hands. The sage's lips bent in a crooked half-smile, and his blue eyes were now a deep, scorching yellow.

He extracted his fingers from within the rings of fire, and on another soft breath from his lips, the holes disappeared and became solid balls, one on each hand. He turned his fingers around them, as if soothing them, caressing them, and they went from swirling angrily to turning tamely, and the surface of the balls began to harden even as the yellow molten liquid threatened to spill out and swallow the house. Short orange sparks flew out, bounced a couple of times on the mud floor, and died.

Durvasa held his hands out to the priest. 'Would you like to hold them, sir?'

The priest shook his head in terror, and Pritha saw that his face was drenched in sweat. She licked her lips and tasted salt on her tongue. She ran her hand over her forehead and saw that it glistened in the orange light of Durvasa's hands. His mouth took on the shape of a small circle once again, and with two soft exhales of breath, he fired up the balls, and looking around, he spotted a heap of wet teak beams in the corner.

He allowed his hands to rest, and with a gentle roll, as though he were setting a wheel in motion, he sent the balls crashing into the beams. Pritha felt as though the breath inside her was being sucked out, as the fire closed in on one beam now, and then on a single point, which the sage pulled out with his right hand. Rolling his fingers under the ball so that it could stay suspended in mid-air, he turned to face the priest. The priest cowered like a frightened mouse and shook his head. A son of the Destroyer, was he? Or the sun himself?

Pritha fell to her knees, intending to prostrate herself at the feet of the sage, but the moment she hit the ground she lost consciousness.

'Pritha?'

She opened her eyes with a start, and found that her hand was wrapped around Durvasa's, and it was cold with sweat. She sat up with a start and leaned back against the beam. He held out a vessel of water for her. She took a sip.

'Kurusti here has agreed to take us to the High Priest, Pritha,' said Durvasa, nodding at the younger man, who squatted on his haunches in the corner. 'If you are well enough, we shall start immediately and get there before nightfall.'

Pritha nodded groggily and got up.

TEN

'I must ask for your forgiveness for the words I used before, my lord,' said Kurusti, after they had settled into his chariot. It was better than Nabha's, Pritha noticed; for one, the cart was drawn not by oxen but by two young, healthy mares. Kurusti tapped his charioteer on the shoulder and whispered something in his year, and upon a nod and a call to his horses, the vehicle lurched forward.

'I keep some dates and apples in my chariot, in case I have to leave in a hurry; the lady can have them if she so wishes.' He bowed in her direction. All his authority and derision was gone; now he was the very picture of deference. He said to Durvasa, 'When I set eyes upon you, my lord, I told myself that you were no ordinary being. May the gods cut off my tongue for the vile things I said to you.'

Durvasa said, 'I have already forgiven you, Kurusti. I only pray that you forgive yourself in a hurry.'

Kurusti joined his hands together. 'I must do penance for this. Tell me, sir, how many years have you spent studying the Mystery of the fire?'

'Not I, Kurusti,' said Durvasa, 'my forefathers. I only reap the benefits of their toil.'

'But you are young, my lord, perhaps even younger than I am! How did you achieve such dexterity in your hands, such knowledge of the elements…'

'I come from the mountains up north, and I belong to a family who studies the Mysteries. We have ways by which we transfer our knowledge to our successors.'

'Like we write them down in books.'

'Yes, except we do not use parchment for this purpose.' Durvasa paused, and Pritha felt that he was weighing his words, groping for the right ones. 'We have other means.'

'The High Priest will be pleased to see you, I am certain,' said Kurusti. 'He must have retired to his bed now, the poor man, and he never sees people at such an hour unless absolutely necessary. But today, I think he shall make an exception.'

'I hope so,' said Durvasa, 'because I am eager to know all about this little Mystery of yours, these black stones that plough your fields on their own.'

'Aye, that is so.' Kurusti closed his eyes and touched the palm of his right hand to his chest. 'If it were not for that stone, Mathura would be nothing but a marshland from shore to shore. There would be no kingdom! And we shall not have our war barges, our trade with Magadha – nothing, sire, nothing on Mathura would be the same if it were not for these special stones.'

'Who first wrote the Mystery?'

'No one did, my lord, until now. The oldest of the Head Priests is a man we call Adhrigu, and it is said that the Mystery came to him when he was all of eight years old, which may have been almost fifty years ago.'

'Came to him, did you say?'

'Yes, that is how the tale goes. He was perched upon the shoulders of his father, and it was a windless day. He saw the lid of the water tumbler jump up and down, he said, with the fire burning away underneath. And then he thought perhaps if fire could be cast into water, then it would make the water move.'

Durvasa fell silent for a moment. All they heard was the clacking of the mares' hooves on the hard ground. At last, he said, 'Fire moves water.'

'Aye, you saw that on our arch when you entered the city, no doubt,' said Kurusti. 'The boy Adhrigu then probed the Mystery his own way, playing with vessels of water at his mother's fireplace. By the time he was thirteen, he had in his hands a fully functional black stone, they say, and on the day he came to show it to High King Ugrasena, there was much jubilation in the court, by peasants and noblemen alike!'

'I dare say,' said Durvasa. 'It was Mathura's first Mystery, was it not?'

Kurusti nodded. 'And he, our first High Priest. King Ugrasena wanted more priests to join him in the study of Mysteries, but then High King Kamsa came to the throne, and he had other plans. He set up a trade route with Magadha, and in return for our black stones, they give us grains, soldiers, and all the other things that you see here. We look as though we are wealthy, my lord, but our only wealth are these black stones.'

'Ah, perhaps King Ugrasena was right. Perhaps you should have waited till you probed the Mystery deeply enough.'

Shrugging, Kurusti said, 'Perhaps, but then people were starving, my lord. They were on the edge of revolt, and many were moving out too, to the Great Kingdoms of the East and the South. I say, what Kamsa did was right for Mathura, but then, you are not wrong, either. I know not.'

'Yes,' said Durvasa, 'it is folly to look to the past. Now Mathura has grown strong to defend herself against the might of the Great Kingdoms. Perhaps that is evidence enough that Kamsa had been right.'

'Ah,' said Kurusti, looking out into the streets, where the lamps had begun to dim and the shutters had begun to descend. 'If only it were that simple. We reached out too much too soon, one feels sometimes, and now, we have strong boats and our lands can be tilled without manual labour, but if we have to extend the stones to other things, we not only have to make them smaller, but stronger too.'

'Well, why do you not plumb the Mysteries further?'

'Where is the time, my lord? All the High Priests and regular priests and all the temples are not enough to supply Magadha with all the stones that she needs. We only have enough time to mend the broken ones and create new ones. Not even the High Priests have looked into the Book of Mysteries once in the last ten years, I dare say.

'And now Adhrigu gasps and grunts on his bed. He has not breathed easy in five moons. Kamsa decrees that he must write down all that he knows into the Book of Mysteries, and believe me, he does try, but the old man has no strength in him any more. I wish that he was one of the black stones himself, and that he could go on living and ward off the lord of death.'

Durvasa asked, 'Does no one else know how to create these stones?'

'Adhrigu knows the most, sire, more than anyone else. They wanted to keep the Mysteries secret, you see, so even the priests know only a little. I know not what I should see if I were to open up this box, and I would love to learn, but not a day goes by without some or the other complaint from Magadha that their stones do not work as they're supposed to!'

Pritha tore open the bag that Kurusti had pointed to earlier, and took out an apple. She borrowed Kurusti's knife and cut it into three equal pieces. All three took a piece each. They had left the city long behind them now, and the smell in the air suggested to Pritha and that they were nearing the riverbank. Whether it was the Yamuna or the Ganga, though, she did not know.

She asked, 'Do you know where King Kamsa imprisons his sister and his father?'

Kurusti narrowed his eyes at her. 'I remember now why your face appeared familiar, Princess. You are the sister of the king of Shurasena, are you not?'

Pritha and Durvasa exchanged glances.

'You need not worry,' said Kurusti. 'But I would think twice before asking that question of anyone else in the country, my lady. Kamsa's guards have elephant-like ears, and they have informers everywhere. If you say that out loud in a crowded place, it will take you straight to the king.'

'I am not scared of him,' said Pritha firmly. 'I would rather come face-to-face with him just so that I could spit in his face!'

Kurusti said, 'I understand that Adhrigu prophesied that Devaki and Vasudev's son will one day kill Kamsa. Perhaps you can ask him if he would consider taking his word back; perhaps only then Kamsa would relent and let his sister and her husband go.' His eyes drooped a little, and his shoulders sagged. 'But if Shurasena would become another ally to us and want some of our stones, I dare say our priests will be sucked to the bone.'

'But you have not answered the question,' she said. 'Do you or do you not know where the prison is?'

Kurusti shook his head. 'I do not, I'm afraid. But Adhrigu may – you should ask him. They say it is up on the hill to the north-west, on the very tip of the kingdom, surrounded on three sides by the water of the Ganga. If it is true, I would say the fourth side would be guarded heavily with men carrying weapons.' He inclined his head toward her in a fatherly manner. 'Not quite the place for a maiden such as you, my lady.'

They got off hard land now and rode into sand and mud, and Pritha could hear the wheels of the chariot spray back murky water as it sped ahead. Only the fires mounted on either side of the charioteer provided enough light. Kurusti raised his hand to his forehead and stared into the darkness. 'I think we are approaching,' he said.

The inner sanctum of the High Temple was different from Kurusti's house only in size, and in the number of candles that had been lit all over the room. Pritha felt the same stifling heat on her ears, and the same layer of sweat bathing her body. As they walked in, a boy looked at them curiously, whispered something to Kurusti and ran away, motioning them to stay where they were. After a few minutes he returned to the doorway and gestured. When all of them stood up, he motioned to Pritha and Durvasa to sit down, and only asking Kurusti to come to him.

Once Kurusti had disappeared behind the door, Pritha turned to Durvasa and said, 'I hope this High Priest knows the whereabouts of the prison.'

Durvasa took a handful of saffron powder from inside his bag, and began to wet it with his sweat. After he had made a paste, he began to apply it to his shoulders and wrists. 'I do not think he knows where the prison is, my lady, but I think not we shall need that knowledge.'

'Why not?' she said, sourness creeping into her voice. They had come here in search of her brother and sister-in-law, and all this time they had been speaking with priests, not with soldiers and guards. 'I think you are forgetting the reason we are in Mathura, my lord.'

Durvasa looked up from his shoulder and smiled. 'My dear, you are angry with me.'

'I am, yes.'

'Pray, give me your hand.' He took her hand in his and pulled at her fingers. 'I have not lost sight of why we are here, Pritha, but you must see how precious a stone this is.'

'Precious perhaps for you. How will it help rescue my brother and his wife?'

'Well, Princess, did you not hear what Kurusti said? It is almost impossible for you and I to rescue your brother and his wife.'

'One moment. What are you saying? Are we ... are we ... to give up, then?'

He shook his head. 'By no means. You heard the priest speak about the Book of Mysteries which tells the tale of this remarkable black stone. If you and I could get our hands on that, imagine how powerful Shurasena would become.'

'But Sage, Mathura already has it, and yet it has not become a Great Kingdom.'

'That is so because they have not yet plumbed the mystery fully, my lady. But if Shurasena acquires this book that they speak of, even if it is incomplete, it shall make your kingdom at least as strong as Mathura and Magadha. Then they shall have no need to fear these two kingdoms, for Shurasena's war barges will be just as strong and fast as Mathura's.'

Pritha snatched her hand away from the sage. 'And do you say that these men will just hand over the book to you? This is the big secret of the kingdom, and I am amazed to see that there are no guards of the High King at this place.'

Durvasa laughed. 'I am certain Kamsa would have wanted guards here, but the priests rule supreme, my lady. They know the Mysteries, and they have not shared them with anyone, not even their own subordinates. So the power lies with them, and if Kamsa does something that angers them, it would not bode well for him.'

'Is that why he wants the priests to write down the Mysteries into a book?'

'That is so, yes. Once the Mysteries are written down, Kamsa could do as he pleases with the priests, because he can replace them with other priests. I am certain the head priests here know that, and that is why they resist writing down the things that live in their minds.'

'Be that so,' said Pritha, 'why will they give you the book?'

Durvasa's eyes twinkled at her. 'Why did Kurusti bring us here?'

'You will show them another of your fire tricks?'

'That is not the only trick in my sack,' said Durvasa. 'I shall talk to these priests, and I am certain that they will help me in my quest – for you see, my dear, they know by now that I am one of them.'

Pritha looked at the sage's face in the light of the lamps, and his eyes acquired the same shade of inscrutable yellow they had become at Kurusti's place, just before he had brought out the ball of black twine from his bag. She wanted to ask him how he was one of them; it was clear that he had studied the Mysteries too. But he was no priest. He was a sage. What was the difference?

But before she could open her mouth, Kurusti came back and said, 'The High Priest will see you now.'

High Priest Adhrigu was in the last year of his life, thought Pritha on seeing him. Rich, dark veins riddled the man's face, and deep ridges appeared on his forehead, constantly changing shape as he peered first at her and then, with more interest, at Durvasa. He held his left hand much the same way as Kurusti had, clutching the white shawl over his chest, and with his right he pointed them toward their seats. As the light afforded him a better view of Pritha, he smiled, and his bottom lip fell away, revealing a single brown tooth on the lower gum.

'I do not see visitors anymore,' he said, his voice hoarse with cough. 'I have much to do, but my body does not have the will that my mind does.' He sat on the edge of his cot, looking down at his flat, battered toenails. 'Kurusti tells me you are a student of the Mysteries yourself, sir.' He raised his head and brought his eyes to rest on Durvasa.

'I am, sir, but my forefathers have seen it fit only to study the Fire Mysteries.'

'Ah, your forefathers, you say, and yet you have practised them enough to handle fire with ease?'

'They have taught me well. Where I grew up, men transfer their knowledge to their successors not through parchments or by teaching, but by fusion of the minds.'

The lines of Adhrigu's face became darker. 'And where might this be, this place you speak of?'

'I come from the north, sir,' said Durvasa, and when Adhrigu continued to stare, he added, 'I learnt my craft at the foot of the Ice Mountains.'

'Ah, will you teach us, perhaps, this Mystery of fusing one's mind with another?'

'It is forbidden among the Northmen to even speak of it, High Priest.'

Adhrigu smiled and nodded. 'Just like our Mysteries, eh, Kurusti? Aye, if everyone spoke of them, they would not stay Mysteries for very long, would they? That is why we have guards at every entrance to our city, sir, because we do not want people watching our farmers and whispering that they may be *shamans*.' He bared his gums at them and fiddled with the hair growing out of his ear. 'The only people we do allow are the men from Magadha; with them we trade for our lives, so we let them in on our secret. Only a little bit, though.'

'I understand, sir,' said Durvasa. 'I have come to ask you about the black stones that you create.'

'I am not allowed to speak of them, sir,' said Adhrigu, smiling.

'By whom?'

'By myself! I am the creator of the Mystery! I decree that no one shall speak of it, and if they do, they shall not understand it.' He waved unsteadily in the direction of Kurusti. 'These men know only the outside working of the stone, sir. Only three of us – just three men in the whole kingdom – know how to build one, and indeed, how to take one apart.'

'Perhaps you could show me how one works, then?'

Adhrigu raised his grey eyebrows at Durvasa and grinned. 'Perhaps I could. But what shall I get in return?'

Durvasa looked straight at the old man. His eyes were hard, yet kind. He sat erect in his seat, much like a man of god giving a sermon, and under his loose upper garment, Pritha could see his hairless torso, tight and tender. For some reason a nameless fear struck her as she saw him at this moment, and she shifted away from him a little, though she found herself unable to wrench her eyes off him.

'I shall give you means by which you can get to the bottom of the Mystery you study,' he said.

A long bout of dry, retching coughs took over Adhrigu's body. When he recovered, he said, 'I am an old man, sir. It does not do you justice to give me hopes that you must later crush. I do not have time to study my Mystery fully; why, I shall be surprised if I even last the year and see next midwinter's feast.'

'I shall give you all the time that you need,' Durvasa assured him.

'Indeed? Do you know what is wrong with me?' Adhrigu's voice grew louder. 'Do you have a cure for my disease?'

'I can examine you. And I can tell you I have not yet seen a disease I could not cure.'

Adhrigu looked up at Kurusti, and Pritha saw the man's feeble eyes perk up in hope. But something held him back, and he shook his head. 'I need to finish my book. I need to be certain that men after me will take my work forward; but I need time. I need time!'

Durvasa went and sat next to him. He took the twig-like wrist in his hands and ran his long fingers over the black spots. 'Do you cough more at night than during the day, sir?' he asked.

Adhrigu nodded weakly.

'And your body becomes warm, does it not, as though someone had set your bed on fire?'

'Yes.'

'You do not feel like eating a morsel of food, and you feel forever weak. So weak that writing even a single word would break your arm in two.'

'Yes ... that is how I feel.' Adhrigu leaned his head on Durvasa's shoulder, and his body shivered against the sage's. Durvasa held the priest with one arm and extended the other arm to his sack, pulling it closer to him. 'I may have something for you, High Priest. Lie down and rest your head against the pillow.' As Adhrigu leaned back with a sigh and supported his neck against the spine of the cot, Durvasa dug into his sack and brought out a bag tied together by animal hide. He untied the cap and asked for a vessel. The boy who had received them scurried away and returned in a moment with one.

Touching the vessel to Adhrigu's lips and holding the base of his neck with one hand, Durvasa said, 'Only take two gulps, sir, and no more.' Adhrigu spluttered and swallowed, and his eyes grew heavy. 'Yes, it will make you sleepy, but tomorrow you shall be well. Let us not speak of the stone today.' Adhrigu nodded with his eyes closed, and before Durvasa could finish his sentence, his breathing had become steady and easy.

Durvasa let the man's head down on the cot, and he placed his arms on top of his chest. Looking up at Kurusti he said, 'He shall sleep well tonight. One of you should keep watch, in case he wakes.'

The boy came forward and bowed. 'I will, sir.'

'Good,' said Durvasa, getting up on his feet. To Kurusti he said, 'If you could arrange for a suitable bed for the lady, I am certain that you and I can then find a little corner for ourselves.'

Pritha lowered herself onto the bed and placed one wrist over her forehead. On the level below, she heard voices of the sage and the priest, speaking in soft tones so as not to wake up Adhrigu.

Something about that day had made her uneasy about Durvasa, but she could not fathom what. Sages were men, she had always been told – great men who had seen a lot of the world, but men nonetheless. She had not ever heard one story of sages performing tricks of the light, as Durvasa had called them. Nor had she met anyone who had seen a sage juggle balls of fire with his bare hands.

Agnayi's first words when she had asked him about Durvasa had been that he would be old enough to be his grandfather.

There was all this talk of Mysteries, but how much did the sages of the north really know of them? She had heard tales of Vasishtha, the great seer of them all, and even he had to give in to ravages of age. Parashurama, Vishwamitra, Angirasa – all these men were old; perhaps they lived to be a hundred or even longer because of their constitution, but no one had ever heard any of these men to be young. If what Durvasa had said was true, if all of them could shed their old skins and creep into young ones, why did more sages not do it?

She had heard that in the forest of Madhu by Shurasena, a priestess had set up her hermitage next to Parashurama's. Pritha had wanted to visit her, learn from her what went into the making of a priestess, and how priesthood was different from being a sage. From her knowledge, what one did, the other did not; was Durvasa, therefore, a sage or a priest? He claimed to be both – but was that even possible?

His laughter came ringing up the steps of the ladder to her ears, and she smiled. Whatever he was, he had come with her to save her brother and sister. He had accompanied her on the Yamuna, disguised himself by smearing himself with ash, and had now come to the High Priest of Mathura, not for himself but for her. And the way he had touched her the night before in Nabha's barn – no man would ever touch a woman thus if he did not love her. Tonight too, he would come to her bed and awaken her, after the lights had gone out. She felt her eyelids grow heavy, but she shook herself away from sleep. Tonight, she would be awake for him.

She rolled to her side, to the edge of the cot, and rolled back to the opposite edge. The bed was not big enough for both of them, but she blushed at the thought. Perhaps it was better that way; the previous night in Nabha's barn, they had drifted away from one another in sleep, and when she had woken up, only his arm had covered her. Tonight would perhaps be a little different.

She did not share his certainty in the thought that the priests would merely give him their Book of Mysteries, but she had seen many faces of him today. She had seen him in the image of the Destroyer himself at Kurusti's house, and here he had cradled Adhrigu and tended to him like he would a child. Her mind went to the arm-sized water vessel made of animal hide that he had made Adhrigu drink from – he said it was just water, but Adhrigu had slept like a babe after that. Sages did not perform cures of this sort, did they?

Her eyes fell again, and this time she did not fight it. He would come, of that she was certain, but her mind began to wander, and soon she knew nothing.

When she opened her eyes again, with a start, all was quiet, and from underneath she heard not a sound. He had not come, she thought vaguely, stumbling to her feet and going to the ladder. She wiped off the sweat from her neck, and licked her lips once. Her tongue felt rough and dry on her upper lip, and when she swallowed her throat ached. She descended the ladder and came to the sleeping figure of Durvasa, and by his side she saw the vessel of water standing erect underneath the sack.

She opened the sack, then the lid of the vessel, and lifted it up to her mouth to take a gulp. As the liquid flowed down her throat, life seemed to come back to her, and she felt as though she had shed two years in that one moment. Her hair seemed to grow richer, her skin softer and more moist, her fingernails clearer. She raised her hand to her eyes and turned it around, watching the black spots on her wrist vanish.

Curious, she looked into the vessel. For a long time she stood there, unable to move. Then she replaced the lid and floated back, like a wraith, to her bed.

ELEVEN

Next morning, when Pritha came down from the loft to the sanctum, she found that the lamps had already been lit. Kurusti was walking about with a brass plate in hand, on which two small oil lamps stood. At each wall he stopped, applied a spot of vermillion to it, and doused it with black fumes. His shawl was white as milk today, she noticed, and only where his hand pressed down on his chest could she see the first gray mark. On the other side of the room, by the entrance to the High Priest's chamber, Durvasa sat on the floor with one knee hoisted up.

'The High Priest is feeling better today,' he said happily. 'He said he feels as though he has become two years younger. He will show us the black stone.' Pritha remembered her aching throat and burning neck from the night before, but now she felt fresh as a morning flower. Her mind wandered to the water she drank from Durvasa's sack. The smell of jasmines lingered in the air, and she realized that for the first time since she had arrived in Mathura, she did not smell cattle dung. She went to Kurusti, offered her palms to the flame, and touched her fingers to her eyes. She broke off a string of jasmines from the bunch and inserted it into her hair.

From inside, the boy came out, a chrysanthemum stuck in his right ear. Solemnly he announced: 'The High Priest will see you now.'

When they went in, they saw Adhrigu sitting up erect on his bed, his eyes glowing like a child's. None of the weakness of the previous night seemed to afflict his limbs, and his long, sinewy fingers seemed to pulsate with energy. 'I do not know what you gave me yesterday, my lord,' he said, joining his hands at Durvasa, 'but I awoke today with my chest clear as a summer night! I still cough, but it is light and airy. You are a magician, sent here by the gods, no doubt!'

Durvasa held the old man's hands in his. Pointing at Pritha he said, 'I came here only because of this young lady here, my good sir. And I am no magician; I am but a man like you, steeped in the Mysteries of the Goddess.'

'Aye, that is so,' said Adhrigu. 'I feel like I can run a league without breaking my hip again, Kurusti. Can you believe that I am stronger now than I have ever been in the last two years!'

'That is indeed great news, sire,' said Kurusti, bowing.

The older man waved him away with enthusiasm. He shrugged off Durvasa's hands and got to his feet, humming a gay tune as he went to the corner of his room. 'We have some work to do this morning, do we not? Our good sir would like to see the black stone at work.' As he began to pick up various things in the corner, the boy came running along to help him. 'Let me hold it, sir,' he said.

Adhrigu paid him no attention. He walked back to the middle of the room and sat down, crosslegged. He placed a small black box in front of him, and opening a little window behind it, he borrowed Kurusti's lamp from the plate of worship. He asked for one more wick, and on receiving it, rolled it around on his finger and dipped it in the oil. He then lit it and let it slip along the side of the vessel and placed the lamp inside the window. With a wave of a finger, he snapped it shut.

'Now it takes a little time to warm itself up,' he said, looking up at Durvasa. The other end of the box had a handle attached to it, much like Nabha's plough had. This one, though, curved downward at its outer end, and its tip had been sharpened.

The whole thing resembled a mother hen out to pick worms in the soil.

Adhrigu opened another small window, this one at the top of the box, and poured into it three thimbles of water. Then he closed it and sat back, rubbing his hands gleefully, his eyes lit with pride. For a moment, nothing happened. But then Pritha noticed that thin lines of white smoke trickled out from under the stone and disappeared into the air. From the sole window of the room, the morning sun flooded in and threw half of Durvasa's grave face in dark shadow. It had been a good month since winter had begun, and it had been no more than an hour since the sun had risen. Why did it burn her arms, then? She rubbed her palms over her wrists to cool them down.

The beak began to move slowly toward the ground. It paused for a moment just as it was about to touch the earth, then rose back up. After it repeated the motion twice, it began to gather speed as the trickles of smoke became continuous streams, and Pritha saw a faint shade of grey in it now. The sound of a whirring top that she had heard on Nabha's farm began here as well, though this was more of a soft buzz, low and content. The beak moved up and down, up and down, up and down, never stopping for breath or rest. She saw Durvasa's one eye that was illuminated by the sun; the blue had darkened so much that it appeared almost black, the colour she had seen his eyes turn into when he came to her bed, slaved by desire.

'Fire and water have often been called enemies of each other, sir,' said Adhrigu, as the beak began to slow down. 'You cast fire into water to put it out, they say, and even the Mysteries of the two elements are studied separately, are they not?'

Durvasa nodded, his gaze fastened upon the stone.

'But perhaps this enmity is something that we humans have set up. Perhaps the Goddess does not discriminate between her five elements.' Adhrigu gazed down at his creation. 'Fire moves water, makes it run, and if we can catch it, we can make things run too.'

'You do the same with your boats, then,' said Durvasa, and his voice seemed soft and childlike, without the usual hoarseness.

'Our ploughs and our boats, yes. We wish to make such stones for everything. The kingdom grows a lot of maize, and too many people grind maize everyday in her farms on grinding stones, by the strength of their arms. If they use the strength of water and fire, they can move all those people into their army.'

'So that is why Magadha is so powerful,' said Durvasa.

'Aye, and that is why *we* are so strong in our defence too. But we do not know enough of the Mystery to make stones for all those other things, sir. We are trying, but we do not have enough priests, nor do we get enough time from mending all the stones that come from Magadha every day.'

'Then perhaps it is better if you do what Kamsa says, and write down the Mystery as you know it.'

Adhrigu smiled. 'I suppose I must,' he said, 'but I do know that once I write it down, the High King will take it from me and cast me away. He will get a new group of priests – perhaps Kurusti will be one of them – and he shall take my baby away from me.' He picked up the stone with the tips of his gnarled fingers and planted a kiss on its smooth edge. He sighed. 'But there is, perhaps, no other way.'

Durvasa stood and went to the window, hands clutched behind his back, looking out at the sun. 'High Priest,' he said, turning back, 'I shall take your book with me, if you permit it.'

Adhrigu's smile vanished. 'I do not permit it.'

'I am a student of the Mysteries too,' said Durvasa, returning to the middle of the room, but standing so that he towered over the High Priest. 'I shall take good care of it, and it shall help the men of my land too.'

'That may be so,' said Adhrigu harshly, 'but I have not written in it the workings of the stone, and if you take it by force and you do not open it the way it is meant to be opened, it will destroy itself, sir, I warn you!'

'I have no intention of taking it from you by force, sir,' said Durvasa. He turned to Pritha. 'Will you leave the room and wait for us in the sanctum, Princess? I shall join you in no more than a few minutes.'

Adhrigu looked at Pritha and then back at Durvasa. 'I doubt if there is anything that will make me give up the Book of Mysteries, sir.'

Durvasa looked down at the priest and smiled. 'You will do me the honour of letting me speak, my lord, if for nothing but giving you two years of your life and freeing you from the dreaded cough and night chills.'

Adhrigu's nostrils flared, his eyes widened in anger; He looked at Kurusti and waved his head in a queer way, upon which Kurusti came to Pritha and bowed. 'If the lady pleases, we shall leave the two men together,' he said.

She tried to meet Durvasa's gaze and gather anything she could from his face, but he refused to look at her. She got up and followed Kurusti out of the room. Just as the door was about to close, she turned around to see that the sage's lips had curled together into a knowing smile, whereas Adhrigu looked up at him weakly, with his forehead set into a deep frown.

TWELVE

They rowed in silence. Pritha wedged her feet against the cold hard surface of the boat to keep her balance against the Yamuna's current. In the water, brown fish scurried up to their oars and swam away as they turned. Only so close to the fall did the water of the river appear so clear. Pritha felt that if she could look closely enough, she could see the bottom. In one of the old tales a princess immerses her hand in the river only to lose her ring, without which her lover, the king, refuses to take her as his wife. But the ring gets swallowed by a fish which gets caught by the royal fisherman, and that very night, when the king sits down for his dinner, he sees in front of him, on his plate, a ring set in white gold.

Durvasa smiled at her. The sun caught the water and beamed into her eyes, making her cover them with her hand. She did not know if her mission had been successful, and since Devaki and Vasudev were still in their prison, it did not appear so, but the sage had coaxed the High Priest to part with his Book of Mysteries, and if, indeed, the people of Shurasena could build black stones of their own, perhaps it would not be long before they could wage war against Mathura and win.

She wondered, though, what the sage offered the High Priest in return for the book, for Adhrigu was adamant that he would not share his mystery with any outsider, even if the outsider saved and prolonged his life. And then she thought of the night before, when she took a sip of the water in Durvasa's sack, and what she had seen when she peeped through the mouth of the container.

They approached the shore of Shurasena now, and Durvasa deliberately veered them away from the fishing settlement toward the woods. Pritha did not protest, for if the sage had given her what she had wanted, she had to give him what he wanted from her. But as they entered the shade of the banyan trees that took root on the edge of the river and threw their branches out onto the river, she once again thought of the water, and the queer little yellow lines of light that she had seen in it, travelling up and down from surface to bottom, rotating about themselves like just-born tadpoles.

She had always heard stories of the existence of an elixir – the balladeers called it by different names; some called it nectar, some called it *soma* – that was fabled to heal diseases and the afflictions of age. Men who drank it, they said, retained their youth and lived forever, and when she thought of that she heard Adhrigu's words ringing in her ears: *I feel younger by two years.*

She had consumed the water too, and how could one describe what happened to her when it slid down her throat? She was as yet a maiden of sixteen, in the prime of her youth, and yet she had felt a surge of life pass through her body, and all traces of fatigue and mental greyness had disappeared, and she had slept as though she had been drugged. When she had woken up this morning she had felt unlike she ever had; she felt ... she felt as though a divine force had cleansed her mind, her body, her spirit.

But the elixir was merely a staple of tales, was it not? Even if it was not, it belonged to the gods who lived up on the Meru and never came down to live among the earthmen. All tales of gods revolved around how much they wished to protect this life potion from everyone else; so they would not share it with men of the north; no, not even with renowned sages. Perhaps they would allow some select men to live with them on the mountain, perhaps they would even share in their Mysteries, but not the water of life.

Their boat stopped, and Durvasa got out to steady it with one hand and extended his other arm to her. His face appeared constant to her; he looked now just like he had in the High Priest's room that morning, half his face mired in shadow and his blue eye aglow with desire.

She took his hand.

When they came up to the grassy mound where they had shed their clothes the previous evening, Durvasa took her hands in his, and for a moment she lowered her gaze, allowing him to pull her gently toward him as the evening shadows lengthened all around them. Just as he leaned in to touch his lips to her cheek, she stiffened and drew back a touch.

'You are not Durvasa,' she whispered.

He did not react in any visible way. The pressure of his fingers over her hands did not change. A little spring of doubt took birth in her mind, so she began to speak, hoping that the words would find their own meaning. Her cheek rested against his, and once again she noticed how his chin and face were completely devoid of hair, even more than hers.

'I know not whether you are a sage or a priest,' she said, her voice still soft, 'and I know not how a sage is different from a priest. But I do know this: sages do not study the Mysteries. Sages pray to the gods of the Ice Mountains and gain knowledge of the *practice* of the Mysteries, but they do not gain knowledge of the Mysteries themselves. Is that not so?'

He did not reply; she knew he would not. But she went on. 'My father, my friend Agnayi, and everyone I knew told me that Sage Durvasa was old. You were not. You told us that the Durvasa before you had just passed on, and the people of my father's court believed you, but immortality is not a boon that men possess, my lord. This is a form of living beyond your death, is it not, this practice of placing your knowledge and memories into the mind of a younger man?' She felt the first stirrings of his fingers, and now she held them firmly with her own. 'If that could happen to sages, why would any man choose to live beyond his youth? Why would Sage Vasishtha hobble on his stick and bear with his old knees? If it could truly happen, why would any sage on earth ever be old? Either it was a Mystery that only you, Sage Durvasa, knew, or you were not Sage Durvasa.' Pritha took a step back and peered into the dark shadow his face had become in the gathering darkness. When he pulled his hands away from hers and looked away, she willed herself to continue.

'Sages do not concern themselves with polity, and they care less about the marriages of princesses in the Great Kingdoms. They retreat to the woods in order to please the gods, in order to perhaps untie the great knots inside their minds, and they often take little interest in worldly affairs of North Country. In the few times we have had visits from smaller sages, never has one spoken to my father about kingdoms; they have only taken to meditation, to courting our waiting-women, and perhaps to give advice on how to perform certain rites.

'But when you came to our court, you appeared to be not only knowledgeable in matters concerning North Country, but you also advised my father that I should marry into the kingdom of the Kurus. I found that a little odd, but your eyes mesmerized me, my lord. They still do.' She hoped that this moment of flattery would make him turn back, but he remained as he was, one hand held up against the bark of the birch tree, the other limply holding his staff of gold. The sapphire at its tip glowed with a deep inner light, like his face had on that first morning.

'Then on our way to Mathura, on the boat at night you covered us with a black fog and called it a trick of the light. In Mathura you summoned balls of fire into your hands and played with them as a child would with bundles of string. The high priests of Mathura, who look no man in the eye, fell at your feet, my lord, and that was when I began to wonder if you really were who you claimed to be.

'Then in the room of the high priest I saw your eyes turning into little yellow balls, much like the sun, and with your words and sights you seemed to affect how the sunlight came into the room. One moment I would see you smile and the harshness of the sun would decrease; the next moment you would frown, and my upper arm would burn.'

'Do you not think, my lady,' he said at last, and his voice seemed to arrive from some place far off, detached from his body, 'that you are drawing mere inferences without substance?'

'If I am, sire,' she replied, 'I am certain that you would stop me. Shall I?'

For a while he did not reply, but then he sighed and said, 'Go on.'

'Until last night, my lord, none of these thoughts were in my head. But I got up from my sleep with a parched throat, and I took a drink from the container of water in your sack, and after I drank from it, I looked at it.' Now his body tightened visibly, and his fingers dug into the tree. 'I saw little yellow lines jump about in the water, wriggling and swimming, and yet when I drank, it slipped down my throat, smooth as juice from a ripe date.'

She took a step closer to him so that he could hear her better. 'It is this water you made High Priest Adhrigu drink to make him feel years younger. When I drank it, my mind seemed to clear, as though something which had forever blinded your vision had been removed from in front of your eyes. I saw it all, my lord; I saw it as though I was gazing through a freshly formed crystal. I saw you – and you are not Sage Durvasa.'

The man sighed again, and he turned around to face Pritha. He took a stride forward, held his staff to one side, and said, 'Then who am I, Princess?'

'You are Surya, the Celestial of the sun.'

THIRTEEN

He first laughed; his hoarse voice seemed to mellow in that instant into something else; the sound of which reminded her of Shurasena's first sugarcane crop, which always got delivered to the royal house of Kunti, on which she always had first claim. Then he tightened his lips and nodded, his face grave. 'It pays me well,' he said, 'for not taking you seriously, Princess. But now I admire your mind; you have no doubt been helped by drinking of the Crystal Water, but the water can only strengthen, it cannot create.'

He held out his hand toward her, but she took a step back, frowning. 'You came with me all the way to Mathura, my lord, and you pretended that you cared about my brother and his poor wife, rotting in Kamsa's prison.'

'I do care for them,' said the man, 'and all that I have done is, indeed, to free them.'

'No,' she said, shaking her head. 'You came to Mathura to get the book of their mysteries, and you have it now. I think not that you ever wanted to save my kinsman; you used me to enter the city, to gain access to the priests, and you got what you wanted.' She stopped, still wishing that her words would somehow become untrue, that he would convince her otherwise.

But he dropped his shoulders and said, 'That is indeed true.' Her heart sank.

'I thought you liked me,' she said bitterly, not able to bring herself to say that other dreaded word that had come to her lips. 'I trusted you, and this is how you repay me?' He reached for her, but she hit out with her hands. 'Do not touch me, you wretch!' she said. 'Thank the gods that you have not taken me!'

A shadow passed through his face. His hand flew to his sack, and he patted it, as though to reassure himself. She smiled scornfully at him. 'You did all this for a book, did you not? You saw it fit to play with a maiden's life for the Book of Mysteries, and you perhaps will crow to your friends back on the mountain that you have succeeded. Well, I have news for you, my lord. You have not!'

His face turned pale. Pouncing on her, he grabbed her by the arms and shook her. 'Where?' he said. 'Where is it?'

She kept laughing in his face. Disgusted, he pushed her away and let her fall to her knees. 'It is at the base of the Yamuna,' she said, and broke into another short laugh. 'I picked it up from your sack this morning at the High Priest's house, and on our way here I dropped it, into the deepest part of the river.' Suddenly a wild thought struck her. Perhaps he would have some Mystery to retrieve it, she thought. Had she been too eager?

Durvasa (no, Surya, she corrected herself) had regained his poise, standing now a few feet away from her, looking up at the sky and stars. Was he invoking some chant, she thought, looking about her, half-expecting the waters of the Yamuna to rise and carry the book to the shore in one large, explosive wave.

But the river remained flat and glittering in the moonlight. The sage said, 'You may think you have foiled me, Princess, but you have only held me back a little.' He turned around and walked to her, smiling. 'You may think that I have no affection for you – no, even I would not say love – but I do. I wish to help you save your brother and his wife.'

'I do not believe you.'

'You do not need to. You have seen through me clearly enough; I did accompany you to Mathura because I thought a maiden such as you would find it easier to enter the kingdom. In fact, that is why I arrived at Kunti; because I knew that you would be burning with a desire to enter Mathura and rescue your kinsman.'

Pritha's eyes welled up, not so much at his words but at the ice-cool voice in which he spelled them out. 'You said that you were mesmerized by me. I must confess that the feeling was mutual. I still am mesmerized by you. But the reason I came down from Meru was to look into the story of Mathura, the tale of this small kingdom that was keeping all the other great empires at bay. We had heard of her war barges – barges that never seemed to break and always cut through water like hungry crocodiles; such tales reached our ears. We had to see for ourselves what Mathura's secret was, and without you I would not have been allowed entry.'

'You used me!'

'I did,' said Surya, shrugging, 'but only as much as you used me.' When she opened her mouth to protest he added, 'We both used each other for our own purposes. There is no disgrace in that, Pritha. That is the nature of a good trade.'

'But you got what you wished out of it,' she spat out. 'What did I get?'

Surya smiled. 'Did I get what I wished for? Did you not cast the book off into the Yamuna?' His smile widened, and it seemed as if the Celestial was now gradually assuming his natural form, now that no pretence was needed. 'But you did not foil my plan as you think you did, Princess. That book only contains what the High Priests already know. There is much in their minds that the book does not have. You thought I was after the book? Ha! It was the High Priests I wanted.'

'The High Priests?' Pritha asked. 'They would never join you. They are patriots, they are students of the Mysteries!'

'They are students of the Mysteries, yes, but they are not patriots. A student of a Mystery loves nothing more than the Mystery itself, my lady. I can tell you that looking you in the eye because I am a student of the Fire Mysteries, and believe me, nothing, no person, no world is dearer to me than my Mysteries.'

She heard Adhrigu's voice in her ear as Surya said this, the thin, wistful longing for some more time that would allow him to complete studying it, so that he could put off writing in the book for a bit longer. Then she remembered the one hour that morning during which Surya spoke to Adhrigu behind the closed door of his room. Was it that hard to believe that given the right price, Adhrigu would give up everything and follow this strange young man back to his land, where he could probe his Mystery to his heart's content? But what was the price? What could Surya offer the old man? Even as the answer came to her she heard Surya's voice.

'Put yourself in Adhrigu's place, my lady. You are old, you cannot move, your breath is rough and your coughs are heavy and dry. You have no more than a year to live, your mendicants tell you. And then, in walks a Brahmin who promises you a long life in which you would have no king to answer to, no broken Magadhan black stones to fix, no priests to mentor, and no disease against which to grapple. You can devote all the time you have to the one thing that you love the most: the probing of your Mystery.

'And when the time came, you can name your successor, and you can live through him forever, and thus you can gain immortality. You can live the life of a Celestial, Pritha. Would you not take that life if I were to offer it to you?'

Pritha now knew what Surya had told the old man to persuade him to give up the book. The book was never important; the book was never part of the plan. What she had to protect was Adhrigu, and she had allowed herself to be swayed by the book. Perhaps it was not yet too late, she thought frantically. Perhaps she could row back to Mathura and speak to Adhrigu, convince him that Mathura and Earth needed him more than the Celestials did. 'I shall not give up,' she said, her voice heavy. 'I shall sail back to

Mathura right now, I shall speak to Adhrigu. I am certain that if he knew – if he knew–'

'If he knew what, my lady?' said Surya sadly. 'He already knows all about me. But you are free to go to Mathura if you wish, though you may find that the High Priest's house is empty when you reach it.'

'I do not trust you. If I leave now, I think I will find him.'

'You are free to go. I do not own you, so I shall not stop you. But will you listen to me some more? Let me speak – after that, if you still feel that you must go to Mathura, do so, by all means.'

Do not agree, she told herself. This was just another ploy – thread after thread of sweet words would make you want to close your eyes and sleep in his arms. Just reject him and run for the boat!

But before she could gather the strength to walk away, he began to speak.

'If I do not steal the black stone from Mathura, my lady, you shall never see your brother and sister again,' he said, and immediately she felt herself drawn to his voice. 'Magadha and Mathura will continue to be strong for generations, until the secret of the black stone becomes known to all kingdoms around North Country. And soon they shall fight and take over the whole land, Kamsa and Jarasandha, once they probe enough of the Mystery to make chariots fly on their own.'

'Make chariots fly!' she said in a whisper. 'You lie!'

'Do I?' he said, stepping closer to her and taking her hand. 'You were present on Nabha's farm. You saw with your own eyes what the stone can do. In a few years, perhaps, no one in North Country would be able to touch Mathura, my lady, be it on water or on land!' He pressed her hand. 'How will you save your brother then?'

She looked into his eyes, blue eyes, which had begun to take on a strange oval shape.

'Your destiny is to rule, my princess, not to serve. With a strong Mathura and Magadha, that is impossible. They shall take over Shurasena, then Kunti, and then Kuru and the rest of North Country too.' He paused to look deeper into her eyes, melting her. 'And after North Country is vanquished, they shall ascend the mountain of Meru, and they shall come after the Celestials.'

'But you ... aren't you too strong for them?'

He smiled. 'We are not, my lady. Even with our knowledge of the Mysteries, we shall not be able to withstand the might of a black stone–led army. Therefore I must take it away, for your good and ours.'

'But, my brother...'

'Your brother shall live,' Surya said, 'and so shall his queen. Without the Book of Mysteries and the High Priest, Mathura shall no longer be able to make new stones, nor will she able to mend the broken ones. Slowly, they will go back to the plough, and they will fill their boats with oarsmen. They have a lot of stones already made, so perhaps they shall be powerful for the next ten years maybe, but slowly, they will crack open.'

'Ten years,' she mumbled. 'That is too long.'

His hands held her shoulders in a firm, tender grip. 'Not too long,' he said, 'just long enough for you to foster Mathura's future king.'

'Mathura's future king,' she repeated.

'That is so,' said Surya. 'When the decline comes to Mathura and the throne falls, Jarasandha will be ready with his army at the gates, and he shall want the land for himself. If he takes it, Magadha shall be the foremost power of North Country. You must prevent that. You must see to it that Mathura's king is ready to take to the throne when Kamsa's reign ends.'

'I do not understand,' said Pritha, holding his wrists tight with her hands.

'That is the only way you will protect your brother and sister,' said Surya, shaking her so that her eyes became alert once again.

'Yes,' she said, suddenly seeing. 'Mathura's future king ought to be saved.'

'He shall be. Now what of you, my lady? What shall become of you?'

He looked at her with such love that she felt her head dissolve and hands drop as she leaned against his chest.

'You shall rule the greatest kingdom in North Country, my dear,' said Surya, rubbing her cheeks. 'You shall be the High Queen of Hastinapur, the capital city that thrives northward of here. Like Mathura it is wedged in between the two Great Rivers, but the soil there is the richest that you shall find across the country, and its rulers, unlike Mathura's, are just people.'

'Who are they?'

'You have heard of Devavrata, no doubt,' he said, and Pritha thought a strange look came to Surya's face when he said that name. 'They call him Bhishma the terrible,' he said, in the same solemn voice. 'His brother's sons, Pandu and Dhritarashtra, are marriageable now.'

'But my lord,' said Pritha, 'all I want … all I ever wanted … was you!'

'And you shall have me, Princess,' said Surya, smiling kindly at her. 'But you shall be queen of the Kuru kingdom, for in the future the Kurus shall rule the greatest kingdom of the age. Devavrata shall see to that. And I shall see to that too.'

'I … I do not understand, my lord.'

'You shall, soon,' said Surya, and with a wave of his staff a blackness came over them, shielding them from the sounds of the river, the smells of the forest, so that she was aware only of his touch, of his smell, of his sight. He drew her into an embrace, and as she gave in to his arms, she found it within herself to ask a question.

'Will I have your child?' she asked.

And he replied, 'Yes.'

FOURTEEN

She opened her eyes just as the sky turned from black to a dark shade of purple. Pain coursed through her, and brought with it a faint memory of the night before, when it had been so sharp that she had feared that she would die in the sage's arms. She sat up, and saw Surya, naked, holding up his loincloth to the breeze. On seeing her awake, he dusted his cloth twice and came to sit in front of her, his hands resting on the balls of his knees.

'You do not think I have erred, do you, my child?' he said with a distant gaze in his eyes.

'I do not yet know what to think, my lord,' she replied, and knew it was true. All she was aware of now was the memory that her body held of his touch, the smell of his exhaled breath on her skin, his teeth marks on her nipples, her neck, her navel, her shins. Only after these signs of his desire had worn out would she be allowed to think; not just yet.

'I ask you that question for I am not certain myself, Pritha. I have come down to Earth to steal Mathura's secret, and I have done that, but I did not think that I would meet you, my dear, and that I would walk down this road with you.' Her eyes must have shown her despair, because he raised his hand at her and shook his head. 'No, my dear, I do not regret our love for one second, for who among the Meru people can claim to be fortunate enough to be slave to your desire? No, it is not that I worry about.'

Pritha waited, and for the first time that morning the breeze seemed to turn into something harsh, sending her hair flying into her eyes and making her eyes sting.

'You shall bear my child,' he said. 'If it is a daughter, she will grow up to be a priestess, and if it is a son he shall be a warrior of note. I do not think that your blood will beget any less.'

He fell silent, the vacant look in his eyes getting hollower. She understood its meaning and said, 'I shall not rear him.'

'No, you shall not.'

'If I am to become queen of Hastinapur, and if I am to marry into the line of the Kurus, they should not know that I have a son.'

'No, they should not.'

'You knew this yesterday too, did you not?'

'I did.'

'And yet you made love to me, my lord. Why give me a son that I cannot have?'

He smiled at her. 'Pritha,' he said, 'giving up your son for fostering does not mean that you do not have him. Once you give birth to a child, he is yours as long as one of you dies. Every mother gives away his son to fostering to some place or the other; that is the way of the world. The Lady of the River who lives on top of the mountain too had to give away her son, and he now champions the throne of Hastinapur.'

Pritha had heard versions of this tale, one which she had thought was woven to keep alive the legend of the invincible warrior that was Bhishma. 'Is it true, then, what they say of him, sire?'

'It is, and if the Lady of the Great River, the foremost of maidens, could not escape the lot that is of all women, you shall not be saddened by it, either.'

'Yes, my lord, but you must know why I must have this child. You foresee great changes in Hastinapur in my time as queen, do you not?'

'The winds of change, my dear,' he said, 'have already blown over the land of the Kurus. In your time as queen, Hastinapur will rise to be the foremost kingdom in all of North Country. The weakening of Mathura will only aid that, and the son of Devaki and Vasudev shall stop the Magadhans from setting up a throne in Mathura, when he comes.'

'So this son of mine – will he rule Hastinapur when it grows to power?'

Surya thought about it, and behind him the first crack of dawn appeared in the sky. 'You shall have other sons too, Pritha, and they will be sired by a king, and they shall have a higher stake to the throne than will my child.'

'Then why, my lord?' asked Pritha, sitting up in sudden anger. 'Why do you give me this son who shall do nothing but live the life of a commoner?'

Surya began to speak, but he seemed to stop himself with great effort. A lark came flying and perched itself on his shoulder, and Pritha saw in its black beak a pink wriggling worm. With a wave of the hand he sent it away, and as the bird took wing, a little part of the worm fell to the soil next to the sage and disappeared into the earth. Surya turned to her and shook his head. 'I cannot tell you this, my lady. Perhaps with your great wisdom you shall see one day why I did this, but now, all I can tell you is that we are trying to shape our futures.'

'Whose future to you speak of? The earthmen's or that of the people of the Meru?'

'Both,' he said. 'One is entwined with the other. We think that the establishment of Hastinapur as the greatest kingdom in North Country is good for both earthmen and the Meru people.'

'But you still avert my question, sir!' she said, feeling her fists curl up into balls. 'Hastinapur shall become the foremost city in North Country whether I do or do not give birth to a child before my marriage. Why, then, did you play this game with me?'

Surya sighed. 'Pritha,' he said softly. 'Shaping the future of a kingdom is not as simple as reading its past. There is but one past and one present, but each instant of the present faces a thousand possible futures.'

'Then I shall not give birth to this child, my lord! I shall kill him within my womb!'

To her fury, he smiled at her threat. 'You shall not be able to, my dear. Whatever you do, unless you kill yourself, you shall bear my child in ten months from now.'

'Then I shall kill him after I have borne him!'

'That, I shall leave you to decide. But you must listen to me, for I have not finished telling you the things you must do.'

Again, she thought, again he was speaking to her in that soothing voice of his, crooning to her and lulling her with words. He had seduced her the previous night with the same jousts, and now he was trying them again. She began walking backward, away from him, when he picked up his sack and pulled out from it a long, stick-like object which appeared to be made of black, rotting wood. He held it out to her.

'What is that?' she asked suspiciously.

'Take it,' he said. 'It is yours.' When she took it she noticed that the surface of the object was soft, and it gave to the pressure of her fingers. She held it gingerly, and when she lifted it up to her eyes she realized it was made of a thick, waxy substance. Five black strings lay curled inside the object, she saw, when she held it against the brightening sky.

'Hair?' she asked.

'Sacred hair from the coat of Nandini, the cow of Vasishtha, and empowered by the chants of Meru's High Priest, Brihaspati.'

'What am I to do with them?' she asked, giving in once again to curiosity.

He stood up, went to the tree where his loincloth lay, picked it up and began to tie it around his waist. 'The strands of hair aid in the Mystery of incarnation,' he said in a voice loud enough for her to hear. 'People on the Meru say that Devavrata is the son of a Celestial by name Prabhasa.'

'Indeed,' said Pritha, taking a step toward him. 'I have heard that too, and he does look like a Celestial, does he not, and they say he fights like one.'

'Maybe he is, maybe not. I know not. But if Hastinapur is to become the greatest kingdom in North Country, it will need the help of more than one Celestial reborn. Your sons will finish what Devavrata started, my dear.'

'But sire,' she said, not fully understanding. 'You said I am to have sons through the High King of Hastinapur, and now you say I shall have Celestials as sons.'

Surya finished tying his loincloth around his waist and turned to the rising sun. 'I shall train you in the Mystery, Pritha, so that you shall bear sons to the High King, but they shall all have the attributes of the Celestial that you invoke.'

'Is that possible, my lord?' she asked.

'If it was possible with Devavrata, my dear, it is possible with you.' After bowing to the sun he turned and walked back to her. Resting his hands on her shoulders, he looked into her eyes and said, 'But remember ... the son I have given you is the only true Celestial, the only one who will have real Meru blood running through his veins.'

'And yet you wish me to give him up.'

'Give him up so that he shall live the life destined for him,' said Surya. 'You shall have more sons after him, and together they will build the golden city of Hastinapur, and your name shall be written about for a thousand years hence, my lady.'

She felt none of the grandeur that his voice carried. As his blue, oval eyes bored through her, she felt something heavy drop in her chest, as if a rope had been tied into a tight knot and lowered down her throat into her stomach. She swallowed, but that only intensified the pain, and when she grimaced, he smiled at her. 'Close your eyes,' he said, 'and I shall breathe into you the words that you shall utter when you lay with your king.'

Pritha obeyed him. Dark, swirling shadows swam in front of her eyes, and all she felt were the calloused tips of his fingers on each shoulder, and a calm, soothing whisper chanting words in a strange language. Without knowing what the sounds meant she began to repeat after him, and in no time at all their voices merged, his throaty and hoarse, hers clear as a teardrop …

When she opened her eyes, she was bathed in sweat, and the garment that had been covering her breasts had flown and caught the branch of the lemon tree to her left. She breathed heavily but steadily, and her lips parted. The stick with the hair lay on the grass between her two feet. She got down on her knees and picked it up with both hands. Then she touched it to both her eyes.

Only then did she notice that she was alone. Surya was gone.

FIFTEEN

The man who entered Pritha's chamber was hefty but moved with cat-like grace. His forehead was plain and smooth, and a smattering of thick black hair covered his strong jaw. He was neither fat nor thin, she thought, neither tall or short, neither fair nor dark. He had a perfectly forgettable face, which was perhaps why they called him the best spy in Shurasena. Over the course of seven years, he had built for himself a career in Hastinapur as a rice trader, but on her bidding he had been ordered to return immediately. Did he leave behind family and friends? Were they missing him now, wondering where he went overnight?

'We cannot bear to think of such things, my lady,' he said, reading her thoughts. 'But I have made arrangements for news of my death to reach Hastinapur in a few days. I think my wife will not miss me.'

A wife. Of course he had a wife. A young man who lived in a city for seven years without getting married would attract notice. He may have even had a child, to ensure that prying eyes would not fasten on him. She felt a tiny prick in her heart; it had been just over a month now since Durvasa had left her, and now, because of her, this man had to abandon his wife. Were men always like this, forever, tied to circumstance, placing duty over love?

222

'They tell me your name is Rishabha,' she said, waving him closer.

'That is the name I took in Hastinapur, yes.'

'And your real name?'

'It does not matter, my lady.'

'They tell me you were a rice trader for seven years. I wish to send you to Mathura.'

'As you wish.'

'There will be danger to your life.'

He smiled at her through tight, pursed lips. 'My life is always in danger, Princess.'

In the faint saffron light of the lamps she did not see his eyes well as she would have liked, and the man had a trick of never allowing his eyes to rest as he talked, so she could not tell for certain what went through his mind. She looked for scars or spots on his face and was able to spot perhaps two or three black moles on his forehead, but then he rubbed it with his swarthy hand and they were gone.

She picked up the linen pouch next to her and handed it over to him. 'This contains all that you need. I have written down your instructions in the book you will find in it. Once you enter Mathura, I shall not be able to communicate with you easily, so I implore you to ask me all questions you may have.'

He took the bag and tucked it under his arm. 'How long shall I have to live in Mathura, my lady?'

'As long as it takes you to secure a job as a guard in the prison.'

'The royal prison?'

'The prison in which they hold my brother and kinswoman captive.'

Rishabha's face hardened just a little. 'You do not know where this prison is located?'

'No,' she said, shaking her head. 'You must find out where it is and enter it.'

His face remained stoic, cold as marble. 'My lady,' he said, 'if I am to free High King Vasudev and Lady Devaki from the prison,

I must tell you right now that it is an impossible task that you have given me.'

Pritha said, 'I do not wish *you* to free the king and queen. You are to rescue the child that Lady Devaki bears without letting it succumb to the hands of Kamsa.'

Rishabha's face softened, and a certain ease entered his stance. 'That is a less difficult assignment.'

'And one at which you cannot fail.'

'I shall try my very best.'

Pritha gave him a curt nod. 'You shall enter Mathura through the eastern gate, where grain traders come from Magadha with donkeys laden with sacks. You shall carry with you a little bag of rubies that will gain you entrance into the city, and you shall stop nowhere until you reach the farm of Nabha, which lies to the western end.'

'I presume, then, that the bag contains the rubies.'

'Yes. It contains rubies, directions to Nabha's farm, and my coronet which you will carry to convince him that you are my man.'

'Very well, my lady.'

'He will take you to Kurusti, a priest whom I know, who will help you get to the prison. These are the only two men in Magadha that you will trust until you begin to make your own friends. And you will need many friends, indeed, to become a guard at the prison.'

'Aye, that is so,' said Rishabha, bowing.

'How many days do you think you will need to do this?'

'Days, my lady?' Rishabha's mouth curved in a sly smile. 'You have asked me to infiltrate the prison of Mathura's High King, and you say it will take me days? I say it shall not be done before next year, Your Majesty, and that too if I am lucky.'

Pritha thought of the last month and the chaos that must have ensued in Mathura after realizing that the High Priests had fled and had taken with them the secret of the black stone.

The kingdom would be in disarray now, which meant that there would not be a better time than this for Rishabha to enter it. But entering the prison was not as easy as entering the city. Kurusti had not even known where the prison was.

But they had time. Durvasa had said that the decline of Mathura would take almost ten years, so even if Rishabha took two years to rescue the future king, it would not be disastrous. The important thing was that Rishabha must not fail.

'You can take two years if you so wish, Rishabha,' she said, 'but you must not fail.'

'I shall try my best not to fail, my lady, for that is the only way I shall stay alive. I shall write to you every second full moon.'

'How will your messages reach me?'

He smiled. 'I shall take care of that, my lady.'

'Do not make use of Nabha or Kurusti for carrying your messages.'

'I shall not. But if you do not hear from me for four full moons, you should assume that I have failed, and you should begin new plans to save the future king of Mathura.'

She nodded.

'I shall take your leave now, my lady,' he said, rising. 'I shall return tomorrow, if you please, to bid farewell before I set sail for Mathura.'

After he left, Pritha leaned back in her seat and rested her head back against the top of her chair. The mention of the full moon from Rishabha suddenly reminded her that it was only two nights away now, and if she had not lain with Durvasa, she would have begun to bleed today. But she had waited with folds of linen ready at hand all day – perhaps the first time in her life when she had so fervently willed it to arrive – but her thighs had remained dry. The weight in her chest reappeared, and she found herself looking past the window into the night sky, at the curved shape of the moon, wishing the night of the full moon would not come, just this once.

SIXTEEN

As she did every day, Devaki threw her arm to her side as soon as she opened her eyes. For the last twenty days that had been her ritual; she had taken to sleeping fitfully and in deep fright fearing that her bed would be empty when she woke up. The guard at the door carried keys on his waistband, she knew, and Kamsa would soon know that she had given birth to a daughter. Somewhere deep within her she harboured a frail flicker of hope that her brother would pardon his niece; after all, how could a girl, who would one day be given away to another kingdom, cause his death?

Her desperate fingers touched the cold flab of the babe's thighs, and she relaxed. On the other side of the bed Vasudev slept. She had often tried to speak with him these past few weeks, but he would turn his head away every time she opened her mouth. In times of trouble men wished to act while women wished to speak; they sought to fight and vanquish while women sought to understand, to feel, to change. He must have felt some of her sorrow, she thought, resisting the urge to reach over and smoothen his brow. So what if he did not wear it on his face?

She began to run her palm over the infant's body, warming it against the gathering cold of the night. Through the window she saw a dying streak of lightning. The rains had persisted well into the winter this year, and she had heard the guards say to one another that Mathura had lost the love of the gods, that their favour left the city with the High Priests. It was now the eighth full moon since the temples had been abandoned, and even from the prison Devaki could feel the air of despair thicken all over the city.

A click on the lock made her sit up. It was well past meal time, and their pitcher of water by the bedside was full. The incense sticks were only half-burnt, and the candles still had not weathered down to their stumps. What did the guard want, then? She drew the baby closer to her and her hand gripped the sheet of the bed.

The guard entered and bowed. 'The High King is on his way, my lady,' he said, clutching his sword tight in his left hand.

Before she could ask why, the door was covered by a hefty shadow, and the next moment her brother stood at the foot of the bed, one leg hoisted upon it, staring at the bundle of linen hidden behind her hand. She had not seen his face for a while now, but it seemed to have aged. His cheeks and chin sagged, and a web of lines had begun to invade his features, starting at the forehead. She guessed that the departure of the High Priests had hit him hard, and even now she found it in her heart to feel pity for him.

'How could you be so foolish, Devaki?' he asked. Vasudev stirred on his bed, and as he sat up, Kamsa bowed to him. Then he clapped his hands, at which two soldiers marched in and held Vasudev by his arms. 'Do not think otherwise, my lord,' said Kamsa, 'but I do not wish you to hurt yourself.'

'Brother,' said Devaki, 'do not take her. Whatever you do, do not kill your niece.'

His eyes came back to fasten themselves on the baby, and it sent a bolt through Devaki's spine. He sighed morosely. 'My sister, do you not see that you have left me with no choice? When I ordered that you should be put in prison, I told you that you must not have children if you wish to keep our love alive.'

'I will touch your feet, Brother,' Devaki cried. 'I will send her away to the farthest of kingdoms. I shall foster her at the humblest of homes. She shall not even know of you her whole life, my lord. I only beg you that you let her live.'

He clapped his hands once again, at which two more soldiers came in, bearing spears pointed straight upwards. Kamsa waved toward Devaki. 'No,' she said. 'No!' One of the soldiers held her in a firm but gentle grip, and the other picked up the baby along with her sheets and returned to Kamsa. With his forefingers her brother lifted the edge of the white hood that covered the baby's head, and he gazed at her for a moment.

'It is not I, Devaki,' he said, 'but you who killed this baby. You killed this baby by having her against my wishes.'

Devaki stopped resisting against the soldier and slumped back against the cushion of the bed. She heard the laboured breathing of her husband on the other edge, hanging by his arms between the two other soldiers, his head bent, his eyes staring at the ground. That sight of him jolted her. 'My lord,' she said, 'if you do not stand up to my brother, you have forsaken your right to share my bed for the rest of your life.'

Vasudev raised his head to look at her, then back again at the ground.

Devaki turned to the soldier and spat in his face. He wiped it away with the back of his hand and held her tighter. 'Brother!' she said, grimacing as his brown fingers closed around her wrist. 'Do not commit crimes against your own kin. The gods will not forgive you.'

'This is not my crime, Devaki,' he said, his face wooden.

'You may tell yourself that is so, and you may believe it, if that helps you sleep well. But the blood on your hands will be washed one day, Brother, whether you like it or not.'

'If you truly care so much for me, you shall have no more children!' he said, and with a wave at the soldiers to release Devaki and her husband, he turned and went out of the room, taking her daughter with him. The door guard stood in the corner, his left hand still clutching his sword, his right arm rigid by his side. After the sounds of footsteps and spears had died down, with the only sound they could hear coming from the thundering clouds, the guard came to the foot of the bed and bowed.

Devaki looked at him. Only now she noticed that she did not recall having seen his face before. The previous guard had been older, with tufts of grey hair peering out at the ears from underneath his crown. This one was younger, bigger, and had a face as lifeless as a mud idol. She tried to look into his eyes to hold his gaze, but found that the man never seemed to look at anything.

'I come here from across the river, from Kunti,' said the man, and at his words Vasudev looked up, his eyes buried deep within the mass of hair on his head and his face. 'I was bade here by Princess Pritha nine moons ago, and I have come to save your child.'

Vasudev laughed and hung his head again. Devaki said, 'You have come a few weeks too late, my good man.'

'No, my lady,' said the guard. 'I did not wish to save your first child; indeed, I did arrive too late for that. But I can – and shall, by the gods – save your next child, should you wish to have one.'

'I do not,' said Devaki. 'I do not wish to see another of my children being devoured by that madman.'

'And you will not. I have persuaded the head guard of this castle to appoint me as your personal guard. I shall be with you always.'

Devaki asked, 'But … why does my child need to be saved?'

'I know not for certain, my lady, but the High Priests have fled the kingdom, and Mathura does not have people who know the Mysteries of the black stone. Word is not out of Mathura's walls yet, but it will get out, slowly, and when it reaches Magadha, Mathura will be under threat.'

'Let it!' said Devaki venomously. 'I do not care if Mathura falls.'

'But if you could do something to save her, my lady,' said the guard, 'would you not?'

Devaki began to say no, but something stopped her. Whether Mathura would be saved or not, the thought of foiling Kamsa's designs tempted her. She did not know whether the priest who had foreseen the king's death was right or wrong, but now, she thought of her child returning to avenge all the wrongs that had been done to her, and she smiled. From across the bed, Vasudev returned her smile, and she knew that he was thinking the same thing.

The guard retreated, and the door shut with a soft click. Devaki looked out of the window at the low purple clouds, and thought of Pritha.

Pritha looked at herself in the mirror. In the last nine moons of carrying her son, her breasts had grown bigger and softer, and now if she stood erect and raised her chin just a little, she could pass for being a queen. A year ago she had hated mirrors and other shiny surfaces, and even now the shape of her nose made her cringe, but she had grown enough at the right places to feel that she was now a woman.

With one hand she flattened the palm-sized roll of paper that had arrived today from Mathura, concealed in the red turban of a travelling fortune-teller. It only had one line, but it told Pritha all that she had wanted to know. 'The bird is inside the cage,' it said.

She looked out at the sky and wondered if she should eat. Carrying a child had killed her appetite; indeed, if Aganyi had not forcefully emptied vessel after vessel into her, only the gods knew what would have happened to the child. Surya had been right; after her moment of anger had passed, she never once considered getting rid of her belly. She had received suggestions – subtle ones from Agnayi, more direct ones from her father – but she had stood firm and insisted on having her son.

She had never stopped to question her choice. But now, as Agnayi was preparing to take him away to the Yamuna and hand him over to the fisherpeople, she marvelled at herself. Did I bear this child all these months only to let him go now? And why do I wish to give him away? Just because Surya told me that I should? Her sons would play great roles in the coming story of Hastinapur, he had said, and she must fulfil her part in the tale; she must ensure that the sons she would bear through the Celestials would all be reared in Hastinapur – it did not matter whether they grew up in the royal palace or in a fisherman's hut.

But all this to what end? Surya said that a strong Hastinapur would lead to a strong North Country, but why did Meru need a strong North Country? She had heard many tales about the Celestials, but from her experience with Surya, they were not very different from men – men who perhaps held deeper knowledge of the Mysteries, but men nonetheless. And men did not embark upon journeys and make plans without selfish reasons. What was Meru's in this case?

Bhishma was a half-Celestial, of that much Pritha was certain. Did the people of Meru wish that their own kin should rule over North Country? Even if they did, her sons would be as much human as Celestial, just like Bhishma. Their loyalties would lie with Hastinapur, for they would be reared there. If Meru was hoping to lend her sons to Earth so that she could gain a stranglehold on the land of North Country, certainly there was a better way than this?

She did not pretend to herself that she understood Meru's part in all this, but the immediate future for her and for her sons looked good, and she could see no storm clouds for as far ahead as she could see. She would do as Surya bade her, then, but she would rear her children to be faithful and loyal to Hastinapur over all else, even their own blood and kin. So when the Celestials of Meru tried – if they ever did – to rule North Country through their sons, they would realize that the High Kings of Hastinapur serve their own men first before anyone else.

Pritha heard the door behind her creak as it slid open, and she turned back to see Agnayi hold a pink silk bundle in her arms. 'Do not enter, Agnayi,' she said firmly.

Agnayi stopped at the door and bowed. In these last few months their relationship had changed; gone was the hand-holding and giggling and open declarations of love. Now, with the birth of a child, she seemed to have grown in Agnayi's eyes to the status of a queen, and Pritha herself felt that Agnayi had grown smaller. There had been a time – which now felt like it was another life – when she had been in awe of her. She no longer remembered why.

'I have told you already where you are to take him,' said Pritha, ignoring the shard of pain that had risen in her chest.

'Yes, my lady.'

'You have dressed him as I told you to.'

'Yes, my lady.'

'You shall take him to the fishermen on the banks of Shurasena that come from Hastinapur. You shall bid them to take him to a nobleman, so that he shall be raised as one.'

'Yes, my lady.'

She waved him away, and forced herself to turn back to the mirror. She had only looked at him once or twice, and he was but an infant, so his memory would pass in no time at all. If she should ever come across him again, she would not recognize him by his face. But if Surya's words came true, she would know him by other ways – by the valour of his deeds, perhaps?

Now was not the time to look back, she thought, patting her chest and swallowing the cough that burnt her throat. Her son would look after himself. Now that she had seen to him, she could set her sights northward, to Hastinapur. On the day of the birth of her son, her father had come to ask her if he should begin arrangements for a groom-choosing ceremony, and she had said yes.

In the silence of the room she felt she heard the gurgle of her son, but she closed her eyes and refused to turn back, for that would mean she would have to look at the bed on which she had given birth to him. She plugged her ears with her fingers and counted to ten.

The sounds died away.

Again the door opened behind her, and she looked over her shoulder at the attendant. 'His Majesty the king has news for you, my lady,' she said.

Pritha nodded at her to go on.

'My lady, the prince of Hastinapur has accepted His Majesty's invitation to attend your groom-choosing ceremony.'

BOOK THREE

THE CITY OF GOLD

PROLOGUE

GANGA SPEAKS

The tale of the Great War is much like the river herself. It breaks off in places, and each tributary flows at its own speed to lands unheard of, until it returns and joins the main river hundreds of leagues downstream. The tale of Amba is, perhaps, the longest such branch, and it would not return to the trunk until long after the weddings of Pandu and Dhritarashtra are but distant memories, until their wives begin to give birth to their children.

In Pritha's tale, by the time of Durvasa's visit to Shurasena and Mathura, Dhritarashtra was already married. Hastinapur had already taken her spot atop the pyramid of Great Kingdoms in North Country. But it was not always so. There exists a rocky land to the far north-west, beyond the lands of Madra and Kamboja, which first settled on the bank of River Sindhu but later migrated inward. They call this kingdom Gandhar, the city of gold.

This was the time when Devavrata was set upon uniting the kingdoms of North Country, so that he could one day lead an army of men against the might of Meru. One of the biggest mistakes that Devavrata made in plotting his battle with the dwellers of the mountain was that he thought that we would not watch him, that we would let him assemble the forces of Earth without raising so much as a murmur.

It was only at the very end, when I came to the battlefield of Kurukshetra to take his mortal body away, that I saw the realization in his eyes, that I, his mother, has been his bitterest enemy all his life, that every moment he has lived on Earth, he has pit his wits and strength against me. I longed to tell him that when I schemed against him, I did not do so as his mother but as the lady of the river whose duty it is to protect and serve the mountain. I longed to tell him that besides being a spiteful foe, I was also his dearest friend, the one person who loved him most, the one person who would shed the most tears at his death.

But before I could find the words, he breathed his last, with the same hurt look of knowing in his eyes. I have often thought of that day in the years past, if I should have hastened to remove from his mind the thought of his mother as a wicked crone, but I doubt if he would have understood, much less forgiven me. So, perhaps, it is all for the good.

For one to win, another has to lose. We play this game of winning and losing with such desperate will that we often forget there is only one victor at the very end. If one were to travel down this line of time far enough into the future, or into the past, one would see only the form of the Goddess, standing alone, watching in silence. And yet we go through most of life fighting our little battles, rejoicing in our petty victories, only stopping when the shadow of death darkens our door.

At that moment we come to know that it was all but futile, and we forgive. We forgive all. On her deathbed I found Gandhari smiling and tearful, and her eyes told me that she had made her peace with the world, that she had come to see both those she vanquished and those who vanquished her with the same eye. But she was not always like this. I remember the time when she sat on the throne of Gandhar and ruled with great hope and wisdom. I remember her and her brother, who were just children but fought with more valour than the bravest of warriors for the good of their land.

I must beckon the listener westward now, and a few moons back in time, so that he can peer through my eyes into the royal castle of Gandhar.

ONE

Even after night had fallen, the rocks of Gandhar seemed to glimmer red. Gandhari felt that if one were to pour water upon the flat surfaces, it would hiss and rise up in smoke in a moment. Travellers to Gandhar's court complained to the queen – only jokingly, but there was truth to even the mildest of quips – that the crumpled land was so hot that they had no need for fireplaces, that whenever they stopped to eat, they could spread their cotton sacks on the ground and break eggs on them. She had heard many such tales in her life, and at first she would jump to her kingdom's defence, but now that she had been on the throne for a good four years, she had learnt to let them pass with a smile. Gandhar was the wealthiest kingdom in all of North Country and they all knew it. If they wanted to poke fun at its weather, so be it.

She ran her fingertips down the length of the copper net that draped the window. The holes shone with hanging water drops – the only leftover signs of that evening's rain. She leaned closer to the net and blew at it, sending silver freckles flying out into the night air. When she had been a child, she would sit on this very sill for long hours waiting for the rain, and when it came, she would watch the net fill up with films of water which had swirling purple spots in them. She would lean her temple against the cold, rusted net and watch.

In the distance she saw the flickering yellow fires standing in a row, along the path that led to the mines. Gandhari tried to squint so that she could see better, but her sight had deteriorated these last few years. When she had been young she remembered she could see well enough to spot the swallow nests atop the branches of the oak trees that towered over the rocks. But now the whole tree was but a smudge. The mendicant that attended to her had said that her eyes would get worse and worse until she reached the age of twenty. Three more years, then, she thought.

She had given up thinking about her illness. The first few days after the mendicant had visited them for the first time – when she was about four or so – she had burrowed her head inside her pillow every night and cried. But thirteen years was long enough to accept things that one did not like and could do nothing about. Now, she could even view it with a sense of indifference. Yes, it would have been a larger issue had she been a man, for it would have impeded her from hunting and fighting. But since she was a woman, even if she had been entirely normal, her soldiers would not have allowed her to enter the battlefield or the woods.

For her duties she needed no more than to look a few feet ahead of her and recognize her courtiers. She had already trimmed the size of her assembly to eighteen from her father's forty-four, and often she asked them to come to the chambers after night had fallen. Shakuni, her brother, came with them and tried to light up a fight, as usual.

The muscles on her face tightened when she thought of him. By the end of next year, on his sixteenth birthday, he would ascend to the throne, and she would step aside to be married off to some king or the other. But the boy carried in him much anger toward the state of Hastinapur, and if he were to do something to disturb the delicate balance that existed between Gandhar and the Kuru kingdom, he could well be overthrown by the people.

She sighed; snubbing him and hoping that he would stay quiet would no longer do. He had to be tutored. She would have to be patient with him.

She remembered that autumn afternoon years ago, when he had been seven and she nine, when he had raced past the rocks and climbed the oak tree, calling out to her to come. She had only trudged behind him, blinking and squinting. By the time she reached the tree, Shakuni had already climbed up to the top, and he was pelting her with dried twigs. She yelled at him to stop, but when he did not, she bent down, picked up a stick, broke it in two, and hurled it into the air.

It missed him by quite a large distance, and he laughed. 'Come on, sister, is that the best you can do?' Through her narrowed eyes she could see him crawl along the branch, legs wrapped tight around it. He reached out for some smaller branches and broke them in his tiny hands. But when he threw them at her they hit her on the back of her neck, her arms, and left red scratches on her skin.

'Do not do that, Shakuni!' she said. 'Or I shall tell father to lock you up in the stables!'

'That is all you can do. You have no fight in you, sister, do you?'

'I do!'

'You do not.' He sent another twig – a big one this time – flying at her shoulder. It drew a wail from her.

'You rascal!' she said, and bent down to pick up it up. When she looked up to face him, although she only saw him as a black fuzzy spot against the blue sky, she leaned back and hurled it at him with as much power as she could muster.

She had laughed at the spiralling twig as it travelled toward its target. She had laughed as it hit him and a look of pain arose on his face. But the next moment she had seen his arms wave, and his legs release the branch. He had tried to cling on, but his fingers had slipped on the tufts of moss that coated the bark. When he had known he was falling, he had shouted to help. She had stood there, watching him drop with a thud and a groan, not on the grassy side of the tree but among the rocks.

She could see the tree now, set against the blue night sky. Whenever she recalled what happened that afternoon, her ankles ached, and they did now too. That day she had turned and run as fast as she could all the way to the palace, and when the guards asked her what had happened she had mutely pointed at the tree. As the men picked up their spears and rushed away from her, she had fled into the palace, not stopping until she had crawled under her bed and lain on her side, crumpled up into a ball. Only then had she realized that her ankles felt as though needles were being driven through them.

Today, she felt that same old pain. She dragged the chair toward her so that she could sit. Just when her breath returned to normal, a girl entered her chamber and announced that her ministers sought her audience.

The four of them entered and took their seats. Gandhari walked away from the window and took the central throne, motioning them to come closer so that she could see them better. Adbudha, her mining minister, moved to the edge of his seat and spoke first. 'I have paid the mines a visit just today, Your Majesty, as per your command yesterday, and I have seen to its operations myself.'

'And?'

'We have mined seven hundred and eighty eight *tulas* of gold this year.' He had little black eyes that retreated deep within their sockets when he spoke. He looked around him derisively. 'It is not, as it was suggested yesterday, any more than it was the year before. In fact, last year, we mined upwards of eight hundred *tulas*.'

Gandhari turned to the mighty figure of Chyavatana, who was in the process of tending to the curls in his moustache. 'Did you hear that, Chyavatana?' she asked.

'Yes,' he said. 'Eight hundred *tulas* last year, was it, Adbudha?'

Adbudha nodded angrily. Gandhari could feel for him. The other three had hounded him as a pack during the last hearing, and they had all forced him on a long ride to the mines just to verify what he had said all along – that the mines had produced the same amount of gold this year as they had in the last.

While Chyavatana pondered in silence, Gandhari gestured at Adbudha for the parchment in his hand. Glancing through it, she saw that he was right; unless, of course, Adbudha had pocketed some of the gold himself.

'However is that possible?' asked Chyavatana, bringing out a parchment of his own from inside his pink silk tunic. 'The prices at our schools have risen, and so have the prices at our mendicants.'

'It is because,' said Devapi, her treasurer, 'our citizens are now richer than they were last year, Chyavatana.' He turned to Gandhari. 'Your Majesty, the honourable minister of schools and mendicants does not believe that Gandhar can get richer, therefore he is always surprised when he sees that she has.'

'But … that cannot be so,' said Chyavatana, frowning at his open parchment.

'All our citizens are today richer than they were last year, my lady,' said Devapi, bowing. 'Last year, each citizen in your country owned seven hundred coins, but today that number has risen to nine hundred. It means, Your Majesty, that the prosperity in your city is rising.'

'May I ask how?' said Gandhari.

'Through the wealth of our miners, my lady,' said Devapi. 'We pay our miners well to bring gold out of the ground, and that wealth travels down to the merchants, the water carriers, the maidservants and tailors. Wages to our miners has also gone up from last year. So everyone in the kingdom is richer.'

Gandhari looked toward the quietest of her ministers, Harayana, who sat in one of the farther chairs, brooding to himself. 'How goes trade, Harayana?' she asked, and he started, as though she had woken him up from a deep sleep. 'Yes, yes,' he said, sitting up and clearing his throat. 'We are trading more and more with Hastinapur, my lady, and that agrees with what Devapi has said. Your people are richer, therefore they are buying more.'

'And the tributes?'

'The tributes keep arriving as they should, Your Majesty.'

'If they are to stop at any time, Harayana, you ought to tell me. Hastinapur shall pay the tributes of war for two hundred years from now, and though it is but a small amount when set against the wealth of our kingdom, they must not know that, for then they will cease viewing us as their masters.'

'Yes, Your Highness,' said Harayana.

Gandhari turned to Adbudha and said, 'So if we have produced the same amount of gold as last year and we have bought more goods from Hastinapur, do we not need more miners for this year?'

'We do, my lady, but where shall I get them?'

'Harayana, let us close the barracks at the western end of the city and send all the footmen in training to the mines for a year.'

Harayana looked up from his parchment and nodded sleepily.

'And because our citizens are richer, let us increase the levy to the appropriate amount, and please be certain that you remind them that this levy shall only be used to better their lives.'

Devapi bowed. 'So I shall, my lady.'

'And Chyavatana,' said Gandhari, turning to the man-mountain to her left, 'you are concerned with the rise in prices of schools and mendicants.'

'Yes, my lady, it is most puzzling, is it not? If people are getting richer ...'

'Let us announce with immediate effect that all families which have children going to schools will be given two copper coins every moon; and for every man, woman and child in the kingdom, let us begin a mendicant's gift of three copper coins every moon. Will that help?'

Chyavatana began to smile, then said, 'Hmm.' He tapped at his parchment with his hand. 'We gave them these gifts last year, my lady, and yet...'

'Then surely we have not done enough,' she said. 'We must do all that we can so that there is no sickness or illiteracy in the land of Gandhar.'

Chyavatana sighed, and made a note with his carver. 'I shall do what you say.'

She could see that the man was not convinced by her, and she found herself growing angry at that thought. Chyavatana was one of Shakuni's staunch followers, and therefore never did – or even said – anything important. Shakuni's pet complaint this whole year had been that Gandhar was losing her prosperity, and even more laughably, he had said that Hastinapur was now richer than Gandhar – that city which had been laid to waste by Gandhar forty years ago in the Battle of Kamyaka.

Once or twice her father had warned her that Shakuni was intelligent and saw things that other men did not; he had asked her to always heed his counsel, but when he spoke utter nonsense so often, it was not easy to take him seriously.

Neither had she any patience with his stooges. She looked at Chyavatana leave the room last, behind all the others, and as soon as the door closed behind him, she clapped her hands, bringing forth two frightened waiting-women.

'Tell the prince to come here at once,' she told them.

TWO

When Shakuni came into the room, Gandhari averted her gaze away toward the window. She had a lurking feeling that the boy overdid his limp when he knew she was watching. What had happened all those years ago should not affect her now, she knew, but it did and she could not help it. That Shakuni knew this made it worse.

He came around to stand in front of her, hands on hips. He was again wearing that ridiculous purple cape that he thought gave him, in his words, a certain royal air. He had always been a small boy for his age, and he had not added significantly to his height during his mature years. Even now, when they stood shoulder to shoulder, he was not taller than her by any more than an inch or two. And that shortened left leg did not help, for it gave him the look of a hunchback.

She looked up at him. He was grinning down at her as usual, with one edge of his mouth raised right up to his cheek. 'I have heard that you have shut down one of the barracks, sister,' he said. His voice dripped with honey, and his eyes bore a peaceful, loving gaze, but Gandhari knew by his tomato-red ears that he was fuming inside. Like all men Shakuni took great pride in military prowess, though he could not shoot an arrow without the use of a raised foot-rest. How was Gandhar going to accept such a

247

man as king? It was to the great misfortune of her people that after being ruled by a queen who could not fight, they would be burdened by a king who could neither fight nor rule.

'I did, Shakuni, yes,' said Gandhari. 'Let me ask my girl to take your cape from you.'

'I shall keep it,' said Shakuni, and gripped the handle of his sword. She had never seen him fight with a sword, but he liked to carry the weapon on him at all times, sheathed in a red scabbard with hand-painted round silver lines. 'I shall keep it, for I shall not be here long, sister. I do not think we have very much to say to each other.'

'No, Shakuni, we do not.' Then she remembered her promise to herself to be patient with him, and sighed. 'Shakuni, brother, one day you shall rule this land. You will not do well if you hate Hastinapur so much. Will you not listen to me?'

'It is not my hatred that is hard to understand, sister, but your love for them.'

'Love?' She picked up the edge of her garment and got up, so that she could look down at him. 'They are a mere vassal state, and they give us tribute every full moon. Why should I love them?'

'A vassal state, sister?' asked Shakuni, clucking in disbelief. 'You perhaps have gone to sleep these last three years, and you refuse to wake up even though I yell in your ear every day. A vassal state! Hastinapur is the strongest kingdom in North Country now, my lady, and you only need to open your eyes to see it.'

'The second strongest, perhaps,' said Gandhari. 'Do you not remember how our army routed theirs in the battle by the forest?'

'That was forty years ago, sister,' he said at length, in a whisper. 'Our good father was but a boy then, and he fought in that battle. I dare say even the old people of Gandhar would have forgotten about it now.'

'What if they have? The tributes for that war still keep arriving every moon.'

'They do, they do,' said he, nodding. 'But do you not see what has happened to Gandhar in these forty years, my lady?'

'Oh, Shakuni, I have heard this tale before!'

'You have, and yet you do not understand! If you did, you would not close down another barrack while Hastinapur keeps adding to her army of elephants.'

'We have enough footmen to ward off any attack.'

Shakuni laughed, with a malice that alarmed her. In her mind she went over the details of Gandhar's army as reported to her the day before by the general. Eighty-four war elephants, one hundred and seventy cavalrymen, seventy-five footmen and fifty archers. All were in prime fighting condition, eager for the call of battle. Shakuni began to nod at her, as though he could see right into that place of her brain where she was checking off the numbers.

'I know the numbers too, my dear sister,' he said, bowing. 'But in the last two years we have closed down six stables and three barracks. We have an army, yes, but do we have the power to produce units at a swift pace when there is battle?'

'Oh, come off it, Shakuni,' she said, 'who is doing battle with us now?'

'One of my men has just arrived from Hastinapur, my lady,' he said, 'and he has brought with him records of their military might. Perhaps you should look at them.'

'Perhaps I will. But do not forget that Hastinapur's gold comes from our mines, and if we stop our mines, then they will be powerless.'

'And our vaults, you suppose, are overflowing with gold?'

'Well, they are.'

'When have you last seen your gold, my lady?'

Gandhari paused for a moment, then said, 'I have seen the records from the head vault-keeper just today.'

'Records?' asked Shakuni innocently. 'Were these records made of gold, sister?' When she did not answer, he continued, 'Forty years ago, when Gandhar and Hastinapur did battle on the edge of Kamyaka, sister, theirs was a poor country. They produced food, but every kingdom in North Country produced enough food. They lost to us, and they began to pay tribute to us – in fruit, grain, linen, brick, thatch and labourers.'

'Why do you tell me all this, Shakuni? I know it all.'

'Then why do you not ask yourself, my lady, how such a poor settlement became the foremost kingdom of the land in thirty years?'

'They say Shantanu made a farmer out of every man, and tilled every yard of his kingdom.'

'Ah, if that were true, where did their army come from? They have been fighting Panchala for their stone quarries now for years. What do they pay their soldiers in, I wonder. In food grain? In pulses?'

'They say that Bhishma is at the head of their army, he of the invincible armour.'

Shakuni bent his head and smiled again. 'Sister, Bhishma is but a man, no matter how invincible. He cannot take on the whole might of Panchala, certainly not alone.'

'They say he is the son of the gods,' said Gandhari.

'Even the gods are not that powerful, my lady,' said Shakuni. 'But consider this, if you will, for a second. What if – *if* – Hastinapur has been stealing our gold?'

Gandhari's breath stopped, and for a frantic moment, her eyes flew to the window, through which she could see the comforting orange smudges that stood in two rows leading away to the mines. 'Stealing our gold!' she said, with more bravado than she felt. 'But our mines are extremely well protected. We have walls, we have towers!'

Shakuni wagged a finger at her with closed eyes. 'Not at the mines, sister, not at the mines.'

'Do you mean the treasury, then?'

'No, not the treasury either. But your people, my lady, do they have the same amount of gold that they did thirty years ago?'

'Yes,' she said, her courage returning. 'Of course, they do.'

'But they do not hold it with themselves, do they?'

'No, they do not. They keep it in our vaults.'

'*Our* vaults, my lady? Who runs the vaults?'

'The traders.'

'And where do the traders come from?'

Gandhari did not say the word out loud, but she knew that most of them came from Hastinapur. But that did not matter, she thought resolutely, for they lived in Gandhar, had families in Gandhar. Their children drank the milk of Gandhar's cows, they tilled Gandhar land, and they paid the king of Gandhar his due every year. How did it matter if they belonged to Hastinapur? They offered the wealthy people of Gandhar a way to protect their gold, and for that the people happily paid them what they deserved.

Now Shakuni had asked the question whether anyone had seen the gold. But then no one but she had seen the gold in the king's treasury, either; that did not mean that it did not exist. He was wrong, of course, she thought, watching his grotesquely bent body and wincing as another pang of guilt shot through her. But he had told the story in such a persuasive manner; how, indeed, did Hastinapur become so wealthy in such a short time? How had they come to be so feared? How had they built an army of such strength that king after king had begun to aspire to be allied to them?

Shakuni was probably wrong, but it would not hurt to check the vaults. She saw a smile spread on her brother's face, and she knew that he knew he had made her think. If Gandhar was destined to survive in his hands, she had no doubt that it would be only on the strength of his mind.

'Summon the vault-keeper tomorrow,' she said.

The vault-keeper came skipping into her room, wearing a white turban that was almost as big as his head. He had a book tucked under his arm, and all his fingers had rings of either gold or silver.

He stood a few feet away from her chair, hands joined and back bent so low that she could see the black spot on the back of the man's neck.

'Enough, Satyapala,' she said. 'Take your seat.'

'I have brought with me all the books that I have shown you yesterday, my lady,' said Satyapala, in his deep, rich voice. 'I shall go over the numbers with you once again.'

Gandhari did not stop him.

'The wealth of your citizens has increased this year, Your Highness. If last year, your average citizen was worth four hundred copper coins each, this year he is worth six hundred copper coins each.'

Gandhari said, 'And each copper coin has a gold coin in your vault, does it not?'

'Oh, yes,' said Satyapala, 'yes, yes. The tributes from Hastinapur are making your citizens truly wealthy, my lady. I often wish that I were born in Gandhar, that I had not had to see the years of poverty that I had seen in Hastinapur.'

'That reminds me, Satyapala,' said Gandari, 'why did you leave Hastinapur and come to Gandhar?'

'Ah, Your Majesty, what shall I say of the tales that visitors to Gandhar told us back in Hastinapur? Fruit bearers, grain traders, merchants, all of them would come to Gandhar and they would be bound by its spell. "How does one go to Gandhar and live there forever?" I ask them, and they tell me that I ought to become a vault-keeper.'

'So you were not a vault-keeper when you were in Hastinapur?'

Satyapala shook his head. 'No, my lady, I was but a fisherman.' His face grew suddenly sad. 'Even though Her Majesty Satyavati has done all she could for our settlements, we are still looked at with scowls back there. Not like here, where people respect us, Your Highness.'

Gandhari recalled the first time her father had told her about the treaty between Hastinapur and Gandhar: Hastinapur would provide everything that Gandhar needed, and the price would be set by Gandhar. After trade had continued for ten years or so, the vault-keepers had come, some of them fishermen like Satyapala, some blacksmiths, and they fashioned large boxes of iron in which the gold could be kept safe from thieves. They issued a copper coin for each gold coin in storage, and soon, the people of Gandhar began to exchange copper coins with one another. All trade with Hastinapur, though, remained in gold because traders from Hastinapur did not accept copper.

Now that she thought about it, it was an odd practice all right. If copper coins were just as good as gold coins, as the vault-keepers told the citizens, then certainly they ought to be good enough for the traders from Hastinapur. But they somehow were not. Every time a merchant from Hastinapur sold his wares in Gandhar, he stopped by at the royal treasury on his way back to exchange all his copper for gold. When the same wares were sold to Hastinapur's traders, though, they were happy to give and accept copper coins.

Satyapala was still speaking about this or the other, and Gandhari waved her arm at the girl at the door, who let Shakuni in. On seeing him Satyapala stiffened a little, and he seemed to mutter something under his breath. Once Shakuni approached them, though, he got to his feet and bowed to him in the same elaborate manner he had bowed to her.

'These books of yours,' said Shakuni, 'I am not interested in them, Satyapala, and neither is the queen. It is her decree that you must show her the gold that is in your vaults.'

'The gold, sire?' asked Satyapala.

'Yes, the gold that your books say is locked up in your vaults.'

Satyapala turned to Gandhari. 'Do you wish to see the gold in all of Gandhar's vaults, Your Majesty?'

'No,' said Shakuni, interrupting, 'perhaps just the main vault for now.'

'Right away?' Satyapala glanced at the sand glass on the window sill. 'It is rather late, the hour of robbery and ruin.'

'Then we leave early on the morrow. I shall have the carriage ready for the three of us.'

Satyapala said, 'As you wish, sire. If I can take your leave then … I shall go to the vault and make preparations for your visit.'

Shakuni grinned at him. 'But it is the hour of robbery and ruin, as you said. You shall spend the night here, at the palace, and my guards will watch you, so if you even think of leaving or sending a message…'

'That is enough,' Gandhari snapped. 'Satyapala is our guest for the night. Let us treat him as one.' She clapped her hands twice, and two waiting-women arrived with their heads bowed. 'Take him to the guest room, and wait on him all night.'

Amid all this, Gandhari saw that the vault-keeper's eyes were moving from side to side, and even when he spoke his smooth voice had cracked. But then he saw her catching his gaze, and he smiled broadly at her and bowed. Rising from his seat, he pottered out of the room behind the girls.

THREE

Very few lived in Gandhar now who still remembered the battle cries that had come from the edge of Kamyaka forty years ago. But every child born on the land could fully narrate the story by the time he attained the age of five. Gandhari first heard it from the lips of her father one long winter night when she was a girl of three, and that one time had been enough for the tale to sear itself into her mind. If she ever wanted to recall it, all she had to do was to close her eyes and it would appear in front of her, as though she had stood in the ankle-deep frozen marshes and watched the diamond-tipped lances crash into bronze shields.

The first challenge was thrown by the king of Hastinapur, and though Gandhar was reluctant at first, she got goaded out into the open, beyond her walls. The Kuru forces had hundreds of archers in them, good archers, and they revelled at fighting over flatlands. Gandhar's battle strategy was to draw them out to the edge of the forest and into the marshlands, in which their archers would sink their feet and not find stable footing. Though that also impeded Gandhar's horses and elephants from moving freely, if Kuru's archers could be blunted, half the battle was won.

The first two days were quiet inside the walls of the city, for men in armour left in droves and none returned. Once every hour or so a trumpet or a neigh would pierce the air and reach them,

255

sending men to ploughs and spades, for they were convinced that
Gandhar would lose and would need to be defended by citizens.
But a never-ending stream of horses and elephants left the stables
and barracks that lined the eastern wall of the city, and the mines
stayed open throughout the night. Bowmen were imported from
Kamboja for gold, and they were deployed on the inside of the
city with their arrows set to shoot.

But the fears of the city were never realized. On the third day
they heard a cacophony of conches and yells, and they knew that
either the battle had been won or Hastinapur had found a way to
kill their whole army with one blow. If they had been able to see
the wetland of Kamyaka, they would have known that the Kuru
forces did kill their whole first army – sixty elephants, eighty-
four cavalrymen and seventy footmen – but the reinforcements
had held the enemy at bay. Once the Kuru archers were killed,
the second batch came only the morning after, and during that
night, without the cushion of raining arrows from behind them,
their cavalry was no match for Gandhar's.

No one knew why Kuru's reinforcements were late in
arriving. Some said the great distance and the rocky terrain
made their travel difficult, but they knew it before they began
the battle. They would have planned for that. Others said that
they did not have the ability to train units at the mindless speed
that Gandhar could, thanks to her ever swarming goldmine.
No matter what the reason, by the time Hastinapur's archers
reached Kamyaka, all they saw was green marsh turned red with
the blood of their kinsmen. Hooves and trunks of fallen animals
were visible in the sludge, along with twisted limbs, gashed
throats and gouged eyes.

It was said that the then general of the Gandhar army, the
legendary Idobhargava, then trotted up to the head of the army,
looked at the small group of archers that stood glancing at one
another, and said with his sword drawn and helmet raised, 'You
may run back to your hell. We shall not give chase.'

And as they turned back to flee, the horses behind the general stood up on their hind legs to pound the wet earth, and the elephants raised their trunks to the sky. It was this cry of victory that the citizens heard back in the city.

In the years that came afterward, men and women wondered why the general had called his forces back when the upper hand was surely with him. Some said that the general was a man given to moments of pity on the battlefield, others said that if Gandhar's forces had gone up to Hastinapur's walls, they would have faced the same predicament that the archers did, and reinforcements would have had to travel all the two hundred miles of rocky terrain and get to the fighting area, whereas Hastinapur's army would have the increased advantage of their towers, which would make their archers invincible. Fighting in the marshes of Kamyaka under the cloak of darkness was not the same as laying siege to a heavily walled city.

But if Idobhargava had pity on the Kuru people, he did not show any, for that very day, upon his return to Gandhar, he sent by the city's swiftest messengers a summons for Pratipa, the old king of Hastinapur, with a threat that if Hastinapur failed to give Gandhar the battle tribute that he demanded, he would descend upon it with the might of a thousand elephants. When he spoke to the gathering of people at the town centre that afternoon, his right arm still bleeding from a searing wound, he spoke not of battle strategy or of war, but of the mines. In the fight between the wealthy and the strong, he said, the victors are always the wealthy.

Gandhar would never forget those words.

The camel caravans started arriving a month after the battle, carrying anything that could be eaten – but not grown – in Gandhar. Every month Hastinapur gave two thousand *tulas* of rice, wheat and pulses in tribute, in addition to basketfuls of apples that grew in abundance on their fertile lands. In the first few weeks Idobhargava would wait at the gates for the caravans, his arm in a sling, and he would personally see to the weighing and the counting. On their return he would keep two of the camels, though what he did with them no one ever knew.

But with time, the caravans began bringing in what the traders called items of value – tiny ivory statues of pretty princesses with their ponies, teak cots whose legs you could fold and rest against the wall, drawings in various colours on tough camel hide, coins from far off kingdoms with engravings no one could read, and other such goods for which the miners of Gandhar paid hefty sums. This practice began at first under disguise, but when the traders saw that Idobhargava himself began to enquire about this marble box or that velvet stole, they came out into the open, and it soon resulted in the formation of the first trade route between both kingdoms.

Soon, the number of camels that came to Gandhar every month from Hastinapur increased almost ten-fold. If twenty camels came from Hastinapur, it was now understood that no more than two would carry tributes. The others went straight to the town hall and set up their stalls, and they sold their wares not only to the wealthy, but also to non-miners. Agriculture in Gandhar had always been difficult; it wasn't easy to coax green shoots out of rock, and here were Hastinapur's farmers, selling succulent apples and ripe corn for almost nothing. If farming had been a fool's occupation in Gandhar before Hastinapur arrived, it died a beggar's death soon after. Now, a mere forty years after the battle of Kamyaka, there was not one farmer left in the kingdom.

Hastinapur did not replace just the farmers. Before the tributes began, Gandhar had been the home of cotton. Kingdoms further to the northwest, where the sun was harsh and the monsoons light, would come to Gandhar and buy their fine gowns and tunics. But once camels from Hastinapur came bearing bales of the soft fabric they called silk, and once they began to sell each silk tunic at half the price of a cotton shawl, tailors began to coach their sons to become miners instead.

The same could be said of carpenters. The teak of Gandhar was soft and soggy, and lent itself to delicate structures with curves and steep angles. Hastinapur's was tough and durable, and as a demonstration, her carpenters would set up stalls in the town hall and challenge anyone willing to try and break one of their cots or chairs with his bare hands. Men who twisted Gandhar's furniture into grotesque shapes could not so much as move Hastinapur's. After a few years of this, carpenters in the city took to creating tiny artistic pieces designed to hold candles.

But all of this did not matter as much as the arrival of the vault-keepers – or as some in Gandhar called them by their later name – the lenders. Nobody seemed to remember when they first came to the city, but most people agreed that it was around the time of Igobhargava's death. They came not on camels but on elephants, and they came not bearing light wads of silken clothes but giant metal enclosures with heavy doors. When they set up their stall in the town hall, one of the miners went to him and asked what their contraption did. 'Nothing,' said the vault-keeper, 'except that it allows you to sleep well at night.'

For the people of Gandhar, among whom everyone owned gold, it was the first brush with fear of loss. Before the vault-keepers arrived, no one had told them that their gold could get stolen, and once they were told of the danger they were in, it refused to go away from their minds. All vaults, naturally, were sold out in no time.

For each coin the keeper put into his vault, he gave out a copper coin which he called a 'token', and in no more than a month, all of Gandhar's gold was in his vaults, and the people who owned the gold had copper coins in their hands.

Soon the people of Gandhar began exchanging the copper coins because all of them knew that the gold was safely held within the vaults, and when the king – Gandhari's father – stepped in and made copper coins the legal tender and decreed that all gold vaults would be kept under the supervision of the king, the tokens issued by the vault-keeper became the money in which Gandhar traded.

The vault-keepers charged a tiny fee for storing the people's gold, and they were paid in copper coins. Whenever they left for Hastinapur they would stop by at the royal treasury and change their copper coins for gold. The traders, too, did business with Gandhar in copper, but everyone knew that each copper coin really stood for a gold coin; so on their way out of the city, the traders would stop at the treasury and exchange their copper coins for gold.

From that day to this, the vault-keepers would come and go, but the vaults would sit in their huts, locked up and filled with Gandhar's gold.

But now Shakuni had seeded the doubt in her mind: *was the gold still there?* Gandhari shifted in the chariot as it rattled along on the rocks with the mine fires flickering in the distance to her right. The morning breeze brought with it remnants of rain in the faraway basin of the Sindhu river. We have a great river of our own, she mused; why do we not use her water to till our own lands? Why do we allow ourselves to be at the mercy of these barbarians?

To her side Satyapala was nodding off to sleep under his heavy white turban, and opposite her, on the hard wooden seat at the base of the chariot meant for the charioteer's companion, sat Shakuni, bent to one side and rubbing his palms together. When they passed an occasional street fire, the ruby in his ring gleamed with an orange light.

The sky had not yet turned grey with the first light of morning, and as they passed the town square she saw milkmen look up sleepily from lugging their brown jars of milk in the dust. If nothing else, Gandhar had once been the city of cattle; people used to say that for each man in Gandhar, there were six cows and bulls – but now even those numbers were dwindling. Milk was milk, whether one extracted it in Gandhar or in Hastinapur. How, then, did their milkmen drive ours out of work?

Shakuni's face was set in a smile, and his eyes danced from her to the bent, sleeping head of Satyapala. 'I have made you think, sister,' he said, in a voice just above a whisper.

'You have filled me with slander and lies!' she said. 'I cannot believe I have let you talk me into digging for our own gold when our citizens are rolling in wealth.'

'Rolling in wealth, sister? Wherever did you hear that?'

'Devapi told me today.'

Shakuni lifted his head and laughed. 'Devapi, the idiot! I have stopped wondering why you surround yourself with such asses, my dear. The only advisor of yours that has been blessed by a brain is Chyavatana.'

'You would say that. I have seen how well he licks your feet.'

Shakuni grimaced at first, but then looked down at his feet. He leaned back and held one of them up for her. 'Then pray tell me,' he said, 'why my shoe is so dirty and yours so clean.'

The chariot sped away toward the eastern gate of the city, where the main vault of the people's treasury was kept. The smooth stone road had given way to loose dust and mud now, and Gandhari made a mental note to herself to order this road to be mended. Satyapala muttered something in his sleep when the chariot began to sway, but soon he fell in with the rhythm and resumed snoring.

'You say your citizens are wealthier,' said Shakuni, leaning in and grabbing her arm. 'Devapi must have told you how many more copper coins your citizens have this year compared to last.'

She tried to pull away from him, but he held firm. 'Yes, he did.'

'But what do they own, sister? What do your citizens own? Do they own their lands? They do not. Do they own cattle?

They do not. Do they own any skill with which they could make something someone else would want? They do not!'

'They own their lands, of course they do!'

Shakuni spat into the wind and smiled viciously at her. 'The vault-keepers bring copper coins from Hastinapur, my lady, and they use them to conduct trade in this country. Why do you think the price of milk is going up as it is? Why do you think your citizens have more copper coins with them than ever before? Ha! Wealth!'

'Yes!' she said. 'Each copper coin is equivalent to a gold coin, as per the decree of our father's law.'

'Sister, my lady, Your Majesty, for one second, will you please think? One copper coin can never be the same as a gold coin. A copper coin is made of copper, by the gods, and a gold coin is made of gold!'

'Oh, come off it, you know well enough that if the number of copper coins is the same as—'

'If, sister, if! Your own Adbudha must have told you that we have mined the same amount of gold this year as last?'

She nodded.

'Then how did the number of copper coins go up? Where is all the copper coming from?'

Gandhari felt her head swim, as it did whenever she let Shakuni speak to her at length. For him everything was a conspiracy, every man a traitor. She closed her eyes and let the wind hit her face for a few moments, and the smell of faraway rain made her smile. She opened her eyes and asked, 'You tell me, where is the copper coming from?'

'They bring it,' he said in subdued voice, nodding at Satyapala. 'To what end?'

'So that each person in Gandhar has more copper coins today than he did yesterday. Then they can price their Hastinapur goods higher, and on their way back they collect gold for their copper.' He bared his teeth in an expression of disgust. 'We have been giving them gold for copper, Your Majesty, for thirty years, one coin for one coin.'

'I do not believe you.'

'You do not have to believe me, my lady. Just look around you. Your own advisers have told you that the amount of copper in Gandhar has gone up, and year after year we send more and more miners into our mines, for the *same* amount of gold. Why?'

Gandhari looked about her. 'Because it is harder to find gold.'

Shakuni slapped his thigh. 'Because we give all the excess gold away to them!'

'But ... but we keep our gold ... our vaults ...'

'That we shall see soon enough,' said Shakuni, sitting back and hoisting his bad leg over his knee. He began to wave his foot with ardour. 'We shall see soon enough.'

FOUR

Upon Gandhari and Shakuni's approach to the front door of the vault, the guards, who had been leaning on their spears, sprang to attention and clicked their knees together. Satyapala waved to the soldiers with his seal on his palm, and behind them, Gandhari held up her ring and Shakuni his bracelet. The guards stayed unmoved.

Once inside, Shakuni asked, 'You have so much gold and only two guards guarding it?'

'Ah,' said Satyapala, laughing. 'The people of Gandhar are good people, sire. There are very few thieves in the kingdom.'

Shakuni looked at Gandhari, and she immediately understood what he meant. *If there were few thieves in the kingdom, what need was there of these vaults?*

Satyapala slid behind a large table and dragged toward himself a book whose leaves crackled as he thumbed through it. On it were numbers and figures of coins. Gandhari narrowed her eyes so that she could see better in the light of the candle. But she was reading it upside down, so after a while she gave up. Shakuni, on the other hand, had gone over to Satyapala's side and was peering over his shoulder.

'Ah, yes, here we are. My lady, if you please.' He turned the book around and pointed at the last row of words on the page. 'The current amount of gold in this vault is seven thousand coins, and the current number of copper coins issued on their behalf, as you will see here, is the same: seven thousand.'

Shakuni muttered, 'You could make words on a page say anything you wish.'

Satyapala laughed good-naturedly. 'That is true indeed, sire. Shall we go then to inspect the vault?'

He picked up a bunch of shiny metal rods hanging off a nail on the wall. Adjusting his turban with one hand and depositing the rods into his pocket, he gestured to them and ambled in through an inner door. 'We keep the vault locked inside three doors, the keys to which are always with me and only me. Please mind your head, my lady, the ceiling of this building hangs rather low.' He reached for one of his rods and applied it to the hole of the door that faced them. After a little tinkering and groaning, the latch opened with a snap and it creaked open. Satyapala pushed it with his arm and waved them in.

'After you,' said Shakuni suspiciously.

Shrugging, the vault-keeper entered with the fire and lighted two fire-stands to his right, bathing the room in dull orange light. 'You must forgive my enthusiasm, my lord, my lady,' he said. 'No one ever comes here wishing to examine their gold. You are the first visitors the vault has had in four years.'

By the time Shakuni entered and opened the door for Gandhari, Satyapala had already lit two more fires in the room. 'My lord and lady,' he said, 'see how carefully we store the gold that belongs to the people of Gandhar.'

Gandhari turned, and in the dim glow of the fire she saw sturdy, black shelves stacked upon one another, and in each one she saw a black silk sack tied at the mouth with a yellow rope. Satyapala stepped over and retrieved the one in the first compartment. The contents jingled when he moved it, and when he placed it in her palm and untied the knot, she saw a gleam that left no more doubt in her mind.

It was gold.

Shakuni drew a quick breath and slunk back against the wall. For a moment Gandhari saw his face darken against the dancing light of the torch he carried, and a pall came over his eyes as he regarded the sack in her hand. She held it out to him, hoping to push him back further, and he began to step away, but something caught his eye and he looked at Satyapala. Then his eyes sprang to life, and he lunged forward and grabbed the vault-keeper by the arm.

'Which is the closest vault to this?'

'The closest vault, sire? You wish to inspect another vault?'

'Not I, Satyapala, you shall come with us. Tell us where it is, by the gods, or I shall slit your throat right here!'

'Enough, Shakuni!' said Gandhari stepping forward and letting the sack of coins drop to the dusty ground. 'You shall not manhandle any of my men, and you shall not threaten a man who has proven you wrong quite emphatically.'

Shakuni did not seem to hear her. His vicious gaze was set upon Satyapala, whose knees had given way and was now kneeling against the prince, hands joined, forehead and cheeks bathed in sweat. 'It is by the north-eastern wall, my lord,' he stammered, 'by the statue of Idobhargava.'

Shakuni let him slump down to the ground and hopped off. 'We shall go there immediately and inspect the vaults there.'

'What if they too are full of gold?' asked Gandhari.

'Then we shall inspect every vault in the city!' Shakuni turned and pointed the sword at Satyapala's throat. 'Lock the door securely and come with us. Not a word comes out of you, man, or you shall see how sharp the blade of my sword is.'

Satyapala joined his hands once again, and glanced at Gandhari as he spoke. 'Lock just this door, sire? What about the ones inside?'

'Just this one for now. Time presses. Let us leave. You shall tell the charioteer only the directions to the place and nothing more.'

'Y-yes, my lord.'

The man jogged to the front door, pulled it shut, locked it and threw the bunch of keys into his knapsack. On their way out the guards snapped up to their feet again and saluted. They reached the chariot and Shakuni knocked three times against the edge of the carriage. A scrambling sound came from inside, and the door opened. The charioteer came out, mumbling and putting on his turban. He made the seats with two or three slaps of his wrists, and jumped out, bowing to the queen and prince. He pointed to the open door. 'Where shall we go, Your Majesty?' he asked.

Satyapala replied, 'To the north-eastern wall, Idobhargava's statue.'

They seated Satyapala in the same seat, but Gandhari and Shakuni exchanged theirs. Shakuni kept his sword drawn, and every now and then he would run his thumb along its edge, looking up to make sure that Satyapala was watching. He tapped his bad leg incessantly against the floor of the carriage, in tune to the sound of the horses' hooves. He shook his head at her.

'Foolish that we are, we told him last night that we would come here this morning. It gave him the whole morning to prepare his vault.' He turned to Satyapala. 'How did you send the message to your goons, eh? Do you have a little carrier pigeon that flies for you?'

Satyapala pushed himself into the corner, as far as he could get away from the sword. 'Please do not kill me, I have a wife and a daughter who is six months old.'

Gandhari said, 'Do not fear, Satyapala. He shall not kill you. You have my word.'

Shakuni moved closer to the vault-keeper. 'She has given you her word, but do remember that hers is not the hand that holds the sword. If we do not see the gold in your other vaults, I promise you that her word shall be of no use to you.'

'Hastinapur will not be pleased with the way you are treating me,' said Satyapala 'It is written in the treaty that Her

Majesty should give vault-keepers at least a week's notice before conducting an inspection of this nature.'

'Ah, now we begin speaking of rules, do we?' Shakuni said. 'The gold belongs to us, Satyapala. Do you understand? It is our gold. Why shall we seek your permission to see our gold?'

'Because our vaults hold it, and we take care of it. It is all in the treaty.' He looked beseechingly at Gandhari, as though pleading with her to make Shakuni take away the sword that he was pointing at him. 'This ... this is quite irregular, all of this, this sudden inspection, and this sudden threat to my life ...'

'Irregular, you say?'

'Quite.' He adjusted his turban with trembling hands. 'If I complain to the authorities at Hastinapur, they shall be most displeased. If anything were to happen to me ...'

'You shall complain.'

'I ... I shall ... if you use that sword!'

Shakuni scratched himself on his cheek and shook his head. With a smile, he said, 'If I use this sword, my man, you shall not be able to complain to anyone. I shall cut you into pieces and feed you to the dogs that sleep at the foot of Idobhargava's statue. Whom will you complain to, then?'

'Enough, Shakuni!' Gandhari said. 'I shall not let him kill you, Satyapala, but you shall do well to learn what not to say when staring at the tip of a sword. If you sit in the corner with your tail hidden between your legs, I shall see to it that my brother does not hurt you.'

Shakuni laughed. Satyapala raised his knees and hugged them tight. His turban bent to one side and revealed balding scalp. To his immense relief, Shakuni now returned his sword into its sheath. He moved to the other corner of the carriage and folded his hands. His bad leg went over the other. He had none of the panache that a king ought to have, none of the elegance. He did not have the ability to fight wars and win them, everyone could see that, but if only he could compensate for that loss by other gifts. Would the people of Gandhar ever unite behind this man?

He picked his teeth with his fingernail and examined it for a moment before flicking it away.

Most decidedly not, she thought.

The statue of Idobhargava had been erected twenty years back, soon after the death of the general. He had died an old, frail man, and people who saw him in his last days spoke of how he had shrunken to half his size, how his voice had become a hoarse whisper, how his teeth had all fallen off and how his skin had become hard and spotty, like that of a garden lizard. But the statue that went up after his death was a younger Idobhargava, the one that led Gandhar's army to victory at the battle of Kamyaka. Though he had been a spearman, he brandished a sword here, and though he had often ridden elephants, here he sat atop a horse with a luscious mane, in full gallop.

The chariot's horses neighed in protest, the whip lashed, and the carriage ground to a halt. The guards at the main gate cautiously set their spears to stop them from entering, but in their faces she could see uncertainty. They looked at her cloak, at his tunic, at their shoes, and their arms faltered a little. When Gandhari held out her hand so that they could see her ring, they fell to their knees, laid their spears down, and pressed their palms to their chest.

With a nod they entered, and at the main table sat a man dressed much like Satyapala, except this man was taller and thinner. He looked up from his book as they walked in and got up to his feet. 'What is the meaning of this?' he said. 'Guards!'

Shakuni displayed his seal. The man looked at it, but his manner did not change. 'You cannot come in here no matter who you are, sir.' He peeked around them at the just entering figure of Satyapala. 'Why have you brought them here, vault-keeper?'

'They … wish to inspect the gold you have in your vault.'

'That, I am afraid, is quite, quite impossible.'

Shakuni reached for his sword and drew it half-way. 'I should say it is quite possible if you have the keys to the door.'

'It is quite, quite *irregular*, this … this … attack on the vault.'

'That word, sir,' said Shakuni with bared teeth, turning to Satyapala, 'is beginning to grate.'

Gandhari clapped her hands twice, and it brought the guards into the room. They stood with their spears held to their sides, their heads bowed. 'If you do not obey us, vault-keeper, I am afraid these guards will hold you down while we get to work.'

'This … this is an outrage!' said the man, standing up on tiptoe. Gandhari looked up at him. He was quite easily a foot taller than she was, but he looked weak, as though a strong breeze would blow him away. 'If I were to complain to the authorities in Hastinapur about this …'

'I suppose,' said Shakuni, stepping up to the table, 'that they will be very displeased.'

'Yes … yes indeed!'

'Then let them be, for god's sake!' He turned to the guards. 'Hold these two men in custody until we return.' Turning to the vault-keeper, he said, 'Give me your keys.' When the man did not reply, Shakuni said, 'Give me your keys or I will strip you off all clothes and get them anyway.' The man then saw reason.

Snatching a torch from the wall, Shakuni led her first through the dusty low-hanging room, then the room full of brass collectibles, and then finally into the room with the gold. It was built exactly as the other one, with shelves on the right holding heavy black sacks tied at the mouth with yellow ropes. Shakuni lit the two fires in the room, and went closer to the shelves, picking up one sack and examining its weight on his palm.

'Well?' asked Gandhari, though the jingle that came to her sounded nothing like gold.

Shakuni gave the torch to her to hold, and opening the knot and tossing the rope away, reached into the sack and brought out a handful of coins. She bent in, so that she could see them better in the feeble light. They were black, these coins, and they left dark spots on Shakuni's hands where he touched them.

'This is not gold,' said Shakuni, looking into her eyes. 'This is copper.'

FIVE

White morning light entered through the open eastern windows, and threw on the opposite wall shadows of the insect screens. Gandhari looked back over her shoulders and instructed one of her waiting-girls to raise them. As much as she liked them during the rains, keeping them drawn on days like this made her feel as though she were imprisoned.

Shakuni followed her into the room. The door closed behind them, and taking the edge of her cloak in her hands, she walked to her seat – the same one on which she had met the ministers the night before – and dusted it with her bare hands before sitting down. A wave of the hand brought an attendant bearing apples and two pitchers of milk; another wave and he was gone, out of sight. Shakuni paced the room with his arms tucked behind his back. Gandhari waited for him to wear himself out. Speaking to him when he was this angry would be unfruitful.

He had been right, about everything. They had not inspected the other vaults in the city, and she had sent soldiers off to do so as soon as they had arrived at the palace, but that was mere formality. She knew that they would find nothing but copper in all of them. Only the main vault had kept the required amount of gold; they would have known that an investigation could occur at any time, and this had been their contingency. If Shakuni's suspicions had not been deep enough, they would never have set out in search of the other vault, by the foot of Idbhargava's statue.

They had dared to loot them under his very gaze. She tried to think what he would do if he had been the person to uncover this. Would he summon his elephant and call for battle straight away? But this time it would be different. Gandhar could not be content with defending herself; now she had to go forth and retrieve her gold.

How much of it had there been? Each vault would hold eight thousand *tulas* at the least, and there were seven such vaults. That meant – that meant all the gold that Gandhar had ever mined. Sure, there were a few hundreds, perhaps a thousand, *tulas* in the royal treasury, but that counted for nothing compared to the amount that was missing. How had they taken it all without the guards ever suspecting? What was now left of Gandhar? Devapi's voice rang in her ear, and he was saying that the citizens of Gandhar were getting richer and richer; yes, perhaps they were, if wealth were measured in copper coins.

Sure enough, Shakuni came to his chair and sat down. He buried his fingers in his hair and stared at the floor. 'Well?' he said.

'Well?'

'When do we announce the imprisonment and execution of all the vault-keepers?'

'You are certain, then, that we must hang them all?'

Shakuni slapped his thigh. 'By the gods! I shall not like it if we hang them. I shall have them whipped to death. Their cries must travel all the way to Hastinapur, and they must bring their king running to us.'

'He does come running to us. Then what do we do?'

'Then we fight him, and we take back our gold!'

'Do you suppose he shall just hand it to us if we ask for it nicely?'

'He will not. He will fight for it, as he should. We do not have any time to think, sister – we must act!'

'For you, to act means just one thing, Shakuni, and that is to draw your sword and go threatening people that you will slit their throats. Now vault-keepers may fear you and that thing you wear around your waist, but real warriors will not.' She set aside her glass of milk on the table and felt anger rush through her, in waves. 'What has Gandhar got, now? Do we have an army big enough to fight Hastinapur? Do we have the means to raise an army?'

'We still have the mine.'

'A mine that produces seven hundred *tulas* of gold in a year. Hastinapur has taken a hundred times that from us in the last twenty years.'

Shakuni slipped forward in his seat and looked at her. 'We have beaten them once, my lady. We can beat them again.'

'What do you think Hastinapur has been doing with our gold these last twenty years, Shakuni? Do you believe their army is the same size as it was all those years ago, when Idobhargava met them on Kamyaka's wetlands?' His face fell, and she softened against her wishes. After all, it was he who uncovered this. 'I do not wish to yell at you, brother, but today we do not have the means to fight Hastinapur and win.'

His eyes flashed defiance. 'We shall not know until we try.'

Gandhari kept her voice soft. 'But what will it do to our own people, Shakuni? If we are to hang the vault-keepers in the town hall, what do you think will happen to the people of Gandhar? They will all wonder where their gold went. They will all wish to see their gold, like we did, and what will happen when we tell them that their gold is all lost?'

He did not say anything, but she saw a glimmer of understanding in his eyes.

'They will turn against us, my boy,' she said. 'They will come and set fire to the palace. They will loot our treasury, and each man will kill his neighbour for his share of the gold. And what do you think will happen when it is all done? Hastinapur will march right into our city and set up their throne in the palace. They will not even have to fight. Do you not see that?'

Shakuni's mouth settled into a grump. 'Then what is to be done?'

Gandhari sighed. 'Nothing. For all that we have lost, we still have one thing that is very precious. The people of Gandhar believe that their gold is in the vaults. As long as that belief stands, brother, they shall not come for their gold. They will hold their copper coins and think that they hold gold – for them, one copper coin equals to one in gold.'

'I find your suggestion preposterous, dear sister!' said Shakuni. 'They have looted all the gold out of our kingdom and you propose to do *nothing*?'

'At least for now. The vault-keepers will report to the king of Hastinapur presently that we have come and seen the vaults. Very soon, the king of Hastinapur will know that we know our gold is no longer with us. I think he will pay us a visit, then.'

'A visit?' said Shakuni, his voice quivering in fury. 'And are we to receive him as a guest?'

'Indeed. What choice do we have?' Gandhari sat back and crossed her legs. She picked up a sliced apple from her plate and bit into it, looking up at the painted figures on the ceiling. 'How strange it is to *know*, Shakuni,' she said wonderingly. 'Yesterday we were the wealthiest Kingdom in North Country, and Hastinapur was but a vassal. Nothing has changed from yesterday to today, except our knowledge of the truth.' She chewed on the piece fully, and swallowed it. 'Nothing has changed, and yet everything has changed. In one day we have become Hastinapur's slaves.'

When Gandhari first saw Bhishma, she admitted to herself a tiny jolt of surprise. She had heard tales regarding the foremost warrior of North Country, and she had expected him to be burly with arms the size of tree trunks, but here was a man who would – if his beard were shaved and if he were decked suitably – pass for a woman. The only marks of combat he wore were on his wrists in the form of pink straight lines. She recalled that Hastinapur was the land of archers who could shoot of either foot and either arm with equal skill. This man, they said, wielded the mace and hurled the spear too, but she could not picture him with those weapons. He had a small face and an easy, boyish smile. He walked lightly upon the carpet of rose petals that had been spread for him, and every few seconds he would brush off the white jasmines that would get stuck in his hair. He wore his hair long, right down to his shoulders. Gandhari suddenly realized that this man was almost thirty years older than she was, and yet he looked to be no more than a youth of twenty one.

She had asked the waiting-women to lead him straight to her chambers after he had freshened up, for the things she wished to speak to him had no place in an open court. She had Shakuni with her, of course, standing by her side, welcoming him, and on his side stood Chyavatana with his arms crossed in front of his mountain-like chest.

When Bhishma sat down in his seat, he bowed to Gandhari, and she found herself smiling and returning his bow. After all four of them were seated, she clapped her hands, emptying the room of attendants. 'I trust you have eaten well, my lord,' she said. 'I have asked for goats from the mountains to be brought down just for your feasting.'

He nodded, with a hint of a smile upon his lips. 'I did, indeed, like it very much, Your Highness. I have brought from Hastinapur some very fine gold and jewels.' His eyes danced to Shakuni and back. 'I am given to believe that the town of Gandhar could use some gold.'

She was shaken out of her admiration of him, and she was reminded of the true purpose of his visit. Her nostrils bristled, and her teeth dug into her lips. 'Why, sir, you certainly are generous to give back part of what you have stolen. Is that the pact of honour these days among thieves?'

He shrugged, and in one swift motion of his hands, untied the cloak and set it aside. She saw that his shoulders were stiff and lean, the shoulders of an archer. 'All of us are thieves, my lady. You steal gold from the bosom of Mother Earth, and we stole it from you.'

Beside her, Shakuni began to rise from his seat, and his hand went to the hilt of his sword, but she looked at Chyavatana, and he laid a heavy hand on the boy's shoulder. What had Shakuni thought, that Bhishma would come and repent for having stolen their gold? Of course he would crow, like victors did and should. One day, on the day of her victory over him and his city, she would crow too. Not today, though.

Bhishma's eyes followed Shakuni's arm, but his pose of relaxation did not change. He wore tough leather footwear that was black with dust from the rocks. When he shook his feet, it dropped onto the floor and powdered the rose petals. He bent toward her, his elbow resting on the armrest and his hand covering his mouth. 'I have come here not to fight, my lady, I am certain you know that.' He glanced about himself. 'I am not dressed for combat.'

'I would like nothing better than to have you killed, my lord,' she said, and saw his left eyebrow jump up, even as a smile spread on his lips. 'But I know that you hold all the strings today, and I must dance as you ask me to.'

'That is indeed true, but it need not be that way, my lady. I have come here not to fight you or to make you dance, but to ask for your hand in marriage to the royal house of Hastinapur.'

She began to laugh, because she was certain that Bhishma was jesting. But when his face remained calm, she stopped herself and turned to look at Shakuni. His face was twisted into the same knot of confusion. 'Did I hear you right, sire?' she said at length.

'You did, my lady, yes,' said Bhishma. 'I do not believe in fighting, because it kills people and it helps no one. We have looted your wealth without your knowledge, but you will admit that we have done so without harming a single person's life in Gandhar.'

'You have stolen the wealth of five generations in twenty years, my lord.'

'And if you agree to become queen of Hastinapur, that wealth shall be neither yours nor mine, but ours.'

'You have quite a cheek on you, sire, if I may say so, for first taking all that is ours and now asking for my hand – for the hand of the queen of Gandhar – in return.'

'Not in return,' said Bhishma. 'I shall not return your gold, but I shall take no more from it after you come to our house.'

She sat up in her seat. 'Does that strike you as a fair trade?'

Bhishma smiled and shrugged. 'There is no such thing as a fair trade, my lady. The battle of Kamyaka was not fair for the people of Hastinapur either.'

'But it was you who came to our gates, you who cast the first stone.'

'And we who lost the most men and the most wealth. It is not fair that we have to work for our gold, Your Highness, whereas you could dig it out of the ground and use it as money. Our milkmen, our merchants, our carpenters and weavers have to *work* to be paid in gold, and yet your men do nothing to get their share of gold. Is *that* fair?'

'We were blessed with the mines,' said Gandhari. 'You were not.'

'So you were. You were blessed with a mine, you did not earn it. And whatever you have not earned, can be stolen. Our scriptures say that, do they not?'

For one moment, Gandhari considered calling for the guards and ordering them to pin this man with spears. Oh, how sweet it would be to smack that smile off his face! How delightful it would be to stare into that angelic face after all life had been sucked out of it. She realized her hands were wound tight together, and her knuckles had gone pink with the marks of her fingertips. She counted up to five, and her anger withdrew, a little.

'I shall not argue with you about whether you are right or wrong,' she said. 'What matters is only that it is done, and what was once our gold is now yours.'

'That is so, yes,' he said, never once letting his gaze waver.

'I only ask you what you will do if I reject your offer of marriage.'

He looked away in the direction of the window, lips pursed, and then turned to her. 'I wish you do not, madam, for the good of Gandhar.'

'What are your terms if I do?'

'If you do not wish to be queen of Hastinapur, then I demand that the city of Gandhar pay Hastinapur four hundred and fifty *tulas* of gold every year as tribute from here on.' Shakuni got up to his feet and took two steps toward Bhishma, who considered him with a weary eye. 'Sit down, Prince. You do not wish to fight me.' Then, turning to Gandhari, he said, 'We shall make that five hundred *tulas*, just so you remember to teach your little brother how to behave.'

'And if I say no to that?' she asked tonelessly, though she knew what the answer would be.

Bhishma leaned back in his seat and laughed, his blue eyes lighting up. 'The only thing keeping Gandhar from revolt and unrest, my lady, is the belief of her people that her vaults are full of gold. But belief – it is such a weak string, is it not? So easy to cut.'

'I understand,' she said.

'Indeed you do,' he replied, and then his expression softened. 'It does not have to be this way, my lady. Let us not fight. Let us bury our past and move forward, together.'

'On my dead body!' said Shakuni, his hand still on the hilt of his sword, though he did not advance past the steps toward their guest.

Gandhari said, 'We shall pay the tribute you ask for, but I shall not become the queen of Hastinapur.'

Bhishma smiled and got to his feet. He clapped his hands to summon the attendants at the gate. When they came to him, he pointed to his cloak and they scampered to pick it up. 'If you show me to my chambers,' he said to the girls, 'I shall retire for the night.'

SIX

Gandhari buried her head in her pillow and wept. The attendants had drawn the insect screens on the windows, so the moonlight threw a chequered shadow on the wall. The silk curtains danced in the dry breeze that blew from across the mines. Darkness had descended upon the whole city, but in the distant northern corner, fires still burned at the entrance to the mines, and if she cocked her ears, she thought she could hear the thumps of spade against rock. She had never gone inside the mines; her father had said it was too dangerous for a maiden. Shakuni had been all but ten when he first visited the mines. She still remembered the envy with which she had burnt that day.

The mines meant everything to Gandhar. When they were first discovered – during her grandfather's reign – the first thing that the king had done was to order walls and towers to be erected all around them so that they could not be taken. The outer wall surrounding the city had been extended to encircle them, and every year from then to now, a few towers would be added to the cluster of defensive structures. Twice in the last seventy years had kingdoms from the north – Aswaka and Bahlika – come with catapults, but each time Gandhar's army had been strong enough to drive them away.

Even today, Gandhar's shrunken military strength would quite easily ward off any direct attacks on the mine. Even Hastinapur would not succeed in taking it, if she tried. They would have known that, of course. Why else would Bhishma ask for a tribute if he thought he could take the city? She did not believe in his righteous sermons about war, but she had to believe that Hastinapur could ill afford an all-out war at this time. It was much easier to hold the reins in his hand and demand tribute after tribute from them every month, threatening to let loose social unrest if she refused to comply.

She tried to narrow her eyes so that the brown smudges on the ceiling would become sharper. When her eyes began to hurt, she gave up with a sigh. What would Gandhar do with a blind queen and a lame king? Even with his limp, Shakuni compensated with quickness of mind. What had she done? If she had heeded his words, would they not have uncovered all this dirt much earlier? Her father had warned her on his deathbed that ruling a kingdom was not the job of a maiden. Marriage, valiant sons, beautiful daughters, managing the running of a household – that was what maidens did and must wish to do, not hold council with ministers and govern the state.

The offer of marriage had surprised her. Now that all of Gandhar's wealth belonged to Hastinapur, she had no doubt that Bhishma's kingdom was the foremost in North Country, perhaps even ahead of Panchala. So it would not be all bad if she accepted the proposal; she would then be queen, and her sons would rule the fertile lands between the two great rivers. Her father would have approved if she had said yes; it would have secured Gandhar's future too; if she married into the royal family of the Kurus, they would not think of destroying her maternal home.

Why had she said no, then? Yes, it was partly the anger at the realization that the thief had now become the master, but there had been something else too. While Gandhar's safety would be assured, it would never again achieve supremacy among the kingdoms of North Country. Gandhar would forever be second to Hastinapur if she said yes, for Bhishma would take over the mines and leave Gandhar just enough to keep her alive. It would assure Hastinapur of generations of untold wealth, whereas Gandhar would need to be content with being secure.

But Gandhar had not yet lost all. They still had the mines and they were nowhere near empty, so if more miners could be employed from among the populace, they could mine more gold than they did now, and in spite of the tribute that they had to pay Hastinapur, they would still have enough left over. Perhaps over a few years they could amass enough gold to put Gandhar back on the path to wealth again.

That would mean pulling out men from the farms, from the cowsheds, from the looms, and from anywhere they could think of, and that would make all the other industries suffer. That would make them lean a bit more on Hastinapur, which would not do. What Gandhar needed was to move away from Hastinapur in trade, and yet produce enough gold to get wealthy *after* having paid the tribute. Right now, Gandhar depended on Hastinapur for everything – from milk and fruits to furniture. Bhishma had been right; what did Gandhar have for herself right now, apart from the mines?

Her eyes went back to the brown figures on the ceiling that looked like bubbles mounted on each other. Back when she used to be a child, the images had been sharp; from memory she knew that there was an archer aiming at a cavalryman who held a lance in his raised arm. They had neither eyes nor ears, these figures, and often as a child her father would tell her that archers represented the bad men of Hastinapur while the cavalrymen stood for the noble warriors of Gandhar. The archers from the plains, fighting on foot, could never hope to oust an armoured man mounted upon a horse or an elephant, her father had said, and for that reason Hastinapur would never take Gandhar.

Her eyes welled up. Hastinapur *had* taken Gandhar, and they had done so without shooting an arrow.

Gandhari woke up in the morning in better spirits. She had had a dream that had left a pleasant sensation in her mind, and all through her bath and breakfast, she hummed to herself songs that her father used to put her to bed with during the old summer nights while servant girls stood on either side of her bed, fanning her with bird feathers.

She was almost done with breakfast when her waiting-girl came and announced the arrival of Bhishma. That surprised her – she had assumed that the prince would find a suitable time today to make a silent exit. Dabbing her mouth with linen, she waved at the girl to let him in. As she waited, a distant part of her cried out in hope that he would leave Gandhar alone. She would not even ask for the robbed gold if that were to happen, she realized suddenly; so desperate had she become.

She did not bother to stand when he arrived, in a white upper garment with his quiver of arrows fastened behind his right shoulder. Though these archers were proficient with both hands, they had a preference, clearly. She gave him a nod to take his seat, and he shook his head at her with a smile.

'I shall not stay long, Your Highness,' he said. 'I have a long day of riding ahead of me, and I must leave if I am to reach Hastinapur by nightfall.'

She took no pains to hide her distaste. 'I woke up today hoping that you had already left, my lord. What is it that brings you here?'

He hesitated. 'I … I could not but help think our council yesterday ended on a bad note, my lady. The presence of your brother, Prince Shakuni, did not help, if I may say so.'

'I do not recall Shakuni saying or doing anything yesterday that I did not approve of, sir, so I am afraid I do not quite know what you mean.'

'Perhaps it was me, then,' he said, shrugging. 'Perhaps I have been uncivil in my manner yesterday. The ride here was not smooth, and it was very long; perhaps we should have waited till this morning before we spoke.'

Gandhari said, 'If you still have the same offer for me, sir, my answer is still no.'

'Do think of it, Your Majesty. I know what you must think of me, but what I have done is no different to fighting. What I have engaged you in is a war of the mind, and you have lost. If all wars could be fought this way, without shedding any blood, would your citizens not be happy indeed?'

Her voice became angry without her knowledge. Her eyes smarted, and her fists closed into tiny balls. 'Do you not have shame, sir, for being born a Kshatriya and speaking of battles of the mind? If Hastinapur had waged war on Gandhar and if they had won our gold from us, I would have gladly given myself to you. But you play games of intrigue and deceit, and you seek to drape them as virtuous deeds. I shall not agree to them.'

Bhishma frowned, lowered his whispery voice even further. 'Of what use is a virtuous war when it kills thousands of people, my lady? And these games of intrigue and deceit, as you call them, have not shed a single drop of blood. I have taken your gold, yes, but you are welcome to try and take it back from me again.'

'If I ever do, I shall come with an army and raze Hastinapur to the ground,' Gandhari replied. Bhishma smiled at this, and it drove her mad with fury.

'Do not think I cannot, sir,' she said. 'I need not remind you of what happened during the battle of Kamyaka. Gandhar's men are filled with valour, and if I call them to lay down their lives for their land, they will not say no.'

'But why must anyone give their lives, my lady?' said Bhishma, springing up to his feet. 'Your biggest wealth is not the gold that I have stolen from you, Your Highness, it is the lives of your citizens. The gold that I took from you has no value; only human life has value. Do you not understand?'

'If that is so, Bhishma,' she said, spitting out his name, 'if it is true that the gold you have taken from me has no value, give it back to me. Why have you spent twenty years stealing something that has no value?'

He averted her eyes, and said in frustration: 'It is valuable because everyone thinks it is so. And now Hastinapur has become wealthy only because all the other kingdoms accept that gold is wealth. But why does it have to be so, my lady? We use it for *nothing*. We make coins out of it, and we hoard it in our vaults.' He shook his head, even as his eyes bored into her. 'That is not wealth.'

At once she felt a great weariness come over her. 'I do not have the strength to argue with you on matters such as these, my lord,' she said. 'I know what you will do if I marry the prince of Hastinapur. You will first take over the mine, and you will only pay Gandhar a pittance for using it.'

'But even if you do not marry the prince of Hastinapur, my lady, you will still give us all the gold that we need.'

'But the mine belongs to us!' She realized she was on her feet too, though she did not remember having stood up. 'We shall mine more gold than we give you, and slowly we will build our wealth back to where it was.'

'It will take you generations.'

'Generations of freedom, yes.'

'You call having to give tribute every month to Hastinapur freedom?'

'It is better than to give you the mine itself, sir, and you know that too.' His face was inscrutable, though, and when he shook his head she saw in him the same expression his father had so often used while talking to her. A wave of resentment lashed inside her, and she had to use all her restraint from picking up the cutting knife and hurling it at him.

'If you want to mine more than you do now,' he said, 'you have to rely more on Hastinapur for your food and clothes and furniture. You will be deeper in captivity if you do not accept my offer, my lady.'

'We shall take our chances.'

'But if you do become Hastinapur's queen, my lady,' he said, bowing to her for the first time since his arrival, 'the very earth you touch with your feet shall become golden. Gandhar and Kuru will be friends, and together they shall become the strongest ruling force in North Country. We can unite all of North Country, my lady, all of it!' When she did not reply, he took a step closer to her. 'You have heard of the legendary king Rama, have you not? In his time, all our kingdoms were one, and all the people in the land were happy. Should we not create that kingdom here again?'

She wavered, caught in the maze of his words. But he was just bluffing, she thought. If he had wanted Gandhar to be friends with Hastinapur, he would never have stolen their gold. He wanted to be friends, perhaps, but he also wanted Hastinapur to be ahead of Gandhar, and that she could not allow. All of this – his whole charade – was not about uniting North Country; it was about spreading the rule of Hastinapur to all of North Country.

'It is Gandhar and its future that interests me, Prince Bhishma,' she said coldly. 'Uniting all of North Country will not happen till the end of time.'

'It is in our hands now,' he said, his voice tinged with desperation. 'It is in *your* hands.'

'I do not want it!' she cried. 'All I want is for Gandhar to be prosperous, and all I know, sir, is that you have stolen our wealth! We shall do all in our power to get it back from you, and I promise you, that we shall not stoop to your level.'

For a full minute he did not speak. Gandhari heard her breath slow down, and her fingers uncoiled, leaving marks at the ends of her palm. 'Is that your final answer?' he asked.

'Yes.'

He nodded, and went down on one knee. 'Then I shall take your leave, my lady, and I shall await your tribute.' Without waiting for her to speak, he got up, turned and marched out of the room.

For a long time after he had left, the sound of his footsteps rang in her ear.

Chyavatana's moustache looked as though it had grown a little from the night of the meeting, though at the same time the impossibility of it struck her. It was probably just that he had begun the day by drenching it in oil and combing it with his ivory comb. She did not know for sure if he owned an ivory comb, but he probably did; Chyavatana was precisely the kind of man who would own – and every day use – an ivory comb.

As Shakuni and he came walking in and took their seats, Gandhari saw a sprinkling of black hair on her brother's chin. Between the two of them, a stranger would think of Chyavatana as the king and Shakuni as the henchman. She had always thought that; her brother did not have the appearance of a king. Indeed, if God were to cast him in a play, he would fit very well the role of a wicked, scheming minister with a sinister laugh.

'You have brought what I have asked for,' she said, at once sitting up and holding out her arm.

'Yes, my lady,' said Chyavatana, and placed two rolls of parchment in her hand. 'All traded items and commodities of Gandhar in the first parchment, and all traded items and commodities with Hastinapur in the second.'

She first opened the Hastinapur roll, and it spilled over onto her thigh. Fruits, vegetables, silk, wool, milk – everything she could think of was on it. When she opened the second parchment the list had just two items: rock carvings from Kamboja and red apples from Kasmira.

She looked at Chyavatana. 'Just these two kingdoms?'

'Yes, my lady.'

'But small kingdoms surround us, Chyavatana,' she said. 'Kekaya, Bahlika, Madra. Why do we not trade with them for all that they produce? I am certain that they will be only too glad to take our gold in return.'

'They will, my lady, and before the battle we did trade with them. But after Hastinapur became our vassal state ...'

'Do not use that word, Chyavatana,' she said, ignoring the smirk that had appeared on Shakuni's face.

'Ever since we began trading with Hastinapur, we have cut our ties with all the other states.'

'And they have not tried to resume trade with us?'

Chyavatana ran his fingertips on his moustache. 'We believe that Hastinapur may have put a stop to their efforts, Your Majesty.'

'Hastinapur? What right have they to dictate whom we can trade with?'

'I have spoken to some – friends – in Madra, Your Highness, and they have told me that Bhishma had come to their kingdom and asked for the hand of their princess in marriage into the house of Hastinapur.'

Gandhari raised her eyebrow. She knew what Bhishma would call this – an attempt to unify North Country under one flag. She just called it dirty statecraft. 'And why would the people of Madra heed his words?'

Chyavatana tightened his lips and said grimly, 'He is believed to have agreed to pay them a certain amount of gold every month, my lady.'

'Our gold?'

'It appears so.'

This was Bhishma's noble plan to unite North Country, then, to steal from one and feed another. A portion of Gandhar's tribute would no doubt be used to keep Madra from trading with Gandhar, and her mouth quivered with anger at the thought. But there could be other kingdoms to go to; there must be at least a few that Hastinapur had not touched.

'So we leave Madra then,' she said. 'There will be a few that will still trade with us.'

'There is Aswaka to the North, my lady, but they have attacked us a few times in the past. It may not be prudent to let them know that we are weak and in need of support.'

'Not Aswaka, no,' she said, remembering the two great sieges of the mines that had happened during her father's reign. 'There is a rice-growing kingdom further southward along the banks of River Sindhu. I forget the name.'

'Amvastha?' said Chyavatana.

'That too,' said Gandhari. 'But further southward, there is another kingdom – I think it is called Sivi.'

'Yes, Your Majesty.'

'Who rules that land now?'

'They call him Mitratithi, and they fight with the image of a crescent moon upon their banner.'

Gandhari inclined her head. 'Send messengers to him and ask if they would be willing to trade their rice with us for our gold.'

'Yes, my lady.'

'And if they say no, offer them double the price.'

'And Amvastha too, my lady?' said Chyavatana. 'A friend of mine speaks highly of the pots in that kingdom.'

'Then we shall buy them. Send riders this very night with messages for the kings of these two lands. And we shall try and awaken trade with Madra; the linen that comes out of that state is worth its weight in gold.'

'I shall see to that, my lady.'

Gandhari leaned forward and set both parchments on the table in front of her. 'Look, Chyavatana,' she said, 'I know not how we shall do this, and how quickly, but we must begin reducing the amount we trade with Hastinapur. If we pay more gold in the process, so be it, but we must shake free of their shackles. Do you understand?'

'Yes, my lady.'

'Whether they are small kingdoms, big, ruled by kings or princes, independent or vassals, we shall ask them all, and at the same time, we are going to put a shovel and a spade into the hands of every able-bodied man in Gandhar, and lead him to the mines.'

Chyavatana seemed to be troubled by that. 'But, my lady, we must ... we will have to tell them why.'

'Then we shall and we will tell them the truth – Gandhar is training an army to take on the might of Hastinapur, and we need the help of all men in the land.'

Shakuni looked up at her when he heard her words, and his eyes gleamed with excitement. As a child his favourite game after the rains was to run up the oak tree and lie in wait for the snails to venture out, and then kill them by stamping on them. He would have the same glint in his eyes as he had crushed them with his feet, and when Gandhari asked his father if his love for destruction would one day turn on him, he had laughed and said that every man was born with the urge to raze.

'So do we reopen the barracks?' he asked.

Gandhari nodded. 'Yes, and we shall open two archery ranges by the western wall and begin training archers immediately.' She turned to Chyavatana. 'You shall send the messengers out this very night, and you shall come back here to my chamber to report to me after they have left.'

Chyavatana bowed. 'Yes, Your Majesty.'

SEVEN

GANDHARI SPEAKS

I do not remember well enough that night on which Chyavatana sent out the messengers; for it is true what they say: as you get closer to your death, you begin to see more and more clearly all that is truly important in life, and all that is not. I remember the young girl who once lived in Gandhar and thought that wealth and prosperity was all that there was to life, and that no price was high enough to pay to achieve them, but I no longer see myself in her. It is as if I see her in my mind flitting from one moment to the next, prodded by some unseen, unknowable force, always restless, always wanting, always worrying.

That girl has grown into full womanhood and become a queen, and her sons have become kings. But she did not stop worrying. Even after she has acquired all the wealth and prosperity that she once craved, even after she had had her vengeance upon the dynasty that had buried the glory of Gandhar in the dust, even after the Great War had come and gone and left North Country an empty shell, she kept wishing, ever edgy, ever filled with grief.

I do not recognize this woman, though she has grown older and become what I am today. Now I have none of the things that

I wished for. Nobody remembers Gandhar or her glory now, and in a few moons even the tale of Hastinapur may get dissolved in the waters of the Great River. My sons are all dead. Bhishma is dead. I stood by him when he breathed his last, and I took his hand to kiss it. He smiled at me and nodded, as though to say everything was well and as it should be, and though I did not understand why, I smiled and nodded back. The young princess of Gandhar would have kicked his head and spat on his face, and she would have blamed him for the Great War and the end of the age of kings. The young prince of Hastinapur, Bhishma, would have perhaps called me a harlot for carrying my tale of vengeance to this bitter end.

But we were no longer young that day. We saw in each other's eyes the weariness of a long life, a life in which you will see everything and everyone you love leave you, without a goodbye or a promise to meet again. We saw in each journey the utter loneliness that is life on Earth; he, once the most fearsome warrior of his age now on a bed of arrows, attended to by his grandchildren, his dearest people, his staunchest enemies. And I, once the princess of Gandhar, then the queen of Hastinapur, now mother to a hundred dead sons.

I know not if the Great War could have been averted if I had said yes to Bhishma's first offer of marriage. When he was alive, I never asked him if he truly believed that he could unite North Country or if it was just a ploy to trap a naive young maiden. After his death I have found many an occasion to ask him that, but he does not reply. I only hear the murmur of the Great River pass quietly by, and I know he has heard me, but I also know that he would rather not speak of it at all.

The seeds of discord had already been sown by the time he had come to Gandhar on his first visit, so perhaps it would all have happened just as it did. Perhaps I would have pursued my revenge with the same passion, and perhaps that tale would have ended in the same way, with me holding his hand on the bed of arrows and watching his eyes close as the western sky went grey. In the old days travellers from the North had a saying that all roads in North Country led to Hastinapur. Perhaps the same could be said of this tale, too. No matter which thread you pick up and which winding path you follow, your journey will end on the battlefield in Kurkshetra.

So I shall not think of whether I could have done something to avert the Great War, for who is to say that the war was not written into all of our fates? Bhishma would disagree, of course, and he would say that any event that took the lives of so many people was a bad event, but I hear sages now already speaking of the war as a cleansing. When the minds of men become corrupt, perhaps there is something hidden deep within Mother Nature that rebels and says, 'Enough!'

Men will return, and among them kings will rise, and they will once again rule over kingdoms. But they will study this tale of the Great War, and perhaps it will keep their hearts from blackening. I shall be long gone by then, though, and that is a good thing, for I belong to an age which has ended. But before I go, I must tell you my tale; if it does not teach you what you must do, it will, I think, teach you what you must not.

In the first few weeks after Chyavatana sent out the messengers, I remember being happy, for the kings of Madra, Sivi and Amvastha said that they would be willing to trade with Gandhar. We set up routes that we thought Hastinapur would not know of, and we began buying rice from Sivi, pottery from Amvastha, and linen from Madra. A few months passed without event, and during that time we took on more miners and produced enough gold to leave us with a modest amount after having paid our tribute.

But as trade picked up with the three other kingdoms, it dropped with Hastinapur, and how I thought that would be acceptable to them, I do not know. Our caravans began disappearing, and our traders began to get killed – by 'bandits', they said. Madra stopped trading with us after she lost one complete caravan with thirty donkeys and forty merchants. Amvastha and Sivi carried on for a while, but soon they would stop too. We did everything we could to protect our route, but the bandits would always know the whereabouts of our caravans, and would always strike when they were unprotected.

So in about six months, all our trade routes vanished, and I received a message from Bhishma on behalf of Hastinapur. It said that it would be a waste of Gandhar's time to try and revive dead trade routes. Why did they need a new route with Hastinapur right at their call? Hastinapur would provide all that Gandhar needed and more, and if Gandhar did not like it – well, Gandhar would have to learn to like it. As a footnote, it also said that the offer of marriage was still open.

Gandhar's future lay torn in front of my eyes that moment, and I thought, perhaps, it was time for me to consider Bhishma's proposal; after all, I would be the queen, and Gandhar would still prosper, enen if under Hastinapur's shadow. Perhaps some time in the distant future, one of Shakuni's descendants would muster up the courage required to wrest the mines back into Gandhar's hands. I had done everything I could to save my city. It was time, I thought, to give in.

But then, a man came from the Eastern Mountains, bearing a pendant of gold around his neck, and changed everything.

EIGHT

Gandhari did not feel part of the festivities. All around her, even in the palace, was frenzied activity; her maids washed the walls and the floor with soapy water four times a day. The granite idol of Brahma that stood in the far corner of the chamber had been cleaned with a tiny brush, and now one of her chamberlains was decking the four heads with vermillion and turmeric. She dared not look out of the window, for she knew that even now, just minutes before sunset, she would find heat waves scurry up the flat surfaces of the rocks.

Her eyesight had deteriorated in the last few months. She extended her arms and tried to look at her fingernails. All she saw were white oval blobs. She could make out the cuticle from the nail, but she could not tell if they were dirty or clean. Only when she folded her arms back did they come into view. She was now past her eighteenth year, and in two more Shakuni's kingmaking time would arrive. No king had come to ask for her hand, which was strange indeed, because Gandhar had the mines. Even if they had, she could not leave Shakuni alone on the throne; he would be picked apart by Bhishma and the other vultures.

It did sometimes prick her that maidens much younger than her in the palace went about carrying bellies as big as they. Shikha, one of her waiting-women who cleaned and replaced the candles every day, had begun to retire to her room a bit too often, complaining of headache or a swimming stomach. She had been in the palace for nine of her fourteen years, and just the previous year she had been given in marriage to the gardener's son. Until she got with child, Shikha had been a tiny slip of a girl, hardly ever speaking and always keeping her chin pressed against her chest. But now she had a light about her face, and Gandhari had once or twice heard her singing to herself in the corridor after the sun had gone down and the candles had all been put out. Shikha laughed more, carried her head higher, and stopped to caress her belly once every few minutes. Gandhari's father had often said that her suitors would come on horses from far and wide, that she would choose the most valiant prince of them all and have a hundred sons with him. He had said that on her sixteenth birthday the town of Gandhar would celebrate her groom-choosing; it would have been three years ago, had it all gone as they had once thought it would. Now was a different time in a different world, it seemed to Gandhari; not necessarily bad, she thought, reflecting upon her pale yellow fingernails and brown knuckles, but different. Even after all this, after Shakuni ascends the throne, perhaps her valiant prince would come on horseback.

She smiled at her own thoughts running away from her. Even now, somewhere deep within, hope of marriage and sons flickered. That was why Bhishma's offer, shocking as it was, had been faintly alluring. Women were made that way, to create and nurture life, whereas men seemed to wish to erect a structure merely to have the choice of razing it to the ground. She thought again of Shikha, who must be lying in her bed now, on her side, combing her hair with the fingers of one hand and murmuring a hymn or a ballad to herself. That was the image that shall endure till the very end of man, she thought, the image of a woman fulfilling life's very purpose: that of creating life.

The feast of midsummer was five nights away, and through the open window she heard sounds of people laughing and plying their tools – the thump of spades against rocks, the snip of shears, the squeak of the water-carrier's balance. Generally she would be in gay spirits at this time of the year, but today her soul refused to warm. The people of Gandhar did not know of the storm clouds gathering in the horizon. They were like her, not able to see beyond only a short distance, ignorant of even the possibility that bad times may be lurking ahead.

The attendant at the door knocked softly, and when she called out to him to enter, he came in holding a candle in front of him. Bowing, he said, 'There is a man who wishes to see you, my lady.'

'At this hour? Command him to return tomorrow, and I shall see him in open court.'

The boy hesitated. 'He has said that if you knew of the purpose of his visit, you shall call him in even at the midnight hour.'

Gandhari sat up, piqued. 'Did he tell you why he wishes to see me?'

'He has not, my lady, but he has sent with me this gold coin that he wishes you to see.'

She waved him into the room and took the coin from him. She bent toward the lamp and held it up close to her eyes so that she could see the engraving on it. It had none. Both the surfaces of the coin were smooth and cool as polished granite, and the edges of the circle had been rounded. She turned it over in her hand to see if she could make out any marking whatsoever. She weighed it in her palm to reconfirm what she had known the moment she had held it – that it was gold.

'Summon him in,' she said, 'and call two of my guards to stand by me while I receive him.'

'As you wish, Your Highness.'

The first thing that Gandhari saw was the yellow gleam of light in which the man's hair seemed to glow. But it was only there a minute, and it could have been a trick of the lamps, for as soon as he stepped in and bowed to her, his hair appeared the darkest shade of black. The skin on his face was as smooth as the discus he had sent her through her attendant, and on each of his bare shoulder blades, she saw two perfect solid white circles. The gold coin he wore around his neck, hanging against his hairless dark chest, was identical to the one in her hand. He wore silver bracelets around his wrists.

He was dressed in the manner of a trader, in loose silks and gem-studded shoes, but he had none of the furtive bearing of one. He looked at her without emotion, as though he had been carved in stone; only his eyes – reddish brown pupils, long black lashes – distinguished him from the idol of the Creator in the corner.

As the man walked closer to her, she realized that his towering height had added to the illusion that his build was slight. In reality his shoulders were broad, and his torso tapered sharply down to his waist and hips. His arms had the smooth, graceful fluidity of a river.

Gandhari felt glad for the two spearmen that flanked her on both sides, though the man appeared strong enough to take care of the guards if he so wished. Across his shoulders a white cloth bag slung carelessly, making a light jingling sound with each stride he took.

She entwined her hands in front of her and crossed her legs. The man bowed again and said, 'Princess Gandhari, I bring you good tidings from the icy mountains in the East.'

'I know of no king or kingdom there,' she said, acknowledging him with a wave. 'Which king do you serve?'

Her visitor smiled a little. She saw a flash of silvery teeth behind black lips. 'Perhaps that is not as important as the issue that has sent me here.'

'Perhaps,' she said. 'But you do not make a good impression, sir, refusing to tell me of your king. What if you belong to an enemy of mine?'

'Do you think I come hither from the court of the Kurus?'

'I know not, and truth be told I have not seen the likes of you in all of North Country, but I must be on my guard, sir.'

He pulled his lower garment to one side to free his legs, and sat down on the seat next to hers, the same chair which Bhishma occupied the day before. Looking at this man now she saw an image of the smug prince of Hastinapur, grinning at her from behind his fingers. She bit the inside of her lips.

He nodded. 'I know your hatred for the one they call Bhishma, for he burns with the same fire against our people, the people of the holy mountain of Meru.'

So it did exist, then, the holy mountain. All her life she had seen sages come from the north and sing praises of life on the mountain, but she had always thought they were tales of fancy, of imagination spruced up by the strange herbs that people said grew in the forests there. If this man had been a sage, she would probably have laughed in his face and sent him away, but she saw in his face a calm she had seldom seen in any other. If this man said that he was from Meru, she felt inclined to believe him.

'I have come to see you, my lady,' he said, 'because it has come to my notice that both of us have a common enemy.' His voice was thin and reedy, yet so deep that it dripped with male energy. 'If you become friends with the people of Meru, perhaps, together, we could gain victory over Hastinapur.'

'You have not yet told me of your name, sir', she said, 'nor have you told me how you know of Gandhar's duel with Hastinapur.'

'My name is Kubera.' He glanced about himself. 'I am the mine-keeper on Meru, but Indra uses me also as a tradesman, and it is in that respect that I wish to speak with you.' He paused to pull his bag more securely around his shoulders. 'As for how we know your story, we have followed the tale of the two kingdoms from the day of the battle of Kamyaka, my lady.'

'Ah,' she said, 'so you know much.'

'We know everything there is to know.'

'But how shall I trust you?' asked Gandhari, keeping her face wooden. 'I have only met you now, and I know not why you seek my friendship when you have a mine of your own.'

'Trust,' he said, looking away at the window. Gandhari saw the distant fires of the mines as little yellow spots on his eyes. 'I do not believe that you have a choice of whether to trust me or not, Your Highness. I have been to all the other kingdoms that you wished to trade with, and I have seen all that I needed to see. You have no choice but to trust me.'

Gandhari thought for a second, then said, 'Yes, that may be so. But why do you do this? If the Meru people have all they need, why do they come to me with an offer of friendship? How do you gain from this?'

'Hastinapur's fall is our gain, my lady,' said Kubera. 'Bhishma's dream is to unite all of North Country and mount an invasion on the Meru, the likes of which we have never seen before.'

'Surely Meru is strong enough to defend herself?'

'Not if all the kingdoms of North Country unite against us. We may still win, but that war will take a lot of lives, ours and those of earthmen. We cannot allow that.'

'Then why do you not invade Hastinapur right away and take it before it takes you?'

Kubera smiled, and she realized that she had spoken like her brother Shakuni would, eager for war and destruction without diligence or thought. 'We do not approve of war unless it is necessary. It may come to pass that Gandhar and Meru shall join forces against Hastinapur in the near future, but for that you must give us your promise of friendship.'

'And what do I get in return for this promise of friendship?'

'Do I have it, by your word?'

She hesitated, and for a fleeting second she wished she had accepted Bhishma's offer of marriage and had gone away before this man of the mountains had come looking for her. But the feeling vanished just as quickly as it appeared, and her sight seemed to sharpen. As she gazed at him, she saw the lines on his arms, the spotless skin that looked like just fallen snow, only in grey, the deep red eyes and the black beady irises. He blinked once.

She looked away. Once again everything was smudges. 'Yes,' she said, 'you have my word.'

Kubera took out his carver and slate from the bag and set it on his lap. 'If you tell me all the items that you trade with Hastinapur, Your Majesty,' he said, 'I shall pass it on to our traders and they will begin delivering them to you beginning next month.'

She shook her head. 'No, we cannot begin so soon. Bhishma's army will destroy your route. We must hide your caravans somehow. We must…'

'You do not need to hide anything, my lady,' said Kubera. 'The path from here to the mountain is laden with mist. Our traders are trained to conceal themselves well, and they have the means to thicken the mist when they need to.'

'Indeed?'

He smiled. 'On the Meru, we devote great portions of our lives to the study of Mysteries, my lady. This is one such, one that Bhishma himself has done much to probe.'

'It is true, then? He did live among the Celestials.'

'Indeed. He is the son of Ganga, our Lady of the River. His childhood was spent in Brihaspati's hermitage, they say. Though I did not get a chance to see him when he lived up there, people still speak of him.'

'Fondly or otherwise?'

His smile steeled. 'Some fondly, some otherwise.'

'I take it that you do not share your people's enthusiasm for him.'

'No, my lady, but I do not hate him, either. He has done more good than harm to the mountain so far, of that I am certain.'

'And yet you wish to see him destroyed.'

'That is because of the harm that he promises to bring us in the future.' He stretched his shoulders once by turning them around in a circle. He prodded at this slate with his carver. 'Now. If you please?'

From under her upper garment Gandhari retrieved the trade parchment that Chyavatana had brought her the day before. Giving it to Kubera, she said, 'This is likely two or three months old, but you shall have a fair idea if you read it.' As he took it and began to scan it from top to bottom, she said, 'I will also need to know your prices, sir. I am prepared to compensate your traders for all the concealment and danger of this route, but I cannot stretch beyond the prices you see on that sheet. Hardly anything remains after the hefty tribute we give Hastinapur, sir; you must certainly know.'

Kubera did not respond to that. His eyes were immersed in the parchment, and his one hand worked the carver over his slate. She doubted if he had heard her at all. She detected a faint odour of musk in the air; it perhaps came from his open cloth sack.

At last he rolled the parchment and returned it to her. 'We shall give you all of this,' he said, nodding at his slate. 'And our items shall be better than Hastinapur's. Our trees are stronger, our fruits are juicier, our milk is creamier, and our lands more fertile.'

'More Mysteries, I suppose?' she asked.

He smiled and shook his head. 'Just the bracing mountain air. Now, coming to your fears of price.' He looked up at her. She stiffened. If he asked for a higher price than Hastinapur, she would have to find more men to work at the mines. That would mean raising the amount she would have to pay them all, and the nature of the 'benefits' they received. Already in her mind she began to calculate how many waiting-women she would have to train, and how many acres of land she would have to let go from the royal holdings.

Then he said, 'We will not take any gold from you.'

'I beg your pardon, sir,' she said, sitting up, suddenly alert. 'Did I hear you right?'

'You did, my lady,' he said. 'We shall give you all of this that you ask and more. We have a mine of our own, as I told you, so we need no gold from you.'

'Then you must need something else? Cattle, perhaps? Land?'

He shook his head to both. 'We just need you to build your treasury as quickly as you can. We will help you by giving you a portion of the gold that we produce, but we use it for trade ourselves, and not much gets left over. But Indra has told me that he shall do whatever it takes to increase our gold production so that we could replace some of your stolen gold.' He raised a finger in caution. 'But most of it must come from you. We will support your populace until then, but you must get more people into your mines.'

She nodded. If they were willing to take the burden of Gandhar on their shoulders without taking anything, she thought, they would come to her at the very end and demand something as payment. Perhaps they would ask her to lend her army, to which she would gladly agree. Even if it were not that, even if they just wanted to raise two strong kingdoms in place of one, in the hope that power would balance itself that way, it would mean that Gandhar would rediscover her path to glory. So no matter what their future price would be for this favour, it seemed to her that it was worth paying, for it meant that her kingdom would live for another day.

'I am deeply grateful to you for this help that you offer, my lord,' she said, bowing to him. 'I only hope that Gandhar would prove herself worthy of it.'

'I am certain that it will,' he replied, setting his slate and carver back into his bag and tying the knot. The smell of musk became less intense. As he got up, he said, 'Think not that we are doing this out of altruism, my lady. Our interests are deeply entwined with Hastinapur's fall, and we think that Gandhar's rise is vital to achieve that.'

'I understand.' She got up and walked behind him to the door.

He turned around and inclined his head. 'We shall talk about the price when we are able to bring an end to everything, just as planned. But I shall come to you after the midsummer feast has passed, on the onset of the first monsoon.'

She bowed to him. 'I shall await your visit.' When she opened her eyes and raised her head, she saw that the man had already left. Only a whiff of musk lingered in the dark corridor.

NINE

The morning after the feast, even though hours had passed by after sunrise, the city did not stir. Gandhari stood at the window and watched the empty lanes and streets. Near the north-eastern wall, the statue of Idobhargava stood out for its stark loneliness. It was customary to have one guard on duty by the foot of the pedestal, but today even he was absent. She wondered if the tall and thin vault-keeper would be found behind his desk, poring over his ledger and muttering to himself. No matter, she thought, the time would arrive shortly enough for those robbers to leave the city.

A knock appeared on the door, and the three men she had summoned arrived, dressed in their royal finery. Only Shakuni came barefooted, his eyes red and swollen. She made a mental note to find out which woman he had lain with the night before and have a quiet word with her. All her maids had been trained in ways and means to prevent getting with child after laying with a man, but one needed to repeat the message every now and then. One never knew when a maiden would get it into her woolly head that she should become a mother. Most of them did not protest, and for those who did, there were other ways of dealing with them.

All in all, things would be much easier if Shakuni could control his impulses. Indeed, did she not have eyes for the handsome men

306

of her court? They would come to her chamber too, if for no other reason but that she was the queen. But they were royals – palace gossip always found ways to get out on the street, so it was always better to kill that flame right when it took birth. But then Shakuni was a man; her father had been the same too, only rarely spending the night in his bed alone. Every time he would beckon a waiting-woman or two, Gandhari would look at him, and he would say that it was a hot night and that he needed someone to fan him to sleep.

Men's desires did not die as simply as a woman's, she had heard her father say, and so when Shakuni began to take maidens to his chamber – around the time he turned thirteen or so – she pretended not to notice. She had once or twice told him to be careful, and he had nodded, but he never had to deal with the women afterward. They came to her, and she would assuage their bruises – not just the ones on their bodies – with some soft words and a gold necklace or two.

Chyavatana and Adbudha took their seats. Shakuni sat opposite them, to her right, draped in black and gold. He had a curious way of leaning to one side even when he sat; she had never understood why. She assumed that he was habituated to being lopsided. She turned to the other two men.

'Adbudha,' she said, 'this year, we are going to increase the amount of gold we mine to two thousand one hundred *tulas*. I understand it was seven hundred *tulas* last year?'

Adbudha's hand stopped on his beard, and his eyes hardened. 'Yes, my lady,' he said. 'You wish to increase the mine's output by three times?'

'That is so. What shall you need to make that happen?'

'Well, for starters, my lady, I shall need six hundred able-bodied men.' He snorted in derision and looked at the other two men.

'You shall have them,' said Gandhari curtly. Turning to Chyavatana, she said, 'Tell all our traders that we shall set up royal stalls in the town centre, Chyavatana.'

'As you wish, my lady.' There was no hint of scorn on his face. For once she appreciated Shakuni's taste in selecting men. 'Shall I ask all the traders to shut shop, or only some of them?'

'All of them. Employ as many of them as possible to man the stalls that we will set up.'

'Yes, my lady. What will these stalls sell?'

'Everything we receive from Hastinapur,' she said. 'Milk, furniture, apples, and everything else that goes onto our trade sheet every month. We will sell our own milk, our own furniture, our own apples – and we shall sell them at less expensive prices than the traders from Hastinapur.'

Chyavatana paused to wedge his tongue against his cheek. 'Our traders have been trying that for a long time now, Your Highness. But the people from Hastinapur do not seem to wish to sell their goods for a profit.'

Gandhari sat up straight and pulled aside the sides of her garment. 'What is the lowest price that the traders are willing to sell an apple for, Chyavatana?'

'Ah, I am not fully certain, my lady, but I believe it is around four copper coins.'

'We shall sell our apple for two.'

'And what if their traders bring it further down to one copper coin?'

A smile spread on her lips. 'Then, Chyavatana, we shall give our apples away to our people without taking anything from them.' She let that statement sink in, taking a moment to survey the faces of the three men. Shakuni was frowning at her and chewing on something. Then she said, 'The traders from Hastinapur will not journey all the way here from their kingdom to give away their goods, will they, Chyavatana?'

'No, my lady,' said Chyavatana, 'they will not. But–'

'Yes, I shall tell you. You have heard, have you not, of the race of men that lives beyond the icy mountains east of here?'

His eyebrow went up. 'I have been told they are mere children's tales, my lady. I do not think it wise to pin our hopes on people that do not exist.'

'Do not exist, you say,' she said, smiling at him again. 'Their chief trader came to my chambers last night, and he left after the feast had begun.'

'Indeed?' said Chyavatana. Adbudha resumed caressing his beard, and Shakuni blinked. 'And what were their terms of trade?'

'That they shall give us all that Hastinapur gives us, but they shall give it to us for free.' She saw a suspicious look enter Chyavatana's eyes, and hastened to add: 'In return, they will take our army when they need it, to quell Hastinapur.'

'But my lady Gandhari, Hastinapur's soldiers shall not allow this trade route to be set up.'

'It has all been arranged, Chyavatana,' she said, mildly irritated. 'We shall need no traders, fruit-growers, merchants or milkmen. We shall need only farmers and water carriers to do their jobs. Of the remaining, half of them shall go to the mines, and half shall be trained as soldiers.'

Chyavatana paused again, looking down at the ground. 'I beg your pardon, my lady, but at the rates we pay the miners—'

'Increase them! Double their allowances, and promise the unmarried ones female company at night.' She thought about that for a second. 'Also to the married ones, with a further promise that their wives will not know about it.'

Shakuni spoke for the first time that morning. 'I shall oversee the selection and training of the soldiers.'

Gandhari ignored him. She looked at Chyavatana, who still seemed troubled. 'What is the matter? You do not think this will work well for Gandhar?'

'I ... I am not certain, my lady. We seem to move from relying on one city to relying on another. What if tomorrow, these men from the north were to withdraw their trade? What shall we be left with?'

'Do not think that I have not considered this, Chyavatana,' she said, angry and impressed at the same time. 'This is not a permanent ploy. Once we have accumulated enough gold in our treasury to rival that of Hastinapur, we shall build our own industry. We shall find fertile land outside of our borders and claim it. We shall do all that we need to be self-sufficient. But for now,' she said, looking out to the mines, 'for now we must throw everything that we have at Hastinapur, and we shall see if Bhishma has the power to withhold it.'

'Yes, my lady.'

Chyavatana's tone suggested hesitation, and she found herself getting agitated at the man's doubt. She asked Adbudha, 'If I were to give you all the men that you asked for, will you give me two thousand *tulas* of gold by the end of this year?'

Adbudha nodded without pausing to think. She beamed at him. 'Then,' she said, 'we shall move ahead with full speed. That will be all, gentlemen.'

TEN

To Gandhari, the beautiful Princess and Queen of Gandhar, the Land of Gold, Bhishma, the Champion of Hastinapur's throne, presents his salutations. I hope that all is well in the royal palace, and that your lands bear enough crop and your mines produce enough gold.

I have begun to notice over the last three months that the amount of trade that your kingdom does with my merchants has reduced remarkably. Indeed, it has now reached a point where my merchants have refused to come to Gandhar, for I am being told that you have set up stalls of your own to rival my people's, and that you give away your items at prices that are near pittances. My traders have thus begun to seek other, greener pastures.

This saddens me. Gandhar and Hastinapur have such a long history in trading with each other, and you know that my kingdom relies on the gold arising out of sale of our items in Gandhar for a great many things. I have always thought that the prices my traders set on the goods that they sell are fair, and they have forever been eager to engage in trade on your terms, my lady. If you wanted them to cut down prices, all you needed to do was to ask.

But I think not that the issue here is that of price. If you have found a way to sell milk, tables, grain and fruit for nothing, then it

311

must only mean one thing: that you have indeed found a way to produce these things for nothing – and that is impossible. There is a cost to producing everything, and that leaves me with two possible explanations to this recent turn of events: one, you have found a kingdom from which you can steal these items without their knowledge, much like Hastinapur did with Gandhar. And two, you found a city that would give these to you without charging a price for them.

If it is the first – though I do not think it is – then I must offer you my good wishes, along with a warning. You cannot steal indefinitely from the same person. Sooner or later they will check their pockets, and when they find them empty, they shall follow the trickle of coins and arrive at your doorstep. Be certain that you are prepared for that day, because it will come, like it did when you discovered us.

But with respect, I do not think you could be as diligent as that. I think it is more likely that you have found a city that would hand out all the goods to you – but then that raises a question in my mind: what do they want in return? And who could these mysterious helpers be? I have instructed my soldiers to keep a strident watch on you and your trade supplies; they have not reported anything, and yet your supplies are reaching you. One of my army chiefs said that it was as though the route has been shrouded by a divine mist, which neither sound nor light could penetrate.

I have seen that mist before, my lady, long back in my early youth, when I served the wise sages in the icy mountains up north. I created a route for the people that live on the Meru, weaving into it a mist of this very kind. I would not be able to find it now, of course, because in these middling years they must have probed the Mystery further, and they must have added to its secrets. But I know whither it comes. It comes from that race of men we – all of North Country – must be wary of in the extreme.

I have lived among them. I know them like I know my own people. I know what lies beneath the fair masks that they wear on their faces. I know what poison lurks under their fair skins and kind smiles. I have seen it. I have tasted it.

They do not wish for the good of Gandhar. They do not wish for the good of Hastinapur. The future of North Country does not matter to them. They wish just for the good of their own people – and perhaps in that respect they are not very different to you and I – but they do so with utter disregard for the well-being of anyone that do not live on the mountains. Today they have come to raise Gandhar up to Hastinapur's level, no doubt hoping that we will go to war. Remember, Princess Gandhari, when two men fight, the beneficiary is often a third who watches from the side.

I know not what price they will demand of you when all this has come to an end, but I'm certain it shall not be to Gandhar's benefit. They wish war upon your land and mine; I do not know why, but I'm sure that their intentions cannot be pure. I will ask you, therefore, to think of what you must do if you are to do good to the people of Gandhar. War cannot be good for them, my lady, no matter how hotly the fire of revenge burns in your heart. Cast off your friendship with the men of the north, for they will spit you out the moment you cease to be of use to them.

I thank you for your tributes; they have arrived faultlessly on the first day of every waning cycle of the moon thus far. I only hope that you have an ear for my word of advice. Let us go back to the trading arrangement we had before this, Your Majesty, and I shall instruct my traders that they will sell you the goods at prices you desire. I am very eager – for your sake and for the sake of all kingdoms of North Country – that you must sever this tie with the Meru people.

I await your reply with great eagerness.

To Bhishma, Prince and Champion of Hastinapur, Gandhari, the Queen of Gandhar, bows with respect.

You will not deny that your previous visit to our palace pushed Gandhar into a corner. When we tried emerging from Hastinapur's shadow by charting trade routes with other kingdoms, you prevented them. You left us with only two choices: that of continuing to trade with Hastinapur, or improve our own industries such that they rival yours. The latter we could not do in a short time, the former we chose not to do because continuing to trade with you would have bled us further. The tribute already hurts us more than you can imagine.

So when the Meru people extended their hand of friendship, I took it. You may be right; their intentions may not be pure, but whose is? Shall I trust you, who have looted us from under our noses for twenty years? Shall I trust mine, which, as you rightly said, are blinded by the need for revenge? Between the three of us, Prince, I think the intentions of the Meru people are the purest; what that says about you and me and about North Country, I know not.

I know you still hold the power of unleashing unrest on Gandhar by telling our people about the missing gold in the vaults. But despite knowing of our new trade arrangement, you have chosen to keep your silence. You perhaps fear that if riots were to break out in Gandhar, we shall no longer be able to pay your tribute, and now that I have friends from the north, your victory over my kingdom is no longer assured. I think the entry of the northmen has evened this battle a little, and now I see you look behind your back and see the approaching corner, just like the one you pushed me into, a few moons ago.

You will no doubt reject that notion, and you will say that you do not wish to see my people die – as you do not wish to see any people die – and perhaps there is truth in that too, but regardless, I must thank you for your choice. The city of Gandhar owes you a debt for keeping her out of civil unrest and riots, though it would be nothing compared to what Hastinapur owes us.

Your tributes will keep arriving, sir, of that you need have no worry. Our mines have expanded, and we have employed more miners to meet your need. But I cannot accept your offer of going back to trading with Hastinapur. As you well know, the men of Meru give me everything I need without asking anything in return, and when you are on the receiving end, gifts are much, much more desirable than trades. What they will ask for me in return as price for this is not my concern, for right now, when I need it most, they have given me their hand. I shall gladly return the favour once Gandhar begins to see better times.

Whether my turn to them will be bad for Hastinapur, I do not know. But put yourself in my place for one moment, Son of Ganga, and tell me if you would not do the same. My first duty is to my people and to my friends. Doubtless that the price they extract from me will somehow plunge into Hastinapur's spine, but that is none of my concern. They have done me good, and my father always said that of all great traits kings are said to possess, loyalty is the most precious.

The harvest festival is but a moon away, and Gandhar is abuzz with its preparations. We have a midsummer feast three moons after that, and we would like it if you could grace us with your presence for that occasion and partake of food at the same table as me and my brother, Shakuni.

I trust you understand my disagreement with you, my lord. May the gods bless Hastinapur.

ELEVEN

Throughout that winter, Gandhar's air had carried a scent of lemon and a hint of fog. Even during middays, with the afternoon son beating down and the dry wind blowing against the glowing fires at the entrance of the mines, Gandhari could see dusty grey wisps flutter and dance forever in her peripheral vision, always vanishing when she focused her eyes. The nights had been chillier than usual, but the mines had stayed open. Ever since Kubera's first visit to Gandhar six moons ago, the mines had stayed open throughout the night, and a file of men always seemed to either go in or out. The ones going in wore clear clothes and had a spring in their step; the ones coming out were washed in fine brown dust. She had heard once that miners took great care of the dust on their clothes, that after reaching home, they soaked their clothes in warm water in the hope that some grains of gold would have accidentally stuck to the fabric. She did not know if the tale was true, but when she narrated it to Shakuni he had laughed and said there was too less gold present in the earth to go around sticking to people's clothes. She had not known what to make of that.

'By the end of spring, my lady,' said Adbudha, causing her to look away from the window at the gathering in front of her, 'we shall have all the gold that you asked for at midsummer.'

Out of habit her eyes sought Kubera's. On the first morning of every month since the mines had opened, Kubera had come to Gandhar and watched over the accounts kept by the noblemen at court. Of matters regarding Gandhar's gold, he now knew better than she did.

His black lips spread in a smile, and the gold pendant on his chest gleamed in the fading light of the evening. He said to Chyavatana, 'And the army?'

'That will take slightly longer, my lord,' replied Chyavatana. 'I would think by midsummer we shall have all the elephants and footmen ready for battle.'

'That will be how many elephants?'

'Three hundred and forty-three, sir, to be precise, along with four hundred footmen.'

Kubera turned to Gandhari. 'Our army will be ready too, by then; a hundred white elephants, fifty-six cavalrymen, forty archers and forty footmen.'

She raised her brow at him. 'That does not sound like much of an army to me, sir.'

'It does not, no. But their armours are tough, my lady, and their weapons are forged by Meru's best blacksmiths. Rest assured that they shall last at least as long as your army does.'

Shakuni scratched his chin and said, 'But we have not accumulated enough gold. Hastinapur has stolen four thousand *tulas*, and they have received a thousand in tribute this year. We have so far only mined two thousand. What about the remaining three?'

'We do not need to mine it, Prince,' said Kubera, and Gandhari warmed at the way he said 'we', as though he was one of them. The three men had at first regarded him with suspicion, but now even Shakuni spoke to him without that unkind tone of voice that he used when speaking to people that he disliked. 'The fear of Hastinapur awakening unrest in people is now no longer present. If they say that the vaults are empty, we will show them that they are, in fact, full.'

'But not all of our vaults are full.'

'And we shall not show them the empty ones. Half of our vaults are full of gold, now. So if any of the people doubt that we do not have the gold we say we do, let them come and claim to see it. We will take them to one of our full vaults.'

'Ah,' said Shakuni, breaking into a half-grin, 'like they did it with us.'

'Yes,' said Kubera. 'But they had only one full vault. We have many, almost eight.'

'So now we begin to plan on how to bring back our gold from those robbers!'

Gandhari said, 'Do not agitate yourself, brother. The Kuru army is a strong one; they shall not surrender as easily as that.'

'Quite,' said Kubera. 'But our army will bring with them jars of water, and I suggest that your army drinks it too. The wise ones on the mountain have said for hundreds of years that it clears the mind of the drinker, and we all know how vital a clear mind is to winning a battle.'

'But must we fight, Kubera, my lord?' asked Gandhari, pretending not to see Shakuni's face darken. 'We have recovered from Hastinapur's theft, and now we can stop giving them their tribute without fear of being attacked. I have found myself wondering, then, what purpose would fighting a war serve, besides killing some men in both cities.'

Kubera smiled at her without showing his teeth. He tucked his bag closer to him. 'With the use of Gandhar's gold, Hastinapur has taken great strides toward becoming the foremost kingdom of North Country, leaving Gandhar behind.' He set his eyes upon Shakuni. 'I know the prince is not pleased with Gandhar being displaced with such deceit.' Shakuni fumed, his eyes burning red. Even the two other men, Chyavatana and Adbudha, stoic men at most times, twisted their lips in anger. Kubera turned to her, still smiling. 'Do you not share the anger that these men feel in their hearts, my lady?'

'I do, sire,' she said cautiously, thinking for a fleeting moment of Bhishma's letter. She had invited him to Gandhar for the feast of midsummer. Would that not be a better, more peaceful way forward now and forget the past? After all, Gandhar still had her mines. It would take them almost twenty years to get past Hastinapur. 'I do,' she said again, nodding. 'But a battle at this time would peg us back more than it will push us forward, will it not?'

'Not if we win!' said Shakuni. 'It will plunge Hastinapur into the dark ages, and I shall see to it that they never awaken.' He was sitting up in his seat, and his fingers were twisting venomously over his scabbard. 'With Kubera's help we shall defeat those daylight robbers, and I shall slit that brigand Bhishma's throat with my sword.'

Gandhari took no notice of him. She said to Kubera, 'Do you really think that a battle is necessary at this time, sir?'

'Battle is never necessary, my lady, Queen,' said Kubera. 'It is a matter of honour, of pride. Can you look at the man who has plundered your gold in his face and smile upon him? Will you invite him to your midsummer feast and make peace with him? Will you perhaps marry into his home and have children that will rule his land?'

Shakuni got to his feet and drew his sword. In a fierce whisper, he said, 'Never!'

'My lady?'

Gandhari thought for a second of Bhishma's warning, that the Meru people wanted no more than to start a fight between two kingdoms and stoke the fire from afar. But here was a man who had given her city food and clothes for seven moons without taking anything in return. Now he has named his price. She could not – should not – say no.

'Prosperity was your birthright, my queen, as it was the birthright of every man, woman and child in Gandhar. You have in your kingdom the biggest mine of gold in North Country. If that does not make you prosperous, what would?' Kubera lowered his voice, and it sounded like soothing notes on a flute. 'He snatched that away from you, my lady. Today, if Gandhar has had to take the help of Meru, if she is in a position where her future is uncertain, it is he who is responsible.'

Gandhari nodded, uncertainly.

'If you will, Your Majesty, put Bhishma in your place and think what he would do. Do you think he would sit with his courtiers and debate the merits of battle? He, who once fought with the kings of North Country at a bride-choosing to which he was not invited? He likes to speak of noble thoughts, my lady, but look at his hands and you shall see they are red with dried blood.'

Gandhari thought of the dust-covered miners slinking away to their homes at the end of a long day. Most of them had wives, children, mothers, families. Most of them did not wish to work in a mine. Until last year they were milkmen, weavers, potters and farmers. Now they allowed themselves to be covered in dust and soot, for whose sake? For hers; because she had asked them to. And who made her do that to her people?

Her father had said that a woman made a good queen in matters of the state, but in matters of warfare, a man trumped her because she would allow herself to be persuaded that violence was not necessary. Would she willingly put so many of her soldiers' lives in danger just to recover some gold? Gandhari's answer to that would always be no, but Shakuni's would always be yes.

I am holding this throne for my father, she told herself, and for my brother. So I ought to do now as they would do.

'Let us begin preparations,' she said.

She waited at the window for the menservants to finish setting her bed, and when they bowed to her and left the room, she walked to the very edge and sat on it, with her hand placed upon the violet satin sheet. The breeze had become cold, and the moon had already disappeared for the night. Shakuni would sleep well tonight, she thought. What he had wanted for years was finally happening, and Gandhar looked like she was going to win after all. If she were Bhishma, she would be worried indeed.

Why, then, did she have this heaviness in her chest? Her tunic disengaged from her hair and fell in front of her eyes. With one hand she caught it and pulled, grimacing as some strands came loose and fell to the bed. After Hastinapur had been defeated and their gold retrieved, Bhishma would no longer wish to have her marry into the royal house. She was in her twentieth year; maidens of her age all over the country were having their fourth and fifth children. At twenty-four, getting with child would be dangerous to the life of the mother, which meant she had four years to have a child or two.

No more than one or two, father, she whispered into the air. *Not the hundred sons you saw in my future, but it is better than nothing.*

At the end of this year Shakuni would ascend to the throne, and her part in Gandhar's tale would come to an end. She would be relegated to the maidens' chambers, and perhaps – just perhaps – some neighbouring king would pass by and ask for her hand. It would not be the same as being queen of Hastinapur, but it, too, would be better than nothing.

A stray thought hit her, then, that she might not get married at all. It was nothing to feel shocked about; maidens in royal houses – the less beautiful, the less able ones – sometimes did not find matches, and they whiled away their lives in the chambers, out of view, caring for a child of a sister or brother. It would be sad if she grew into that life, she thought, and for a moment she thanked fate for having taken her father away before it happened.

But what did her life matter? She folded her tunic twice, wedged it under the pillow. She unclipped her hair and let it fall over her shoulders. Gandhar's future would be secured, and if the life of one princess had to pass without marriage for that to happen, it was a small price to pay. She understood that, but somewhere deep within her a voice asked why that princess had to be her. Looking down over her shoulders, she noticed her hair was thick and long, and when she let it loose it covered her big ears and framed her face rather well – not well enough to be called beautiful, because her eyes squinted and blinked too much, but enough to be called passable, perhaps.

She asked herself if she hated Bhishma, and she did, with one part of her. But the other part, this little girl in her who wanted to marry and have sons and watch them become kings, that part of her longed for him. In her whole life, he had been the only man who spoke of marriage with her. Ever since the death of her father, the king, all that she had heard from courtiers and courtesans alike had been how she must live up to his legacy, of how she must uphold Gandhar's honour, of how she must mould young Prince Shakuni into a worthy king ...

But Bhishma had come, and on his first visit, had spoken of marriage, of making her queen. That part of her who had governed Gandhar and lost sleep over its welfare hated him, for he was a thief and a rascal. But that same thief and rascal gave her the only chance at a life which she had always dreamed about.

A knock was heard at the door, and she asked harshly, 'Who is it?'

A tentative female voice replied. 'It is Lord Kubera to see you, my lady.'

'Bring him in,' she said, getting up and setting her face in a smile. Two attendants came in, one ushering Kubera to his seat and the other going around the edge of the chamber, lighting lamps. In no time at all, the darkness was gone. She found her mood lifting when she saw his languid smile. Pushing herself off the bed, she went to her seat and stood holding it with one hand.

'Yes, my lord,' she said.

'You look quite fetching this evening, my lady, if I may say it.'

She wished to smile but did not. 'Certainly you do not go to a maiden's chamber in the dead of the night to tell her how comely she looks. Is that the way of life up on the Meru?'

'It is not,' he admitted. 'I came to see how you were faring, for I know that this battle weighs on your mind.' When she did not reply, he said, 'Does it not?'

'I am a woman, sir. Taking lives does not come easy to me.'

'Aye, that is so.' He leaned back in his seat and gripped the arm-rests on both sides. He looked straight ahead, into the distance. 'I have heard our Lady of the River say the same thing, that death does not come easy to women. Mother Nature has created us to give life, Kubera, she would say to me. We are the image of the Creator, and man that of the Destroyer.'

She looked at the chamberlain who still waited at the table with her head bowed. She gestured to her to leave.

'I do not have the wisdom of the Lady of the River,' she said, turning towards Kubera. 'But I must do that which is good for Gandhar; that is my duty as queen.'

'Duty is one thing, Princess Gandhari, and want is another. You have told me what your duty is, but what do you want?'

'Do you not know, my lord?' she said. 'Kings and queens do not have wants of their own.' He smiled, but she continued, 'If you ask of Bhishma what he wants, perhaps he shall give you answers that surprise you.'

'Perhaps,' he said. 'But we already know what Bhishma wants, and that is why I am here, my lady, guiding you by the hand and making you fight this battle.'

'But why, sir? Is all this killing necessary? North Country is in its longest period of peace. No blood has been shed for years now, and people like it. Kings like it!'

Kubera opened his sack, and her nose immediately woke up to the intense smell of musk. 'I have here with me oil taken from one of the trees that grow on the slopes of the Meru,' he said, and although she wanted to ask him about the war, the image in front of her eyes grew dreamy. 'I have been told that I must give it to you, to wear over your eyelids.'

'My eyelids,' she said.

He nodded. 'This has been blessed by the Lady of the River herself. She said you could use some of her sight.'

'Her sight.'

'Her sight. You cannot see very well from afar, I have been told.'

'Yes,' said Gandhari, her eyelids growing heavy. 'Cannot see ... well ... far off ...'

Kubera stood up and came to her. Taking her hand in his, he placed the container of oil into her palm and closed her fingers around it. 'You shall take this, then. Inside this little box you will see a parchment describing what you must do to make it work.'

'I can see?'

He thought about it for a moment. 'You can see,' he said, 'but not with your eyes.'

'I can see ... not with my eyes. What ...'

'You shall see soon enough,' he said, and leaned in to blow a little current of air along her earlobe. She felt herself fall back, and his arm cradle her neck. He lifted her up and carried her to the bed. All that she could feel was the cold brass box of oil around which her fingers were wrapped. She wanted to let go but could not.

'Will you sleep with me?' she asked, and even in her trance, she hoped that he would say yes, that he would fill her with his fragrance.

But he said, 'No. I shall take your leave now, Princess. I have given you that which I have come to give.'

TWELVE

Gandhari, the Queen of Gandhar, salutes Bhishma, the Champion of the Kurus, the foremost dynasty in all of North Country.

Spring has come and gone here in Gandhar, and midsummer is but three moons away. I have once invited you to our kingdom to join us in our festivities to celebrate the night of the solstice, but between then and now certain things have happened – things that have regrettably forced me to withdraw my invitation.

The people from the mountain have sought their price. They wish to free Gandhar of Hastinapur's clutches, and they wish to free Gandhar's gold from Hastinapur's vaults. They wish for the tribute of gold to cease, and they wish for Gandhar to be declared by one and all to be the strongest kingdom of the land.

For all this to happen, my lord, the only course of action available to me is to declare war between the two kingdoms. I know not if this comes as a surprise to you; indeed, if my spies are to be believed, you have expected this outcome many moons ahead and have begun to train an army. I am certain that your spies have informed you that we have done the same. We have mined enough gold in the last one year to reduce the threat of riots and social breakdown in Gandhar if you were to throw open the empty vaults to public view. So to begin our open antagonism toward Hastinapur, I withdraw with immediate effect the tribute that we have agreed to pay you. From this month on, you shall receive nothing from Gandhar's treasury. Gandhar's gold shall stay within Gandhar.

Also with immediate effect, we will imprison your vault-keepers and hold them for ransom. If you wish to free them, you shall pay us all the gold that Gandhar has given you in tribute this previous year. I do not plan on keeping them alive for more than two months, though, so make your decision about them before our battle begins. I have shown mercy to their wives and children, and they will be sent to Hastinapur safely on mules. I have asked my infantrymen to accompany them, so you need not worry about them succumbing to beasts or bandits.

I shall allow the next one month for peace to prevail between the two kingdoms, in case you wish to conduct talks with me. But on the same day of the moon during the next waking cycle, I shall declare war to begin. I have informed my generals of this, and their armies are ready, eager to put their trained muscles to test. Men have also arrived from the Meru to embellish our forces, so if you feel that we could be swatted away with minimal effort, perhaps you should pause and ponder.

The people of Gandhar are aware of these developments. I, the queen, and my army, have the blessings of the people, and we shall come to Hastinapur to take back the gold that has forever been rightfully ours.

To Gandhari, Queen of Gandhar, Bhishma the Champion of Hastinapur's throne submits his humble salutations.

I wished to invite you to Hastinapur as queen, as wife to the son of my dead brother, as future mother to the kings of North Country. But you choose the path that shall take us away from each other, my queen. Gandhar and Hastinapur ought to be entwined as one entity against the men from Meru, for it is our interests that are alike, and theirs are but mere mirages just like their lives.

But your mind appears to have been made, and you claim to have the blessings of your people. I wish it were true and that you do not say it just to strengthen your resolve, for I know from long experience in statecraft that people never, ever, wish their kings to go to war. They know what comes out of war; the promise of bounty is sweet, but bitter indeed is the fear of ruin. I have kept close watch on Gandhar for the last year, and I admit I do not know for certain if ruin is what awaits her, but Hastinapur is not the same kingdom it was forty years ago, my lady, when Idobhargava drove us out of Kamyaka and demanded tribute from us.

Now we are stronger by at least four or five times, for now we are wealthier. Our army is more powerful; no longer is it only full of skilled archers. We have spearmen atop chariots, and armour-clad elephants that trample everything in their way. We have swordsmen who are as good with two blades as they are with one.

And do not forget, if you are to take our gold – though you keep saying it is your gold, my lady, it is in our vaults, which means it is *our* gold – you must fell the walls of Hastinapur. All of this last year we have strengthened our defensive structures, and when you arrive on the shores of the Yamuna, you shall be greeted with a maze of walls and towers the like of which your soldiers have never seen. We have our best archers patrolling these, and I must tell you, Your Majesty, that I have picked them out myself from the winners of our archery competitions. Whether the target is moving or still, big or small, they do not miss.

We have trained macemen in the last ten years that specialize in killing elephants. I have seen some of these men bring an elephant to the ground with two blows, one under each eye. And for good measure they carve out the tusks and make necklaces out of them, which their wives and young ones wear. We have footmen who can strangle the swiftest horses with their bare arms.

I am telling you all this not to scare you, my lady, but just so that your generals – whether they belong to Gandhar or to Meru – would not be shocked on the day of the solstice when they do not see just a line of archers along the edge of the battlefield. Our archers are still the best in North Country, but now our army comprises of so much more.

So whoever is advising you that you must fight us, I shall be wary of them if I were you. One – of us – does not need to go down for the other to rise. That is the code of barbarians, of mindless savages. We have built kingdoms, we have tamed the water and land to our will; certainly we can think of a better way, a way in which blood does not have to be shed. Blood is blood, whether it belongs to Gandhar or to Hastinapur.

THIRTEEN

'I would not believe everything he has written, my lady,' said Kubera, putting down the parchment and turning to face her. After him, Shakuni picked it up and scanned it, his left eye twitching the whole time. His hands shivered, and he seemed to her like a curious bouncing ball, forever on the verge of pulling out his sword.

'But even if some of what he says is true …'

'I would not worry about it, Your Majesty. Your generals command a great army, and you have our own units to help. Our cavalrymen alone could account for all their archers and elephants, and your archers shall take out their macemen before they can even reach our elephants. We are every bit as good as Bhishma at battle strategy, Your Highness.' He smiled. 'After all, he learnt everything from teachers on the mountain.'

'He also speaks of their defensive structures …'

'I have only today spoken to our blacksmith, my lady,' said Kubera. 'He will fashion for us forty iron catapults that will fell their walls in a day, and their armour will be tinged with diamond dust, which means not even the sharpest arrows will pierce them.' Looking at her still apprehensive face, he reached out for her hand and patted it. 'This is how battles are fought, my lady. First they attempt to scare you, for then they have won without a hurl of a spear.'

Spread before them on the table was a map of North Country. The path from Gandhar to Hastinapur had been marked with two red lines that slithered around River Iravati and first went eastward, toward the mountains. Then it slid down from between Trigarta and Pulinda – two of Hastinapur's vassal states, and came to a stop near the point where the Yamuna broke off from her sister Ganga.

'On the southward bank of Iravati shall we build our camp. The people of Trigarta – or of any other kingdom – shall not see us, for we will hide under a curtain of mist. There is enough mist that settles on Iravati, so we shall have enough to use our Mystery and create a film that will hide us well.'

'Mist in the summer?' said Gandhari.

'Aye,' said Kubera, 'the same mist that hides our trade route, my lady. We shall create more of it and build a few barracks and stables on the riverbank, for we shall need reinforcements during the battle.' He turned toward the map. 'We will draw them out to the clearing here.' He carved a circle at a point next to the eastern tip of the Kuru kingdom. 'The land there is soft and muddy, much like the wetlands of Kamyaka, so their archers will not find solid footing.'

'And it is flat too,' said Shakuni, 'so they will have to shoot their arrows into the air and hope that some of them pierce our armour shields. They cannot aim at us directly like they could at Kamyaka.'

'Yes,' said Kubera, 'that is so.' He said to Gandhari, 'I do not expect Hastinapur to fight us on open fields and win, my lady, but if at any point they take our gold mine, our reinforcements will suffer. We must prevent that at all costs.'

'I have already stationed my best guards at the gold mine, and the towers there will not allow any intruders to pass.'

'That is good for now,' said Kubera, 'but once the battle begins, we must see to it that the mine is well guarded.' He thought for a moment, looking away. 'Perhaps I can persuade Indra to part with a few dozen footmen. They're the best fighters on the Meru. With them guarding your mines, you will have nothing to fret about ...'

'But you say they belong to Indra,' said Gandhari. 'Will he allow them to guard our mines?'

'I shall do my best,' said Kubera, smiling and patting her hand. 'You must not give much of your mind to this, Your Highness. You must think of what you plan to do once you recover all of your gold.'

In spite of the shadows in her mind, she smiled back. The evening heat made her vision wavy, or perhaps it was the oil that she had become used to applying under her eyelids before she went to sleep every night. She reminded herself that she must ask Kubera how it worked; even after a month of constant use, she had not seen any improvement in her sight. Her dreams had become more vivid and clear, but the figures she often looked at on the ceiling in her room still appeared as smudges. What had Kubera said when he had given her the oil box? Something about the sight of the mind – tonight, perhaps, after the lamps had been put out, he would steal into her chamber like he had done a number of times recently.

She was beginning to get addicted to his smell; no, not the smell of musk that he carried, but the light green must that tingled her nose when he held her close to his bosom. On the nights when he had slept in her bed, she had slept without dreaming, and she had woken up feeling like a lotus in full bloom.

She did not know if Shakuni guessed it, especially at times like these when Kubera did not hesitate to take her hand in his. Her wrist strained a bit when the thought struck her, and she pulled it back. But then in a flash of indignation, she thought: *So what?* How many women had he not lain with over the years? If she liked a man enough to invite him into her bed, why should she look for Shakuni's approval? As long as the matter did not cross the palace walls – and she would ensure that it did not – nothing mattered, at least for as long as she was queen and he a mere prince.

'I do not wish to think of a victory that may or may not come, my lord,' she said to Kubera, not telling him that she did not dare think of the war coming to an end because that would mean it would be time for him to return to Meru. 'All of Gandhar shall have you to thank if we, indeed, manage to win.'

'There is no question of us not winning!' said Shakuni, getting up and limping out to the window overlooking the mines. 'I shall kick Bhishma's face into the dust, and I shall bring back with me his crown. Hastinapur shall belong to Gandhar!'

Gandhari held her hands together and frowned as she looked at her brother's face. She found herself worrying, curiously, for the welfare of Bhishma and Hastinapur.

Gandhari sees a moving mass of black cloud in front of her, and every few seconds a flash of light falls upon it, illuminating it for just long enough for her to make out what is going on, and then it goes away, leaving her staring at blackness again. First she sees the swarm of soldiers, elephants and horses moving on the rugged terrain, crossing River Iravati and moving northward, just as Kubera had said they would. At the head of this group is Kubera himself, leading his cavalrymen by subtle shapes on the fingers of his raised arm.

Then the footmen crouch and the horses neigh. They stop at the edge of the Kamyaka forest, and her warriors trade glances with one another from behind their armours. Kubera turns and says that they would wade through the jungle and light fires in the thickest part of it so that the enemy could not see them, and he warns his troops that this part of the jungle is teeming with hyenas. When one of the front men chuckles, Kubera silences him with a gaze of steel, and says that hyenas could tear open a man with less effort than a tiger.

Now they are passing through the forest, and Gandhari hears the breeze rustle in her ears. The smell of corpses and vultures hits her. Wolves howl. Bats fly in bunches, screeching. The men move ahead, not turning their heads once, swishing their torches from this side to that, leaving orange arcs in the night air. The wooden sandals clack against the rocks, the dead leaves stick to their soles. Kubera jumps up on a ledge by a brook and says, 'We shall camp here for dinner!'

Nibbles, licks and sighs of pleasure. Smoke from the fires, the taint of burnt flesh. Here a man sucks out the marrow from a yellow bone. There a horseman feeds his steed a bag of oats and gram. To the far side, with his legs immersed in the brook, an archer holds a bamboo tube to his lips and begins to breathe into it. Legs tap, hips begin to sway. They all gather round him, and over their heads a swarm of bees wade into the sky against the half moon.

The marsh is frozen, but then she recalls that it is not possible for it is midsummer night, so the icicles drop away, and sludge replaces them. The army walks through it with care, examining their feet after each step. The mendicants warn the soldiers to look out for leeches, and every few moments someone would cry out in pain, and the man with the bandages hops over with a knife to scrape the animal off, along with a layer of dried skin. The elephants skirt along the edge of the mire, keeping to hard ground. The mahouts whisper sweet nothings to their animals and sing songs of old travellers.

Now they are passing through a narrow lane, flanked by stone on one side and thick shrubs on the other. In the firelight she sees fear flicker in the eyes of the footmen, and when they hesitate, Kubera chides them and goads them on, telling them that the camp is just on the other side of the passage, with the great clearing just beyond. The footmen enter first, then the horses, then the elephants at the end.

'We are trapped!' someone yells.

'Stay quiet!' says Kubera.

'The entrance, it is blocked with trees!'

'A trap! We have been ambushed!'

Darkness engulfs her, and she sees nothing but hears arrows whizzing, men wailing, the feet of elephants thundering against the rocky earth. She feels herself pushed back against the cold flatness of a rock, and she looks up straight into the open aiming eye of an archer, with his shaft pointed straight at her. Before she can open her mouth the man has released his arrow, and she sees it slice into her heart, and yet she feels no pain.

Then she sees an elephant buckle, first trembling on her hind legs, then heaving to the front as arrow after arrow pierces her sides, causing the trunk to rise and point to the sky. She waits for a moment on her front knees, and tries twice to haul herself back to her feet, but fails, each time sinking deeper toward the ground. Then a maceman leaps into view, and turns around himself twice to gather enough momentum to land a blow on the animal's forehead. This time it does not make a sound, but it drops down. Her eyes close, and her trunk falls away, limp and lifeless. The maceman gets out a machete and jumps at the tusks, and with two quick swishes, they are in his hands. He launches his mace onto his shoulder and looks about himself, eyes alert, his nose sniffing for new prey.

The archer who played the bamboo flute at the brook lies dead among the fallen leaves, his chest broken in, his mouth red with blood, his eyes peaceful, fixed upon the moon in the sky. In his one hand he holds the feather-tip of the arrow he meant to shoot at his attacker, but his bow is cut in two, though the string has survived, waving in the night breeze. He has the face of a miner who whistled on the way back from work, with his mine turban hanging lopsided on his head. Gandhari thinks that he would have been in the habit of waving at young women on the way back from the lake, who would giggle at him with their hands clapped over their mouths.

Then she sees the moment in the clearing, where rows and rows of kneeling archers rain arrows on footmen emerging from the pass. Some horses charge straight at them in useless valour, only to be dragged down by spearmen. The elephants are all frightened to a corner by a group of soldiers wielding torches, where the macemen pounce on them and pound them to the ground. The mahouts have their skulls broken.

A stream of armoured horsemen then rides into the pass with lances in their hands, and they break into the archers who were frantically forming a circle of their own to combat the enemy. Some of them get pinned back against the rock, some of them have their limbs broken, most have their lives snuffed out before they can set their first arrows to their bows.

And in the midst of all, she sees Kubera at the head of the clearing, along the edge of the jungle of Kamyaka, atop a white horse, silently watching. She sees his eyes, and finds no anger or lust. Behind him stand his cohort of horsemen, and none of them breaks out to attack the enemy archers. Gandhari runs to them and screams at the top of her voice, but they do not hear her. They do not see her.

The carnage is ending. The last few men are being chased and slaughtered. Dismembered limbs and bleeding pieces of flesh hang off every bush. A horse's head looks up at her from the ground, as though the rest of its body has been buried. Yell after yell – both of the victors and of the killed – rend the air. She slaps her hands over her ears and runs. Just as she is about to exit the clearing and enter the pass, she sees, through the corner of her vision, a lone chariot bearing a red flag. A yellow rising sun is painted on it, and though the breeze is strong, the flag seems to extend out to its full length and stand steadily.

She does not see the man standing in the chariot, for he is hidden by shadows, but she knows who it is. She turns and resumes running, through the pass of death, toward home, toward the warmth and quiet of Gandhar.

Gandhari woke up with a shriek, covered in cold sweat. Gathering her nightclothes she tumbled to the window to look at the fires at the mine. They were glowing as usual. She could see movement there, of white and red spots meeting and colliding, but even when she narrowed her eyes, the vision did not improve. Perhaps everything was okay, she thought, perhaps it had all been a dream.

The doors flung open, and Chyavatana came running in. She turned to him, her gown fell away. 'I beg your pardon, Princess!' said he, falling on one knee. He was bleeding from the arm, from the tip of his ear. 'We have been led into a trap! Our army … it is no longer …'

Her eyes opened wide, but she said calmly, 'I know.'

'And the mines, my lady! The mines have been attacked. All your guards lie dead at the gate, and the enemy has taken over.'

FOURTEEN

Gandhari went into Shakuni's room. He stood with his back turning away from the window, and she knew at once that he had been staring at the mines. The torches had been extinguished now, and the guards that stood by the gates wore a different uniform and carried maces and bows instead of spears and swords. He looked at her with disgust in his eyes, and he clutched his arm and dragged it across the front of his body as he limped over to his bed. She went to his side and laid a hand on his shoulder. 'You shall be all right, brother,' she said. 'Bhishma will let you rule independently if you let Hastinapur take all the gold they need from our mine.'

'Well,' he spat out, 'is that not rather kind of him?'

'It is, rather. We ought to be glad that he has not killed us.'

'Even death would be pleasanter than living like this, as a slave.'

Gandhari sat on the bed and looked at her brother. She held his cheeks in both her hands and turned his head so that he looked into her eyes. 'Brother, do you not see, that I burn just as much as you do? Do you not see that all that has happened here this last one year has just been one big plan to get hold of our mines?'

His roving eyes focused.

She nodded at him. 'Why should some unknown man from the mountain come and offer us help at the very moment that we needed it? Why should Hastinapur fail to locate this one trade route, even though they had been so efficient at sniffing out all the others? Why should Bhishma, our mortal enemy, be so peace-loving and generous towards us? Why should the man from the mountain goad us into war though we were uncertain of winning it? Why should he offer soldiers of Indra to guard our mines? And why should they fail to fight against a band of archers that have come from Hastinapur, and why did they surrender our mines? So many questions arise tonight within our minds, do they not? And yet, there is but one answer to them all.'

She released his face and looked away into the corner, where Shakuni's assortment of swords and scabbards were kept. 'From the beginning, Shakuni, from the very beginning, the man from the north and Bhishma have worked together.' A sharp intake of breath came from Shakuni. 'Accept that for a moment and look at all the questions that I have asked you. Do they not all disappear? The man called Kubera appeared when he did because he was sent here by Bhishma. He offered us all the help that he did so that he could gain our trust, which he did.'

He gained my trust too, she thought. Was that just part of the plan too? Or had there been genuine fondness in his gaze? Her face hardened as she remembered the way his lips touched her body. She shivered in sheer revulsion, striving to push the memory out of her mind. 'Everything he did, every strategy he implemented for us, he did with the aim of bettering Hastinapur's chances of winning. He was fighting for them, Shakuni, from our side.'

'My sister,' said Shakuni, taking her by the arms. 'What is it that you say? The same Kubera who gave Gandhar all the goods that she needed? The same Kubera who gave us forces to fight with!'

'Whose idea was it that we should fight Hastinapur, Shakuni?' she asked. 'You remember the night when I asked him if war was necessary, and how he argued that it was – he was more passionate about fighting than you and I were, brother. Ah! If only we had seen through his coat of wool. I wish that I had him here in this room; I would slit his throat with that sword of yours!'

Tears came to her eyes. 'We did not doubt anything even when Bhishma allowed trade with the Meru people to flourish. We thought that he was helpless because the mountain men were stronger than Hastinapur. Bhishma did not stop us because that was what he wanted us to do all along. How foolish of us, Shakuni!'

'And the constant refrains in his letters to you, saying that war was bad for everyone?'

'He knew. He knew that the more he restrained me from fighting, the more I would be bent on doing so. It must have been their ploy all along, that Bhishma would speak against war, giving the impression that he was afraid of our might, and that Kubera would encourage us to fight and take back what was ours by right. How well they played it, and we are such knaves, brother, to be fooled by the same man twice.'

'I cannot believe this,' said Shakuni, shaking his head. 'I cannot believe this.' She felt a faint wave of pity toward him. His eyes had a dazed look about them, and his hands trembled. Gandhari thought again that there was no king in him; never had been, never would be.

'Think to yourself, Shakuni,' she said sadly. 'How else did we lead our army straight into a trap on the bank of the River Iravati? How did all of Hastinapur's army attack our west gate and fell our towers? How did the supposed guards of our mines lose so easily, and where have they gone now? Where is Kubera now? He is not dead, oh no, he is perhaps sitting with Bhishma now, and they must be sharing a pitcher of wine, laughing at us. The mines … the mines are gone …'

Her eyes welled up. She craned her neck so that she could see the extinguished torches lining the path to the mine's gate. Brighter fires had been lit at the gate, and she saw two rows of armed men guarding it. They did not need to be there. Gandhar's army had been decimated, and they had no resources to raise a new one. Gandhar was now utterly routed, nothing more than a slave city to Hastinapur.

'Yes,' she said. 'They are gone.'

'We shall never reclaim them again!'

'No, we shall not.'

'Then all is lost, sister. You say I shall be king, but there is nothing to rule but rubble, and there is nothing to do but beg from Hastinapur, from Bhishma, the man who killed us all.'

She thought of the slender, smiling figure of Bhishma in her chamber, and rued the day she had let him return to Hastinapur without ordering his execution. If he had been killed that day, things would have turned bad, but not as bad as this, surely. She remembered the letters the man had written her, the number of times he had implored her to not take up arms, though he had known – he must have known – that she would not listen, that she would believe, like Kubera had wanted her to, that Gandhar had the power to take Hastinapur.

He had played them once with the vault-keepers, and he had played them again. A sour lump took shape in her throat, and she swallowed with purpose. She closed her eyes, and an image sprang up in front of her eyes, one that equally surprised and pleased her. She cried out loud, for in front of her she saw Bhishma – not as he was now, but older and greyer – prone on the ground with his arms thrown out, arrows sticking out at every possible angle, some long, some short. And there was blood, everywhere.

She saw him smile, and when his lips parted she saw no teeth or tongue but just a red mass. He spat on the ground and held out his arm into the fog. In the distance she heard footsteps approach, and from the film of smoke emerged a woman about as old as he was, and this woman had a blue satin band over her eyes.

Gandhari opened her eyes with a start, and saw that she was bathed in sweat. She had recognized the woman that had stepped out of the fog and taken Bhishma's arm, but she could not understand why tears were flowing down her cheeks, why she had not spat on his face.

And if it were really true that Kubera and Bhishma together plotted all this, why had he given her the oil for improving her vision? And this image she had just seen, what did it mean? She looked about her, at the ceiling, at the weapons, at the pitcher of water, at the puzzled face of Shakuni. She called out to a mother she had never known or seen. *What do you want of me, mother?*

All that came back to her was silence, and yet in that very moment she knew what she must do now. Shakuni was right; Gandhar's mines were lost forever. From now on, Hastinapur would perhaps give Shakuni a tiny amount of gold, just enough to run the town, and take most of the bounty for themselves. Now Hastinapur would become the wealthiest and strongest kingdom of North Country, stronger, perhaps, even than Panchala.

But – that did not mean there was nothing to do.

'Is all lost, then, forever?' muttered Shakuni.

She smiled at him and ran a palm over his cheek. Then she shook her head.

Gandhari watched the round red blobs on the ceiling coalesce into one another. It did not bother her any more that she could not see the shapes. When she closed her eyes and reached into her mind, now, she would see images sharp as tacks. They had been flimsy at the start, staying in place only for an instant or so, but now, after four months of practice, she was able to hold an image for five or six seconds. Soon she would be able to make them move, she thought, not wondering about where that knowledge came from.

She thought of the vision of herself blindfolded, her hand twined with that of Bhishma on a bed of arrows. They shared a lot of traits, she and Bhishma; not least in the love they had for their lands. Now Gandhar was no more, and its star would descend. In less than three generations from now Gandhar would be but a distant memory, but Hastinapur had won, and with Bhishma at the reins, it would go on to become a true paradise on earth.

Not if she could help it, though. There was little she could do now, with the battle fought and lost, but just over forty years ago, Hastinapur had been as Gandhar was now. They had clawed themselves back, and by sheer power of will (and more than a little subterfuge), had placed themselves ahead of the clutch of kingdoms that littered North Country. At that time Bhishma would have been as old as she was now, so perhaps now was not the time to give in to despair. If she could pick herself up and plan well enough, was it possible that in about forty years from now, Hastinapur could be brought down to her knees?

She thought of the vision again, and tried to see again the folds of skin on her cheeks, the grey in her hair. She looked as old as sixty in that image, and in a curious way it made sense, because that would put it exactly forty years into the future. Perhaps this battle was not the conclusion, then, as much as it seemed like one. Perhaps it was only a prelude to a bigger event that would come, that she would orchestrate. And on that day her revenge – and Shakuni's revenge too – would be complete.

Bhishma was about to arrive in Gandhar the next morning. She closed her eyes, and hoped that her sight would show her something that would tell her what to do. But nothing came to her; all that she saw were black shadows whoosh about, and strange dark shapes forming wherever she looked.

Just as she was about to slip off to sleep, she had a vision where she saw herself standing to her full height, streams of water flowing down her naked olive body, a black ribbon plastered across her eyes, neck craned toward the sky, her black nipples erect. She realized at once that she knew what she must do.

Her path of revenge and deliverance had finally come into view.

When Bhishma was ushered into her chamber next morning, Gandhari, dressed in a white sari, gown and tunic, looked less a queen and more a chamberlain, which was befitting, for she was now no more than Hastinapur's slave. She hoped that Bhishma saw that. She looked up when the sound of his footsteps came to her ear.

He had a bloody gash on his right cheek which disappeared into his beard, but he strode into her chamber like a king, holding the hilt of his sword in one hand and letting the other arm hang loose. Gandhari got off the bed and fell to her knees, clutching her chest with both hands.

'Your slave, Gandhari, my lord,' she said, 'at your service.'

He made no motion to pick her up. He sat on the same throne that he had taken on his last visit. He folded one leg over another and rested his elbow on his thigh, looking at her with amused interest.

'I wish it had not come to this, Princess,' he said. 'But you forced my hand and left me no alternative.'

'Please do not have mercy on my life after all this, my lord. Use your sword and slit my throat, and end my life right here.'

'Why do you wish to die, Gandhari?' His voice lowered a touch when he said her name. 'You will rule the city of Gandhar yet, but now your tribute to Hastinapur shall increase, for we have to recoup the losses of war.'

'I shall not rule Gandhar, my lord,' she said, looking up to meet his eye. 'My brother will. And there is no king in the land who would take the hand of a maiden that belongs to a kingdom as poor as Gandhar.' She looked out of the window, and she longed to see the torches at the mine gate alight again. 'Without the mines, Gandhar has nothing. Shakuni has nothing. I have nothing.'

'It is perhaps true,' said Bhishma, 'but death is not the answer, my lady. We all but live once, and we must make the best of what life gives us.'

'That is easier to say when you are a victor at war, sire. I am a woman, and I have already passed my twentieth year. Who shall marry me? Whom shall I bear my sons to?'

'I am certain any nobleman in Gandhar would be pleased to marry you, my lady.'

'Noblemen?' she said. 'Do you think that Gandhar still has noblemen, my lord? All we have now is dead bodies of soldiers, and the living corpses of farmers and miners. Nothing more!' She spread her arms in his direction. 'You have taken much from Gandhar as spoils, my lord. Take me also, and I shall serve in your palace in whatever capacity that you see fit.'

The suggestion seemed to catch Bhishma off guard, for he buried his chin in his palm and thought for a while. At length, he said, 'The job of a chamberlain is hardly worthy of a queen of your stature, my lady.'

'I am no longer a queen, my lord, Bhishma. I am but your slave, and I shall do your bidding and serve you for as long as I live.'

'Then I offer you the same thing that I offered you last summer. You said no one would marry you because of your poor kingdom. I have in my court my nephew, whom no one wishes to marry because he is blind.'

Gandhari raised her head, and in the moment it took her to blink, she saw in front of her eyes the frozen image of a bare-chested warrior wielding a mace. His eyes had no shape or colour, and they appeared to be mere glass holes. She knew that her physical sight would be like his in a few years, and they shall have to be waited upon by servants and maids.

'Dhritarashtra is his name,' said Bhishma, as though he knew what she had seen.

Dhritarashtra. He would suit her much better than the strong Pandu. It would allow her to lay low, behind the palace walls, hidden by the curtains, and put her ideas to work. They would never make a blind man king, and they would never take notice of the blind man's wife, who herself could not see well. But if she could push herself further away from public view, if only she could find a way to practice her Mystery in peace, to strengthen the effect of the oil on her lids. Kubera had said the only way was to close her eyes …

When she trained her eyes back to Bhishma, she saw him look at her in a puzzled manner. She joined her hands and bowed to him. 'There shall be no greater honour, sire, that you can bestow upon a woman as lowly as I.'

'You are the highest of all women,' said Bhishma, getting to his feet and helping her up, putting his hands gently on her shoulders. 'You shall be his eyes, then, and may you have a hundred sons by him that will unfurl the flag of Hastinapur high against the wind for years to come.'

'Sire,' she said, bowing, 'May the gods grant me the hundred sons that you wish for Hastinapur. But I shall not be my lord's eyes.' Bhishma's face changed. 'Do not think I will not take care of him, sire, I will with all my love, but I shall not see the world when my husband and lord cannot. The scriptures say that a wife must share in all of her husband's joys and sorrows, and that she must see the world as he does. I will therefore see the world just as Prince Dhritarashtra does, my lord, and not as Gandhari has for all her life.'

As she said those words, and not a moment before that, she understood the full meaning of the vision that she had seen the night before and the dark path that lay in front of her was now lit by light – not of lightning that was there this moment and gone the next – but that of the constant, resplendent full moon.

Bhishma said, 'I do not understand, my lady.'

In answer Gandhari tore off the end of her sari and folded it in her hands. She laid it over her eyes and pulled it back over her head, tying the two ends in a knot above her neck. As her eyes closed, she took a sudden backward step as image after image flashed in front of her closed eyelids, each one appearing for too short a time for her to make sense of them. Her breath quickened, and her palms became wet with sweat, but the relentless flash of visions kept attacking her, hitting her with a force so strong that she buckled on her knees and fell forward against the sturdy arms of Bhishma.

'My lady, Princess, Gandhari,' he was saying in his hoarse, whispery voice. She heard the steps of the worried attendants, and she heard cries of alarm from the women. But all this came to her as though from a distant world, a world that the blindfold had cut off from her. Now she had to awaken to a different world, the world of magic, the world of the mind, and she had to sharpen the sense of her sight so that these figures would slow down and move to her will, so that she could speak with them and they would show her what she needed to see.

'You shall be the wife Dhritarashtra would be proud to live with,' said Bhishma.

She had fulfilled her first objective. She had gained his trust. Now all that she wished to do was to slip away into sleep and allow her mind to awaken.

And to devise Hastinapur's downfall.

FIFTEEN

Ganga, Lady of the River, hunched down in front of her hut and filled the earthen vessel with water. She took out a bunch of berries from under her cloak, plucked them out, and laid them on the ground next to the water. Leaning on her stick, she got to her feet with a mumble. She looked around her. The mother doe was nowhere to be seen. She would come, though, once the light disappeared. She had kept an eye on this doe for a while now; she preferred to come lumbering in just after sunset, and left the hermitage, after having had her fill, while the moon was still yellow, almost touching the horizon.

She went to the edge of the cliff to look at the great white rock in the falling light, and at once she remembered the morning on which Prabhasa had come to teach her the Mysteries. She had often heard her mother say that after a while one did not remember which events belonged to her life and which belonged to those of her predecessors, and now Ganga felt the same. On that morning, she felt that she had been both nine and twenty-nine, that she had been both the child who partook of the Mysteries and the maiden who sat cross-legged on the porch, watching.

A black spot appeared on the brook far off the west, and as it became larger and larger, it took the form of the barge that once brought her here from Hastinapur. A dark man with white spots on his shoulders descended, looked up at her, and smiled. She could not see his face well, but he walked as though he were tired. She kept her eyes on him all along as he came up the mossy steps, barefooted. When he arrived at her side, she turned to face him, and he kneeled on one knee and bowed his head.

'Arise, Kubera,' she said. 'I am glad to see that you have come back alive.'

He got up to his feet said solemnly, 'I am too, my lady.'

'I trust you have done all that was asked of you.'

'I have, my lady. I have returned to the mountain, in fact, a few days ago. But my limbs were tired, and I rested them a little before making the journey up to see you.'

'A few gulps of the Crystal Water would have helped, I am certain.'

'I have had more than a few gulps, my lady. I have only lived on Earth for a few months, and yet I have so desperately missed drinking of the Lake.'

She nodded; she knew only too well of that burning in the throat, of that stinging thirst that would never leave a man who had tasted the water of the Lake. Only Devavrata had escaped its clutches – or had he simply learnt to live with it?

'Give me news of Earth, Kubera. How does Devavrata?'

'They call him Bhishma now, my lady Ganga,' said Kubera, 'Bhishma the terrible. He is known to be the fiercest warrior in all of North Country.'

'And not a bad strategist, either, I hear.' The words bore only a little of the pride she felt tingle within her heart.

'No, not at all. He has with his own hands now put Hastinapur at the top of all the kingdoms of North Country. In a few days, Dhritarashtra will wed Gandhari, the Princess of Gandhar. And with that Hastinapur will come into possession of the gold mines.'

She turned and walked toward the hut, nodding at him to come with her. When they reached the porch she sat on the edge and held her staff out to her side. She looked at the bushes in hope, but the doe was out of sight. From somewhere below her she heard the sounds of children playing in Vasishtha's courtyard. The mountain air was thin and clear; one had to only quieten down to hear the smallest sounds from leagues away.

'They are marrying the princess of Gandhar to the blind one, are they not?' On Kubera's nod, she took a long, deep breath. 'It is as it should be, then.'

'But my lady,' said Kubera, his voice low, 'we had set out to weaken Hastinapur and quell the power of Bhishma. But we seem to have made it stronger than ever before. Have we not put Meru in danger because of that?'

Ganga looked at Kubera and tried to discern his real age. The water of the Lake kept people young, but if you knew where to look, you would still find signs of wear. She saw that his fingernails were yet white and had not begun to turn clear, which meant that he was yet a mere cub, new to the ways of the Mysteries. He would have learnt well, no doubt, at the feet of the old Kubera. But as the sages said, there was no better teacher than life itself.

'Kubera,' she said, 'there is one thing that you must always remember. We have yet to find and probe the Mysteries of time. We are yet to find ways to be able to predict the future. Some say the sight – which some men are blessed with – belongs to the Great Goddess Bhagavati, and it is she who sees through the tiny hole that connects us to the future. But I do not agree; the present faces not one but many futures, so perhaps even the Goddess herself sees but one or two.

'So whether what we have done will turn out to be good or bad for us, no one knows, my boy. The Wise Ones do not know, either. The high sages that come to the Meru every year tell us that the wiser you get, the more you realize that you know nothing.'

'But my lady,' said Kubera, 'we have done the exact opposite of what was needed.'

'It appears so, on the face of it, does it not? But have we?' Kubera's face reflected puzzlement, so she smiled and said, 'We have three strands here, Kubera, that all come together and converge upon Hastinapur. First there is Amba, whom Devavrata has wronged and who has become a priestess and is now rearing a child of her own. Then there is Kunti, the princess from the southern kingdom who shall bear sons in whose bodies will flow the blood of the mountain. Then we have Gandhari, who shall see a lot through her closed eyes, using the Mystery that you have given her.'

Kubera said, 'I still do not see, my lady.'

'Neither do I, Kubera, for as I said, no one sees the future. But do you not see that even though Hastinapur is the strongest kingdom of all, seen from the outside, there are fissures deep within it, and all we have tried to do is widen them, and keep them wide enough for long enough so that one day, they will crack.'

'Do you refer to the blind prince?'

'The blind prince has no ambitions, Kubera, so we cannot do much with him. But look at the princesses. Gandhari, the queen of Gandhar, wronged twice by Bhishma and Hastinapur – if she had married into Hastinapur the very first time that Bhishma asked her, she would have been a happy woman, mother to sons who would make Hastinapur truly great. We did not want that, so we sent you to deepen that crack that existed between the two cities, and you have done admirably, causing a battle and seeing to it that Gandhar lost.'

'But even now Gandhari is marrying into the royal family of Hastinapur, my lady.'

'She is,' said Ganga, 'but she does so out of revenge. She does so with the sole ambition of plotting the downfall of the Kuru race, and it is vital for this purpose that she is married to the more docile prince, Kubera, and that she does not become queen, because now she will have a lot of time to think about the wrongs done to her.

And the longer you think of your misfortunes, the bigger they seem to grow, and the more they begin to trouble you.'

He nodded, but his face still looked pained. 'And what about Kunti, my lady?'

'She is the second strand, and perhaps the most important. We did not plan for her; indeed, when Surya came to me on the day before he was to set out for Earth, his sole purpose was to find out what was happening in the town of Mathura, and he only saw her as the easiest way into the city. Without her help, we would not have taken the black stones from that city, and we would not have weakened it like we did, for if Mathura had continued on its path of studying the Mystery of the stone, I suspect it would have become a close rival to Hastinapur by now.'

'And we did not want that.'

'No,' said Ganga. 'We wished for Hastinapur to be the strongest kingdom. Also, the black stone is a marvellous Mystery, and it will do for us a great amount of good. If we use it right, we may never have to fight a war with any kingdom again.'

'About Kunti–'

'Yes, Surya was smitten with Kunti, and he thought she would make a great queen to Hastinapur. She would be the other half, with Gandhari being the first. She would bear the powerful sons, the sons of the Celestials, and she would arrive at Hastinapur expecting to rule it, expecting to be the Queen Mother in time. So you have ambition on one side, and entitlement on the other.'

'But there was another son, my lady,' said Kubera, 'the one that Kunti bore Surya.'

Ganga's mouth twisted at this. The sun had begun to sink in the sky now, with only half of its shape visible over the horizon. She had the feeling that the Celestial was hiding his face from her anger. For he had been strictly forbidden from bearing any Earthly maidens children, and yet he had gone ahead and done it. He had said that the boy would grow up in Hastinapur and play a 'great role' in its destiny, but it was hard to believe him. For one, Celestials always believed that their sons were destined for great things.

'He,' she said, scratching her forehead with one finger, 'was a mistake.'

'A mistake!'

'A small one,' said Ganga, 'but a mistake nonetheless. He will be in Hastinapur, so perhaps Kunti will take him in and rear him as her own. Perhaps he shall play no part at all in what is to come, I know not. But he adds one more ingredient to the broth, Kubera, and when you try and shape the future, perhaps more is not necessarily bad. We shall find some use for him, for after all, he is the son of a Celestial.'

Kubera nodded. 'I am still troubled,' said he, 'because I fear for the future of the mountain.'

She patted him on the cheek. 'The mountain shall be safe, Kubera. With the Crystal Lake and now the black stones with us, I think not that any kingdom on Earth shall ever touch us. No, not even Hastinapur.'

'But you said there were three strands—'

'Yes,' said Ganga, and even as she said it, her heart grew heavy. She had told Kubera that no man or woman could foretell the future, and yet whenever she thought of Amba, her vision blurred, her stomach turned. Somewhere deep within her, she felt that she knew the answer. But she dared not give it voice. 'The third strand is Amba,' she said. 'She is another of those women that Devavrata has wronged, and we have nurtured her and seen to it – through the High Sage Parashurama – that she has borne a child, a female child, who shall grow into a maiden.'

'The father is the king of Pachala, I hear,' said Kubera.

'Indeed,' said Ganga, smiling. 'Panchala and Hastinapur have been enemies for a long time now. Drupad has not had a child before – or even after this babe – so he shall have no choice but to accept her as his. And she will grow up a princess, then perhaps she will grow into a queen, but wherever she goes, she will carry within her heart her mother's hatred for Devavrata.'

'I see,' said Kubera, and for once she saw the knot in his eyebrows smoothen, and the creases on his cheeks vanish.

'You do see,' she said. 'There are two ways to fight your foe, Kubera. One is by force, by battering him down repeatedly, making him weaker with each blow, until he falls down never to get up again. That was the way of the Dark Ones before us, but we – we think it is better to strengthen your enemy and make him bigger than he has ever been, but make sure that you build in these little cracks in the founding pillars, so that you can later find and widen them as you need to.'

'All of this,' said Kubera, 'to get at one man?'

The sun had disappeared, and the stars began to twinkle in sight. When Ganga turned her head to the other side she saw the yellow crescent just about to begin her rise. Like she had on that unforgettable night all those years ago by the peepal, she looked for a star at the tip but found none. Any time now, the mother doe would bound out of the bushes for her berries, and she did not wish to be around to scare her away.

'It is never about one man or one woman, Kubera,' she said, standing up. He got to his feet too, and bowed to her. She touched her palm to the hair on his scalp and murmured a blessing. 'There are always bigger tales afoot than yours and mine. Remember that.' She saw his face crumple up again at her words, and before he could ask her a question, she gestured him toward the stairs. 'It is time for my evening prayers. Perhaps we could speak of this at a later time.'

'My lady,' he said, and turned away. She did not wait to see him descend the steps and make his way to the boat. She hurried away to her front door and let herself in, giving her eyes a moment to get used to the darkness of the hut. She groped with her free hand and found the firestone. At her fireplace, she gathered some hay and began to scratch the stone against the hearth. The first two sparks were too weak, and they fizzled out after they touched the hay. But the third caught fire, and Ganga reached for her blowpipe. Just then she heard the sound of hoof against stone on the porch, followed by a light gurgle. The mother doe had come.

She smiled to herself. All was well, now.